A TIME TO REMEMBER

CHARLES HENRY POINTER

 www.trafford.com

North America & international
toll-free: 1 888 232 4444 (USA & Canada)
fax: 812 355 4082

PROLOGUE

The idea for writing this book came about when I wondered where the subject matter would come from to do my third book. I wanted to write a book which I felt strong compassion for and I remembered when I was a senior getting a Bachelor of Science degree in secondary education, with a major in history and minor in English at Southern Illinois University at Edwards, in 1974, which became my teaching areas to teach on the high school level in the state of Missouri and part of the graduation from the history department required its students to write a historical paper on any topic they were interested in. With the encouragement of my professor Dr. Herbert Rosenthal, he said I should write it on Stokely Carmichael, leader of the civil rights organization called SNCC, which meant Student Non-Violent Coordinating Committee, who made the term "Black Power "popular because Stokely wanted black people to control their own destiny and build an economic base of power for themselves.

Stokely felt if black people elected their own representatives; they could get better living conditions for their people and challenge the Jim Crow laws, which operated in the north and southern parts of the United States. My research showed Stokely developed the ideas of Pan-Africanism whereas blacks in America would unite for a common cause and fight for equality over here and elsewhere in the world. I met Stokely when he came to Washington University, St. Louis, Missouri and gave a speech. I told Stokely I wrote my theses on him and his organization fighting for civil rights in the southern states for African Americans.

I wrote a fictional book based on the difficulties John Carol my fictional character experienced growing up in the town of Jackson, Mississippi the main city where most of the story originates and a main character, United States senator Big Jim Wilson, who gave John a difficult time when he and his father Peter Carol and his wife Sarah share cropped with Kobe Wilson, Big Jim's father and enjoyed a great relationship. All that changed when Big Jim took over control of the plantation when Kobe died and cheated the Carol's out of their money when they cashed in their crops in the fall because Peter and John both could not read or write and John stopped going to school to help Peter with the crops like all the black students did and their one room cabin schools had thirty students in it and the instructor taught nine grades which were inferior to the white schools and given more money, educational books, supplies, and better buildings to learn in.

John Carol and his friends walked many miles to get to their school while they lived next to ones close to them but only white students could attend them. To make matter s worse, John Carol fell in love with Betty who was Big Jim's daughter and they played together with Sandy who later became a lawyer and her brother Kirby Wilson who had political ambitions but his ideas conflicted with his father Big Jim's pro-segregationist ideas.

Sandy clashed with Betty because she did not like the integration of black and whites on an equal bases and did not favor the idea of Betty and John running off together. Peter and Sarah tried to tell John not to fall in love with Betty but he would not listen and they both left and made a living in Canton, Mississippi. Earlier Betty told Big Jim about her love for John and he feared not getting reelected to the United States senate from the state of Mississippi and because of the disturbing news, Big Jim would kill anyone who got in his way to keep him from winning reelection regardless to who it was family or friend. Big Jim sent word to his political friends to make life hard for them if possible before Betty would tell of his plans to take valuable lands from the farmers because he was told oil was on them and he wanted them for himself and his businessmen friends of Jackson, Mississippi.

Being in love with each other and romantically involved, Betty told John she was pregnant and having twins and when they are born the genes in their blood systems produce two girls with Dora being black and Dianna white. To avoid problems with the authorities, John left Betty and the twins telling her he would come back to them but they were separated for several years with John being put in the army against his will to avoid going to prison for being with a white women, to fight in the Korean War while Betty raises the twins, but has to leave Dora in an orphanage because she felt Dora would suffer being raised in a white community with her and Dianna and hoped a black family would adopt her. Through the years a black woman by the name of Dr. Lilly came to the orphanage and saw what a problem she was experincing and adopted her.

The twins meet without knowing it when they competed against each other in basketball games that Betty attended but never told Dora she was her real mother but felt she could not because it would hurt her business dealings with her white pro-segregationist business associates.

Coming back from the army a war hero, John runs for the United States senate seat and loses because he wasted so much time not going to the people trying to explain what he could do for them if they elected him to the high office and but comes back and wage a gallant effort to win the senate seat against Big Jim Wilson who never lost an election in his political career.

To stop John from winning the election, Big Jim did many things to stop him, campaigning on a pro-segregationist platform, but gets rid of his white wife Mable and sleeps with his black mistress Polly and carried her to every social gathering regardless to what his associates felt about it and morns deeply when she is killed in the middle of Big Jim's efforts to destroy a civil rights meeting Polly's brother s was attending to attack Big Jim's agenda to deny civil rights to black and white farmers and how they rallied to get John Carol elected and were impressed with his ability to get a college education despite the prejudice he faced to be able to write laws which could help and protect the people of Mississippi both white and black citizens in a book written called A Time To Remember.

Charles Pointer, the Author, MS-ED

CHAPTER 1

'A Time to Remember by Charles Henry Pointer

At the Wilson plantation Senator Jim Wilson ate his favorite catfish and sneered at what he read in the newspapers about civil rights workers both black and white people coming to Mississippi pushing for voting rights for black people and he shouted out loud, "God dam it those white and black liberal son of a bitches are coming down here trying to get our black folks the right to vote. I'll submit this anti legislation to stop it." Jim got his name Big Muddy when he saw one of his black friends strolling down the banks of the Mississippi River with one of the girls he liked who worked on his father's plantation and he had a secret love affair with her and no one knew about it. As Jim approached the couple he hit Roger Jones in the mouth and he went flying through the air landing in the river and Jim dived in after him and the both of them hit each other violently and mud got on their clothes and the crowd yelled "Big Muddy kick the nigger's ass because we're going to lynch him anyway! "Big Jim wanted to finish Jones off but the people watching the fight grabbed Jones and hung him to the nearest tree. Ever since that time people called Jim Big Muddy but as he got older he went by the name of Big Jim Wilson and he felt the name Big Jim made him looked more dignified. "That dam nigger show could hit hard," he said to one of his friends.

The alcohol helped Big Jim figure out how he could please his voters who elected him to office.

He weigh about 200 pounds and Big Jim loved touching his beard when he thought about what was best for the people he represented in the state of Mississippi. The year of 1960 was when no race mixing among blacks and whites was popular in his state. Big Jim wore his favorite suit which was a white colored one with matching tie and cup links and he admired looking in the mirror as he did his work. "Man don't I look pretty? "He said to himself and did not care who was near him when he repeated it. On the wall hung pictures of the generals of the civil war and old confederate guns and flags lined his walls. Suspenders hung from his big shoulder on a 'six by six' tall body frame. Smoking enormous Cubin cigars consumed many hours of his work time and he played golf in a segregated country club where black people could not enjoy this privilege. Ceiling fans circulated air where his many awards were placed in trophy cases and pictures of him showing the number of German aces he shot down as an American combat bomber pilot. All type of medals showed honor and duty to his country. As a combat flying airman, he did not know about the black fighter pilots from Tuskegee who never lost a bomber when they were used to escort and protect American bombers from German enemy fighters. Coming from the state of Mississippi, everything Senator Wilson grew up around showed black people living in segregated conditions and he was raised in Jackson, Mississippi where black people could not go to the movie theaters with white people and if admitted sat in the black only section away from the white folks attending it. Big Jim never went to school with black people or associated with them and did not believe in integration whatsoever. Even in Europe the black airmen could not go into the white officer's clubs and these fellows were college graduates just like the white officers. The only thing Big Jim knew as a kid is he saw black people on his father's estate living as share croppers and getting treated kindly by his father Kobe who paid decent prices for their crops, but Big Jim resented it and vowed to change all of that if he ever took control of the plantation which he later did by paying lower prices for the crops the share croppers sold to him and he made huge profits from it. Being a kid did not stop Big Jim from playing with the black kids whose parents plowed the fields and picked the crops from the early morning starting at seven a.m. and finishing at eleven p.m. in the evening, and the climax of those friendships ended when Big Jim grew older and chose not to associate with his black friends anymore.

When Big Jim saw President Harry Truman integrate the armed services he vowed he would not support him but what could he do? President Truman wanted the armed forces integrated with all deliberate speed even though one of his top generals, General Douglas MacArthur was dismissed for not trying to comply with his order after Thurgood Marshal went to Korea and turned in a report on the discrimination black soldiers experienced under their white commanders.

The valor of the black airman was never spoken about even when one of them saved Big Jim's bomber from being shot out of the air by a German fighter when a black pilot got in back of him and shot at the enemy aircraft which exploded in midair. Knowing it was a black pilot who saved him, Big Jim did not tell his fellow white officers what really took place because they would not believe him anyway. In a conversation with a fellow congressman, Big Jim rubbed his soft beard and said, "Who in the hell do he think he is that President Truman. Our white southern troops are not use to this integration with colored troops."

"We never spoke to the black airman when I was in the air force fighting against the Germans. Every civil rights bill Truman tried to get through the congress I voted against it and encouraged the other senators and representatives to do the same thing." Big Jim said to a newspaper reporter.

This was 1951 and an election year for Senator Jim Wilson who claimed his election history showed he never lost an election when running for other political offices in the state such as Alderman, or State Treasure, State Representative, and Secretary of State and the legislation Big Jim wrote kept various institutions segregated and to

3

get reelected he wrote bills that pleased his constituents who voted him back to the United States senate so no changes would take place to enforce civil rights laws for the African Americans to get full equality in the state of Mississippi.

Generation after generations of Wilsons since the revolutionary war took land from the Indians and enslaved black people who tilled it, built the big mansions, and helped build up the richest plantation in Mississippi. Cash crops like sugar, beans, cotton, corn, and tobacco were grown in abundance but when slaves escaped they paid dearly for it when they were brought back to the plantation and beaten to discourage other slaves from escaping to freedom. The Wilsons did their own business of buying slaves to help with the crops and did not allow them to learn how to read or write. If caught reading a newspaper, they could be hung or sold off to other plantation owners. When news of Nat Turners slave rebellion reached the Wilson plantation, during that time period, the Wilsons kept a tight hold on their slaves and sent money and men to help stop Turner, who 's band killed many plantation owners and their love ones in their raids which terrified many owners' of slaves.

On the Wilson plantation lived the Carol family who were descendants of slaves who grew up on the estate like Peter and Sarah Carol who raised a son named John Carol who was very energetic and played with the Wilson children as they grew up on the plantation together and never questioned each other about the color of their skin until orders came from the owner of the plantation that such friendships must end immediately because the black kids had to know their place and could not be equal to the friends they grew up with because the way of life at the plantation was the white people were supposed to be superior to black people living on the plantation. Growing discontentment among black farmers who sharecropped with Big Jim Wilson developed because they never gained anything from it.

The farmers borrowed from him to buy supplies to plant their crops and he cheated them by charging large interest rates on the loans and the black farmers could not read or write lost all the time because they could not understand the wording in the contracts they usually signed with an x for their signatures. The thought of forming a union came up when the farmers got together and talked about his policies in private picnics hosted by Big Jim but were too afraid to organize themselves into a union.

After paying off Big Jim, Peter Carol came home with ten dollars in his pocket and tears in his eyes because he felt with all the hard work he did, he should have more money in his pockets but as usual he accepted things of the transactions without questioning the results. Many times his son John Coral told his father he was being cheated by the senator but Peter Carol trusted Big Jim Wilson's word. Big Jim Wilson's father Kobe died and he and Peter Carol were close friends which resulted in much jealousy shown by Big Jim because it. Kobe and Peter went fishing together and developed a great friendship. But for now the thoughts of reelection occupied Big Jim's activities and he tried to keep his mind off the Carol family and the other sharecroppers on his land and money from them would help finance his reelection. All the agreements Kobe made with the sharecroppers were changed by Big Jim where he would get the lion's share of their money.

John said to his father, "One day I am going to change the way you and the colored farmers are cheated and I will become senator and defeat Big Jim and take his senate seat. I do not have much of an education but I will learn how to read and write and present bills that can stop the corruption which is hurting our people such as yourself."

"Son you're day dreaming again because the white man will not let something like that happen."

"Now Peter do not say that. My son can do anything he sets his mind to. Let's encourage him not put him down. There are many colored people who became successful and my son will be a success despite the racism and prejudice we face down here. One day a change is going to come." Sarah said Power was something Big Jim wanted and he said he never lost a reelection and would stop anybody who stood in his way with any means possible. If it took lying to the people Big Jim did it and if it meant threatening the voters to vote for him he did it. If it meant burning down the headquarters of the opponent running against him he would pay an underworld figures to do it and have no regrets about the damages done to his political enemies.

Listening to his favorite music, Big Jim looked into the large mirror and shaved his hair down to a comfortable length and put his best cologne on but he shouted when he saw his best ties were missing especially tailored to match his suits.

"God damit my maids have stolen my ties. You just cannot trust those niggers anymore. They are always stealing from me."

"Daddy why are you fussing and blaming our colored maids for stealing from you when your ties come up missing. I think you like some of those black maids because at night I see Polly coming out of your bedroom and this has occurred many times. What if your anti-black friends found out about? your love affair with her? You will be the laughing stock of this state and they would not support you in your efforts to win in the next coming reelection." Betty said to him. "Momma might come home and catch the two of you together and all hell will break loose."

Putting on his white suit and pants Big Jim said, "Now Betty I like my maid Polly and that's a private matter between me, you and her. I see that strange look in your eyes now what's on your mind?"

"Why are you smiling? Now let me have it?"

A big smile appeared on Big Jim's face because he thought Betty would tell him some good news which would make his day pleasant. Different thoughts dashed through his mind like is his daughter going to marry a rich white boy with lots of prestige, money, and power which was one of his requirements for the person Betty would marry.

"Do not bring me a poor sonofabitch for a son in law or I'll disown you."

Before going into her father's office Betty reflected on the times she spent with John Carol and how they played as kids and the summers swimming in the lake in back of their plantation and the stigma was well remembered when Big Jim took the kids to town and John could not go to certain facilities because of his skin color. At that time Betty dressed in a colorful long whitish blue dress and she remembered how John cried when he could not enjoy the same opportunities as the other children and in her heart she always said to herself these prejudice feelings against the black man must end and the discrimination laws would one day be abolished.

If any of the black servants joined the local NAACP, they would lose their jobs and sometimes against Big Jim's orders Betty sneaked and attended the meetings especially if it was meant to attack the Jim Crow laws in the South and in the state of Mississippi and when Big Jim found out about her going to those meetings he would make orders telling Betty to confine herself to her room for a week after coming home from school which had no black students in the classes.

The black students walked or hitched hiked to get to their school which was a wooden old shack with all the grades from kindergarten to the 12th grade being taught but during harvest time black students stopped going to school and helped their parents so they would sell their crops to companies buying those fruits and vegetables.

John Carol took an interest in reading when Betty attempted to teach him but it was difficult because John worked in the fields and did not have time to study. The black folks were supposed to be happy with growing and tilling the crops. Thoughts of aspiring to be a positive person such as a doctor, lawyer, or teacher did not dawn on the kids who were black because they only felt their role in life was to stay on the plantation and share crop with the white plantation owners. After moments of reflecting on how she lived in a time period when segregation was the law of the state of Mississippi, Betty started not to say anything to her father and hoped he would understand her feelings as to what she wanted to reveal to him.

Betty remembered her father going to a black church and telling the congregation he tried to pass civil rights bills to get the votes of the black people who could qualify to vote if they passed the literacy test but it was all lies to make them think he cared about their plight of living in a segregated system life style which degraded them and made them feel like second class citizens. Maybe Big Jim, Betty thought might change his mind about his feelings about pro-segregation after he gave his speech to the black church members.

Gradually Betty tiptoed towards her father and said," Daddy I want to speak with you about something you might want to hear so you relax and put those papers down and hear me out."

The sound of Betty's voice echoed through the room and she stood behind Big Jim and hugged him and said, "I have always relied on you when I had problems I could not handle. You always said you would rather see me come to you than anyone else when I am facing difficult problems"

As his favorite music played Betty said. "Will you dance with me on this lullaby?"

Smiling at Betty, Big Jim said, "Ok daughter", and held his daughter and kept stepping on her toes as he could barely keep up with the music's beat.

After the music stopped Big Jim said, "Well you must have something on your mind because you cannot seem to tell me."

"Daddy I want your permission to marry John Carol. I have loved him since we were kids growing up playing on the plantation together. I loved him a lot. I know you wanted me to marry a rich white man but not a colored boy. I just could not help it. It's the same as you loving Polly."

A serious look appeared on Big Jim's face as he said," Betty you cannot say things like that because it is not making sense. The daughter of Senator Big Jim Wilson marrying a colored sharecropper's son would make me the laughing stock of the whole state of Mississippi. You must be crazy. I will not have no such thing happening. What impression do you think the people will get of me when I run for re-election on an anti-civil rights agenda and against mixed marriages? They will not vote for me thinking I support what my daughter is doing"

Not to be discouraged, Betty said," Who gives a dam what your supporters say. It's none of their business about my love for John Carol. He's inspired me to be someone and never give up while I attempted to be a doctor, lawyer, or anything that would give me independence and not marry some promising white boy who has power and money who can help your political gains such as running for the United States senator of Mississippi or maybe making a run for the White House."

"I do not care about your love for this colored man but marrying him could keep me from being re-elected. The only thing colored folks can do is take care of my land. They have oil on it and I plan on getting my fair share at any cost. If you marry John Carol, I will have his family evicted off the land."

With tears in her eyes, Betty grabbed a picture of him shaking hands with some of the field hands and threw it against the wall. Glass from the picture scattered throughout the office and it made much noise as pieces of it hit the floor. Running out of her father's house brought back memories of the times when Betty's father said he loved the Carol family and they could always stay as they desired. Betty saw her father lied and just like most politicians said what he felt the voters wanted to hear.

With anger in his eyes, Big Jim slapped her but regardless of the tragic circumstances a contract existed between Peter Carol and Big Jim's father Kobe Wilson which he thought about getting annulled that said the Carols could not be evicted from the land Kobe Wilson gave Peter and if oil is found on it they would be able to own it. Being a popular politician, Big Jim felt he could persuade the probate court officials to destroy the document or make up another one, but somehow it posed difficult problems because there were witnesses present when the contract was written up and they could be counted on to say they were there when it was signed but if it meant bribing them to say they did not witness signing the will, Big Jim would do it and he would have them killed to have his way because other rich minerals were on the land but the black farmers never thought about trying to drill on it.

Immediately Big Jim ordered Betty's room to be cleared of her possessions without telling Kirby his son and youngest daughter Sandy. Big Jim not marry Mable for love but for her family's influence who could help him win his election for United States senator after he came home from the war and needed someone in a high political position help him gain the senate seat and Mable's father Tommy Hat seat could do it. Tommy said he would order his daughter Mable to marry him and in turn he would see to it that Big Jim became the next United States senator from Mississippi and Big Jim would write bills designed to protect Tommy's business interests.

Before the marriage was to take place Tommy called Mable into his private chambers and said to her." I want you to marry Big Jim Wilson who I will help become the next United States senator from Mississippi and he will look out for our business interests in this state and write some legislation so I can get some of the land belonging to the colored farmers which I think has oil on it and other properties my railroad wants to lay rail tracks down to carry my goods to other parts of the state and states outside of Mississippi."

Mable who looked attractive did not like the idea of her father ordering her to marry someone she did not know or love and she said," Father I cannot marry Big Jim. I do not love him and plus he is not faithful to women and is not liked by many of my friends. "

"I will disinherit you from my will if you do not marry Big Jim. I will make millions when he's up there in the senate getting bills passed for my railroad and business interests."

Because of Big Jim's racial attitude about colored people and people who did not have wealth, Mable did not want to marry him because he only married her to further his political career. People in her family made her realize the advantages of marrying Big Jim would keep her in her father's will and she would inherit much of the businesses Tommy owned valued at millions of dollars in revenues for the family who lived a life of splendor which could not identify with the masses of poor people who worked their land as share croppers. Mable and Big Jim did not share the same bed after Sandy was born but their marriage was more ceremonial because in public it appeared as if they were a happy family but behind closed doors Big Jim's appetite for women grew and Mable tried to ignored it but it was impossible because his relationships with other women was the talk of the town in Washing D.C. where he spent some of his time when the congress was not in session.

Regardless of his beliefs his son Kirby did what his father wanted him to do and argued with Big Jim in private and disagreed with him but in public stood united and fought anyone who said insulting dangerous words against his family and he would die for the honor of the family and there was Sandy a younger sister who sought recognition from the family because Betty 's achievement s outweighed her's in the community and his wife Mable got tire of him cheating on her and left and no one knew of her whereabouts. As a younger child Mable abused Betty and Big Jim never did anything about it. Betty could not turn to her mother who hated her because Betty ignored her pleas to stay away from John Carol who she could not accept as an equal because of her upbringing that black people were not on their cultural or economic level.

Her great grandparents told her how the Union soldiers invaded the plantations and stole everything insight and burned their property and how the black and white carpet baggers bought the land from the famers at low prices and the railroad owners from the north took their land and built the railroad tracks on it and did not give them a fair price for it. Mable resented her husband because he married her for her money and her family's connections which helped build his political ambitions.

CHAPTER 2

Tension and fear raced across Betty's face as she ran towards the Carol's track of land as sweat poured down her skin and her hair flew wild into the air. It was a modest tract of land which had a variety of crops on it. Being a jack of all trades, Peter built everything with wood and if he did not know how to do the job he sought the advice of other people who were good in that trade. The house consisted of two floors with a lot rooms. The sound of insects echoed through the forest and animals like the deer ran back and forth and her feet hurt hitting the rocks and tree branches covered by leaves. The shoes she wore were not fit for traveling over rough terrain but nevertheless Betty was determined to reach her destination regardless of what obstacles stood in her way.

A knock sounded on the big white door and it awakened Peter and Sarah as they attempted to sleep and not answer the door. One problem which made it difficult for Peter to overcome was his constant snoring and Sarah waked him so he could breathe without disturbing him. "Peter I hear something. Could you go see who it is."

As he tried to put his head under the pillow, Peter did not want to get up so Sarah hit him in the face with her pillow and Peter shouted at her.

"There you go disturbing me when I am trying to get my rest. You know I have to work in the fields tomorrow."

"Now Peter get up and see who it is. It might be someone who needs help."

The six foot tall, Peter strolled down the stairs and his dogs kept barking and making noises as Betty knocked on the door.

"Ok I am coming so wait. I'll be there."

As Peter opened the door he could not believe his eyes and there was Betty out there crying and as she came in Sarah called John to come at once to see what problems Betty got involved in. Being a hard sleeper like his father, John did not enjoy being awakened by anyone as he slept. But the family dog came into his bedroom and jumped on him licking his face. This was a custom his dogs did when they wanted John to go to the door. In his ears, John heard someone crying and got out of bed trying to reach a light so he could put on his pants.

John went down the stairs with his Long Johns on with big black buttons on them.

"Now John you shouldn't come down here in your Long Johns. We have a guest and most of all it is Betty and she has a problem." Sarah said," Betty and her father probably had an argument about her wanting to marry you."

Big Jim got angry about what Betty told him. Smoke filled up the room as Peter took puffs off his favorite cigar and Sarah said," This is a fine time for you to be smoking when this lovely girl has come to us in pain and tears."

Gently putting the cigar in an ashtray Peter said, "Now Sarah I always smoked when problems came up. I remember when I was in the great World War One and the Germans were closing in on our positions. I held my cigar in one hand and the good book in another and puffed a while. I figured out what to do with the Germans. I stayed calm and prayed. The Germans retreated after that and I kept on smoking and reading the good book. I always do this in times of trouble."

Getting some coffee John said," Betty what brings you here so late at night? You should not be out here in the dark. It's too dangerous. You should have come in the morning."

Betty looked into John's face and hugged him.

"Now what's all that for. Tell me who has hurt you because I cannot stay happy if you are sad," John said.

Giving her a cup of coffee," Sarah said." Now take this coffee and relax. We are here to help you so settle down."

As Peter pranced the floor smoking, he tried to put everything into perspective and said," I know you two have played together as kids but I did not think it was a good idea for both of you to get too close to each other because of the way things are down here. Many years ago when the first black folks were brought to Jamestown, Virginia in 1619 black folks and white folks married up a storm until the 1700 but now a colored man could get lynched for doing such a thing. I loved Betty and she never gave me any problems and she always spoke out against her father when he wanted to buy our land because it might have oil on it. We thought about leaving after the Second World War but we just stayed here because this was our home."

John listened to everyone talk but he had much to say as he made a motion with his hands and said, "Now what is the best thing for us to do?"

"I have some money saved up if daddy has not closed the account. He will do anything to keep me from marrying John and raise our kids in this place."

When Betty said this everyone looked at her in disbelief as Peter said, "When are you going to have my grandchild? I cannot believe it,"

John said. "There is no way we could raise our children in this state of Mississippi. People will not accept it. We might have to go up North and maybe I could find some work."

Taking her bank book out, Betty said "I have some money. Maybe I can take it out and get us a house in another state. I could not do it in Mississippi because my father know too many people and they will come where John and me are staying and make things very rough for us. They might even hang John."

The big old clock struck 10 and a wooden owl jumped out and made a loud noise and the smell of boiling corn traveled into the living room as Sarah managed to get some food prepared.

"Come and get it folks. I know you cannot talk on an empty stomach," Sarah said," And you know Peter the doctor said you must eat more vegetables and chicken instead of pork. You know your blood pressure is going to explode because of your greediness for pork."

Several cars approached the Carol house going at great speeds and when Sarah came out with the food she said, "You better hide Betty in the basement of the house where they will not find her."

A big muscular man knocked on the door and waited for someone to answer it.

Seeing it was taking too long for Peter to come to the door, Jack Benson kicked the door open and stumbled in.

This made John angry as he said, "Why in the hell did you kick the door in for? I was coming to let you in and what is it you want anyway?"

"Have you seen Betty Wilson? She and her old man had the damdist argument last night. Betty has not been seen anywhere and Big Jim wants to know where she is at."

Grabbing John by his shirt Benson said," Hold your mouth boy before I have you taken out side and horse wiped." At that moment Sarah rushed towards Benson and pleaded for her son.

As he let John go, Benson said," I know you and Betty were sweet on each other but if you think of marrying her we will string you up to the nearest huge oak tree."

"You niggers sure eat well around here. Fetch me some black coffee with no cream."

At first everyone looked at Benson in a rage but Sarah who wanted her son to be left alone got a cup of coffee for Benson because he would probably leave. Being satisfied with drinking the coffee, Benson pulled up his large pants and strolled out the door cursing up a storm and said, "If we catch that nigger son of yours with Senator Big Jim Wilson's daughter we will hang him and set his body on fire."

To intimidate people was Benson's way of getting what he wanted just like Senator Wilson who got what he wanted at any means possible. Benson was the man who did Senator Wilson's dirty work to establish he ran everything in the state of Mississippi. To keep his self –esteem up, Benson tried do beat John when he was overseer on the plantation but Peter stepped in and voiced his disapproval to Senator Wilson's father Kobe Wilson who immediately stopped Benson from beating the field hands cruelly.

Taking big steps Jack Benson went to his truck and drove off cursing as his tire wheels scattered dirt into the air. Benson was a big man who did jobs for Senator Wilson on his plantation and kept things in order for him.

Kirby and John played together as kids and Benson resented it and felt John's place on the plantation was to labor all day in the fields instead of running around in the forest hunting, fishing, and playing Robin hood with Betty and her brother but there was nothing he could do about it. Betty, John, and Kirby knew nothing about color barriers that kept them from socializing with each other. John and Kirby got into fights when they called each other racial names like nigger or honky sometimes for fun. It turned into bloody fights with Betty trying to break it up but they dared not tell their parents about it for fear they would not be able to play with each other again.

Big Jim's father Kobe allowed the colored and white kids play together as long as the chores were done on the plantation. Big Jim did not like his son playing with colored children and know them because he felt John's place on the plantation was to labor in the fields all day instead of roaming the forest hunting and playing with Betty, Sandy, and Kirby.

On Christmas the three of them exchanged presents and Peter and his family came up to the big house to eat turkey, greens, dressing, peach cobbler, fruit, corn on the cob, nuts, smoked ham, liquor and many good foods. White folks eyes got big when they saw colored folks eating at the dinner table. On the plantation porch hung Christmas ornaments, and red ribbons. The mansion was built by black slaves and it stood out as an architectural masterpiece.

Now the Coral family and Betty faced great problems because of Betty and John's love for each other brought conflicts which were going to make life difficult for them. Blacks and whites marrying each other was forbidden and their feelings could not be hidden from the pubic but they tried anyway. Betty was taken upstairs and all three of them sat and discussed how to solve the problem.

"You two are going to have to leave before your father catches the two of you together," Peter said, I'll lend you my truck so the two of you may go up North. You cannot live in this city as man and wife."

Taking out her dentures, Sarah said," I want the both of you to be happy and I have about two hundred dollars to give you. I know it's not a lot of money but if I can help you two in any way I will."

Working in a rush John brought out some boxes packed with clothes and a gun he kept since childhood.

"You think we can make it in that old Ford truck of yours. You know what usually happens when you go pass the speed limit in it," John said as he hugged his father.

"Well the two of you better go and write and tell us where you are going," Sarah said, "John's a good man who will take care of you."

"We will get a telephone in so you'll be able to call us." John said

With their blessings John and Betty got in the Ford and raced down the road to maybe a safe place in Canton, Mississippi.

CHAPTER 3

When he was a younger boy, Kirby said he would go into politics like his father Big Jim. Kirby debated in the manner his father did. He admired the way Big Jim debated other senators to get his legislation passed for the people he represented. When Big Jim was away in Washington, Kirby would put on his father's clothes he wore to the senate gallery and practiced speeches as if he was defending his point of view or debating other politicians about bills he proposed and as a high school student Kirby found himself into student government and he was not a bad student. He mostly got good grades in government and the social sciences and felt studying math and science was a waste of time. Giving equal rights to colored people became a problem when he felt there should be equal rights given to them and he became unpopular at school because of this. It was difficult trying to stay neutral with his father who was a segregationist and he and his father clashed on this issue of equality for colored people to where his father punished him for it.

Instead of going to class, Kirby skipped them and studied at the last minute for final exams and he managed to hide the fact he dated colored women but he kept it away from his father who would punish him for it because he preached separation of the races and to find out his son courted colored women all hell would break loose. His sister Sandy knew about it and Kirby did not get alone with her most of the time but Sandy could be trusted and when Sandy asked Kirby for a favor he reluctantly said yes and did it because she threatened to tell Big Jim about his love affairs with colored women.

Sandy disagreed with her father's views on race relations in the South and the way black people were treated. Sandy said to him," I hope you will one day change your attitude about colored people because you're wrong. There are some good colored people who work for us."

But now Kirby saw Jubal Short Dog Black get on the podium saying remarks which would keep him from becoming governor of the state of Mississippi. For two years Kirby campaigned throughout the state of Mississippi and lied to the people mostly white people that he cared about their rights and as governor he would pass legislation in their behalf and welcomed information from people telling him how he should work on the issues his opposing candidate failed to speak on.

Running for political office under his father's contacts would not suit him and Kirby hated how they lied to the people saying his father helped the people so they should support Big Jim's son to become elected governor. There were many people out there who did not like Jubal Short Dog Black to become governor because of his position to let big time politicians and big businessmen take the land belonging to the poor famers and put up fancy apartments on their land to gain wealth and build tourist attractions and not give them the fair market price for their land.

Kirby was a pro-lifer and opposed abortions and the people who were for abortions were at his rallies booing him every time he spoke about problems state officials were having to let the women have their babies without the state telling them they have a choice in the matter on if they want their children to live or not live. In many cases, Kirby told the people what they wanted to hear because he did not want to gain enemies but only to make the people in the audience think he had their best interests at heart. If he got word he would speak to a colored group of people he spoke about equal rights legislation and if he saw no colored people at the rally he spoke about preserving the rights of white people when it came to integration of their schools with colored children.

So many times pro-lifers came close to getting shot by people in the audience who opposed their viewpoints to stop women from getting abortions and pro-lifers and pro-abortion people often clashed with each other on this issue. The issues of states' rights to determine who could come into the restaurants and who could not always came up and Kirby looked at the amount of colored and white folks who were in the audience before he made a comment on the subject because he did not want to lose votes to the other candidate.

Sometimes Kirby's ideas on civil rights differed from his father who would not compromise whatsoever. Kirby's friends kept telling him to stay consisted with his father's views against pro-civil rights and not oppose them.

Before debating people at his rallies and fundraisers, Big Jim's rich friends told Kirby he would not get their support if he spoke out against the ideas his father stood for like letting colored people vote or hold public office which the white folks have enjoyed since the formation of the state government of Mississippi. Kirby as a young man witnessed how his father cheated the black and white share croppers out of the money when they sold their crops back to him for seed and fertilizer. Kirby told his assistants he would stand up for those farmers both colored and white and see they got a fair deal when selling their crops to Big Jim's friends and that his father was wrong for cheating them.

This political day Kirby and Jubal Short Dog Black would square off in public debate and the crowd mostly anti segregationist could not wait to listen to the next man who would be governor for the great state of Mississippi. His opponent Short Dog Black owned land in different parts of Mississippi and hated northern college students coming down to their state on the buses getting colored people to better themselves and live off welfare hoping the wealthy people would fund government programs designed to force the affluent people in the state to pay the bill.

The polls indicated Kirby lacked the strength to muster up the votes to win the masses of people in the state to be elected governor. There was a section of the audience where colored people could sit but there was no race mixing going on. Outside civil rights groups paraded back and forth shouting and singing and held up posters supporting Kirby to win. It seemed he was their only hope to get someone in the governor's office who would represent their interests even though they knew Kirby could be for civil rights when he talked to colored citizens who would listen and white folks who he knew did not foresee colored people getting their rights.

These two politicians did not like each other from the start because of their beliefs and some people felt they would have a bitter political fight to the end.

In politics a person who wanted to win in Mississippi usually won if they played ball with the wealthy land owners in the state, and they held secret meetings and decided which politicians shared their views on civil rights, and welfare programs, and health insurance topics supported by the wealthy land owners of the state and decided which politicians shared their views against giving civil rights and welfare programs to the poor colored and white farmers. The announcer came up to the podium to introduce the two candidates for governor by the name of Joe Miller and he was dressed in a comfortable white suit and Joe said,"

"Man how are you doing out there. This is a fine time for a debate. These two fine southern fellows of Mississippi are going to talk about the issues and problems affecting us and how they are going to do something about it."

People in the crowd were anxious for Joe to sit down because they wanted to hear from the candidates so they could make the best decision on Election Day.

As Short Dog strolled by Kirby, he pushed him and a fight started and the crowd broke them up and bad blood between these two men was shown in their faces every time they looked at each other but the crowd wanted to see a good debate on the issues they both stood for.

As Short Dog gave his speech Kirby threw missiles at him and this made Short Dog angry but nothing was done about it. For the second time a fight broke out between them and punches were thrown and as usual the crowd separated them as newspaper reporters recorded the events as they took place but lied on their opponents they supported to always make them look good so they could win votes. As they fought the people who wanted their candidate to win gave them support by yelling for their candidate to knock out the person they were fighting. The people who supported Short Dog felt he would put an end to the bus loads of white liberals and colored people coming to their towns in Mississippi stirring up the colored farmers to organize into unions and keep them from collective bargaining where the cotton pickers would get decent wages for their work and medical benefits for their hard labor working in the sun from morning to dust in the evening.

The people who shouted for Kirby to win consisted of many colored people because they needed the welfare programs and the right to vote for the person who would represent them. Many of them wanted their children to attend the white schools because they were better built and had much more to offer and plus many of the colored students walked many miles passed schools where only white students could go to and this is why they hoped Kirby would win because he was their champion who they felt would stand up for their rights.

Many of the people in the audience which were colored and white saw how the poor white and colored people could not attend school full time and worked in the cotton fields in the hot burning sun scorching their bodies. They realized if the colored man's freedom were locked up their own rights would be threaten too. Kirby supporters were against the rich plantation owners who formed corporations and bought up all the fertile farm land and gave nothing back to the poor white and colored famers for their hard labor.

Many times those supporters of Kirby faced the stigma of not being treated fairly only to see that Short Dog wanted to buy up their land and not give a fair price for it. The supporters for Kirby were moderate to liberal with a touch of being conservative on many issues and stood by Kirby to beat the hell out of Short Dog.

Sweat poured from both Kirby's and Short Dog's face, forearms, and body parts, and they looked like trash men pulling and tiring each other's clothes off. Hotel police came and broke the fight up.

Still filled with hatred for Short Dog Kirby said, "I challenge you to a duel. I get tire of you always speaking up for the colored people and pretending to be their friend against white people."

Short Dog was not going to be out done in words by Kirby and to intensify the conflict, he said," I get tire of people talking and saying your sister is sleeping with a nigger. She should be wiped and tied to a tree. No decent white folks would do a thing like this and there should be laws against it."

It took three men to control Kirby as he said," You do not know anything about my sister. John and Betty have known each other for years since they were kids. I do not think you should talk about her like that. You are mad because she never fell in love with you when you came courting her."

While Kirby tried to straighten out his suit and look more decent Short Dog saw a waiter bringing some drinks on a tray and pushed him into Kirby spilling the alcohol on his suit causing more heated calling of names at each other and Short Dog shouted with a big grin, "Your sister is pregnant and has been seeing Dr. Jamison and the colored boy John Carol is the father."

With that comment Kirby said "Ok hot shot we will go to another state and get this over with because the honor of my family is at stake and I will restore it when I shoot a bullet at your head and it lands in your big mouth."

Being a big drinker like his father, Kirby could not figure out where he was at and could barely walk but he was all fired up after drinking a lot of booze and he hated Short Dog. His friends kept telling him to go home and forget about what took place at the rally and what Shor Dog said. A lot of people heard what the both of them said and to back out of a duel would bring shame to both of them. None of them wanted people to think of them as cowards.

In his drunken state of mind, Kirby remembered going to school as a youngster and saw his colored friends working the fields instead of being allowed to attend school and one day learn a trade so they could get better wages and take care of their family needs. This drinking made him think he could do something to abolish the shame his sister and John brought on the family during a campaign year he decided to run for office. These thoughts kept running through his mind and it made him hurt inside to witness people laughing about the mixed relationship between his sister and John.

CHAPTER 4

As Sandy, Kirby's sister, and Mable, Big Jim's wife, showed up at the debate, strolled out the political hall they looked for Kirby but he could not be found and they wanted to take him home with them. Kirby always went home with his aides who supported and work with him. When Kirby got drunk, it was difficult for him to keep in control of himself and the slightest irritations made him vulnerable to attacks causing him to rebel against anything he did not like. Getting high off alcohol made him irresponsible and he respected no one when those drinking spell hit him. Other times Kirby took a drink to keep him on task to complete a project.

This dilemma confronting the Wilson family was one concerning murder and revenge to take out the life of someone who dared to attack their family and love one's reputation. Sandy who possessed a high voice and light skin presented a big smile and fine teeth and a round face, weigh about one hundred and fifty pounds wanted fair treatment for colored people and often argued with her father about his anti- civil rights for colored people to have equal rights as white people. She expressed much anger at many of the dinners her father gave at the plantation when his wealthy friends wanted to take over the farm lands in the state of Mississippi which might contain oil and Sandy spoke out against the segregation laws which said colored people had to sit in certain sections of the movie theaters or could not eat in a restaurant with white people or had to give up their seats to white passengers when riding on public busses but Sandy tried to explain to her brother about this inequality so he could embrace and fight for the civil rights colored people were being denied like the right to serve on juries or to live in any community they wanted to reside at.

With this great commotion taking place, Kirby felt honor must be restored back to the family because Shor Dog spoke nothing but lies about him wanting to make it better for colored people.

As thoughts of killing Short Dog came crashing down on him like a meteor, Kirby felt he would be the coward on the plantation if Short Dog was allowed to get away with those insults he said about his family in front of all of his good friends and enemies and most of all his father who would not think highly of him if he did not defend the honor of his family.

The sound of rain danced on the window near the driver's side and hit Kirby in his pale face and he tasted it as he tried to push it down his throat and it burned the soft tissues of his jaws. He could not tell what he drink because rainwater drifted into his mouth and if he dropped some of the whiskey, he took his lips and sucked it off him. His blue eyes appeared blood shot and you saw his hair hanging down. His nice neat blue suit became stained with alcohol and rainwater and his body smelled like the whiskey he drink. Lighting darted across the dark bare sky and hit several trees and their branches touched the ground making a loud noise as if you were experiencing the sounds of a haunted house and the wind blew the tree timbers back and forth as the wild animals hid for safety but these two men wanted blood spilled all for the sake of honoring their families. The raining stopped at one a.m. and an alcoholic personality Kirby staggered out of the car and Short Dog met him at the same spot but all of that fire water Kirby drink at the rally slowly left him and he realized he might kill Short Dog and probably spend the rest of his life in jail.

The alcohol posed such as great demon in him and his badge of honor made Kirby say to himself who would defend the rights of the people regardless of their race or did the colored people feel both Short Dog and Kirby were sincere in helping the plight of the white and colored farmers who barely made enough money to feed their families and buy supplies and seeds to plant next year's crops? Most politicians gave broken promises to those they would one day represent but currently many of them felt northerners would come to their homes and dictate the way they were suppose live. Who would decide which of these candidates were best suited to represent the people of this state as governor?

To duel against Short Dog meant standing up for the family name. The Wilsons have always stood up and fought for the honor of their family when someone insulted a relative. Many people felt Kirby could not measure up to his father's reputation as a great communicator when getting people to accept his ideas in the manner he wanted things done in the state of Mississippi which meant the life or death of his policies on segregation or integration for the people of his great state.

Now Kirby felt this was the chance to have his father speak highly of him when he entertained wealthy friends of the family. Political friends told Kirby he would go to jail and he heard dialogue from his cousin Steve Wilson," Kirby don't duel with this man. It would ruin your political career."

"Ah shut your mouth!" Kirby said as he drink more and said," This man must be killed for talking about my sister sleeping with a colored man."

Steve Wilson a cousin said, "You have to think about this cousin Kirby because spending time in jail is not worth it."

"I have to honor the family name! Maybe my father will be proud of me to silence this man who bought dishonor to our family who never did great things for Mississippi citizens."

Kirby and his second whose name was Randy faced Short Dog and his second Teddy as both of them were given their dueling guns. The two of them looked at each other in the eyes and the second of Short Dog said, "You two gentlemen walk 15 paces and after the counting stops face each other and shoot."

Their long 18th century pistols could not miss their target if pointed in the right direction and Short Dog's string of dueling victories caused Kirby to become afraid because Short dog's reputation made people attending betted 10 to one Short Dog's great shooting would win them a lot of money and before the dueling began money passed from one hand to the other hoping they betted on the right man.

The spurs on their boots made a sounding noise and insects such as lighting bugs flashed off and on in the dark forest and a night owl made sounds as if they were in a hunted forest with ghostly figures watching two men thirsting for death in the early morning when they turned to fire at each other and Kirby at the last minute decided not to take part in this fatal dilemma. Being a Christian man, Kirby remembered his pastor saying killing was sinful and he could not accomplish anything by killing people to honor the family name.

Deep in his heart Kirby did not want to kill this man who said his sister was sleeping with a colored man but his pride could not let him get away with those comments he said in public with many of the richest people in the state of Mississippi looking and watching to see what he would do to uphold the family honor. Maybe his actions would win him votes Kirby thought to himself but now all the frustration mounted on him and historians would record his finest hour to make people see they needed a brave and courageous governor.

As Kirby pulled the trigger, he stopped and shot into the air but after the smoke cleared Short Dog laid dead on the tree leaves.

"I did not shoot him!" cried Kirby, "Someone else did!"

As Short Dog laid in a puddle of blood coming out of his body someone shouted, "I see some smoke coming from distant trees!" one of the people at the dueling area said but Short Dog was motionless with a bullet hole in his forehead between his eyes.

Knowing he did not intend to kill Short Dog Kirby said," Another person shot Short Dog and I fired into the air.'

Someone checked his gun but chose not to tell anyone about it as Kirby pondered what took place. As Short Dog laid in a puddle of blood and his eyes remained opened with a smile on his face as he slowly drifted away to meet his maker.

As he laid in someone's arms Short Dog said," Kirby please forgive me. I did not mean the things I said about your sister. I just wanted to blow off some steam." As he coughed up some blood which dripped from his pink lips.

"Maybe we can get you to a doctor to get patched up. "Kirby said, "People say things in anger and when they come to their senses, they say they did not mean to express themselves in such an ugly way."

Looking at Short Dog, Kirby said, "This is a horrible manner in which a man is supposed to die, No man should end his life in pain like this. There must be better methods to solve disputes between men which can bring about a better solution instead of killing and bloodshed."

Still a little disappointed in what took place Kirby said, "Shot Dog died as he lived and the good book said you live by the sword and you will die by it. I know I did not kill this man because I never fired a shot at him. I fired into the air instead because I am not a man who handles or practices shooting guns."

To hide any evidence, Short Dog's friends took his body from the spot in which he laid and any other evidence left at the scene of the crime so no one would know what took place. Kirby was too overcome with grief to know what events place.

Still sad of the shocking situation, Kirby strolled on the moist ground making a crackling noise with his shoes which touched the fallen leaves laying on the ground and said," At this time of my life, I've made a stupid mistake of dueling and I am accused of killing someone I know I did not kill. I do not want to spend all of my life in jail. Maybe my father might be able to get me out this trouble and a lighter sentence."

His cousin Steve said," That is impossible because he did not want to see you get more powerful than him. Maybe your father could keep you from serving so many years but he's made a lot of enemies. He is a powerful senator up there in Washington but you know the elected boys always tell you what they want you to hear when they run for office."

Being in a delirious mood Kirby got away from the crowd and strolled down the dark lonely road and he reflected on the challenge of being able to beat the charges of killing Short Dog and his father's enemies loved seeing Big Jim's son going through trials and tribulations.

A gust of wind blew his hair as he scrambled through the mud with each step and the leaves sticking to his shoes made this a terrible sight to see. The atmosphere presented to Kirby a passion to pick leaves off the trees and smell them like a bee getting nectar from a flower but Kirby's favorite tormentors were insects tying to bite him as he drifted in the wilderness towards home. Dueling with Mother Nature became hard enough because mosquitoes tried to make a lucky bite and dine off Kirby's blood.

With each bite from the little flying creatures, Kirby shouted, "God Dammit the devil is coming after me!"

In a loud noise like a lion, Kirby envisioned demons coming at him from all sides spinning him back and forth and he saw in his mind being tied to a pole and different creatures dancing around him like the Indians did when they were about to kill an enemy of their tribe, and his other signs of life which were left made him want something to eat.

His thoughts lingered on what would his mother Mable think of him getting in trouble because she was strict on him and he and his mother always battled each other while Big Jim concentrated on politics and Mable took to drinking to forget her husband romanced many women who were friends of hers and rumors circulated Big Jim slept with his colored maid Polly but by now Mable tried to shut out such gossip by getting drunk and stayed in her room thinking about how to deal with her husband's womanizing ways while she stayed at the plantation for a long period of time before she left Big Jim knowing he did not love her and only married her for her wealth and her father's political clout.

Big Jim said this about Kirby, "The boy's a man who can make his own decisions. I cannot always be there for him. It's a shame I paid someone to shoot Short Dog so Kirby could be sent to prison to keep him from running for governor and plus he spoke out against my Jim Crow agenda."

Many times when Kirby got drunk he shouted," I could never measure up to my father's ambitions as my mother always told me!"

Kicking a nearby tree and breaking many small branches, Kirby kept on repeating, "Every time I tried to talk with that son of a bitch father of mind he would not let me say anything in my defense when a problem came up. His judgment was always right and the only one. There are two sides to everything."

With a no give up mood, Kirby drifted into a nearby road which smelled like new pavement was placed on it. For years the politicians ignored building and repairing the roads which the people complained about but the state authorities were interested in putting gambling houses in the city of Jackson, Mississippi so they could get the rich people's money and the poor people's money living in the state. Stubborn pride appeared on Kirby's face and he said to himself, "I'll hurry up and get to the house and tell my side of the story. I did not kill Short Dog but they are trying to frame me!"

Traveling so many miles his feet ached and he worried about what his ultimate fate would be if he turned himself in to law enforcement people controlled by his father who never gave convicted people a fair deal when they arrested them and only the rich felons received lighter sentences and probation.

When Kirby reached the road, he heard the sound of a car. A women driver noticed Kirby strolling down the road and she stopped and said, "I wondered who that man was drifting down the road. You looked so untouched by reality as if you were in your own little world not wanting any intruders to enter it. I hesitated whether to pick you up because you might molest me."

As she approached Kirby, he avoided talking to her but being drunk herself she knew she had to stop the car to avoid having an accident and she had a bad driving history of accidents where she was driving while full of gin and her favorite beer.

"Get in I am driving you away from this god forsaken place. Where are you going in all of this darkness? You must be on a mission and you look a mess and it appears you look as drunk as me. This is wilderness country and the insects will bite you all night if you continue to stay out here or you might get mugged by some strangers. These are hard times and people up to no good will stop you and kill you for a little of nothing. Sometimes they will do it because you don't have any money."

Wiping the dirt off his shirt and coat jacket Kirby said," I have been framed. Those no good bastards are the cause of this. I might get life in jail and my political future will be ruined."

Trying to keep her eyes on the road the girl said," My name is Chilly Wicket but most of my friends call me Wicket because I like to talk a lot and once I get started its hard for me to stop."

When Kirby looked and admired this small lady with long hair and a pretty smile he patted her on her legs and she slapped him in his face.

"Damit why did you do that? Those legs looked very good to me. You should be glad to have a man tell you how sexy you are."

"I am no tramp and I want to be treated as a lady if you catch the drift of what I am saying. You pick up a bomb on the road and he tries to feel on you. I could have ridden on but I saw you needed some help."

"By the way, man your breath smells bad. You have been drinking, wine, vodka, and gin on the rocks. You cannot survive out here in your condition."

"May I have some gum? I hate having people talk about me like that. I would not have killed Short Dog if I was not full of that fire water which was 100 proof alcohol."

"Give me fifty dollars and I will give you some gum."

"What do you think I am a complete fool, that's too much to pay for a stick of gum? How about five dollars. I do not have much money."

"You must be lying to me. A character like you wearing those fancy clothes got to have some lean naked presidents to spend on a bitch like me. I am no cheap whore. I need money for inspiration."

"You want to hear my story with a bad breath?"

"Hell no!"

"Well give me the gum so my bad breath won't run you out of the car."

"I can accept your proposition but you have to write me an IOU for seventy five dollars with interest. Baby I got to get paid to listen to your story which might be a pack of lies and plus there are two sides to every story."

"You look like someone I know. I've seen your face and picture on television on several posters. I know you must have the girls beating down the doors trying to flirt with you and get those greenback dollars in your bank account."

Still thinking about his ordeal, Kirby chose not to say anything because he felt it was none of her business and wanted everything to be a secret as he said, "You might know my father and his name is Big Jim Wilson and he is a United States senator. You know he signs a lot of bills that can help the people of this state and he will do anything to win an election. Sometimes the person running against him comes up dead. Mostly it was when the other candidate road in cars or flew in airplanes to talk with their supporters in different towns in this state."

Wicket's car scrambled around each curb and it appeared the drugs affected her vision.

"Take it easy!" "I want to make it home in one piece. I have a lot to live for."

"All you politicians do is lie to the people. You still tell people what you want them to hear and once they get elected into office they forget about all the promises they made to the people who voted them into office."

"Now look dam it! I will not take shit off of you so let me out of your car right now."

"You are being uppity and ignorant. You will need me one day. I am opposed to your father and his racist policies and one day we will chose a candidate who will beat Senator Big Jim Wilson. He's cheated many people out of their land like my father and I'll get even with him. If you are like your father I will not vote for you. Your father is nothing but a snake in the grass!"

With that being said, Kirby jumped out the car and slowly made his way back home looking a horrible mess.

CHAPTER 5

On the way home from the rally, Mable, and Sandy listened to the radio and cried when they heard Kirby was their suspect in the killing of Short Dog Jackson.

One night many years ago Big Jim bought a prostitute home he met at a night club and promised to give her $ 5oo dollars for sexual pleasures and he said to her, "My wife went to see her relatives and won't be back for a week. It will be ok to come home and sleep with me."

Sneaking her into the house when everyone was asleep, they went to another room and took off their clothes and commence to make love and Mable heard the noise and came into the room to investigate and realized what was happening and grabbed an umbrella and hit the both of them with it and she did not ask any questions and this commotion woke up the whole house and Kirby, Betty, and Sandy came into the room and broke up the fight. Big Jim did not know his wife left much earlier to come home.

"Mam you better get dressed and go home because momma is going to kill you!" Betty said.

"I'll go to the newspapers if he does not write me a check for $ 500 dollars!"

"Write the check out for the bitch because if this hits the newspapers it might hurt his vote in the Christian community! "Mable said," They think he is a saint and would never cheat on his wife!"

"You should know better than to do a thing like this which could make you and momma break up. Do you have any respect for your family than to bring another woman to our house and have sex with her!" Betty said, "Where is your dignity daddy!" Her father's actions with the prostitute angered family members.

The heavy drinking that night took its toll on Big Jim and he could barely remember what occurred between him and the prostitute. When he got a chance to talk with Mable he said." I was out on the town and drink too much. I cannot tell how I got involved with a prostitute. Can you forgive me for this? A man will be a man. Sometimes I get lonely when you are a way and want to have the affection of another woman. I cannot make any promises but I 'll try to stop doing my womanizing."

"I don't know about you keeping promises because you always break them all the time."

"Mable I am not perfect. I got to stop my drinking and settle down with you."

That flashback suddenly went away and Betty said, "I hope Kirby did not do any foolish things like attempting to duel with Short Dog to defend the family honor. This incident would ruin Kirby's political ambitions but it will brighten Big Jim's future more because his supporters and financial backers in future elections are looking forward to seeing their candidate fight for the rights of his son.

"Momma you know daddy has much influence on important people in this state and he could get Kirby a lighter sentence. He does not want to give much power to his son because Kirby tried not to identify himself with his father when he talked about not giving equal rights to colored people. These anti-integration policies have been in his thoughts and values ever since he was a small boy. Most of the judges owe their appointments to him. "Betty said,

Big Jim was not at the house when Mable came home with her kids and wanted it this way.

"That's one of the reasons I left your father. I told Big Jim to help your brother with his political campaign and raise money for him to become governor but Big Jim seemed to not be interested when he saw pictures of Kirby kissing little colored kids and shaking the hands of young white and colored people who joined the freedom rides who came down here in the south trying to get colored folks registered to vote and form unions so they could get better prices for their crops after the harvest was over.

Kirby's clothes were dirty and smelled bad but he managed to come back to the mansion. Looking at the spots on his suit made him look like a leopard with black little marks on him. At the big mansion all types of sounds generated from room to room as Sandy and her mother came into the big mansion which had five big marble pillars. To touch the white columns in front of this massive building made you think of the rich heritage of the black slaves who worked and built the beautiful mansions for their white plantation owners.

When family members saw him, Kirby had a gun pointed toward his head and he threatened to kill himself if anyone tried to stop him.

"What are you doing with that gun?" Sandy shouted at him," You will not prove anything by killing yourself. You are my older brother and the family needs you."

Still trying to put the pictures back in order of his terrifying experience Kirby said," My political life is ruined because of Short Dog's death. I did not kill him. Another person did it. They will not believe me so I should kill myself and end it all. They will not have me to be picked on this year."

"Listen to me son. I am your mother and I always told you to stand up for your rights and not try to find an easy way out. Just think what your father would think if you did something like this."

"I never had a father who stood by me. I always disagreed with him on equality for colored people because of the way they were being treated and I still don't like it. One day those prejudice laws against the races being able to enjoy their civil rights will end if I have anything to do with it."

"But son," Mable said," You should have been silent on civil rights talking about those anti-civil rights laws he was for and when he was trying to get them made into law."

Getting up and walking to the door, Kirby made it to the front of the mansion and fired five bullets into the air and dropped the gun.

It was a difficult time for both Kirby, Mable, Sandy, and Betty who was out of town called and spoke to him about it and Betty and Kirby clashed about him speaking too soon against the segregation laws in the South because he would need his father's support to become governor of the state of Mississippi but Kirby ignored her when she tried to tell him this because Big Jim had a lot of influence with the local and state politicians and supported them when they ran for election and reelection.

It appeared Kirby developed a mental health condition. This worried Mable and Sandy because Kirby was her heart but Big Jim treated Kirby in the old tradition of bringing up a boy making him do hard work and one main thing he instilled in him was he wanted his son to be the best he could be. Big Jim would accept nothing less from his son and when he caught his son lying about skipping class he confronted Kirby when he was with his friends beat him for such conduct and called him disrespectful names.

Sandy said, "You need your father's influence because the thought of you going to jail is hurting the family members. I know you and father had a bad relationship when you were much younger but he wanted you to be better than him in whatever you did."

"But momma you never tried to stop him from being hard on me. When he gave me a beating in front of my friends you never said anything to him and let daddy have his way. He called me so many names and said I would not be anything but a bomb of a rich senator."

I said, "I wanted to be my own man and not modeled into something I don't want to be to please my father."

Big Jim gave Kirby a direct order he must go to college and he recalled a time when he visited a prison as a class project and he witnessed a project designed to keep people who were on probation from going back to prison and his nerves got unsteady as he heard about the prison gangs and prisoners killed each other in secret without the authorities knowing about it and how they were sprayed by guards to keep diseases off of them.

Kirby remembered one prisoner telling the boys on probation the following: "The food is bad and you have to wait to see a doctor for at least five months and there is only one doctor treating four hundred men."

One of the prisoners said, "You can forget about your girl because she is not at home waiting for you to get out of jail. She is seeing another man. We can get any weapon we need to kill someone and drugs are one of the things we can obtain."

"Now we will show you a film on what can happen to a person who does ignorant things like killing and shooting innocent people. "One of the prisoners said.

"Man I've never seen nothing like this showing a man being electrocuted before my eyes. His skin peeled off his face to the bones. Crime does not pay." Another prisoner said whose face was covered with cuts and bruises.

Another prisoner came up on a boy who was on probation and said, "Prisoners have to join a gang to survive in here."

When Kirby thought about the times he took those boys up to the prison who were on probation he said to Sandy and Mable, "Please forgive me for my behavior. I will not go to prison. They will have to kill me if I have to live the life of a prisoner. I just cannot see myself in a prison with killers, rapist, and people who made a living in crime and doing wrong."

A loud noise echoed through the door as the sheriff kept knocking on it.

After several delays, Big Jim arrived from Washington, D.C. and he took part in a filibuster to defeat civil rights legislation giving colored folks the right to vote.

"I could not support the right for those niggers to be given the right to vote, "Big Jim said to himself out loud, "When they got the right to vote because of the Reconstruction period too many of them became uppity. That cannot happen again."

What surprised him was seeing his wife Mable who he had not seen in three years and his son looking a dirty mess.

Before he could speak to everyone, Big Jim said, "At 12:00. Am. at night who could be coming out to our mansion at this time of night.

Can't they see it is time for us to be in bed? I have a lot of work to do when I get up in the morning."

"Son what is this all about? You are looking bad and who have you been fighting? You look awful and your face is cut badly."

"Now Big Jim your son needs you. Don't be so hard on him. The law enforcement people feel Kirby killed Short Dog in a duel across the river."

"What the hell, why would you want to do a godam thing like that for which could cost you your political future in this state?"

Sandy said," There is no time to argue about what your son should have done because we are family and must support Kirby. He did not kill Short Dog. Somehow pistols were shown with his finger prints on them but Kirby saw fellows shooting at a long distance from where he and Short Dog dueled."

"Wait a minute!" Big Jim hollowed at the sheriff." I've got to get dressed, "as he rushed up the stairs and ran into his room to put on his pajama pants, shoes, and a shirt.

"Where are my sleeping clothes? I cannot find them."

Sandy said, "You took them to Washington. I did not see them when I did the wash."

The sheriff kept beating on the door outside and his knocks on the big white door sounded like a musician beating a big drum.

In a frantic hurry, Sandy strolled into Kirby's room and got his sleeping clothes and gave them to her father who was too small for him but he got them on anyway.

As Big Jim opened the door a slender man stood in the doorway holding a warrant in his hands for Kirby's arrest. His beard touched his chest and his hair was long and his big boots looked like the ones worn by paratroopers and around his waist contained many bullets. A big flashlight hung on his waist and a big western caliber pistol and he said, "My name is Sheriff Early and I want to search the house.

"You cannot do this without a search warrant."

"Here's my search warrant, "and Sheriff Early hit Senator Wilson in his mouth knocking out his front teeth.

Not to be out fought, Big Jim lived up to his reputation of defending his family when trouble came to his house and grabbed a chair and hit Sheriff Early who felled to the floor. This did not stop Sheriff Early as he grabbed a fishbowl and threw it at Big Jim who ducked and he used a hip throw to toss Sheriff Early into his couch.

Sheriff Early got one of Senator Wilson's swords used in the Civil War by one of his great grandfathers and Big Jim cried out. "Don't touch that sword you might break it. It is worth one hundred thousand dollars." Big Jim said as Sherriff Early threw him another sword to protect himself with as the two of them squared off like the Knights of the Round Table. Sweat poured from their underarms as each of them tried to cut each other and Sherriff Baker's sword tore off part of Big Jim's clothes as he thrust it at him.

Dodging the sword Big Jim shouted with a grin, "You liked to have got me but I am too good for you."

Mable and Sandy watched as the two of them tried to stab each other to death.

"Stop the two of you!" Mable said, "The both of you might get killed!"

Kirby hid in the cellar of the attic and watched the two people nearly kill each other and wanted to stop the fight between his father and Sheriff Early and he sneaked into the room where they fought and it was no easy chore because both of them were extremely good. Picking up a vase Kirby stood in back of Sheriff Early getting ready to hit him but Sandy pushed the vase out of his hands and shouted: "The two of you must stop before someone gets killed as she pointed a gun at the both of them getting ready to pull the trigger.

"All I need is for my father to go jail for killing Sheriff Early. I cannot bare such a thought. I know my beliefs of integration of the colored and white folks differ from my father and I do not want to see him die because of it."

Everyone settled down and got their composure and Kirby said, "Daddy I did not know you would fight for me when my enemies want to have me killed for my pro civil rights convictions and another thing, I did not kill Short Dog. A no good evil person who hated Kirby shot him"

Sheriff Early said, "You and Short Dog talked a lot about dueling with each other and all of a sudden he comes up dead. We have to take your son in for questioning and he might have to stand trial for killing to see if he is guilty or not."

Kirby did not like what was being said by Sheriff Early and said, "You know I will not get a fair trial because my father and I disagree on how integration and segregation cannot exist in society at the same time. The judge and jury will be against me because most of the jury I know and do not like my thoughts about colored and white folks integrating. They do not want to integrate the black and white children and they are against busing. They will be against me and not be fair in their decision making."

"Hold your horses, "Big Jim said, "I know most of the jurors and they owe me favors. They will not give you a harsh sentence if I have something to do with it."

As Kirby heard what Sheriff Early said an angry look appeared on his face and Sandy knew her brother could be very explosive but before Sheriff Early came to the plantation he told his deputies to tire down the door if he had not called them in thirty minutes.

Seeing Big Jim's door was not locked a strange fellow strolled into the house without knocking and Kirby shouted at them, "Who gave you the authority to drift into my house without knocking."

As Marvin who was one of Sheriff Early's deputies and the other officers came into the house, Kirby threw a punch at Marvin with his fist knocking him down and as Marvin went to the floor Sheriff Early hollowed and the other men wrestled Kirby to the floor and placed hand cups on him.

"Ok" said Marvin who weighed over two hundred pounds of solid muscle and could press two hundred and fifty pounds of solid weights when he did his weight exercises kicked Kirby in the stomach and cursed at him and said," Godamit you should learn how to respect the law enforcement officers who come to the house. "Marvin said as he let Kirby up and sprayed some mace on him which made him very sick and Kirby coughed and other family member ran out the house and Marvin carried Kirby to his car.

As they stood outside in the front, "Mable said, "I' know Big Jim you framed my son to keep him from getting bigger than you. You did not want your son trying to appease the civil right groups coming into this state trying to get colored people to vote and eat in the restaurants where white folks could only patronize. I've read some of the racist books you have and how the white racist groups were attempting to keep things just the way they were when President Rutherford Hayes took the union troops out of the South after the War Between the States ended."

"Mable I would not set up my son to have him framed because we disagree over our civil rights issues. In some cases I changed my viewpoints on the issues on civil rights," he said as he pulled up his suspenders and said," I would not mine my son following in my footsteps and maybe holding a big political office in the state but the murder on my son's record will hurt his chances of becoming governor of this state."

Not being outdone Sandy said, "Well I think you have never tried to spend a lot time with your son. All you did was run for political office and lie to the people. Depending on the crowd you told them what you wanted them to hear."

As they stood on the front porch Mable said, "Sandy this is my house and I will not tolerate this type of talk coming from you. You will be going to law school next year and your father will be paying your tuition. I want you to work in one of my businesses the family owns."

"You cannot be too friendly with the colored folks around here. I won't hear of no such thing. If I pay for your schooling, you will work for the organizations who are very rich people. I've already got it arranged," Big Jim said.

"I cannot let you run my life for me or tell me who should I work for or not and I do not care if you are paying my tuition. You cannot tell me how to think and I do not share your views on segregation of the races."

As Kirby was put into the police car, Sandy said, "Goodbye Kirby I will come to see you and be at your trial. I'll testify in your behalf too. I' believe you if you say you did not kill Jubal Jackson."

Officer Marvin and Sheriff Early slowly pulled out a journal and wrote on it charging Kirby with first degree murder.

Tears fell from her eyes as they took Kirby to jail, and Sandy said," Now daddy I want to be a lawyer for the poor people both white and colored people around here. I do not care why you expect me to help you when you are pretending to be for the poor colored and white farmers in your senatorial district. You wrote a bill that stopped northern integrationist to come here to organize colored sharecroppers so they could get a union."

"I am going to pay for your law school education and you will work for me. I am not sending you to law school to learn how to stop my beliefs in segregation of the races plan and I plan to get the oil on the colored people's land who lives outside of Jackson, Mississippi. Who gives a dam if many of those farmers will lose their lands? I want the oil on that property."

With that comment, Sandy gave him a frown and said, "Well it looks like you might win on this issue because I need your influence and help to succeed." Sandy said this to please her father but she did not mean it but inside of her was a burning desire to see people of all races are treated fairly.

A big smile appeared on Big Jim's face when he heard Sandy say that and said "That's the spirit Sandy you have to help protect your father from his enemies and I have a lot of them. Many attempts have been made on my life but I manage to escape each one of them."

Little did Big Jim know Sandy would rebel in later years against his racist policies.

CHAPTER 6

Noise from conversations drifted back and forth through the courtroom and the smell of cigarette smoke danced in the hallway because you could not smoke in the courtroom. People sat on the wooden benches in the court and in the hallways. Kirby would stand trial for the murder of Short Dog a favorite son of the people of Mississippi who wanted to keep the colored people from getting equal treatment to enjoy going to movie theaters, getting the right to vote without having to know how to read or write or serve on juries. Short Dog was for men of evil keeping minorities from living in several white communities because of the color of their skin. One of Big Jim's lawyer friends was supposed to represent Kirby but his father did not give the lawyer any money to pay Kirby's legal fees so a public defender took over the case but he was not to be trusted because he usually followed the orders of Kirby's father which might mean disaster for him which were not in his best interests.

Before the trial Sandy visited Kirby and spoke with him and she said," Try to get another lawyer because the one who is given to you will not represent you fairly. Father is up to his old tricks again. The jurors are his pals and will rule in favor of what he proposes. You cannot trust him Kirby."

The courtroom was filled to standing room only. In back of Judge Ben Wallace hung a confederate flag and pictures of great people of the southern states who made a name for themselves like General Robert E. Lee and many relatives of confederate soldiers were at the court room proceedings.

A section for the black people who wanted to support Kirby waited patiently for the judge and jury who would decide his faith. The sounds of people talking in quietness were heard as they tried to figure out the outcome of Kirby who could get life in jail because all the evidence led to him being convicted of a crime of murder in the first degree. It was illegal to duel in the state of Tennessee anyway and many legal experts felt this state had jurisdiction instead of Mississippi. Many of the people in the audience sucked on tobacco and you could see them spitting on the floor after getting all of the juice from it. This hideous behavior could be a five dollar fine if they were caught doing it, and if caught carrying a gun without a permits a person would get a $500 dollar fine.

Even though the officers and sheriffs checked people for guns sometimes they would let their friends in the court without doing it and who could easily shoot at Kirby who did not like what the verdict would be. Outside the court room people sat in small groups making bets on if Kirby would get life or manslaughter but the safest place to make bets was in the restroom which many people did to make some money if a verdict of $ 5000 dollars would be imposed on the people doing illegal actions but the fines imposed on these people would be divided among the judges and court personnel instead of going to the city of Jackson, Mississippi. Corruption took place and this would become a time to remember. A section of the court reserved for colored people were divided in their support of Kirby because they felt he was for the same segregationist ideas his father possessed. This was not the true belief among some colored people who supported Kirby who they felt could speak up for them because on some occasions he visited colored schools in the city of Jackson and saw the public schools were segregated and in bad shape lacking up to date books with nothing in them talking about colored people who made contributions to the history of the United States.

Kirby saw no modern heating facilities in many of their schools and rooms for nurses to treat the kids and one doctor to give all of them their booster shots before interring school which was an enormous task. Looking at the bare land in back of the schools, Kirby saw no baseball diamonds or track fields for running track and field events and he cursed at politicians in his thoughts because they were for the rich citizens only and not the middleclass or poorer people who they took an oath to protect and write legislation for the people they represented. When Kirby came to the school, the children booed at him because they knew he was Big Jim's son and felt he would give them broken promises he would not keep like his father Big Jim and he promised he would try to improve their schools in the neighborhoods they stayed in which for years were neglected and not brought up to modern standards of the day to educate students.

When the students saw his sincerity, they embraced him with open arms. When attorney George Wilmore visited Kirby while he was in prison he spoke about his war experiences and said," The Germans attacked our position and they only gave me the Blue Cross. They should have given me some whiskey and a million dollar trip home but they patched me up and sent me back to the front with Patton. What a lousy way to get rewarded for getting shot in the leg. The doctors said I could not fight on this leg but I had to pay them $ 500 dollars to have that done and they would have shipped me home but I did not make enough money in our army pay to do that and plus I loved to gamble my money away when I got paid."

In his hands, Wilmore carried information about what took place at the crime scene and he looked through his wide rimmed glasses and said, "My name is Wilmore and I am going to represent you. I am not a criminal lawyer but I'll represent you the best way I can," and he smiled in a suspicious manner and further said, "Morris Parks your father's lawyer could not come today because of out of town business and plus he hits the bottle too much. I wonder why your father puts up with him anyway. I've chosen to handle the case because of your father."

"It would have been nice if my father would have given me a selection of lawyers for me to choose from because the ones he knows can be bought off which can mean I spend time in jail by being appointed a lawyer I do not approve of."

"If you plead guilty of involuntary manslaughter you will get out of jail in two years and probation after one year of prison. There are many civil rights workers coming into Mississippi trying to encourage colored people to vote and organize their own political parties and we do not want them to see you are treated unfairly because they might cause a lot of unrest and those college kids whose parents got money to give their kids will come to our beloved Mississippi trying telling us how to live our life down here.

The conversation attorney Whitmore brought to Kirby did make him too happy as a frown appeared on his face and he crossed his leg in a fold over the other one and said, "I won't have a chance with you because I would rather take our chances with our family attorney Morris Parks. He served my family good and I knew him as a kid when father took me to his office millions of times and they always came into conflicts with each other because daddy wanted to tell Parks how the law should be applied to their legal problems but he was the only lawyer who did not let my father have his way with him."

"This took me by surprise because attorney Parks called me and said for me to take the case and he'll be out of town for a few months doing some work for your father."

Giving Whitmore an angry look Kirby said, "I want you to get out of here at this moment because I'll represent myself. You will not work in my best interest. My father probably paid off the jury and the judge presiding over the case to be against me as usual. I'll get my sister to get an attorney for me. You look too unprofessional to represent law abiding citizens."

Gradually getting up from the chair which made loud noises Kirby went into the courtroom and a judge waited for him to see what he would say but it was rigged into a bench trial. Judge Willcut asked what he knew about the incident and Kirby said, "I did not shoot Short Dog. I pointed my gun in his direction but I did not fire a shot at him even though I wanted to get even and silence those evil red lips of his for saying words which dishonored my family's honor. I did not pull the trigger and as a matter of fact I saw another man running away from the crime area when Jubal fell to the ground."

Judge Harry Willcut looked at him and said," The lab technicians examined the gun and it has your finger prints on it. Several people at the crime scene said you fired the fatal shot which killed Jubal Jackson and by the way where is your attorney? A man representing himself is a fool and will hurt himself all the time."

Kirby unbuttoned the top of his shirt and said," I did not want an attorney to represent me because most of them are crooks and will sell you down the river. My father pays them off when they try to sue him and he controls state politicians because they owe him favors and will not stand up against him. My father will be the next Huey Long."

The tension between the two of them flared up and Judge Willcut said," That's enough of that kind of talk in my court room. Your father and I have clashed many times but he is a good friend of mine. I promised your father I would give you a lighter sentence for non-voluntary manslaughter."

Banging his fists into a desk, Kirby said, "You haven't proved me guilty and besides I do not have a lawyer to defend me or jury to decide whether or not I am guilty. I was full of alcohol and did not know what happened when the shooting took place."

Taking off his glasses and throwing an ashtray at Kirby, who ducked, Willcut said, "You signed this document saying you did not want a jury trial and I would decide your fate on this matter and based on the evidence I sentence you to 20 years for killing Short Dog to the Mississippi State Prison. Guards take this criminal out of here!"

When Kirby heard this he said, "Just as I expected. This is wrong and dam it you and my father will pay for this illegal proceeding because I never killed Short Dog in the first place. I have a right to a jury trial which I did not get and to face my accusers. I do not see their lawyer or their people who said I killed Short Dog in this court room."

Saying he had business transactions in Washington, Big Jim said he could not make the trial and all the family told him his son needed him in this time of trouble but Big Jim laughed and said, "Kirby should not have killed a man who supported me and my anti- civil rights legislation and my efforts to get those oil rich lands the farmers are living on but doing nothing to get oil from it."

Much commotion took place when the verdict was issued and Mable his mother and his two sisters were angry when it was read and Mable stood up and said, "This was not a fair trial because the writing on this confession is not my son's signature. You can barely see it. My son was drunk when he came home after the duel. He could barely stay on his feet and he is entitled to a trial by jury."

Sandy said, "You gave orders not to let me and my mother see Kirby and advise him of his legal rights which violates his Fourteenth Amendment rights. I'll go to the media and tell them about this injustice."

"Kirby my dear brother control yourself. They will not get away with this injustice, "Sandy said," I'll try to do what I can for you."

Looking with curiosity Betty did not say too much because she and Kirby clashed over his liberal views on civil rights and equality for colored people and knew if she openly supported Kirby it would anger her father who supported her when she wanted to do something with her life to develop her businesses and Big Jim could influence bankers to give her loans.

Sandy's plea's did not matter because Kirby ignored her and cursed up a storm and spitted on the armed guards who hit him with their clubs and shouted. "You dam nigger lover you deserve everything you are getting," as he hit Kirby in his back.

With blood dripping from his forehead, Kirby still had the strength to say, "I'll get even with the no good son of a bitches who did not give me a fair trial. I did not ask for a bench trial and I have a right to a lawyer. Momma do not let me go to jail and where is my old man and has he forsaken me!"

Filled with so much emotion and giving everyone he faced an angry look, Kirby said, "Damit I knew when Betty hooked up with that nigger John Carol this bullshit would happen."

While Kirby is taken to jail, Big Jim sat in the judge's chambers and later paid him $10,000 dollars for sending his son to jail in an unjust manner. To keep his power and influence, Big Jim would do anything to stop other people from getting in the way even if it was his own son. Big Jim never left town.

At Axter Prison clashes between the guard and prisoners took place all the time while Kirby was there and they lived under harsh conditions. Prisoners made license plates and were paid five cents an hours while the big money went to state officials leading up to Senator Wilson who wrote regulations for the state representatives to pass legislation making it ok for the prisoners not to get their fair share of the money made from the sale of license plates. To justify their actions, prison officials said by using cheap prisoner labor it gave them something to do with their time because sitting in a prison cell all day would make it hard to reform them. The longer they stayed in jail the more money could be made off their cheap labor.

Axter prison held some of the toughest prisoners in the country who enjoyed a life of crime. Pressure came from the relatives of prisoners who were missing to find out what had happened to them without anyone knowing what took place or the causes of their deaths. Outside the prison was a huge mass of concrete containing 60 feet walls above the ground with barbed wire and electricity running through them. A ten feet moat filled by water had alligators swimming in it surrounded the prison and a wire fence placed around it. Many prisoners got ate up by those reptiles who thought they could escape out of the prison trying to get away from the harsh prison conditions which the outside world knew little about. Letters sent to their family and friends never reached their destination. A draw bridge was built to let in people coming into the prison and at each of the fifty feet towers guards carried 45 automatic pistols and automatic shot guns. Visitors coming into the prison got searched with metal detectors. One doctor treated three thousand prisoners and they went for weeks before a doctor saw them. A prison riot took place before he came to Axter Prison but it got repulsed by the guards.

CHAPTER 7

With all of this drama going on Betty and John secretly traveled to Canton, Mississippi with John driving because people would think he was her valet escorting her around to different places of business. When Betty went into a place which rented out rooms, John could not go in because the signs indicated colored people had to enter from the back door. John sneaked into the room when Betty paid for it

"Now John wait out here while I try to buy some property in this place of business."

Mr. Larry Woodson, who weighed 250 pounds and wore glasses and long hair down his back said, "What brings you to my office so early in the evening?"

His office did not look too business like and dust laid heavily on his desk and you could see rats trying to eat food left in one of the rooms which did not bother him and the head of a big deer hanged over the fire place and a picture of him standing next to the deer he killed on a hunting trip many years ago and he wore a wrinkled suit.

'Well sir, "I am looking for some property and hope to settle down in this town. My servant is driving me to different places."

"Will he stay with you at this house?"

"Yes he will. My daddy recommended him and he has been driving for our family for years. This is a special assignment for him and later he will go back to my father's plantation to work."

"I do not think our company can sell you the house because the white folks will not stand for a white girl living with a nigger so take your money and look somewhere else."

Not to be outdone Betty and John knew the social atmosphere for race mixing would be hard on them. With Betty being pregnant, John constantly worried about her condition and sometimes wanted to leave her so she could get a hotel room to sleep in but she insisted on staying with him no matter where it was.

With a lot stubbornness Betty yelled at him and said, "You are the father of my kids and I will not get shelter in a place you cannot enjoy too."

"John I want to get married and I want our child to have your last name and I want to raise our family also."

"You know that's a good idea but it's too impossible because no white or colored ministers will marry us. It's hard for us to even stay together at a hotel and difficult to own a farm. I remember when we went to a justice of the peace saying we were going to get married a mob formed outside when they heard about it and you and me sneaked out the back way."

John, and Betty kept talking and she said, "I am a woman and just like it is hard for colored people to buy property in Mississippi they make it difficult for a white women to have equal rights too. And if you are a wealthy white woman they tend to get everything they want."

"What do you have in mine?" Maybe your idea may work so tell me how this problem will be fixed."

"Let's get a white man to do it and his name would be John Carol. They do not have to know it is the name of a colored man."

"The only problem is what white man we could get to do something like this. Most of the people know Big Jim and who could we trust?"

"I have a great idea," and she looked like a car wreck in her head of hair from sleeping on the car seat and being pregnant did not help matters either.

"A friend of mine lives not too far from here," Betty said." In a town called Law and Order who might be able to help us for the right price by the name of Snake Eyes but I do not know if we can trust him because he has a reputation of being dirty and dishonest but if you want something done illegal you could always count on him."

"What will you do to get him to help us or betray us? You cannot trust everyone with your money because times are hard enough without people plotting to steal from you. Just be careful."

"All we have to do is give him one hundred dollars and he will sign up for the property and we will be able to move on it and make it our home."

Well let's try something because I am tire of sleeping in this old car and plus you are pregnant and need a proper place to have our baby. He should not be born in a car. I guess what you are proposing might be ok."

Her friend's name was Snake Eyes and he constantly looked at his watch because he never knew when the police would be knocking on his door to raid his place of business because he kept himself on the wrong side of the law selling moonshine gin which him and his friends made in the nearby forest on government property and he always put his women on the streets to keep his prostitution program in order. If his girls got caught by the police, Snake Eyes acted as if he did not know anything about it and pay off the mayor and he kept them from being put in jail.

"You look really dapper Snake; it's been a long time since I've seen you. You owe me a great favor because I got my father to bail you out of jail and the charges dropped when you were caught having sex with a girl who was fourteen and you could have went to jail but instead he got you a 30 day sentence for you to get counseling."

Rubbing his hair down and putting on his favorite cologne, Snake said, "I remember but part of the deal was for you to have sex with me too."

"I would not dare because you had so many bed maids; I did not want to catch a venereal disease because you went to the doctor all the time for shots because of your appetite for having sex with anything who wore a skirt. Now let's get down to business because I need your help."

When Snake looked at the beautiful women, he took his hand and rubbed it over his hair styling it back in place and in his office were pictures of him and the mayor shaking hands with each other and on his wall hung picture of him singing in the night clubs and standing in front of a big bear he shot on a vacation to Alaska.

"Well let's get down to business. I am tire of sleeping in this old car plus I am pregnant and need a proper place to rest before I have my baby and he should not be born in a car."

"Come on in. Who's the nigger. You know they can lynch you for driving around with a colored boy and you know it. What brings you to my office to see me? Betty the years have been good to that fine figure. I might reduce my cost for a little sex."

Getting up and slapping Snake in his face, Betty said, "You better respect me and my man because I love him and will not accept your racist remarks."

"Now Betty I was only kidding. I like to flirt with the women who come into my place of business."

"I see you are still trying to rip the people off by saying you are a lawyer and breaking the law at the same time."

"I need you to buy some property for me. I am a woman and I have John with me and every time I go in to make a deal I get turned away. I am pregnant and need to be resting in a house so will you do it?"

The clock clicked quietly as Betty and John looked patiently to see what he would say because everyone they approached said no and did not give them an explanation for denying them the right to buy some property. As they waited for Snake to say something his phone ringed constantly which kept him on it for fifteen or twenty minutes and Betty turned up the radio very loud and Snake hung up the phone and blew kisses through it because the person he spoke to was one of his many female friends he developed an ongoing relationship with.

To make matters worse, a knock was heard at the door and a gentlemen came in and two other gangster looking men accompanied him.

All of them dressed in pin stripe suits and carried guns and the last two men to come in did not say anything but Snake said to John he had to speak with the fellows on some business

All four of the men walked into the room and spoke with each other and an argument erupted over some money Snake owed them and a fight started and one man came flying out the door with a broken arm and Snake shot the other one in his leg and he scrambled out the door begging not to be shot again. The intruder tried to hit Snake but he grabbed a bat and slammed it into his leg and threw him out of the office.

While this was going on Betty and John ran into the restroom and did not come out until Snake told them to.

"The nerve of those thugs asking me to pay protection dues. Nobody tells Snake how to protect his place of business. I run things around here and that's the way it's going to be."

Coming out the restroom quickly Betty said "I know you do not have time to think about what to charge us so I think we will have to come back."

"Wait a minute just give me $ 5,000 dollars and I can do it but it must be given to me right now. ".

"What in the hell do you think you are. How do we know you will not take our money and run off, $ 5000 dollars is a lot of money these days? Betty will have to go with you because I do not trust you."

When Snake saw himself getting into difficult money problems, he placed a smile on his face and took out his comb and pulled it through his rough long hair which made him look like a hippie and quickly strolled in front of them moving his hips in a sophisticated manner like he was a holly wood producer and said, "You have no choice nigger. I am all you got. Once they see you they do not want to make a deal with us and I can always say Betty is my sister but you cannot say anything that would not make them too suspicious. You have to let me make the deal because I am good at it. Five thousand dollars is too much money to turn down plus I know Big Jim and he cheated me in a dice game years ago before he became a no good senator for the state of Mississippi."

"I'll tell you what. Come with me Betty and we will talk with some people who can sell the both of you the house but John you have to stay at my place of business and wait for us to come back." Betty gave him the $ 5000 dollars.

"I still will not go along with that and how can we know you can be trusted and I did not like the way you keep looking at her."

"I am having your baby and I cannot keep resting in this car. I have some money to buy the property. Snake will bring me back. I got the money out of my account before coming to your house before my father decides to stop payments in the account he set up for me."

"He'll better or I'll break his back".

"I'll be back in a minute John with the deed to our house," Betty strolled out of Snake's office where he had all types of stolen cars in his parking lot and they proceeded to the Bell Montgomery Mortgage Company where Snake might make a dream come true for Betty and John.

Snake could not keep his eyes on the road from looking at Betty and as they drove a loud noise sounded off as bullets broke the windows of Snake's truck.

"Get down you might get hit with a bullet!"

"Who in the hell is trying to kill you? I want you to help me get this house!"

"Hang on Betty I think I can out run them. Take this gun and try to shoot out their tires so we can get away."

"What time does the mortgage company close?"

"I might hit someone if I shoot at the people chasing us."

"Don't worry about that keep on shooting until you hit a tire!"

As Betty tried to shoot out the tires her stomach ached with much agony and she shouted, "My stomach is getting upset. I need a gas pill or I am going to faint!"

As Snake turned a curve and headed west, he saw a drug store and said, "I'll stop in front at the drugstore and hold them off while you go and get something for your stomach ache. Betty you go in and buy some pain pills."

Quickly Betty ran into the store and Snake pulled another gun from a holster which fitted around his leg.

Scare and shaking, Betty scrambled into the store as Snake and his enemies shot it out at with each other and Betty asked the clerk, "May I have something for my stomach ?"

"Take one of these and get the hell out of my drug store. You and those gangsters are destroying my store so take these pills and leave!"

"Thanks sir you are very brave. I can use those pills."

Bullets ringed inside the store as several people screamed and shouted hoping not to get hit by them and as Betty held up the bottle of pills one of them hit it and pieces of glass scattered across the floor.

"Hurry up I am running out of bullets! I cannot let them catch me!"

Ducking and dodging the bullets, Betty rushed and jumped into the car as Snake started the engine and it made a loud noise and he drove down the street going pass the speed limit.

"Why are they trying to kill you?"

"I owed Bulldog some money from a crap game and he wanted to collect but I would not pay him because the cards we played with were fixed. No matter how the card game went he kept winning with the same cards, I lost $ 5000 dollars."

Holding on the cross which hung around her neck, Betty prayed and said "Oh God please help us get out of this dangerous situation we are in. Please protect Snake and give him the power to rid himself of this trouble he's gotten himself into."

It appeared Betty's prayers were answered because Bulldog suffered a stroke as his blood pressure went up very high and he ran into a fire hydrant causing much water to shoot into the air.

"I do not know what you did but Bulldog and the boys are no longer following us no more."

Wiping sweat from her face," Now take me to the people who will sell us the house."

"Ok Betty I'll do it."

By now John is wondering was everything ok. Two hours passed by since Snake and Betty left to hopefully buy a house. His stomach growled like a lion and he needed something to eat and John searched in his wallet to see if money was in it to buy a sandwich.

Trying to think about how to remedy his hunger pains, John remembered Peter gave him a check to buy needed food in an emergency and he looked at the folded document and $ 10 dollars made out to him showed so brightly when he read it. The cramps in his stomach hurt him as John went to the bank to see if he could get money to buy food. The bank looked like a civil war museum, and in the colorful lobby a picture of General Robert E. Lee hung and a picture of him riding his horse Traveler, and a picture of Jefferson Davis former president of the Confederate States of America, and the names of soldiers printed on a piece of paper who died for the southern states which succeed from the Union. Flags of the Confederate States lined the walls, pictures of the Battle of Gettysburg, displays of civil war weapons, a picture of Lee surrendering to General Grant could be seen, and black and white people protested outside because they would not hire black people as officers of the bank.

A female clerk approached John and said, "I'll have to check with my manager to see if I can cash it. I am not familiar with the name and address of the person's name printed on it."

Wearing a bright yellow dress with black polka-dots on it, and much makeup, and strong perfume, and short curly black hair she said," How do I know you are not trying to cash a bad check? Your kind do bad deeds like this so often."

"That's my father's signature and he's never given me a bad check which bounced."

"Just sit in the colored section of the bank and I'll go and check this signature."

Talking to Mr. Tim Walls who blanked his blue eyes and shook his head from side to side and kept on humming as he looked at the check.

Mary Times said, Mr. Walls there is a colored boy out there trying to cash a check and I think he is forging it. I looked at the signature and I cannot make out the name to see if the man had an account with us."

"I'll call the police and have him come to your desk and try to detain him."

Miss. Times said," The police will come out and arrest him. Big Jim always placed his signature on any of his worker's checks and it is one of his checks."

Mr. Walls said, "Senator Wilson is the only person's whose signature was supposed to go on the back before he wrote or gave out a check to his workers. I do not see Senator Wilson's signature on that check or any other signatures on it. I'll call the police and get to the bottom of this."

Two big policemen strolled into the bank and one of them said, "Nigger what in the hell are you trying to do? It appears you want to get over on the bank officials and you cannot read or understand you are not supposed to sit in this section of the bank with white people. The sign is visible for your eyes to see where the niggas are supposed to sit in this bank."

"Go to hell. I'll sit where I please and you cannot do anything about it."

Hatchet Jones did not like what John said and he let his K-9 dogs go.

"Attack the nigger!" and the Black German Shepard chased John around the bank and he jumped on a big mahogany desk.

"Get that dam dog officer. I am so sorry. He'll chew off my leg. Call him off. He is tiring up the place and most of all he's trying to get a part of me!"

"Settle down Rufus. I think this smart ass nigger has learned his lesson!"

"Well let's go to jail and by the way what is your name?"

"I do not have to tell you shit! Plus I need a lawyer!"

"Rufus this time finish the job and the nerve of him getting smart with me."

Seeing Rufus would eat him to bits, John raced around the bank again and as Rufus tried to bite his leg, John grabbed a heavy fire extinguisher and hit him in his head just as he was going to bite into it and he only came to cash a check and not get in trouble. Rufus's head was so hard the blow did not hurt him at all.

As officer Jones takes John to jail, it is time for the both of them to have their ribs with sauce on it and when Rufus cannot have his ribs every day's he gets angry and is hard to live with.

"Rufus we will go to Cindy Good Rib House and get your favorite dish of pork ribs, Nigger want something to eat?"

'Yes sir I am hungry."

"Well wait until me and Rufus come back. Come on Rufus you got to eat some good food. If you bite that nigger you might get blood poisoning."

John noticed Jones left the keys to his hand cups on the car seat and thought about how he would get them off the seat so that he unlock the hand cups.

A ten year old black fellow by the name of Prince strolled by and saw John hand cupped to the inside car door handle which could not be pulled opened.

"Why are you locked up on the inside of this car with the windows shut?"

"Can I help you?"

"This is Officer Jones's car and I hate him,"

"His dog Rufus bit me and nothing was done about it."

This little boy's complexion was a high yellow color and Officer Jones disliked him. His hair was thick and he wore brown field hand clothes and he sucked on a candy cane and wore black boots which were too big for him.

"Little man if you help me I'll give you some money but I don't have it now. If they take me to jail, I won't be able to be with my wife so can you get the extra keys close to the gas tank and open the door? I heard him say he kept an extra pair in a special compartment under the car just in case they lost them chasing thugs in emergency situations."

"Times is hard and I need some bread to give to my momma so can you kick me out some money for helping you?"

"I do not have any money but I might be able to help you when I become the first colored United States senator. I'll try to help the poor people in this state and some of them will be your relatives."

"Ok I'll crawl under the car and get the keys for you so keep your promise to me."

Inside the restaurant Rufus and his master ate some ribs and both of them drink their share of beer and consumed red peppers.

"You two dogs get out of here. They will tire up the place." Cindy the owner shouted.

A big Black German Shepard who was a male came crashing through the door after a female pit-bull who was in heat and Cindy who weigh about 139 pounds grabbed her broom and swing it at the dogs and by this time Rufus got the scent of the girl dog and he left his master to chase after her.

Cindy's Rib House sat over two hundred people who ate in there during lunch time.

Getting angry at what took place Cindy said "Get the hell out of here. I should have called The Humane Society the last time those two dogs came in here trying to make love,"

Cindy shouted," Do not get too close to the dogs they will make you drop your trays of food."

It did not matter because the dogs bumped into her and she accidently threw her pies and cakes at the customers away from the fighting dogs who chased the female dog.

Hollowing at Officer Jones, Cindy shouted, "Get that no good mutt of yours out of here. You are ruining my business and my customers are running for their lives."

After Rufus ran away the male dog he got in back of the female pit bull and had sex with her and they got stuck together.

Meanwhile Prince managed to locate the box containing the car keys and struggled to get John the box.

"What's keeping you? Officer Jones is going to come and take me to jail,"

"I cannot find any tools to open the box. I'll go out and get some."

So much commotion was going on that an armored car driver coming to get the cash receipts arrived at their regular time to carry off Cindy's money for the week totaling $10,000 dollars.

When the guards left the truck, strange looking fellows fired gas smoke gun shells at them and they did not know what took place as they fell to the ground holding on to their throats hitting the concrete pavement.

Two armed men wore gas masks and held machine guns in the hands told the guards to throw their guns on the floor and let them have the truck.

"Do as I say and you and your friends will have to hand over the cash you have collected for the day."

"It's over in the box man. Let's us go this gas is hurting me. I cannot breath."

While Rufus tried to get unstuck from the female dog, he smelled weed on one of the robbers and broke away from the dog and ran towards the back to search for drugs on the men.

"Godamit Rufus you picked a good time for chasing for drugs. That black brother in the car will escape if we don't go back and take him to jail."

As officer Jones went towards the back of the restaurant he is overcome by gas and he cannot go any further. He went into the kitchen and grabbed a towel.

"You cannot use those towels, "Perry said, "Cindy paid 10 dollars for each one of them so give them back, who in the hell do you think you are"

At once Perry and Officer Jones fought each other to get control of the towel which eventually tore apart with Officer Jones hitting Perry in the head with a pan knocking him out as he rushed towards the back of the store to help his faithful companion who wrestled one of the robbers.

Officer Jones approached the men, and shot one of them when he saw he had a mask on and was about to shoot Rufus as he chewed the robber's hands off and licking the bloody hand at the same time.

By this time Prince came back with a brick because every time he tried to borrow some tools the people he asked said he was too young and plus he was a minor so he slammed a brick into the cage surrounding the box holding the keys which could be used to get the hand cups off John.

Prince crawled under the car and slammed the brick against the cage which came off and he took the box out from under the car. Immediately the alarm went off and Officer Jones was busy apprehending the gunmen and he did not realize Prince was unlocking John from the car so he could escape.

"Use the key Prince because it should unlock the hand cups."

"There are twenty of these keys to fit and it might take me a long time to open the lock, ".

After going through 19 keys which could not fit, Prince tried the last one as the car exploded from banging on many parts of it near the gas engine and sparks set the gas tank on fire because fuel leaked from the tank. As John exited the patrol car it exploded and the both of them scrambled away as the crowd gathered around the burning vehicle.

When Officer Jones and Rufus came back to the patrol car, it was a blaze and his face looked sad as reporters asked him questions about who was in the squad car as it burned.

"Well it was a nigger in the car. I do not know how this fire started. I was busy apprehending the robbers who were trying to rob the armored car and take Cindy's cash receipts for the day. Rufus and I got those robbers and I feel sorry for the nigger for him to die like this. I kind of liked him."

Rufus and Officer Jones got an honorable medal for their valor but as for John Carol they thought he was dead and burned up but never did he realize John escaped from the burning patrol car and only after they found no bones in the car would they put out an award on him for escaping from a police officer.

There was so much smoke but John and Prince got away without being detected and John said to Prince, "I'll never forget what you did to help me. One day when I beat Senator Wilson I will hire you, so stay in school and get a good education."

"Well Mr. John Carol you got a point but if you're going to be the next colored senator from Mississippi, the white folks will not like it but you cannot give up your dreams of helping our folks both colored and white. Senator Wilson must be stopped. Senator Wilson cheated my father all the time especially when it came to dividing the money from his crops with my daddy. Daddy got ripped off because he could not read or write and never complained about being cheated. He only says "Yes sir" "No sir". I am going to be a lawyer and fight for my people and maybe I might be your lawyer by the time you'll become a senator."

After talking with Prince, John went back to the car lot and waited to see if Betty and Snake made it back. This time he decided to go to a shed and wait until they arrived back with some good news about buying a house and some property.

CHAPTER 8

After having a hectic day, Snake drove Betty to see a man who sold rehab houses and his friends called him Cool Collins and he wore a gray conservative suit and his face appeared to be clean shaven and his long hair came down his back and he sported a thick mustache.

Going into his office, you saw all types of awards for selling houses and on front of his building was a sign which said," Cool Collins Mortgage the Best Honest Housing Realist state Man in the Country. Come to Cool Collins For the Best Deal in Town."

Inside the office carpeting covered the place and soft couches for sitting and rich aromas made the office very comfortable but Betty could not stand the fragrances coming from the air deodorizers.

The outside of the building were dark brown and beige curtains on the windows with a second floor and 10 rooms and many women and men traveled upstairs for a night of pleasure.

"This place looks suspicious and those girls are prostitutes."

"I know all of them. I am one of their clients on a regular time when I want to have some fun."

"Let's hurry up and get away from here and if you touch my legs again I am going to scream I am being raped so keep your hands to yourself or I'll tell John about what you tried to do and he will kill you because of how you treated me.

They left the car and a big man came out of a door and said, "What brings you to my place of business?"

"Man I smell some good food coming from the kitchen."

"Now Betty it's too late for you to be eating. We have to hurry up and get back to your husband because he will be worried about you."

"I know you want a house and I got the perfect one for you." Cool said, "I'll sell it for $15,000 dollars."

"It looks pretty on this picture and I would love to see it."

Pulling on his suspenders and looking at his schedule of appointments Cool said," I am sorry I cannot do that and I do not have the time for site seeing. If there is a problem with the house I'll get some repairmen to fix it."

Opening up her purse and pulling out the money she said "Ok I'll buy the house."

"This map will show you how to get to it. It is a beautiful dwelling."

"What's that siren I hear? "Betty said,

"It looks like the police are coming to raid the place again. "Cool yelled, "I thought I paid those police to not raid my place for illegal prostitution."

Upstairs people danced and gambled which was illegal but Snake and Betty managed to get out of the place as the police surrounded it and they attempted to bring out those people breaking the law. Policemen took axes and tore up the gambling tables and pulled prostitutes and their clients out of their beds with the men complaining they did not get what they came there for because of the disruptions from the police.

"I bet it was that Big Jim who did this to me because I did not send any money for his reelection campaign.'

The police stopped Snake as he got into his car but while the officer looked in another direction, Snake hit him in the jaw and the officer fell down. By this time the church people came with picket signs and protested and celebrated the closing down of Collin's place of business and they knelled in prayer but as this took place some of the church people drink beer and passed it around when their pastor disappeared talking to other people.

Again Snake broke all speeding limits and the police gave chase.

"Pour some of this on the street Betty as they get much closer to us!"

"Ok Il do it," and she poured the oil on the street as the police car got closer and it made driving difficult for the driver and he slid into a big window at a grocery store. Finally they made it back to Snake's place of business and found John in the back of a shed surrounded by his dogs ready to eat him up.

"Darling where have you been, "I've had a hard day and I am hungry!"

"That's no problem because on the way back home Snake stopped and robbed a store and took some groceries for us to eat."

"Did we get the house? You know you are pregnant and we cannot keep on living like this."

CHAPTER 9

The house was not what it looked like on the pictures Collins showed them but no one could bother them too much. There was no running water or lights on the property or furniture in the place.

"You mean you bought a house with the utilities off."

"Do not worry John I will get everything tuned on. There's a lake not too far from here. You can get some water from the pond when you need it." Snake said as he counted the money Betty gave him to get Cool Collins to sell them a house. Give me some more money to have the utilities turned back on."

They listened to Snake but John did not go along with giving him more money because he did not have much trust in him and his history of having a criminal record.

Betty's morning sickness affected her and she constantly rubbed her stomach because the unborn baby moved back and forth causing all types of hell.

The house was two stories and a brick house surrounded by trees and farm land black slaves cultivated for hundreds of years to grow tobacco, beans, rice, cotton, corn, and other crops.

John looked in the back and said," I see many carvings on the barks of trees and dates on them. Its good President Lincoln freed the slaves. Forty acres and a mule did not work and black people were free but they had to go to your father for seeds and tools to farm the land and they were in debt all the time after paying them back the loan money they borrowed to start the next year's crops. How could they get any money from the fruits of their labor?"

Looking disappointed in his face, John said, "We do not have any furniture in this house. How are we going to live without it? There are some burlap bags in the cabins and we can fill them up with weeds and make beds with them. Plus I have to break out the boards in the windows to make this place look presentable so it will not get too much attention."

Not wasting time to get their home functional John looked at the place up and down.

"There is some wild corn growing not too far from here and some apple trees on the property. I'll go and pick some of them. We need some gas turned on but I see there is a fireplace in this house that we could use to get some heat in it. I cannot get cold in here. I think it will be difficult but times will get better. I'll try to get some work and help take care of my family,"

Trying to keep his thoughts centered on what to do about the situation, John said, "I wonder what will happen once our child is born. Why should we bring our child into this world when we know most of the white and black folks will not accept him or her? Maybe it was a mistake to get involved with each other. Will the kids in this union between you and me be treated as people instead of half breeds?"

"I know what you are trying to say. Here we are in the middle of nowhere in this house and there is no furniture or modern utensils to use and we have to set a fire in the fireplace to keep warm."

Lying down beside Betty in the dark room with candle lights burning and the sound of insects making noises and the smell of many flowers drifted into their house. The crackle of weeds in the burlap sacks made noises as Betty and John struggled to get some sleep and as he began to talk, he rubbed Betty's shoulder and said, "It's too late to think about that now. We are together the three of us and God will keep our enemies away. I want you and our kid to be proud of me but I cannot read or write. I am a shame I cannot measure of up and be intelligent like you."

"Now John you cannot help the situation you were placed in. You know they did not build enough schools for your people to go to but that does not mean you cannot do something with your life. You might be able to complete school and graduate from college."

As he starts to laugh, "You must be kidding. A colored man the son of a share cropper going to college, that's unheard of in these parts of Mississippi."

At that moment when John spoke his opinion on the subject, Betty slapped him and said," I've seen you try to study my books when we laughed at the pictures but you kept asking what was this word or that word. You talk about wanting to change things for the betterment of your people and that you hate the way your people are cheated by the white man but you never think in terms of doing something about it."

"Betty your wrong. A colored person would get lynched if he got out of his place and you should know that but someone must stand up for equality and maybe it might be me who will defeat your father in his reelection campaign.

"Our kids will be mixed with your blood and mine. Discrimination will be heaped on them because they hate colored and white folks living together and having mixed blooded children." Betty said, "As far as education is concerned there have been many colored people like George Washington Carver who came from a poor background and overcame it and succeeded and made a contribution to the South by inventing so many products with the peanut and people like Booker T Washington who founded Tuskegee Institute. If they can succeed you can too."

"You might be right Betty. I got to get the slave mentality out of me and do something about it. I might even run for senator and write legislation for civil rights for all the people."

"John this is a beautiful night. I hear the crickets and the noises of foxes and wolves hollowing."

The night settled in as John and Betty looked in the sky counted the stars shining in it and comets dashing back and forth through the midnight sky in a majestic sight. The wee hours of the night ascended on the both of them and they heard owls echoing a quiet sound and the perfume Betty wore made John move closer to her smiling and showing all of his pretty white teeth but everything did not seem ok because they faced an uphill battle trying to survive in a hostile southern environment.

"I smell smoke and hear someone shouting in the woods John. Let's go and see what is going on."

Taking their time Betty and John quietly tip toed towards the woods and saw something that surprised them.

"Oh John I see a burning body and it is a white woman and black man tied to a cross."

"Betty, people doing these crimes are kids not adults. These are sick teenagers and small kids out there doing wrong to people just because they are black. We better get back to the house because they might attack you and me and get away with murdering us."

All of a sudden drivers in four cars drove up and one of the men with them was Big Jim who said to the boys," Job well done. We will get rid of all those people who are of different colors and burn them alive. These two people were civil rights workers who came here to register black folks to vote against me." and he paid the boys twenty-five dollars apiece for killing them.

As they both raced back to their house which had no lights or gas, thoughts ran through their minds as they spoke to each other in conversation and the topic seemed most disturbing such as how would they be able to survive in an environment which was against racial couples marrying each other ?What would Big Jim do if he heard his daughter lived with a colored man named John Carol and what type of respect would Betty get from her neighbors if they found out John Carol was Betty's lover instead of her helper being paid by her father Big Jim.

Could they endure this type of life style? They knew Big Jim looked for them because his daughter's actions damaged his public image and she did this to defeat his political ambitions and he would do anything to stop Betty from shaming him by being with John Carol.

CHAPTER 10

The next morning John went outside to do chores where farmland could be used to grow beans, corn, wheat, and cotton but obstacles stood in his way because he did not have any farm machinery to till the soil and it kept on raining making the soil soggy and the land looked like you could not grow anything on it but John was willing to grow crops to make money to take care of his family.

"If the rain keeps on falling it will flood the fields, I cannot plant seeds until it stops raining so I can grow some crops. I hope the land will dry out."

"John the land is good for growing crops but the rain makes it too moist and plus who will sell us a tractor to plow farrows so we can grow crops on them?"

"When will our lights be turned on?" John said, "We have to live in a comfortable house but a lot of work needs to be done around here. We have to build a well so we can use it for washing and cooking. There is no inside plumbing and I do not want to use an odd house."

"Maybe I'll be able to get some of the farmers to come and help us. We cannot live like this and I will see what I can do and I being a woman I might be able to get some discounts."

"No way you are pregnant and cannot be running around here handling responsibilities I should be doing."

"Now who's going to believe you when you ask the white farmers to help us?"

"I'll make up a big lie to tell them you will write a letter introducing me to our new neighborhood saying I work for you and do little jobs for you, it just might work."

"We have to be careful John because if daddy finds out it would be your funeral because he is dead set on keeping our baby from coming into the world. He'll do anything to keep white folks from knowing his daughter had a baby by a colored man."

CHAPTER 11

Roosters echoed their morning ritual noise as the sun rose in the east and dogs barked and farm families began their everyday chores of going to the fields to cultivate their land and throw fertilizer on the ground and spray insecticide on them. One of the farmers spotted locust in a county and warned the other farmers about it but they ignored him and did not attempt to do anything about it.

Mary Florence a landowner who lived five miles down the road noticed John and Betty on the porch arguing with each other and heard John say, "Godamit Betty I am no slave and will not do any women's work!"

A rabbit darted across the front yard with grass in his mouth but quickly spit it out because plant life on the property was dead due to the lack of water to keep the property irrigated.

"Those birds are trying to get their share of the grasshoppers and crickets and they will later eat the worms hiding in the earth trying to get away from them," Florence said to herself.

Florence's face, wrinkled from years of the fast life worked as a hooker in a saloon before she found God at a church and intended to save the lost souls who turned away from God and felt she could get John and Betty to come to their church and pay her respects to both of them.

I bet she is very nosy," Betty said, "I can tell a hypocrite when I see one and she fits the description."

Dressed in a bright yellow dress and wearing a hat with little colored Easter eggs on it, Florence strolled in front of the house and gently knocked on the door and waited for someone to open it.

"Is someone here? I need some help. Could someone open the door?"

"Do not answer the door maybe she might go away and think no one lives here? We don't need people to know our business anyway," John said, "Besides I don't want to act like a field hand in front of her."

"If you do not it will cause suspicion and bring in the local sheriff if you do not act the role of colored field hands. We got too much to lose if they put you in jail for being with me."

As Mary Florence knocked on the door, John did do some chores but he made his choice to perform it slowly or fast or just lay under the big apple tree.

"I do not have any makeup or nice clothes to put on to look like a real lady."

"It doesn't matter Betty. You cannot be what you want to all the time. She will have to accept you as you are."

Tears came to her eyes as John said this because memories of her getting dressed up going to dances and parties flashed back to her when she was on the good graces of Big Jim and anything she wanted her father got it for her. Big Jim spoiled her to death and now the good life was over and Betty said to John, "I'll never live this dreadful life style again and one day I'll live in splendor as I was accustomed to having and wearing the best of everything."

When Betty opened the door, Mary was not good at meeting people and talking to them and she said, "Hello I am Mary Florence president of the auxiliary and I decided to come over and tell you I live a few miles down the road and would like to help you in any way I can or send you news about what is going on."

"That was nice of you to think of helping people who are new to the county and want to make a living.'

Betty said, "We do need help and will let you know when that occasion comes up when my handyman and I begin farming on our land."

As always Mary Florence knew she would ask more questions and said, "Where is your husband? A pretty girl like you should have someone to help with the chores around here. I know many fellows who would love to hire themselves out to a cute girl like you. The next thing you know you will be getting wedding proposals but make sure he has money to support you. Too many of the lazy men want a woman to take care of them. There's no romance without finance. That's my philosophy."

"I would invite you to have some coffee but we do not have any running water so we go down to the creek to get some. We do not have any lights or gas either but I am working on getting this place together so it can become productive. We can sit on the back porch where there is a lot of shade and I can introduce you to John my aide who helps me but sometimes he gets moody and indignant and uppity. I've known him for only a few days and when I decided to buy this farm I asked him would he like to be foreman when I get more men to help with the farm."

As they made their way through the house Mary said, "This place looks a mess. It's not fit to live in!" and she noticed John sleeping under a tree and said, "What's that colored boy out there doing laying under the tree. He should be trying to dig a well or paint this house. It's about to fall down and it smells bad. He should be acting like a servant instead of a foreman who owns the place. He got his nerves. You should beat him for this."

"Miss. Florence do not take what John is doing too hard. His grandfather was a body servant to a Confederate general during the war between the states and as a result he freed his grandfather who received a pension. John's father and his family avoided slavery because their great grandfather helped Confederate soldiers during the war. He assisted doctors and treated wounded men injured in battle.

"So that's why John is acting this way as if he's been a free black person all of his life, "Betty said, "He's is as gentle as a lamb. No one but him offered to help me until our first crops came in but John."

"You might be sorry if you start planting because there is word locust were seen in another county and are coming this way so be sure you check with the agriculture college before you plant anything because locust are known to come through here and eat up all the crops our farmers grow in these parts of the country."

Still probing Mary said," Where will you get the money to pay for this raggedy house. How will you pay the taxes on it? Paying the taxes is important because if you do not pay the money, they will throw you off the property."

Giving Mary a stern look, Betty said, "Now Mary you're getting too much into my business and should not probe into my private life."

"Why are you holding your stomach? You have not been eating. I'll get Dr. Jamison to come and see you."

"John!" "John!" Betty cried as John could hardly awaken himself to come and help her.

Seeing the serious condition Betty was in, Mary went to John and scolded him and threatened to beat him with her night stick.

"Get up and help Betty because she is sick before I give you a beating with my cane boy."

"I do not think so lady. I am not taking a beating from a white lady or man anymore. You'll have to kill me before that happens to me again. You better best go on home before I get mad and throw you off the property myself."

Seeing John would make an enemy of Mary Florence Betty said, "Now John treat Mary with some respect and do what she tells you to do. You know how you are supposed to act around white people."

"I will not treat her with any respect because she had no good intentions on treating me with love or dignity. This is not slavery times and she is going to have to get it in her head colored people are not going to be second class citizens to bigots like her."

John said, "But if it was not for Betty I would curse you out. I get tire of white folks coming around here telling us what to do. They should mine their business and let us take care of our own welfare.'

"How dare you will insult me like this. I'll spread information about your uppity hired man to my relatives and they will deal with him!"

Grabbing some hard mud, John hurled it at Mary and shouted "Do not come back here no more trying to tell us what to do!"

At about two in the morning a bright light casted a glow into their living room and John said," What's that smell Betty? Someone has put a burning cross in our yard without us knowing about it. That Mary Florence had something to do with this. Are you feeling much better Betty?"

CHAPTER 12

As John walked back and forth in their bare living room with no tables and chairs to use he counted the change his father gave him before he left.

"Look at this place. We have to do something about the way it looks. It can be productive but it will take a lot of work."

Betty stared at John, "It would be nice to have a catfish pond with water flowing into this area and have catfish mating with each other. We could sell catfish to the farmers and anyone else who would buy the fish."

"I have about $ 200 dollars daddy kept saving for me. Momma told me to keep it for times like this. The only problem is daddy liked to blow the money gambling and buying drinks for the boys. He had a hard time explaining to his wife why the money was lower each time she checked his banking account."

"So you're saying there was more money than the $200 dollars left in the bank for you."

Holding John Betty said, "At first I did not like your parents because they were colored and my father Big Jim filled his kid's heads with racial bigotry and he wanted his kids to think negative as he did about colored people."

"There was a terrible feeling my parents had about you. They felt I would get in trouble with the law by playing with you, Sandy, and Kirby because this was the law to keep colored folks separated from white people"

"Despite what my father thought, I realized I loved you and your mother and father found it hard to believe one day we would become lovers and friends. I'll give birth to their grandchild. They want the best for us but they know people in these parts cannot accept colored and white folks associating with each other and getting married. John they will lynch you if you attempt to show affection towards me in public. It will cause much suspicion from white residents in this area. Those prejudices from the white residents might change but right now I do not think so."

"What people do not understand is you cannot measure love by someone's skin color. When we played with each other as kids I saw a person not a white girl. I loved the things we shared together and the childhood games we played, "John said.

"I pretended to be Robin Hood protecting you from the king who was your brother Kirby who was a bad king. Kirby was brain washed by Big Jim to hate colored people and his mind got twisted and turned in many directions about the true meaning of equality and civil rights and who he was supposed to love or hate. He hates me for the problems he has to face for me being with his sister. I have to make up for the problems I have brought to him."

Holding John much closer, "There's something I want to tell you that's been on my mind,"

"What is it Betty?"

"As we grew older and attended high school I did not want to have nothing to do with you and I regretted it. My father felt I was much older and did not need any colored friends. I argued him to death about it but it did not do any good and I never stopped trying to see you."

"I do not believe it. You probably developed the same prejudice feelings like your father."

"That's not true because daddy felt his white friends in big political circles would object to it. They would say how it is Big Jim is preaching anti-civil rights and his daughter is sleeping with a colored boy. Daddy said it was difficult to come up with a reason to defend my actions."

"Why is it you are now telling me this? Your father cheated the colored farmers and kept them from getting loans to plant their crops or buy or fix their farming equipment used for planting and harvesting them."

Lying on the floor and looking into the ceiling John said, "I wondered why you stopped coming to the house and later my father and mother talked to me and said many people kept telling your mother and father they saw us kissing in the woods and he immediately wanted us to stop seeing each other."

Rubbing her little hands through John's clinky hair Betty said," Your right because my brother Kirby said his friends constantly teased him and said his sister was sleeping with a colored boy. Kirby knowing how his temper could become violent got into so many fights defending me and my sister against the negative news about out puppy love relationship. My brother never allowed bad words to be said about me in his presence or when I was not there to hear it."

Both of them were hungry by now as it grew darker and their utilities were not turned on yet and Betty who's morning sickness got to her said" I want some fish and I got a taste for it. Can you get something for us to eat? There is a lake down the road and you can catch something for us to enjoy a meal."

"First of all I do not have any bait or fishing pole to catch the fish,"

"Look who's trying get out of getting us something to eat. You always told me you could bring home a big catfish now back up that talking. At about 5.p.m I expect to see catfish on the table for us to eat."

Looking at Betty in a curious way John said, "I like to have challenges brought to me and especially from people who do not think I can do the feats I talk about."

Feeling his empty stomach early in the morning John reflected on Betty's challenge and went fishing to a nearby lake. The forest echoed with noises coming from birds and insects flew back and forth getting nectar from plants and two bears fought each other because of the mating season. As John looked at the rows of plants grown by the other farmers he said to himself, "Will I ever measure up and be able to make this farm productive?"

Those thoughts lingered in his mind and John looked through the woods and he spotted a wild deer and heard shots coming from the rifles of hunters who chased him in wild suspense to bring home a large buck but they killed the deer illegally.

The loud sound of guns going off did not scare John because as a young boy up growing up in a rural farm area, he hunted rabbits and deer's but fear gripped him when he had a sure kill and sometimes freezed once he knew the deer or rabbit would be dead because of him. This time John saw the greed of men who sought nothing but killing wild animals for sport instead of killing to make a meal to survive. In many cases the hunters left the meat of a deer stay on the body only to get the skins off of it. As the hunters approached the killed deer they argued over who would get its beautiful skins and a fight erupted between the two of them.

"This is my deer and I shot him. "Dirty Larry said to Goose Matson.

Getting angry Matson yelled back, "I shot this buck and I will take the skins off of it."

"Over my dead body you will take the deer skins away from me. I will make a coat out of it with the skins for my wife." Dirty Larry said.

"No you want I killed this deer for Senator Big Jim Wilson. He is always sending us out to kill more than enough of the deers and gets us to share in the money from the sale of the animal skins we bring in,

"Matson replied back.

"If I do not sell these deer pelts for Big Jim he will put me and my family off his property. I will kill you to protect my family." At once Matson tackled Dirty and they wrestled and the gun went off killing Dirty.

Dirty grabbed his stomach and placed his hands over his wound hoping to stop the blood and watched it drop from his body and he put his blood drenched fingers into his mouth and tasted it. His body was a bloody mess and his body stood frozen as he knew he would probably die from the wound. As Matson stood up he looked at Dirty who was stunned by the whole incident which took place but instead of being humble he laughed up a storm as Dirty struggled to stay alive.

"I'll finish you off Matson said, "You always tried to persuade the senator from getting the job to be his assistant. Revenge is a mother." After saying that Matson shot him again and again as John heard and saw all of this because Betty's father was getting money from hundreds of illegally killed animal skins which was against the law. All around Big Jim's estate were heads of bears and deer's and other animals from such activities. The hunters sold animal furs to buyers and Big Jim influenced state officials to let the hunters continue hunting when it was supposed to be over. For his kindness the hunters paid Big Jim money rewards.

Trying to concentrate on fishing was difficult to do because Matson saw John run away after he shot Dirty but John ran as fast as he could and hid in some bushes where no one could find him. Marching quickly to complete his objective after witnessing a murder and seeing Big Jim got kickbacks from people who hunted year round instead of the allowed six months for the deer season, John did not want the killer to see him.

It took hours for John to find Lagoon Lake surrounded by trees and the shoreline contained a lot of brown rich soil. He saw the lake appeared to be dirty without fresh water in it. Rumors circulated the best Cat and Buffalo fish could be found in the lake.

On this day groups of people came to catch fish and camped around the lake and fished into the next morning slapping insects thirsting for their blood and got drunk and cursed up a storm. To the dismay of the older established fishermen, teenager's loud music scared fish away which sparked much conflict between them and the people who wanted to catch trout. The lake had a long history of fights between the fishermen who often got into fistfights with the teenagers about this problem. State park rangers stopped the fights when they broke out.

John placed some bate on his hook and he heard a loud noise in the water and saw a man trying to swim out the lake. His big body dropped liked an atomic bomb and water splashed high into the air. The stranger's boat rocked back and forth before it sunk. Fishing and sitting with the hot sun beaming on him, Jack Benson drink a lot while he did everything in his everyday life. Intoxication followed him in whatever he performed and he did not care about the consequences of his actions. Knowing he could not swim, Jack never wore a life preserver and broke all the rules of safety when it came to boating. Now a problem faced John as he contemplated trying to save Benson from drowning because he had not been swimming in years and he was allergic to the plankton in the water which caused him a bad reaction to it. But nevertheless John broke all the doctor's orders and plunged into the water to save Jack who cried out for help.

As John swam towards Benson a poisonous water moccasin was disturbed by him and Benson feared for his life because one bite from it would mean instant death. Realizing he wanted to protect himself, John grabbed the snake and cursed up a storm and it bit him in his arm. This was a poisonous snake but during his rescue mission John did not realize he was bitten by him. Grabbing the snake John hit him in his head and he threw him ten feet away from where they were at. After his decisive battle with the snake, John had the challenge of saving this big intoxicated man and keeping him from drowning in fifty feet of water. This was not an easy feat because the man weigh over three hundred pounds sank into deep water and he hesitated at first when he saw how big the person was and thought about abandoning the huge task of saving him.

He said to himself," Why should I risk my life saving a white man because all of his life he saw how Big Jim treated his father Peter and the other colored farmers and built up a deep resentment for white people who were plantation owners and now this white man needed help and all at once John took a deep breath and dived into the water with little fishes swimming around him and Benson. As John grabbed the man he tried to hold on to him and John hit him in the face so he could calm down. Instead of calming down Jack Benson grabbed John with his strong fingers in a balled fist which hurt him and needing air very badly John hit him with some finger stabs into his eyes and broke away from him and swam towards the surface gasping for air.

"I cannot let him drown! "John cried, "I got to save him!"

Grabbing a small piece of floating log John dived again and swam towards Jack Benson who swallowed much water but could not hold his breath for a long time and as John approached him he held the log in his hand behind his back and Benson could not see the log and John hit him in his head which looked like a big ball of steel. Grabbing him around his back John pulled him to the surface and to the shore.

"Man are you ok, I thought you were going to drown!" as he tried to get him in a blanket to keep him warm from catching a cold which laid a few yards from the lakeshore line.

Benson looked rugged in his face and sported a beard and his head contained black hair and he weigh over three hundred pounds. It was miracle John pulled him out of the water at the risk of his own life.

"What happened? I heard a loud splash in the water and saw you struggling and I could not stand by and watch you drown so I jumped in to help you."

Rubbing his head, Benson said," I was trying to catch this big Catfish and he gave me a hard time bringing him in. The sonofabitch pulled and I pulled. He must have won because he got the best of me as I lost balance and fell into the water."

"It looks like you got bit by the snake. I can see where he bit you.

"Oh it was nothing just a little scratch. I'll put some alcohol on it."

"I think you better get some medical attention before an infection sets in."

When John said that he fell to the ground and Benson sucked the poison from his wound and after a few minutes John came back to life.

Waking up after Benson helped him, John said, "I did not know what took place and I just fell out,"

"I had to suck the poison out of your wound so you would not die."

They both laughed about the incident as Jack said; "My name is Jack Benson and yours?"

It's John and I live with my boss lady on the small farm a few miles away from here. I promised her I would bring some fish home for dinner but it looks like I will not be able to."

"For saving my life I owe you a great payback and I want you to take the fish I caught and at lease you might win the bet you made with her. I would not want to see you lose to a woman. You have to make sure the woman realizes who the breadwinner of the house is even if you do not have a job earning a decent salary."

"I see you have camping gear with you. Do you have some coffee? "Benson said handing him a cup.

"I'll make you a cup and boil us some."

The sickness of the snake bite took time to wear off but he tried to stay in good spirits.

"I heard of your name before Mr. Benson. Mary Florence came to visit us and she mentioned your name as someone who could help us irrigate our property to grow crops on it and you were a powerful man in this state."

"Well John I own a lot of property in this county and hope to get some of the land the black farmers live on and they are letting their land go to waste and not trying to farm it but ask for handouts to keep from being productive. I heard much oil is on their property and me and Big Jim plan on getting their property in a legal way if they continue not to raise crops on it. We do not know what method will work but it will take time. We plan to get the property from the white farmers too. No people will be spared except the ones who support us."

"What do you know about Big Jim?"

"I heard he is very wealthy and gets his way and everything he wants he'll do anything to obtain it.

"He owns his bootleg whiskey business,' "Benson said.

"You must be kidding. The senator is in the moon shine business but how can he get away with this without getting caught?"

"Well Big Jim made legislation where no one could touch the state property for veteran's facilities but he had his whiskey business in a private building on it and sends out shipments of booze liquor to stores who will buy it at a cheaper price and he shares some of the profits with the veteran's administrators who are selected by him."

"Big Jim can play a good hand of poker and out drinks you to death especially if its scotch whiskey. Every drinking contest he's in he wins it and one time he pulled out his gun to shoot the other person when he felt his competitor was going to win. The moral of the story is not to complete against Big Jim in anyway because he hates losing. For a while many people came up dead who tried to take control of the bootleg business and Big Jim put out a hit on those people and every now and then you saw their bodies floating down the river with bullet holes in their heads."

John tried not to renew the frown hidden behind his smile and he vowed to stop Big Jim who felt he was bigger than life and could have anything he wanted at the cost of innocent lives and said, "Well Mr. Benson I cannot write but if you can write my address down I would deeply appreciate it. I'll tell Betty that you are coming to see us."

"For saving my life why don't you come out to my plantation? Maybe I can hire you out for five dollars an hour. I can use some hired hands. I might need a foreman because my colored workers did not like Jake who is white and treats them too unkind at times. I need someone who will be kind to them and make them productive. Little did John know Benson meant him no good and he lied to John because he was the only supervisor over his colored workers.

CHAPTER 13

With that taken care of with uncertainty, John went home and told Betty about what he thought was good news.

Looking at John in an angry manner Betty touched the fish and smelled it and heard the birds outside hoping to get their fill of the left overs and she looked at John and said, "Of all of the people you could invite to the house it would be Jack Benson. He is no good like my father and everything of value he got in his life he cheated and stole it and did not care how he obtained it and killed people who opposed him."

"How do you know Betty you were too young to know what Big Jim and Benson talked about so shut up?"

At once Betty slapped John and he said "Look damit why did you do that, and if you were not pregnant I would kick your ass but listen to me. I am the man running things around here."

"John I am sorry for slapping you but not for you inviting Benson here but listen to what I have to say this time."

Trying to compose himself John said, "Ok tell me your side of the story because I never listen most of the time but you might have a point so just tell me what I do not know,"

"Jack Benson always came out to the plantation to talk with daddy about taking the farmer's lands unable to pay their property taxes especially the poor black and white farmers who could not read or write or who were willing to take low prices for their property. Those farmers who resisted they had them beaten into submission. Big Jim drafted legislation making the property taxes too high and many farmers lost their land as a result of this and state senators and representatives passed the unlawful legislature giving them the power to take lands from farmers who could not pay their property taxes without notice or due-process. Someone discovered oil on the land where the poor white and colored farmers lived for years. Daddy and Benson tried to buy them out but for some reason the farmers will not give in."

"If Benson comes to our house do you think he will recognize you?"

"I think he might but we have to not associate with many people around here and remember my father is trying to find us anyway and he'll do anything to keep us apart even if it means killing the both of us."

"I understand but I was only trying to help better our situation."

"That will bring people on our farm who might attempt to lynch the both of us."

John said, "I want to do something positive for the family but I do not know at this time what it is."

"You see what my father is doing to the famers down here. Why don't you get an education and run against him five years from now."

"Me the son of a colored sharecropper running for the United States senate seat. You must have lost your mind. Never in the state of Mississippi will they elect a colored man for the high office. Most of them are white and have millions of dollars in assets."

"How in the hell do you know unless you get out of that slave mentality and do something about it."

CHAPTER 14

Impressed by what John Carol told him, Jack Benson came to call at the home. Betty and John Carol were sound asleep as the both of them slept on cardboard boxes. Betty snored up a storm which kept John from sleeping soundly. The smell of fish occupied the rooms and plaster kept falling on the floor making loud noises and birds flew in and out of the roof because the aged wood had holes in it.

Bugs ran back and forth across the walls and getting food from the left over fish John managed to cook in one of the fire places in the house.

Despite the horrible house Betty purchased, she felt she and John should be safe from her father who desperately searched for his daughter and placed rewards out for the person who would tell him about the whereabouts of his daughter.

But now one of the dirtiest men in the state of Mississippi came to see what these two people were all about. A big 300-pound man came to call on them. Would this be the final curtain call for Betty and John to be with each other? Fear marched through both of their hearts as Benson knocked on their door several times before they decided to answer it.

Betty did not want to come to the door because she wore no makeup or a suitable dress and she wore the same dress when making her escape to John Carol's house.

"John I look a mess. I am not in the mood for seeing anyone at this time."

"I know but he will keep on knocking and will not give up."

"Ok I'll go and let him in."

Betty could not dress in the good clothes she was accustomed to wearing but to get Benson to leave would be her goal and avoid people who would tell he father where she and John were living in Calhoun County, Mississippi

As Betty opened the door and looked at Benson, this man she disliked intensely, Benson said, "Now I did not know a pretty woman like you would be answering the door. Your servant did not tell me you were so beautiful looking. I should have dressed much better than this. Would you accept my apology?"

"That's ok sir. You do not have to dress so uppity to come to this house. I was busy with my chores. I cannot talk with you too long. Now what brings you up to my house? I do not speak to strangers too often but there was something about you that made me open the door."

With that comment Benson's wide smile appeared on his face, he ran his fingers through his beard, and he tried to knock the dust off his clothes as he approached Betty and she could not wait for him to leave.

"Man this house is in an awful mess. How can John and you live in this place? It needs an overhaul. It seems as if I've seen you before but I cannot tell where and how can you wear such dirty clothes?"

"By the way what is your name? "Betty said, "I've have never seen you before in all my life. If I had some running water I would make you a cup of coffee but our house does not have all the comforts I am accustomed to. I plan on doing something about our living conditions and fix this place up before it gets condemned by the state inspectors of housing. They give you thirty days to fix up the house or they make attempts to have you evicted and they take over your property."

"I have to see you make the coffee."

"I would not do anything to hurt you."

Still rubbing his thick mustache Benson said, "I have to be careful because there are a lot of people who do not like me too much. I want to treat people right but I just cannot seem to. I do not trust people and because of that it's hard for me to get alone with society and all of its ills."

"Well what brings you over to my house on such a bad day when I am feeling very poorly in my stomach? It seems as if you could be out there chasing the pretty women especially at Jake's Lounge? They have everything going on at that place that's corrupt like prostitution and wild drinking with much loud music."

"One of my neighbors Miss. Marry Florence said you needed some help with your farm because it looked so bad and your hired hand John needed assistance to get the state to irrigate your land so you can get your crops and needed water to bring in a good cash crop for the year."

"Man you have been told a lot. How do you know it is true what those people told you? "Betty said, "You have to hear both sides of the story."

"It will not be a problem Betty if you do the right thing and plus I will have a pond built so you can raise and sell catfish who will mate and make more baby catfish to rise into adulthood."

Trying to show her huge pride in getting help Betty said, "I do not need your help. I think we'll be able to use other resources to irrigate the property and get the catfish pond started. Besides I do not know how long we will be living here."

Grabbing a glass of water and drinking it, Benson spit it out and said, "Where did you get this water. It tastes like oil."

Betty pointed to a small creek about 30 feet long away from their farm and said, "Why do you ask?"

His eyes spied on the girl who looked so attractive to him and he enjoyed touching her hands that felt like burned toast and he could not hear many of the things Betty said because of a war injury when he fought in world war two and was hit in his ear when he refused to obey a Japanese officer to shine his boots for him.

While he was in their prison, Jack was indoctrinated with anti-American brain washing and he had a long time rehabilitating to rid himself of this mental problem.

Benson wetted his lips and admired that fine shape Betty possessed and a humble smile appeared on his face and he said," "Now Betty this is a wonderful place to live in and the neighbors can be nice and they can be uppity and clown right dirty too. They will not like the idea of you staying with a nigger."

Looking at Benson in a defensive manner Betty said, "Do not call John that ugly name. He's a good natured fellow and I need him here helping me all the time."

Instead of saying something to Benson he chose not to because of fears Benson would have him turned in to the law enforcement people and John was needed to be there with her baby. Staying quiet about what Benson said did not make him comfortable.

"You'll need help from these people to get your farm prepared to be productive. I know the crackers in town who can probably help you get loans to get your farm going but you have to court me. I am married but we can hide from her and I can be your secret lover. She knows I have to have another woman every now and then. A man like me has to have more than one woman to keep himself happy."

"You no-good dog. Benson I cannot mess with a married man. I have lost my trust in men but we can be friends not lovers. I and John do not need a lot of people coming over here. I just want to be by myself and be taken to the hospital."

Still rubbing his head Benson said, "Well Betty Dr. Jamison is the best doctor in these parts of Jackson Mississippi so why don't you go and see him. He's always treats his patients good but you have to watch him because people have filed malpractice suits against him also."

Still determined not to give in to Benson's offers of help she said, "I have to see a doctor but we will not get any help from people to help irrigate our farm lands."

With a reluctant look in his face Benson said, "Well your pretty stubborn but Benson gets his way or else. To get water on your property for farming purposes you have to get my permission."

When Betty was told information, she did not want to hear, she escorted Benson to the door and wished him a blessed day as a frown appeared on his face as he left knowing he would probably get his way but he did not understand Betty wanted to be independent from him and other people.

CHAPTER 15

When John and Betty woke up, Betty's stomach felt bad. The nearest doctor was twenty- five miles from where they lived and most of them left Mississippi to practice in the big northern cities.

Looking at Betty in a disappointing manner, John said, "Most of the people who get sick were given home medicine made by their mother or father or friends. Many of my relatives died because they could not get medical care or a doctor who would not come into the black section of town and the closest white hospitals would not treat black men and women which were nearer to where they lived."

Betty sat in the back seat of their 1954 Ford sedan when Betty went into labor. The night before the red dress she left home with was washed in the creek. The water tasted like oil and it smelled bad but there was no other choice to have cleaner clothes and as John drove the car, he could not stay on the road because it dodge from one side of the road to the other scaring Betty to death.

"I cannot stop the car Betty. Benson must have done something to the brakes. I should have watched him leave the house. He does not like to be told no when he wants a favor from you."

Seeing he could not stay on the road John hit a tree and a beehive fell into the car.

"The bees are stinging me!" John screamed, "We got to get out of this car or they will kill us."

"Stop the car John and we will run into this building and go to the top floor."

As they ran towards the elevator a butler carried a big birthday cake on a tray and they bumped into him and the cake flew into the air hitting two or three people who were present as Benson and three other men rushed into the building and they pushed people out of the way trying to get John and Betty and cursing disrespectful words which came from their voices.

John and Betty did not know who was following them but they rode up to the fourth floor and scrambled out of the elevator. Instead of going out the exit door to escape downstairs they went to Mr. Moon's place and knocked on the door.

"Hello me and my assistant are checking all the plumbing and electrical outlets, "Betty said, "It will not be too long."

"Where is your identification?"

"We left them at the office so let us in."

"I cannot do that because you have no identification. You might be part of the criminal element around town selling drugs and illegal liquor."

"Here's your identification information you enquired about" and after that John hit him in his jaw and he and Betty rushed into the apartment. Not to give in without a struggle both of them fought for at least three minutes and Mr. Heavy Moon who was a big guy grabbed John and threw him through the air in a hip throw but John managed to get up and grabbed a chair and threw it at him and he jumped out of the way. While John defended the honor of his family, Betty went into the kitchen and got a plastic bag and put some food, knives, plates and forks in it since they did not have any and there was such a great smell in his kitchen that suggested he was a gourmet cook.

"I better get back in there and see what is happening. "Betty said to herself.

"Oh no do not kill my John! "As Mr. Moon was getting ready to end his life and she hit him in his head with a glass pitcher of beer and knocked him out.

"Where in the hell were you? I needed your help!"

"You did not need me John. It appeared you were doing all right for yourself fighting this man. Let's get the hell out of here and go out the back way where no one will see or know what we did."

As they attempted to open the back door it was locked.

"God admit he has a combination lock on it and only Mr. Moon knows it! We need to revive him or those gangsters will catch us. I do not know why they are doing us like this!"

Trying to wake Mr. Moon up John said," We'll give you one hundred dollars before the year is out if you help us escape from here. I think my wife's father has his thug friends coming after us."

When he heard that Mr. Moon went to his bed room and got his pet skunk and lightly opened windows in the back room where he John and Betty hid. He placed his skunk in the living room and the thugs kept trying to tire the door off its hinges.

"What's that smell!" one of the men said who wore a big black hat and white shirt and blue jeans and sporting sunglasses. At once he took his hat and swings it in the air and said, "Man we have to get the hell out of here and go to the doctor. Mr. Moon's skunk saved us with the grace of God."

John grabbed Betty's hand and strolled towards their car and shouts were heard from protesters mostly black prostitutes because the white businesses refusal to hire black people and they could only sit in the colored sections to be served or waited on.

"They picked a fine time to picket the store in front of my car, "Betty said, "We'll be caught and taken back to my father. He does not want us to be together."

"Do not worry Betty I'll figure something out."

Seeing the group of colored prostitutes were angry and itching for blood John shouted, "The Klan is forming groups and coming this way!"

The militant group of citizens ran toward the excited group of Klansmen who they thought posed a threat to their civil rights. As the group left, John and Betty got into their car and left to see a doctor. The police went to the scene to stop what they thought would be a confrontation between the Klansmen, and militant group of protesters who thought they must protect their rights by any means possible.

As John turned on the engine to his car he cried, "What have I've done? The white and black folks are fighting each other. I've caused a big mess."

In the street police broke up fights between the white and black citizens and Klan members who wore white robes. Later the fireman arrived and turned the water hoses on anyone who would not disperse and go home.

They felt safe driving towards the doctor's office and a protester who shouted for equal rights ran up to their car and begged them to let him ride away from the people who were fighting each other.

"What are you trying to do? I cannot take you with us, "Betty said "We do not know you and you are probably running from the law."

A bullet hit the fender of their car which came from the fighting coming towards them.

John could not start the engine and Greenback Higgins, the name of the stranger was called by, said, "I will help you fix this car if you take me with you!"

"By the way my name is Greenback, "who looked like a lumberjack with long white hair and he helped John open up the hood and checked it out. Greenback was very charcoal black in skin color who always had the answer to problems anyone had in their life. The only problem is you could not trust him because he lied all the time.

"I see what is wrong. The battery cables are loose and they need tightening. We cannot start the car unless we can get plyers. I'll try to get some and Greenback ran to the hardware store down the street and pulled out a gun and said, "I do not have any money but I'll write out an IOU and pay you back. I need those plyers hanging on the hook against the wall, "The clerk said, "Please do not kill me I have kids to support and take care of."

"This is no robbery and I will come back and pay you with interest."

The clerk's big German Shepard awakened by the noise went after Greenback as he opened up the door and ran towards him and caught on to his pant leg and tore off the material and continued to chew it with his teeth. It appeared the dog was having a fit and went after anyone in sight and people jumped on cars as the dog tried to bite at people near him but Greenback smashed into a window and scrambled away from the dog with the plyers tightly held in his hands.

"That mutt could have hurt me, "Greenback said as he screwed up the cable end of the battery and John started up the car, As they drove down the street the three of them felt uncomfortable because of their past ordeal.

At last they finally made it to Dr. Jamison who examined Betty. All three of them strolled into Dr. Jamison's office and Betty said, "Both of you come on in with me and wait for the doctor to give me a checkup."

They saw a Dr. Jamison who wore silver glasses and his height was about 5'8" and he wore a white doctor's outfit and his shoes were highly glazed and he had dimples on each side of his jaws and his hair was in a close nit style and when he talked he made gestures with his hands.

"Now what brings you to my office and by the way the two colored boys must sit in the colored section in my lounge area. That's the law. I do not want my white patients to be run off and never come back because I am serving a white girl and two colored boys."

His comment enraged John who said, "When will this bigotry stop. We want to be treated equal and not as second class citizens."

Betty supported John by saying," The doctor was cruel to treat these two fellows with no dignity whatsoever because they happen to have colored skin. Many of their relatives got called into the great civil war between the states and now they cannot sit in the group of people as a whole. Their relatives fought in World War one and two and now in Vietnam."

A weird look appeared on Dr. Jamison's face as he said; "Now you're going to give me a lesson on black history. When I was in school, they did not teach us anything about your people. Where colored and white folks sit in public places will have to be done by state law which said white and colored people cannot sit in a place like this together. If you do not move to the colored section I will call the law and have him and his friend arrested."

With a frown on his face, John said very little about the ugly remarks Dr. Jamison repeated about the segregationist laws of the South.

"Let me teach this fellow respect for colored patients. I do not mine killing him anyway. I heard he charged colored folks more than his white ones, "John said, "I should report him to the authorities but they would not listen to me anyway because of my race and he is white."

"Do not do anything stupid like this to get us lynched now get your hands off the doctor!" Betty shouted at John," Besides he has to give us information on taking care of a new born baby."

His pride was hurt and he did not like what was going on but to get into an attack mood to hurt Dr. Jamison would get him and Greenback put in jail or lynched and he did not want that. Betty needed the help of this doctor so he or she would come into this world without any problems.

"I do not want to be placed in jail and I guess I will go to the colored section of your office even though I feel the people who make these laws are unjust. One day even though I am uneducated; I will get my high school diploma and a degree and run for public office and write laws to change these controls on our civil rights."

"Doctor. I need your help to make sure I deliver a good birth," Betty said as she sat in the patient's seat. On Dr. Jamison's wall hung everything but his license to practice medicine.

"Where are you licensed to practice medicine in this state? "Betty said,

"That's none of your business. Big Jim got my license for me. I went to medical school in another country. Plus colored folks cannot go around here asking white folks questions like that. You both are going to have to stay in your place especially when speaking to me. Do you hear me?"

Dr. Jamison put his stethoscope on Betty's stomach and said, "I hear two heart beats. I declare you are going to have twins and this will keep you from working in the fields. You have to get lots of rest and watch your diet and come back to see me for prenatal care."

"Doctor I am afraid because I have never given birth to babies before."

"I have to run some more tests to make sure the babies are doing just great."

As Dr. Jamison examined Betty he rubbed her thighs and kissed her at the same time. Before he knew it, she hit him in his mouth and Dr. Jamison's head went back.

"Why did you do that?"

"I came here to have a medical evaluation not to get laid by you or be flirted with. My man will kill you if I told him what you did."

Still trying to get prepared for a patient client relationship Betty and Dr. Jamison tried to act more professional and said, "I'll have to get some more test to make sure everything is ok."

"Where are my clothes Dr. Jamison I am sure you have them. I cannot stay in your office all evening. I have to go back to the farm with John and Greenback. I want to take off this garment and put on the garments that your patients wear. You will pay for this inconvenience."

Sitting in the colored section John and Greenback grew restless. They knew it should not have taken this long for Betty to take the prenatal examination and Greenback said, "Why is it taking so long for the doctor to examine your wife. I bet he's trying to get some love and affection from her."

"I beg your pardon she loves me and no one else,"

"You must be kidding. Love affair between you and a white woman. Who are you trying to fool. What does she want with the likes of you?"

Grabbing Greenback John pushed him into a chair where a white person sat. Other people got between them and broke up the fight.

"By the way what brought you here to this town anyway," John said, "You talk like a white boy so uppity and proper. Is this the way colored people talk and where do people live who talk like you do?"

Tucking his shirt back in his pants as they sat in the colored section of Dr. Jamison's office Greenback said, "I am from a small town in Nebraska and I grew up on a farm and I hated the work but our family through the years bought land and grew all types of crops."

"Well you do not talk like you worked on a farm before. It appears from your conversation that you have some education."

"I went to college and I majored in farming and agriculture but I could not it finish it because I read in the newspapers about the freedom riders traveling into the south and colored people sitting in the colored sections of hotels and places of entertainment and decided to do something about it."

"You are the perfect liberal. You could have stayed in college and graduate and be something and by the way were you threatened by anyone and is this why you came running after us? You can get killed coming down here to the south trying to fight for equal rights for black people. This is not just a fight for the colored people's rights. White folks have died to get equality for the colored people. If you do not stand up for your rights no one else will."

"I wish I had the education you have. I do not know how to read or write. One day I would like to run for public office like a governor or senator. I want to better the lives of my people and see the colored folks have decent schools put in their little towns. I remember taking off time from working in the fields and going to school."

"You know how to do farming. We need someone around here who can do farm work and when our farming problems appear and we will pay you weekly wages and maybe you can teach me reading and writing. I would be deeply grateful for that."

"I do not know John. I have plans to go back to New York and complete school."

As Greenback and John spoke to each other the atmosphere in Dr. Jamison's office changed when Betty said, "How would society accept my children who has a white mother and black father who struggled to maintain his manhood in a proslavery atmosphere where the colored people were field hands who did not get an education that could uplift their spirits and move to skilled jobs making more money."

Many thoughts raced across her mind as Betty put on her clothes. It was getting late and many things had to be done at the farm which needed much work. Reaching into his coat pocket Dr. Jamison gave Betty some pills and said, "I hope you plan to come into town without John because the white folks are not going to like you living with him. They get tire of the civil rights people from the north trying to integrate the colored folks with us. The white business owners can decide who they want to serve in their places of business."

Taking one of Dr. Jamison's suckers he gives to children who visit him, Betty said, "I know people are not going to like the way I decide to run my life but I have the right to live as I believe and if my lifestyle with a colored man upsets people I could give a goddam about it. I am not going to tell people who they can sleep with or love and will not be their friends if they cannot accept me and my mix-blooded friends and my children and I will have nothing to do with prejudice people. Dr. Jamison I do not have any money to pay for the visit but once I get to the bank I will mail it to you or have John bring it back to you."

"I normally do not give credit to colored folks but since you are white I will give you the benefit of the doubt."

CHAPTER 16

"Well it's good to see you are through with the visits to Dr. Jamison. We have not paid him and he never complains about it. I wonder why. What little money we give him he gives it back. I cannot figure him out. He talks segregation but he shows kindness at the same time and understands most of the people who are black do not have any money to pay him. I'll try to be a good father for our kids."

"The doctor heard two heat beats and it looks like I will be having twins."

Overhearing their conversation Greenback said, "Are both of you crazy. I think you all should go to Canada. I hear there is much prejudice in the north as it is in the south. In Canada many colored folks went there to escape slavery and it was safer and harder for slave catchers to come there to bring escaped slaves back to the southern states."

Fear only gripped John and he knew the price he would pay for driving Betty around town and the danger of him being discovered as the father to Senator Big Jim's daughter and especially if they knew John, a colored boy, was the father to his daughter's children all hell would breakout.

"Betty you cannot sit on the front seat with me no more because the police will stop us all the time."

But without failure to not say anything on the ride back home Greenback said, "Segregation in the south would be hard to stop because most of these white folks have been taught by generations of their ancestors colored people were inferior to them and they have always been slaves without knowing black people contributed to this county in many ways. You cannot change the hearts of people who do not want to embrace the ideas of people who want to give true equality to the colored people but that's why winning a civil war between the states took place to stop an end to it."

As John drove back home memories of growing up with a loving mother and father came to him and with reluctance still treated Betty as family when Big Jim gave out orders for her to stay away from the colored children. Peter and Sarah tried to caution John as the children got older they would not be able to play with each other and be equal to their white friends on the plantation. Growing fears of John getting hurt came up as a topic of conversation because they knew black men and women living together would mean lynching for the black men who defied southern life styles. Too many times Peter got into fights when his friends teased him about John's social relationship with Kirby, Sandy, and Betty. Now the biggest challenge came to John and he wondered would he survive the pain and prejudices of people who frown on his fight to keep his family together.

CHAPTER 17

Quietness surrounded them as Betty, Greenback, and John drove the car towards his farm. Against Betty's wishes John said, "Betty get in the front seat and Greenback you get in the backseat. There comes a time when you have to tell people they cannot direct your life and they can go to hell if they attempt to."

"Ok Mr. Liberal before we get home we will be stopped by the local Klan or the sheriff because Betty is sitting in the front seat. Now when we get stopped tell them you are her servant working for her father."

As John drove towards their farm a deputy sheriff got in back of them and signaled for them to stop. Out jumped a big man wearing a dark brown and beige uniform and his shoes made loud noises as he walked on the muddy road and the scent on his clothes smelled like he had been eating steak.

"You know it against the law for a colored boy to be driving a car with a white lady sitting on the seat with him and the fine will be $75 dollars."

Greenback tried to control John's behavior so he would not challenge the white deputy because he knew it would mean jail time for the both of them or even death.

"He looks like he is a hippie and he is mean looking, "Betty said, "I hope he does not send us off to jail. The police can be very evil about things like us being in this car together,"

"Just do as we are told and he might give us a break, "Greenback said "You must use self-control and show him some respect."

When things tended to go the way Greenback wanted them to react to the officer John disagreed with him.

"Officer show us the law which said a colored boy could not drive a car with a white girl sitting in the front seat."

Looking at John, "Boy what did you say? I did not hear your comment so say it loud enough so I can hear it."

When John did not say a word the officer slapped him and as he slumped down kneed him in his lip.

Betty saw what happened and she pulled the officer's gun out of his holster and pointed it at him. "Let my nigger alone. You have no right to beat him. He is only saying what is on his mind. You cannot beat him for that because he has First Amendment rights to say anything he wants to. By the way I want you to dance for me Mr. Policeman."

At once Betty shot at the policemen's feet and he jumped up a storm hoping she would not hit his feet.

"Now, I want you to start walking in the opposite direction to where we are going."

The officer had no other choice but to do what Betty was telling him and she said, "Take off your pants! "as she fired a bullet into the radio so he could not call backup. As they drove off, a pack of wild dogs came and tore into the officer who were starving and desperately wanted to have something to eat. All three of them could see the dogs eating his body leaving only bones. He yelled for help but it was in vain and no one was there to get the dogs off him.

"He got what he deserved," John said," They got their nerve thinking colored folks are going to take this abuse any longer but I better get us back home, Betty I did not know you were such a good shot. Did you see the look on his face as he dodged the bullets and how his eyes got mighty big showing a worried face?"

Looking in a panicky manner, Greenback said, "You know they are going to come back after us if they can. Betty you must be crazy. That fellow's friends are not going to let you get away with what you did."

Posing a question at Greenback, John said, "How can a skeleton talk? The dogs were hungry and wanted to eat and attacked the police officer."

"Well you got a point John the dogs ate him up but Betty left the gun at the scene of the crime and they may check for finger prints and if they can use them it could give them a lead as to who did the shooting."

"We do not have time to think about that now. Let's get going." And John stepped on the gas to gain a higher speed.

CHAPTER 18

The sweet smell of flowers and trees came into the car as John drove on the road. "Man these trees smell like the ones we use to play around chasing each other. I could live in the rural wild farm land for ever. I like the long country roads with mother nature's creatures darting back and forth through it going about their daily lives."

When John said that, Betty grabbed her stomach and gave him a loving stare.

"You are going to get all of us lynched. By the way how far do we have to go?"

Never caring about what Greenback said. "No matter what ever happens to me raise my kids and keep them together. I know it will not be easy but we have to work things out but have faith in God and nothing can stop the way we feel about each other."

"The two of you are living in a dream world of make believe but I give much praise to you. It looks like both of you will live as you believe."

"I do not think we are going to have any good luck this time and as Betty said that a car with three white men followed them and they were forced to the side of the roar. John tried to put more acceleration on the car but he could not because of the car's engine age reduced its ability to go at high rates of speed.

"You have to slow down John or get a ticket or a big fine." Betty held his hand, but John still applied pressure to the accelerator and made swift turns with the steering wheel.

"If I stop this car they will probably lynch us."

Greenback's eyes were ready to pop out. "Man keep on driving. I am not ready to die!"

Trying to hold John as she moved closer beside him. "If you do not slow down you might injure me and your two newest babies coming into this world. I want our kids to born with no broken bones or defects because you are afraid we will be killed by sick people."

By making requests to John it made him think but he did not want to stop the car to see what the strangers wanted. Reluctantly thinking about the safety of his unborn babies and Greenback's screaming and hollowing, he stopped the car.

"Oh John you're going to have to tell the biggest lie ever told. In the meantime, I'll pretend I am deaf and dumb." Greenback said.

"Now John you stay calm and do not get smart with them. I think they do like us riding together with two colored men and a white girl did not look good."

A big hand containing cuts and scars with a lot of hairs hanging from his head opened the door and grabbed John by his shirt and pulled him out of the car. A big black patch covered his one eye and his face had scars on it and he had not shaved in two months and his grayish black hair made him look like a ghost of the night and he wore all black silk clothing and each time he spoke bad breath came out of his mouth and he saw Greenback on his knees on the back seat praying to God to keep from getting killed. There were so many plans Greenback had to do to make something of himself and getting killed would not be one of them.

The big man weighed about three hundred pounds and as he spoke pulled Greenback with the other hand and he hit John in the mouth and said," I do not ever want to see you riding with a white girl sitting beside you again because it does not look too good with my white friends who do not like this type of socializing with white women."

Two of the other men were just as big holding John but they chose to drink whiskey while their buddy made John and Greenback pay the price for ridding with a white girl.

Josh who did the beatings on John and Greenback thought he would have no problems but the two of them grew tired of the beatings and John and Greenback hit Josh with their fist and he fell to the ground and the other two white fellows attacked John and Greenback and John laid in some mud and it was covered over him and he managed to crawl out of the dirty water before he could inhale it into his nose. Betty seeing what happened went to the trunk of the car to get a wrench but did not find one.

"I'll get a spare tire and roll it into one of the men fighting John and Greenback." She hollowed.

A big tire came rolling towards one of the men hitting John and it rolled into him and seeing he was distracted from John paying attention to the tire and John grabbed a big branch and hit him in his head lying beside his body.

Meanwhile one of the fellows held Greenback with a choke hold in some grass and Greenback rolled him over and he hit Greenback in his mouth. They both got up and the man he fought threw a punch at him and Greenback who knew judo caught his arm and did a hip throw on him and Betty finished him off with a kick to his mouth.

While this fighting was going on Betty pleaded for them to stop fighting. One of the bleeding white fellows stood at a distance from them and said, "All three of you will not get away with this. If you continue to be with white women we will drive you out of town where ever you may be. It is against the law for you to be with white women."

When he said that he helped the other two injured police officers to their car. With triumph written on their faces the three of them scrambled to their cars.

CHAPTER 19

Both John and Greenback were bruised and battered with blood and sweat coming from their foreheads and faces. Their clothes smelled from the blood which stained them.

"I told you not to drive the car too fast and you ignored me and look at this situation and we almost got killed by some white bigots." yelled Greenback.

As they made that long trip home the car slowed down and rain drops danced on the window shields and John's windshield wipers could not keep water off the front window as noise from the raindrops became much harder.

The ordeal Betty faced affected her because tears came to her eyes as her memory reminded her of the ways those white men beat John because she rode in a car with them and they could not accept that type of relationship among them.

The thoughts kept coming back to Betty as she wondered if she would one day have to separate their families because their children would be mixed with white and black identification. Driving through the woods at night gave her a frightening feeling because of the different sounds of insects, animals, owls, and the cry of wolves and farm animals like the cows, sheep, pigs, and chickens ending towards night time.

Greenback slept outside and he made a loud noise as he snored but inside the house, John and Betty had intimate conversations of concern.

"Betty I feel bad. Why do people have to hurt me because I refuse to stop loving you. This is the price I must pay to stand tall and not let other people tell me who I can love and be with."

Putting bandages on John. "We cannot let our dream die because other people want to hate."

"I know one thing I am getting banged up by these white folks who are still sick about the colored people living in the same local communities as them."

"John I had mixed emotions about getting involved with you but there was something different about you that I loved."

"And what was that? I hope it's a good reason," as he smiled.

"You do not have a formal education but you always wanted to make something of yourself. I'll never forget the times when you tried to read from the books I brought home from school. I taught you your ABC's against my father's will. He felt if you learned how to read he would not be able to control you. One day you will be someone special but promise me you will go on to college and get an education."

"I do not have a grade school education. You know the colored schools were not up to date. All the grades were taught in a one school cabin with no air conditioning or fans to keep you cool and the books we used were out dated but we managed. I stopped school and helped my father with the chores and plowing the soil and assisted him in the planting and collecting the crops for harvesting. I spent more time in the fields instead of school anyway."

"We cannot the let the dream die because other people want to hate. One day all of this bigotry will change but we have to believe in God for this to take place."

"I hope it will not take two hundred years from now. I will never leave you unless you want me to. What kind of life can I give you and my kids that will be born pretty soon?"

Still prancing the floor, Betty said, "I told you not to drive the car and have me sitting in the front seat. I know you have your pride and feel you are free to do as you wish but you cannot do this in Mississippi. When you did not care, all it got you and Greenback was

113

a beating. I am having your children and they could have been killed when we fought the police."

Drama took place in Betty's thoughts and she wondered if she would one day have to separate their families because of having biracial children.

Would they see mobs of white citizens protesting the transfers of black students into white neighborhood schools? This dilemma troubled her a lot and she knew anti -white folks might continue to work against any form of integration of the races and that dream of blacks and whites in the state of Mississippi going to school together was only a joke of misbelief. In her heart, she wanted her children to be raised in an integrated community because if they are raised in a society of just one race they would develop racist hatred for people they do not know anything about. Plans to attend medical school was stopped when her father threatened to not pay the tuition and with his connections she would go on a scholarship but she had to denounce John and this is something she did not want to do but said to herself she would get into medical school with or without her father's help.

Many of the farmer's families could not afford doctors and when illness hit their love ones. They went without medical treatments and died because of this which could have been prevented and some of the women could not afford prenatal care when their babies were born and were delivered in a house instead of a hospital. Seeing these growing medical needs for the farmers both black and white, Betty hoped to one day build a clinic for all the people both black and white could be treated in despite her father's efforts to block integration at all cost to further his political ambitions.

As she looked at John's back it made Betty hurt inside but she was happy the fellows who fought him did not kill him. What type of life would they live in? Would they overcome the prejudices and become a united family and would John take his anger out on Betty because the stigma of segregation would inflict emotional harm in John more than her? Would John strive to get a much needed education and run for public office and learn how to read and write and argumentation and debate? Would her children be able to attend school together and socialize with children of their race and would their teacher's judge them by the content of their character and not because they are racially mixed?

The answers to these questions did not forecast a bright future for Betty and John but for now the situation presented a challenge to them and they both were fighters determined to live the way our constitution said and being with each other was a right and many people died to preserve the meaning of that document into reality and not be just mere words on paper talked about but not enjoyed.

One evening John drove to town to buy some food but he had to go to the colored stores owned by his own people and he forgot Green back was at home with Betty. As John drove back to the house he heard a loud noise indicating he had a flat tire and at the same time Greenback attempted to molest Betty and he chased her in the house but Betty put up a good fight and she threw so many things at him as he tried to rape her.

When he finally changed the tire, John came home and saw Betty struggling with Greenback. "I know I could not trust you. You are probably working for Big Jim now get away from here before I kill you."

"John she needs a man like me not a field hand who cannot read or write."

Hitting Greenback in the mouth, he dropped to the floor and then John kicked him in the stomach and grabbed a stick and hit Greenback in the back of his head.

Greenback rushed John and tackled him and he got on top of him and threw punches at his face.

"Do not kill my man!" Betty hit him in his jaws knocking him off John and Greenback slapped Betty and scrambled out of the house in a rage.

"I always knew he was no good. His plan was to get close to us and take you away from me," John said.

CHAPTER 20

At Baxter Prison Kirby found it difficult trying to survive and he could not adjust to the prison life he hated so much. His former lifestyle was one of luxury with nothing to worry about and colored convicts would or would not try to help him depending what you gave them for their services. The prison represented nothing but great resentment to the law enforcement officers who ran it. There was much bitterness between the prisoners, the guards, and prison administrators who hated each other with daily clashes among them with one side pitted against the other. Prisoners made license plates and they were paid 5 cents an hour while the big money went to state officials leading up to Senator Big Jim Wilson who wrote tough legislation making it hard for the prisoners to get protection. The longer they stayed in jail more money was made off the products constructed by the convicts.

Baxter Prison held some of the toughest prisoners in the country who enjoyed a life of crime and pressure came from relatives of prisoners who came up missing without anyone knowing what took place or their cause of death. Outside the prison the large fifty feet walls raised above the ground contained barbed wire with electricity running through them. A ten feet moat filled with water had alligators swimming in it surrounded the prison and a wired fence was placed around it too. Many prisoners got ate up by those alligators who thought they could get out of the prison swimming across the water to dry land and safety, trying to get away from the harsh prison conditions, and the outside world knew little about the letters sent to their families and friends which never reached their destinations. A drawbridge was built to let in people coming into the prison and at each of the 50 feet towers guards carried 45 automatic pistols and shot guns. People coming into the prison got searched with metal detectors. There was one doctor to take care of a thousand prisoners and men went for weeks before a doctor treated them. Bitter prison riots took place before Kirby came there but were repulsed by the guards and at times the guards came up missing. Gangs dominated prison life and everything you wanted like drugs was available to them. When relatives came to visit the prisoners, a thick piece of glass separated them from their love ones. Many a night a prisoner sat and cried when they heard their girlfriends left them because a great majority of them served life terms.

When they were released from the prison to go on probation, within days they were back in prison because with their long prison records, it was impossible for them to get jobs. DNA was not available at the time when Kirby was sent to prison and many of them were put in jail with no evidence leaking them to the crimes they were accused of doing.

The warden Mike Hard times was a war buddy of Senator Jim Wilson, who always got his friend to stop legislation to have reform at his prison because better treatment of the prisoners would result from it. Against the orders of Warden Hard times the prisoners did their own legal work and in some cases proved their innocents and got out of jail. The longer the prisoners stayed in jail the more money was made from their cheap labor fixing and digging highways. In the winter these men froze to death because there was little or no heat coming from the fire places built on the floors and many prisoners died from living in cold cells in the winter months and during the summers it was hot in their cells for lack of air conditioning which made it hard for them to breathe.

Instead of having exercise machines to use, they never provided any type of recreation for the prisoners or educational programs they could earn a GED or a trade to use once they were released from prison and placed on probation and Warden Hard times made sure they would not abolish the death penalty.

With Big Jim 's son in the prison, Warden Hard times meant to make life miserable for him until he decided to make decisions in favor of his anti-segregation views which Kirby found it difficult to do.

Warden Hard times walked the prison walls making sure everything was ok wearing a bright red prison uniform with a walking stick and the tops on his black shoes made a familiar sound and when he approached the security officers they saluted him and if they did not he deducted money from their pay.

To check on his interest at the prison, Big Jim visited the facility to get his take of the money from the cheap labor the prisoners did to use it for his re-election and personnel use. Big Jim never announced he was coming to the prison to inspect it and all he wanted was the money to spend on his workers who canvassed the state drumming up support so they could get citizens in the state to vote for him every six years.

His fine cologne smelled many yards away as Big Jim wore his pin stripe suit and he was well shaved and his black mistress Polly accompanied him to different state functions but stayed at the hotel in town and did not have to sleep in a colored part of any hotel Senator Wilson went to because it was understood Polly was his maid and no one asked anything about it because they feared what Senator Wilson would do to them. Big Jim often hosted lavish parties at the various functions he attended at his expense.

Getting use to prison life did not appeal to Kirby and he hated being confined in a cell with one room mate who was black who weighed about 200 hundred pounds and made a loud noise when he snored. With all of this snoring, Kirby could not take no more of this and a fight broke out between the new inmates who always takes the top part of the bunk beds and Kirby did not want to sleep on the top.

"Why did they put you in this cell with me? "I do not like white boys because as a kid I was beaten by them so you have two minutes to call the guards and take you out of here." Smithy said, "Plus you have to sleep on the top bunk anyway."

"Over my dead body," Kirby shouted and hit Smithy in his mouth but the only thing resulted in Kirby hurting his hand and Smithy picked Kirby up and slammed him into the bottom bed.

The prisoners smoked pot and made bets on who would win the fight as Smithy pulled Kirby out of the bed. Kirby hit Smithy in his groin area and Smithy fell to his knees. Kirby was going to finish him off but one of the guards who betted twenty-five dollars on him to win grabbed his hand and said, "That's enough Kirby! You won the $ 100 dollars for me." and hand cupped Smithy and Kirby to the bars keeping them away from each other.

"If the two of you fight each other again we will make both of you fight over the bridge of death with the alligators to eat the one who loses and gets knocked into the moat."

"Now Kirby stay out of trouble or they might make you walk the Bridge of Death," his father replied. "I've got to finish my business with Warden Hard times about getting better living conditions for the prisoners."

"Go to hell daddy. You do not give a dam about me anyway. If so you would have done something to help me. You did not give me love and support when I needed it."

Instead of responding, Big Jim smiled and walked away. The sight of Smithy made a person want to fear him but Kirby was not going to let a colored man boss him around and would fight to the death to keep Smithy from showing his authority over him. Sweat poured from Smithy's body and he smelled because he never took a shower but he always stole a weaker prisoner's plate of food at breakfast, lunch, and dinner time and the prisoner went hungry and angry as a result.

Smithy served life for killing a man he discovered having sex with his wife and he went madly insane in the heat of passion and murdered his wife and lover and the jury at his trial found him guilty but because he did not have a sane mind at the time of the killings the jury gave him life.

Much disorder took place in the trial because many of the spectators in the audience felt Smithy should have received the death sentence. Seeing Kirby and the colored prisoner would not get alone,

Warden Hard times made both of them fight each other on a bridge over a deep pit containing ten feet of water where the alligators stayed.

As they approached each other Kirby threw punches at Smithy and he kicked Kirby in his stomach and Kirby went tumbling down but held on to the narrow bridge for dear life. The sounds of the alligators made a welcoming salute to the losing victim whose fate was sealed for their evening or morning meal leaving nothing but bones which settled at the bottom of the twenty feet deep moat. The alligators waited to tire into the flesh of the loser who would fall into the moat and their large jaws holding so many teeth would get their exercise in slicing up human flesh with no regrets. The sounds echoed back and forth from the reptiles anticipating the meal they would consume when the losing party comes down after the fight, falling into the moat of water.

The constant pounding from Smithy took its toll on Kirby and bruises appeared on his head and the fear of defeat for only a slight minute and he kept bleeding from the punches inflicted on his face and his hair looked like a wet mop used over and over again.

Kirby's tongue stuck out of his mouth and his breath barely made it out of his lungs and as Smithy started to finish him off he smiled and said, "You are too rich for me to kill!" and jumped into the moat with the alligators who immediately ate him up.

Kirby was not the model prisoner and did not get alone with their rules because he broke them. He resisted the guards who wanted to spray him with a powder to kill lice because it made him a shame because the guards treated him like he was an animal and censored all types of communication leaving the prisoner's cells. Kirby fought for his meals because the inmates knew he was the senator's son and they felt he acted too uppity.

Working for the prison posed a problem because the majority of the jobs paid 5 cents a day and it was against the law for prisoners to have five dollars on them. It was hard to uphold that law because many of the prisoners sold drugs and anything they got on the outside world they could get it in prison. Big Jim controlled the decision making on who would be let out on probation or not and he lowered the sentences of many of them who raised money to pay him for such a privilege. Homosexuality existed in the prison and many times they approached Kirby but he got into fight after fight because they attempted to be his lover. This sort of behavior was new to him and he grew to dislike it.

He often wondered how men could want to have sex with each other as lovers. He saw how the prisoners beat up homosexual lovers because of their sexual preference. In one incident Kirby defended a fellow who was being beaten up because he was a homosexual which he did not like.

Getting drugs in prison wasn't a problem, but Big Jim and Warden Hard times fussed about the money each of them was to get. Big Jim paid off the commissioner to help take care of the prisoners. Always ready to help finance his large life style and reelection campaign he made sure the trucks carrying the drugs got to the prison where it was dispersed to the inmates who paid money to buy them. Most of the prisoners walked around high all the time. Some of the men said they would tell the authorities if their drugs were not delivered on time but if they leaked out this information their bodies would be found in their cells dead. It was difficult getting prisoners to work on the chain gangs because they were high off of drugs and often fought each other.

A tragic event took place when Kirby ate some food which was poisoned by his new cell mate Lonely Heart but no one could prove it and he nearly died. The reason they called him Lonely Heart was because he held a picture of his girlfriend to his chest at bed time hoping he would see her again but since he served time for life for killing her the prisoners called him that name. Lonely Heart hated Kirby with a passion because of what Big Jim did to help operate the selling of drugs to the prisoners for profit and vetoed bills which would assist the prisoners complete their GED's. This action done by Big Jim hurt the prisoners and most of them had no formal education and read on a first grade level or no level at all. Kirby never found out who poisoned him and he chose to stay in his bed and treat himself to homemade remedies made by the prisoners who liked him because they felt taking medicine from the prison guards would be tainted with poisons especially if they had bad confrontation with them. A prison guard happened to be making his rounds after taking drugs to the prisoners saw Kirby struggling for dear life. "Lonely Heart why didn't you call someone about this man's condition. He is dying?"

"Before I go get the doctor this rich kid would have to give me one hundred dollars or he'll die!"

Opening his eyes Kirby said, "Look bastard I do not have any money. It is against prison rules to have a lot of money on yourself. I am sorry but I need some help!"

The guard slowly took out a joint and lit it up and waited for Kirby to communicate something in favor of him getting his money. The other prisoners shouted at each other. "I bet you twenty dollars Kirby dies in twenty minutes and another prisoner shouted, "I bet you a carton of cigarettes Kirby dies within an hour."

"I'll take that bet brother."

There was much chattering as Kirby tossed and turned in his bed." Please take me to see a doctor. I do not want to die in this godam place!"

Another officer saw what was happening and rushed to the cell and began to open it. "Who told you to open that cell with Kirby dying in it? No one can move him unless this prisoner pays me one hundred dollars!"

Tallman as the prisoners called him hit the unkind guard in his head knocking him out instantly. He opened the cell and ordered his cellmate Lonely Heart to help him take Kirby to the doctor. "I will not do it. Let the punk die. What's in it for me if I help you?"

"I'll make sure you get time off of your record doing work on the chain gang. I know you hate working all day in the sun so I'll get you a job in the kitchen fixing food for your fellow prison friends."

"It's a deal so when do I start?"

"Right away just help me get Kirby to the doctor."

The both of them took Kirby to see the doctor who was in another room with a woman and they were naked in bed.

Looking very unconcerned as Dr. Houseman came out of his private room where he treated patients. "What's the problem?"

"My prisoner is sick. Can you do anything for him?"

"I do not have a lab to test to see what is wrong with him. Leave the white boy on the floor. We do not have any beds for our sick people when they come in here."

"What has been happening to the fans the state sends to these men. It's a dam shame for them to be treated this way."

The two men left Kirby in the doctor's office and he went and got a book out of his drawer to see what might be wrong with Kirby, He was not a doctor and made a guess on what he thought was the problem with him. Many men died because Dr. Clyde Houseman, as he was called never finished medical school. There was an old saying that if you went to see Hr. Houseman you might as well say goodbye to the world of the living. This was senator Big Jim's son so he called a licensed doctor to treat him and that was what he did most of the time when he treated patients. When so many men came up dying an inquiry was made but with Big Jim's influence Dr. Houseman kept his job and a well-known doctor was sent to work with him. The inmates complained about the miserable prison conditions and hated Senator Big Jim Wilson who made sure they received no civil rights benefits because of the anti-prison reform legislation he wrote depriving them of their rights to have a law library at their prison.

There were no religious ceremonies at the prison or no effort to rehabilitate them to learn trades they could use to get a job after completing their sentences and many of them found themselves back in prison because no one hired them because of their history of living a life of crime. The prison officials managed to add more years to their sentence because of them getting into gang fights and you had to join a gang to survive in prison but Kirby was a loner who did not want to conform to any prison life and found himself in solitary confinement most of the time for weeks with no light in the small cell as he was punished for cursing out prison guards.

The doctor who treated Kirby, by the name of Magic Touhill looked at him as he laid in a specially ordered bed because Kirby was considered a VIP being the son of a United States senator.

As he checked Kirby over Dr. Touhill said "It looks like someone tried to poison you. It was probably an enemy of your father who thinks you have the same ambitions as he in running the affairs of this state. I am part of a group of people who are opposed to the way your father is serving the people of Mississippi and need help in getting him out of office. We have evidence he had you framed so he could keep you from getting elected into public office because he fears you will talk against everything he stands for when it comes to getting civil rights for the black and white farmers in this state."

"I thought him and Warden hard times were on good terms with each other."

Sitting in his chair. "That's all a mirage. The reason the prisoners do not have no basic rights is because of your father. He is a very powerful man in this state and the prisoners fear him."

"Why haven't any of your people tried to bring him to justice?"

"Everyone who tries to do an investigation on his activities in the state comes up missing or dead or ran out of town. The warden cooperates because he fears for his life and position because your father is ruthless and has the reputation of getting anything he wants,"

"How do the drugs get into the prison and why has nothing been done about it?"

"Your father paid someone to put poison in your food?

Trying to keep tears from coming from his face Kirby said, "Why would he do something like that? I know we disagree but why would he want to kill his own son. It does not make much sense?"

"You are different from your father. You are conservative but you talk about equal rights for colored folks and white farmers. Big Jim and his powerful friends have bought elections and state land from all the poor people especially the ones who have lived on their property a long time and were productive but many of them failed to keep their farms because of high property taxes and not being able to compete with the big commercial companies which hired people to farm on their property."

"What we want you to do is get on the good side of the correction officers and guards and find out who is your father dealing with to get the illegal drugs back into this prison."

"I would like to know who was responsible for raping me after I jumped on the trampoline. I do not get alone with those men but they tease me a lot because of the rape. I was in a dark part of the gym and this ugly thing took place. I am still hurting from wounds one of them made when he stabbed me in my back. One of the inmates who liked me put a dressing on it but my back gives me a lot of pain when I try to lift heavy objects

"Guards nearby heard all the commotion and came to rescue me because I nearly died from the blows to my body. Those beatings to my body left permanent damage because I have to walk with a cane but most of the time I try to get around without one. I feel like an old man using a cane. I cannot be myself using this cane all the time."

"Why is our mail suppressed every day? I cannot receive any mail in this prison. I bet I get lots of mail they will not give me. I've written the probation officer board after so many months and they have to let us apply for it but I never get any mail. I think my two sisters Betty and Sandy do not love me."

"That's why I am asking you to work with us and we could get you out of here as soon as possible and clear your record of any killings of Jubal Jackson on the night of the duel."

"I shared a good relationship with my sisters and always fought to defend the honor of my family even when we disagreed with each other on certain issues pertaining to civil rights."

As Kirby kept talking, Dr. Touhill handed him two hundred letters from friends and supporters who wanted him to get his freedom and win political office against his father who they felt was ripping off the people and favoring only interest groups who paid him huge sums of money to support his campaigns.

"Dr. Touhill I want to get out of this prison as soon as possible. I will give you an answer in two weeks. I do not want to turn against my father but he is not doing anything to help me get out of this prison. He did not come to the trial and attempt to use his influence to get me out of jail. You will get an answer in two weeks."

CHAPTER 21

While John and Betty are sleeping John hears Betty scream and gets up immediately and John is snoring and cannot be woke up because he took some sleeping pills. Dealing with the problems and stress he and Betty experienced, it became difficult for him to sleep at night. They slept on the floor on blankets he found in the cabins outside the house which he washed in lake a few miles from the house. Grabbing a pitcher of water Betty threw it on John who jumped up and shouted, "What in the hell you did that for. I was having a good dream about you!"

"Oh John I think I am going into labor. Please help me get into a hospital so I can have our children!"

"Ah Betty it's not the time. You just have a stomach ache and besides the doctor said our children will come in two weeks. Just go and take something for it. I got some aspirin lying on the floor. I'll get some sleep."

"Ouch, why did you kick me in the ass? That hurts!"

"Godamit John I am expecting and you are picking the wrong time to be playing around with me and Betty started crying." I have gone through this before."

"I'll get some clothes on and we'll be there in a few hours. I hope its two boys. We always wanted something like this to happen."

"Ok Betty I am sorry and I will do my best to help you."

Going into the closet, John looked to see if there was something for Betty to wear and he pulled out a grown he got from the goodwill. It was a red and white blue grown he felt would look good on her.

John was not with Betty when she bought the gown but he did not know a Confederate flag was on it. Even in this time in the early birth of her two kids, Betty did not want to put on any kind of gown but she did not know wearing it would cause a bad reaction to come from John.

"I cannot have you wearing a gown with that dam rebel flag on it. Why didn't you let me see that dress before you bought it? It's a disgrace to me and my race for you to own such a piece of clothing with that hateful flag on it and I will not let you wear it."

Grabbing the gown Betty said, "My great grandfather was a Confederate general and many of my relatives fought for states' rights against the federal union under former President Abraham Lincoln until the war ended. Many of them died for what they believed in. I bought this gown to honor them even though I did not believe in what they fought for to preserve slavery. Now get me to the doctor's office or I'll have the babies here and they might die so make up your mind."

"Ok Betty you win and I'll get you to the hospital!"

Grabbing her by the hand, John escorted Betty out of the house and the floor cracked with each step they took and as they approached the door it would not open.

"What's the problem now John!"

"I cannot open the door because the lock must be struck. I'll get an ax and knock it off."

"You know this lock is old and will not open up the way that it should."

"Oh my stomach it hurts! Hurry up and get the lock off!"

Seeing Betty cried in agony John started the engine but nothing happened and he cried out loud because the moment when he needed things to go as planned it did not work out. In the car Betty kicked and screamed because she wanted to get her new born children into the world.

"John what's the problem. You have to get me to the hospital before our kids are born or we will lose them?"

Prancing back and forth in front of the car John spotted a car on the road heading toward their farm. It surprised John to see it traveling toward them and it was a miracle of God to what was happening.

"May I be of some help to you? I was headed towards Jackson, Mississippi which is my home town and I spotted you and her as I drove by."

"My friend is having a baby and I need someone to take us to the hospital."

The stranger who sported a beard and long hair looked at Betty and John. "A colored man and a white women running around with each other will get stopped by the county troopers. Let me take you and her to the hospital. I doubt if they will let you in and by the way what is your name? I'll do what I can even though I do not like the idea of a colored man running around with a white woman."

Getting angry, "I do not give a dam about what you think. This is my women and I love her. No one will stand in my way even if I have to carry her to the hospital in my arms, I'll do it. I am getting so dam tire of people telling me who I must love. There is no law in the land which says I cannot love this woman because of her skin color. God made us to be free and love whoever we want to. Now are you going to help or not?"

The stranger who was Betty's brother did not like John's uppity attitude but he admired the way he spoke up for his sister and said what was on his mind and did not care how a white man felt about it.

"John please do something about this. I am hurting and the both of you stop debating and get me to the hospital!"

Her brother had much hair on his face and Betty or John could not recognize him and his high pitched voice was a bass tone quality. The stranger looked at John and Betty and saw who they were but he did not tell them who he was and disguised his voice even more and wore a long beard on his face. If he told them anything he would have to reveal who he was and how did he get out of jail or what his intentions were.

Kirby said, "My name is Rick Hunter and I will take you to the hospital but do not ask me anymore questions."

A black hat covered his head and a black patch took up the space over his right eye. His shirt felt like a cotton made one and his blue jeans made him look large in his legs and his feet wore big army boots. His assignment to get the confidence of the prisoners proved to be successful when he spoke to them and informed them his father was behind the dirty conditions they lived under which took pressure off their warden who cut the papers to say there was no identification of Kirby as the one who killed Jubal Jackson and Kirby was freed by the justice department to run for governor of Mississippi using a moderate stand on getting civil rights for black and minorities which Big Jim opposed and he knew he feared for his life when Big Jim knew he'll be running for the office of governor opposing his views on segregation laws which had been placed in the state constitution of most of the southern states.

Dr. Touhill helped Kirby and was later killed by Big Jim's men. Now he was not accused of killing Jubal Jackson and could run for governor of Mississippi and use a moderate stand on civil rights for black people and other white folks who supported him against Big Jim who was his father. Kirby knew he could not trust a lot of people associated with his father because whatever he tried to do in his efforts to campaign for civil rights would make Big Jim angry because Kirby opposed the anti-civil rights laws which were one hundred years old and he said he would fight to abolish them because of the black codes started after President Rutherford B Hayes pulled the Union troops out of the South so he could become president of the United States.

Both John and Kirby got Betty to the hospital but on the way a big tree fell on the road in front of them because a storm was in progress and lighting hit the huge oak trees and set many of them on fire. In a hurry Kirby and John got out of the car and attempted to push the tree off the road but it became difficult to do this. They managed to tie the tree with some tree limbs to their car and drove it out of the way so they could pass. They gradually made it down the road and a deer darted in front of them. Kirby turned his car into a spin to avoid killing the animal. Still determined to keep his eyes open because this was his dear sister and memories came back to him on the times he always defended her in her battles with society ever since they were children even though they argued about the issues of equality for colored people. This was the sister who encouraged him to become something he wanted to be instead of following the desires of his father even though they had bitters quarrels on his womanizing, drinking, cursing a lot, and gambling away allowance money Big Jim gave him all the time to buy things he needed for school.

They got on the road and behind them a driver followed as Betty's screams echoed out of her mouth with her two front teeth missing as she kicked her legs into the air.

Who is in back of us," John said, "If it's the same white folks who beat me. I am going to shoot at them before they do it again."

"Now you are thinking crazy because they will kill you. Let me speak with them."

The driver in the car motioned for them to stop. Kirby walked towards the car and he said to them,

"I am part of the local white patrols of the Southern Allegiance Organization. We are taking the screaming white woman to the hospital. She is having my baby at such a time like this. She's acting crazy from those effects of having a baby and I have had no sleep all day trying to help her."

The men dressed up in white and black uniforms said, "We were going to shoot out the tires in the car . . .We do not like the idea of a black man riding in the car with a white lady. Why is this taking place?"

"That's my nigger and he does work at my plantation. He's a good nigger and he picks much cotton for me doing harvest time. He's too valuable to let him go. I needed his help to comfort my wife as we drove her to the hospital."

"Ok let's get back to our work of patrolling this countryside and go home. I guess everything is ok."

By this time Betty is screaming. "Please hurry to the hospital. I cannot take this pain any longer!" as she pulled out her 45 caliber pistol getting ready to shoot John and Kirby as the babies kicked up a storm.

"You cannot come into the hospital John. Let the white hospital workers help me bring Betty into the operating room."

This upset John who wanted to rebel and curse the people out who did not want him to be in the hospital because of his skin color.

In the hospital there are many babies and mothers having newborns. Groups of people came in and out and the smell of medicine circulated through the air coming out of patient's waiting rooms. The cries of children were heard who were sick from flu and other sicknesses. People who suffered from drug abuse could hardly stay in their seats. In the office treatment areas dentist struggled to pull teeth and patients moved back and forth in their seats when it took hours to do root canals in an unprofessional manner. The social workers refused to give grants to people who could not afford to pay for their medical treatments. The interior of the hospital needed cleaning and it took hours for them to treat the patients. One problem was there were many groups of foreign people from Asia, and Latin America who could not speak English and posed difficult problems for the doctors to understand their language which resulted in them not being able to know what was making them sick. Some of the Mexican patients escaped from across the border into the United States looking for work but it was impossible for them to get good jobs in their own country and many of them picked fruits and vegetables in the hot summer sun and during the harvest season and those types of jobs did not have health insurance and they were refused service because of Big Jim's requirement they have identification papers and proof they were citizens in order to get medical treatment especially if they did not have insurance. Kirby and a staff worker placed Betty in a wheel chair and on the way to the operating room the big wheel stopped moving.

"Got to get another wheel chair and if that do not work I'll carry her to the operating room myself!" Kirby said.

Instead of waiting for the wheelchair, Kirby picked his sister up and carried her to the operating room and when he got there two of the doctors played dice with each other. They were not even dressed in their scrubs and ready to help deliver any babies.

Kirby gave them a dirty look, "What in the hell are you doing not getting ready to deliver this baby. I'll have your license revoked if you do not get dressed to help this women!"

One of the doctors looked at him." We heard one of the babies would be black and the other one white. We do not deliver those type of babies and besides I am throwing a mean hand of dice so she is going to have to wait until we finish because I got a good streak of luck going at this moment. So shut the hell up!"

Betty could barely speak when she pulled out her 45 she always kept with her. "Stranger take this gun and kill both of them if they do not get to the work and deliver my baby!"

The two doctors stopped throwing the dice and helped put Betty on the operating table and she kicked and screamed many curse words. Kirby ran into another room and pulled out his gun and said, "All the doctors in here come and help the patient who is having a baby!"

Kirby fired a shot into the ceiling and both doctors stopped throwing the dice and helped put Betty on the operating table and she kicked and kept pulling on the doctors' uniforms with her hands.

He hollowed at other doctors and they darted down the hallway to where Betty was having her babies. Hospital officials called the local police and they rushed to the hospital and located the area where Kirby fired his shots. Hearing the police coming to get him Kirby realized he might get caught by police officers his father controlled and he went to the kitchen and the officers followed the dogs smelling for his cent which would be let loose. As the dogs came into the kitchen Kirby opened fire and killed one of them but he could not fight off the other big Doberman who got a holt to his legs and bit his calf muscle but John tried to see his children come into the world and Kirby was taken back to the same prison as a result of Big Jim learning of his departure from it and ordered tight security. His friend

Dr. Touhill was killed as a result of his enemies at the prison telling on him for helping Kirby get out of jail.

Meanwhile John grew restless and went into the operating room and he risked being put in jail for breaking the segregation laws of the state. At that moment John saw delivery people bringing some medical equipment into the hospital and they dropped some packages on the floor and John said to himself "That's my ticket to get to the operating room to see my children come into this world. I can pretend I am a delivery man working for this garment company."

As John made his way through the hallway holding packages, he was spotted by a security officer by the name of Easy Money who weighed about 250 pounds and carried a big shot gun and had a reputation to take no mess off anyone especially his own people.

"Where are you going? You do not belong in here so get the hell out of the hospital. They will fire me if they find you in this building. They do not allow colored people in this place."

Pointing his shotgun at John who said, "Man you're going to have to kill me. I am going to get to my woman to see my children born into this world if I have to die doing it. I am getting tire of people trying to keep me from the woman I love."

"Man you got your nerve willing to die to see your children get born to come into this world. I could blow your head off if I wanted to and get away with it. They do not care about a black man killing a black man. If you were white, they would lynch me for killing you."

"Follow me. I like you because you were willing to die for a cause. There are not too many people willing to take a bullet to see their child come into the world. Come into this room and I will get you some scrubs to put on and I'll tell the other guards you're with me and no one will mess with you."

All the hospital prisoners knew Easy Money who fought in the second world war and rose up to rank of first lieutenant and won many medals when he wiped out several German machine guns nests when they had his platoon pent down. When he came home after the war, it was difficult to get a job but he saved the life of a hospital official by the name of Dr. Jamison who was being robbed who later got him a job at the hospital. The doctors happened to be dressed in scrubs as John walked into the operating room and a big oval light was shown over them and Betty ached with pain and every curse word she could say came out of her mouth in agony. "The two of you are dismissed because I heard you did not want to help deliver this woman's kids into the world because of your prejudice ways. I will have you fired in the morning so get out of my operating room." Dr. Jamison said,

It was a good thing Betty was in a modern up to date hospital and many of the women of the state had their babies born deformed because they did not have prenatal care before their children were born.

When the nursing attendants saw Easy Money they did not question who he was bringing into the operating room. As John came in, he saw the nurses cleaning new born babies and smiled at what took place and saw Dr. Jamison getting ready to perform the operation.

Dr. Jamison tried his best to perform a good delivery. "There is more than one of them and they are different races. One was white and the other one was colored. I have never seen anything like this before."

John's emotions overcame him and he wanted to shout to the world these were his two daughters but Easy Money told him to keep his composure and he could sneak him into Betty's room so he could see her as she preferred to breast feed her babies and not be given formula milk. If this was a normal society, John could let the people know he was their father and wanted to pass out cigars to the people in the operating room and enjoy holding his children and consoling his lover Betty who loved him dearly regardless of how society said a black man and white woman could not love each other.

Easy money was called on the radio to come and stop a disturbance because a group of civil rights workers who were outside protesting about the segregated conditions in the hospital and denied full equality because they had to be segregated in every manner when using hospital facilities and since this hospital was funded with taxes taken out of their incomes they felt compelled to demand equal treatment when coming to it. They could not provide blood to the regular blood pool where every white person's blood was placed. A section for black blood was put in with the words colored blood only painted on several signs. They marched back and forth shouting full equality and equal treatment by the staff.

A security officer guarded the door where Betty slept and asked John. "Are you a surgeon and why are you up in the white section of the hospital?"

"I am a doctor and I need to see Betty Wilson and check on how she and the twins are doing."

The security officer who was white said, "I have not seen any new doctors on my list which were just hired and plus the hospital does not employ colored doctors."

A loud announcement came over the public speaker saying, "Security officers to the demonstration area immediately."

When the officer heard this, he forgot about John and left to help put down the demonstration. Tiptoeing up to Betty, John did not realize Betty was not sleep and said as he approached her, "Oh John you look odd in the uniform. I am glad to see you. I know they gave you a hard time to get in here."

"Who was that man who helped us? His voice sounded like my brother Kirby's"

"I do not know who he was, "John said as he moved closer to Betty and looked to see if anyone was looking and kissed her. With all of her might Betty managed to hug him as she kissed him.

"Your hair looks a mess. It looks like you are going to have to gain some weight." The both of them stared at each other in bewilderment because of what they both were experiencing and John said," How are my children?" I heard we have twins where one is colored and the other is white. It must have come from genes in our families."

"Is there a problem with this? John they are your children and I went through living hell bringing them into this world."

Sitting in a chair," I know we have twins but I did not think one would be white and the other one black. Have you thought of a name for the twins yet?"

++ Opening up her mouth, "Let's name them Dianna and Dora. We 'll name the colored one Dora and the white one Dianna."

Resting his back against the back of the chair. "There will be difficult days ahead of us. How can we raise the children under those types of conditions? The town's people will beat Dora up badly with insults because of their prejudice towards colored people in general. Dianna will be treated much better because her skin color is white. I would have to take Dianna to school for white people only and with you being colored you'll take Dora to an all colored school."

Feeling very sad he looked at Betty and held her. "They might grow up hating each other because of it. We have to instill in them to stick together and be strong and not have a divided family."

The nurse brought the twins into Betty's room and she held Dianna in her arms. "This is a beautiful child. She makes so much noise when I try to feed her."

Trying to see who was talking, Betty said, "May I hold my baby. She looks just like my mother Mable, beautiful with blue eyes and soft blackish brown hair and a fat rump. By the way where is my other child? You know the colored one which came after the first one came out of my stomach?"

The nurse pretended not to hear her but asked to repeat her question. "I did not hear you at first."

Rising much higher out of her bed, "I gave birth to a set of twins and one was colored. Could you bring the colored one to my room. I want to have both of them in here."

"Ok I'll go and get Dora so she can be with you."

The nurse never came back to honor Betty's request. John looked at the situation. "I bet the nurse cannot bring Dora in here because she is colored". The nurse did not give an explanation for her actions.

"I'll go and see where my daughter is and I'll raise hell if they are keeping me from seeing her."

As John walked out the room, he stopped and waited to hear why they did not bring Dora to see Betty. As the nurse who was white approached both of them she said, "There is a rule colored babies cannot be brought up here to be with their mothers in this maternity ward. I know you do not like this but that's the law in this hospital."

Trying to keep from dropping Dianna Betty yelled, "Get my baby before I kick your white ass. I do not give a dam about her color. She is my child and I will sue this hospital if you do not bring her in here and I do not mean tomorrow!"

The nurse left with an angry look on her face and felt determined not to bring Dora into the room fearing she would lose her job if she broke the laws of the hospital. Getting upset Betty grabbed anything in reach and threw the articles which went sailing through the air and as Dr. Jamison came in he moved out of the way because they would have hit either him or anyone else coming into Betty's room.

"Now you keep on raising hell like this or you might have a heart attack or be sued by someone who happens to be hit by one of your missiles causing damage to them. The only thing you could say is you are sorry for that ugly behavior and you did it out of anger."

Another nurse came into Betty's room holding Dora and she was Dr. Jamison's private nurse. Grabbing Dora Dr. Jamison made a comment. "Here's your baby. I cut an incision on both of them for identification records just in case one of them might need a blood transfusion."

Smiles appeared on Betty's and John's faces and Betty said, "I have some beautiful kids.

I know God will take care of them and the mother and father."

Sitting on a chair Dr. Jamison said, "You see Dora has sickle cell and will one day need a blood transfusion from Dianna because only her blood could be used to save Dora if she was to lose a lot of it and needed a donor. Please remember. This is for the child's own protection. I know you do not want to hear this but I'll have to tell you anyway."

"Tell me what?" as she played with the both of her kids.

"It's the same thing I expect to hear from everybody that my child is black and will not be accepted because of her skin color and these Jim Crow segregationist laws."

Feeling more comfortable to speak, "Well Dr. Jamison I cannot give up because of the situation. I might have to travel to Europe because you do not find too much prejudices over there. During World 1 many colored soldiers stayed in France because of the way they were treated. They did not want to go back to the south and be treated like an animal or lynched by some sick white people who hated you only because their skin color was black."

"You will not do something like that. You might go over there in Europe but this is your homeland and besides do you want to learn another language?"

They both laughed at what he said.

"When are you going to get rid of your for colored only section and let the patients sit together both white and colored. It does not make sense to segregate your patients like this because they all have something in common when they come into your office and that is to get well after you treat them."

As he picked up her clothes, Dr. Jamison looked at Betty in a curious manner. "Sometimes I think about this and want to change but I might lose my big paying customers like the local politicians who run the state. Maybe one day I'll change but I do not want to lose my livelihood because of it and by the way there is one thing they have in common is that they are sick all the time."

"Many of the places where people reside near water they get very sick and some of them live close to livestock have been buried. My father always writes legislation to keep money from the farmlands to clear out the pollution to develop it with shopping centers. He never does anything about the insets which invade the crops and eat everything in sight."

"Well Betty your father has all the politicians under his control and on the payroll and me too. He cannot be stopped in his plans for corruption. I owe him because he kept the state from taking my medical license when they found out I did not have certain medical courses I should have taken in medical school."

"My father has a way of controlling everything he wants to but not me. I'll live as I believe. The hell with what my father wants. He cannot control me and John's life."

"You are up against a stone wall Betty. I hope you and the kids will survive this ordeal. You know some people are not ready for race mixing around here. Many people are thinking ugly things about you John, and the twins."

"You cannot change the way people feel about my having twins of different colors. I will love both of them as equals."

"What are you going to do when you cannot take Dora into a theater or places to eat with you?"

This comment did not deter Betty from feeling the way she did. "I'll go to another place where we can enjoy some happiness together."

"You might have to go north to Canada but down here in Mississippi you do not stand a chance. Your colored daughter will not be able to attend the same school that Dianna would be going to. They might grow up and become bitter enemies because of this."

After leaving Betty and going back to the hospital to take Betty and the twins home, the hospital officials would not let John to do this claiming he was not the father of twins because he did not have his last name on the birth certificates and there's no way a colored person could be driving a white girl home because he might get stopped and arrested.

"But I am the father of these twins!" as he slammed his fists against the counter tops.

Making his daily visits to see his patients, Dr. Jamison saw the commotion going on as John tried to explain he was the father of Dianna and Dora. "He is the father," Dr. Jamison," said, "I will drive the twins and their mother home. John you can follow us."

Realizing it was a losing battle John relented and tears fell from his eyes because he felt he was being treated like a second class citizen and he did not want to raise his kids in a prejudice manner. John knew the conditions he lived in as a colored man and he tried to convince himself maybe he'll be able to do something to end segregation in the state of his beloved Mississippi, but will his race stand in the way to keep him from learning how to read and write?

CHAPTER 22

During Big Jim's political life, he made enemies and destroyed people who stood in his way. One such person was Digger Fox who Big Jim promised he would give support to when he wanted to be secretary of the housing department. Instead of supporting Digger Fox for the office, Big Jim was given $500,000 dollars for indorsing Lefty Pete who beat Digger Fox badly in the election. Digger Fox spent four million dollars on the election and vowed to get even with Big Jim Wilson. Big Jim Wilson made sure his people counted the votes at the polls and instructed his workers to throw out Digger Foxes votes and he came out publicly and endorsed Lefty Pete for the office of Secretary of Housing in Mississippi and ran a smear campaign of printing negative ads on him to influence people to vote Lefty Pete into office.

With the problems Digger Fox faced, his main ambition was to keep Big Jim from influencing the state elections coming up this year and paid over a million dollars to get Kirby placed on probation if he could run for office. As Digger Fox approached Kirby's cell, the guards questioned why they were coming to see Kirby.

"I do not need an explanation as to why I want to see this man. So just let me talk with him."

The guards were not going to back down from Digger Foxes' body guards and drew their guns out too. As usual bets were made as to who would win the shootout.

Overhearing the conversations almost ready to end in blood Kirby shouted, "Its ok this is Digger Fox the wealthiest man in the state of Mississippi. I've been waiting for him so everybody put up their guns."

"Digger give these prison guards a fifty dollars apiece and tell your people to put up their weapons."

"My boys were trained to protect their boss at the cost of their lives."

Why didn't the warden tell us Digger Fox was coming to see Kirby?" said the prison guards.

"You know the warden do not tell us anything. He does what he wants to do. He's gone on vacation and he forgot to tell the prison guards about our meeting with Kirby."

Immediately, Digger's men paid the four prison guards fifty dollars apiece and Digger was let into Kirby's cell to talk with him.

"I am glad you came. I wrote just about everybody I knew indicating I was innocent of killing Jubal Jackson. I think I was framed by someone but I do not know who it was and it dark and I was lit up like a rocket and much alcohol drifted through my system when I fired a shot at him. They captured me at the hospital when I tried to help my sister have her twins, and Dr. Touhill got me released without my father knowing about it."

Digger took out a bottle of whiskey and a glass set for social drinking and said," I need your help Kirby to run for governor of Mississippi. You were slandered by your father's political allies."

"I have a prison record and the citizens will not vote for a man with a murder charge against him who has done time for this crime even if I was able to beat the charge of murder the first time"

"I understand Digger Fox said," I can make things right for you and get your crimes dismissed at once. All you have to do is play ball with us and I will get you out of prison."

"I know you did not come to this God forsaken place to get me out of prison and get nothing in return so tell me what you are planning to do?"

"We will get your sentence dismissed for lack of evidence on who killed Jubal Jackson because witnesses saw other people running away from the crime area when Jubal was killed and they were captured by the police and indicated they shot him because he owed them a lot of money."

"We will help you win the race for governor and you will give us permission to buy out the lands which many of the poor white and colored farmers have oil on them and we can declare imminent domain and put corporations on the property. We will pay the farmers top money for their property. We will say the land is contaminated with chemicals that's destroying the land, spreading disease, and it's killing the babies of expectant mothers in that region of the state of Mississippi."

"That means many people including my father and his friends will lose their property and everything they have worked for."

. "I have to think on that because my father and I do not have a good relationship but my two sisters Sandy and Betty still live there and are in line to inherit the big estate."

Pouring his whiskey Digger said, "Your father plans on not giving the estate and his millions to your sisters. He is still messing with his colored mistress Polly and the word is going around she will inherit the estate."

"That's a lie and only fiction and not the truth."

Out of his hand Digger showed Kirby a will indicating a maid by the name of Polly was to get most of the estate leaving his sisters nothing signed by Big Jim.

All rage broke out in Kirby's eyes as he read the will but could it be a forgery he thought. He knew his father wanted power but to give his estate to a colored mistress just did not make sense to him and felt it was not the justified thing for his father to do.

Digger said, "Polly is in the background of everything he does and civic functions your father attends she is his secretary and not a maid. Some people say your father is fascinated with her and spend much of their time together at his estate in Washington acting as his private secretary. Look at these photographs of the two of them laughing and enjoying the company of all those important people but their life together after business is very private and the only people who know about it is his staff."

"Getting angry Kirby said, "Just help me and I will do anything you say. I am sick and tire of sitting in this cell. So when do I get out of here; I cannot wait to get even with that father of mine and that colored boy John Carol who my sister will probably marry. We cannot have any colored blood in this family."

Taking another drink of whiskey Kirby said, "Will this information hit the press"

After hearing that, Digger combed and stroked his hair and took out some cologne and placed it in his hand and patted it on his face and said,

"We'll put it in the press the state of Mississippi proved by the evidence there was another person who shot Jubal Jackson and the police captured him. The politicians in some parts of Mississippi are getting tire of your father controlling everything and are willing to take power from him."

"I will need money to take care of myself."

"We'll set you up in one of our plantations and get you a part time job but most of your time will be running for governor and spying for us and voting on legislation favorable to us and what our organization wants you to do is to protect our interest and that is to keep your father from stopping our efforts to develop the civil engineering projects in the state of Mississippi."

Kirby said, "That shouldn't be hard but what about the federal government? They will not give funds to federal projects that will not hire colored people."

"That's why we want you to be governor because any anti-discrimination legislation for the federal or state level you can voice your opposition to or veto it on the state level."

"I'll do what I can to help you so give me the orders and when they should be carried out."

CHAPTER 23

It took time for Betty and John to settle down at their house and being black John could not get a loan from the white bankers because of his skin color but being white Betty could easily get one. The reality of getting rejected became a way of life for both of them and when she applied for the loan and got one the banker sent letters back to them saying they could not do it because she lived with a colored man.

. One evening Betty ate at one of the restaurants in town and as she finished her meal a young girl choked and could not breathe and Betty seeing what took place rushed over to girl and put a hemlock hold on her forcing the food out of her throat. At first the men in the restaurant pushed Betty to the side and said, "You're a woman and this is men's business."

The men could not get the food out of her throat and Betty saw an old loaded shot gun laying behind the counter and grabbed it and said, "Who ever do not get out of the way and let me help this girl I'll blow their brains out."

"Ah that gun is not loaded," One of the men said as he got in front of the shot gun.

"Sounds of the girls breathing could not be heard and her pause was dying out and Betty fired the gun just to see if it was loaded and pulled the trigger and aimed it at the ceiling and it went off hitting the electric fans circulating air to keep people cool.

At once all the men left and Betty ordered them to leave the restaurant and they did not have any problem in obeying her command. Betty immediately applied the hemlock maneuver on Mira Racoon and she spit up the food and began breathing.

Mr. Racoon said," Ok, thanks for reviving my daughter Mira. I thought we would lose her."

His wife Laura Racoon said, "Is there anything we can do to help you?" My husband is the president of Daisy May Bank and helps people get loans to take care of their homes and farms if they qualify for the money."

"Well Mr. and Misses Racoon I need help with a loan to fix up my farm, I tried to get a loan at your bank but the loan officer Mr. Teddy Udall saw me with John who is colored and said no without giving a reason. This has been the story every time I tried to get a loan from the local banks."

"Come to the bank and I'll make sure you'll get a loan for forty thousand dollars to fix up your house and build up the farm and when the crops come you can pay the bank back and there will be no interest on the loan. We owe you for saving our daughter's life and I'll make sure you will obtain the money to get started on your farm to pay for necessary expenses."

Within two weeks, contractors came to repair the house to bring it up to code for good living conditions, which included rooms with running water being pumped into their house. Misses. Racoon ordered contractors to fix up the interior of the house and made sure John had the machinery to cultivate the land for farming. Even though they received the funds to build their farm up the racist forms of bigotry came up. John could not talk with the white contractors and when they found out he was living with a white women and they refused to do their already paid for contracted work which led to a breach of contract in many cases.

Discrimination from colored contractors resulted in them not liking John having a white women and one of them said, "Of all the colored women in this state you had to get with a white women. Where's your allegiance to your own race? I will not do any work for you."

Knowing John was outspoken in his beliefs he said, "First of all who I sleep with is my business and you or no white man is going to tell me who to have my life with."

Life as usual took place and things seemed to be bad all the time because Big Jim's people kept creating problems to keep them from bringing in a good crop like setting fire to their corn fields and poisoning their cattle or stealing them when they were not at home. This worried John because he had to pay back the loans he borrowed to get started to make a life for him and Betty. Trying to get help from the law was useless because they were controlled by Big Jim who cared very little about the farmers who he felt had oil on their property and would not sell it to him. It was difficult to get hired help because Big Jim's people threaten to kill them if they helped farm the land.

CHAPTER 24

Every one left out and Kirby and Digger Fox spoke to Kirby about making a deal with him.

"I want you to run against Lefty Pete for governor ousing oSt SSS and I have paid over $1,000,000 dollars to spring you out of jail. When I pay off the right people I 'll able to cut the red tape in getting you out of this. Your warden was paid so get your clothes and leave with me."

As they drove down the road, Digger is giving Kirby instructions on what he wants him to do as a result of him getting him out of jail. Have some hamburger I know you are hungry."

"That's ok I ate before we left the prison."

"Go on and eat. This is good food."

"Well I do not want to eat. For all I know the food might be poisoned. I cannot trust a person who is an enemy of my father."

Before he knew it one of Digger's men put a rope around his neck and choked him to death.

As he choked Kirby, the killer said, "Your father paid us real good to take you out. You would do many things to hurt him if you win public office."

CHAPTER 25

Mary Florence visited the house and saw how it looked. The roof did not leak and the house looked in much better repair and somehow they had a bathroom with running water coming from the nearest creek. With the loan money Betty brought needed things for the house and even farm machinery to help plow up green beans, and cotton. As she ringed the doorbell a rich aroma of food came drifting through the air and the sound of John running the tractor made a humming noise and Betty dressed in finer store bought clothes because without the conveniences of a washing machine she made many walks to the lake to wash clothes for the family by hand and trying to do this made her angry. The first thing she did was to get a washing machine even though they had a problem keeping the lights and gas on because of people trying to get Betty to sell the property. The water had the smell of oil in it which made them sick at times but it was very low.

"Who is it."

"It's just your neighbor from next door. Miss. Mary Florence president of the Local Auxiliary and my group is giving a party for the area girls and would like to know if your children would care to join us."

As Dora and Dianna came strolling out of their rooms, they could only say momma and daddy and a few words. Dianna's skin was very white looking and Dora's skin was black as coal. Relaxing in a love seat, Betty said," I would love to have them go and meet other children of their own ages,"

After looking at Dora, Miss. Florence said "I am sorry but I cannot let your colored child come but Dianna would be the right child to bring. The other parents will reject her for her skin color and the kids too."

"I will not segregate my children from each other. Either you take both of them and not at all and get out of my house and do not come back!"

CHAPTER 26

K nowing reelection was about to come for the United States senate seat, big Jim held a press conference at his estate for the press only.

Dressed in his best clothes, he wanted to impress the newsmen who could write coverage on his plans to rip off the citizens of their property with good defined lies.

"Fellows I invited all of you to hear what I will do if reelected this year. I am always friendly to the press especially during election time and this is my platform: As Senator Wilson prepared his speech to the reporters his servants passed out refreshments and food. A bowl of cigarettes was in the middle of the room as Big Jim invited them to a heavy meal. At his side was Polly who sat patiently and ate her food without saying too much to anyone. Everyone looked at Polly who was very beautiful with mixed blood and she kept looking at Big Jim as he greeted various guests he invited to his many social functions. When these activities took place Polly stayed at Big Jim's side at all time and would not dance with the black invited guest at many social events and was there if he needed her.

"Fellows this is what I have in mind. I want more law and order because the laws against white collar crimes are too strong and need to be changed in every state especially Mississippi. We must get together federal and state laws to stop the violence made by these people."

"I do not want the integration of students. Things must stay the same and we should be able to send our kids to the schools they want to go to. People around here do not want government officials from Washington telling them how to get their children educated and not being educated in a classroom with niggers is only going to hurt them."

One reporter field a question at him. "What is this thing about you sleeping with a colored woman? There are rumors circulating and plus you are uptight about your daughter running off with a colored man by the name of John Carol. Now senator you are not practicing what you preach. Your daughter is practicing integration in your family tree against your wishes and when you speak to us you are anti-integration. You do not stand a chance of winning reelection if your family members cannot live up to your beliefs about the segregation you preach so proudly about."

"Senator are you for colored and white folks marrying each other? "A reporter said as he finished drinking a glass of wine and eating his favorite chicken soup.

Big Jim tried to avoid the questions but the press would not let up.

"If you look at my record, you'll see I have been fair to the colored people in this state and wrote legislation so they could attend their own colleges even if it meant going to another school."

"I heard you are planning to steal the farm lands of both the colored and white farmers because there is the possibility of oil and gold in that region of Mississippi."

"That's a dam lie. I have no interest in taking over any oil rich lands in this state. This is hearsay information with no concrete evidence."

"I've seen some bills given to me saying you are talking to people about writing legislation for the state senators to create what we call imminent domain and you have stopped all legislation to improve the area. I'll write a column about this information. I will not sit back and have you take over this oil rich land. You know you like to control and get anything you want and do not give a dam about how you get it."

"All this is hearsay and no evidence and I want you to print the truth like I said it. I'll influence the state legislators to help lower the taxes not raise them. I want to make sure the people get good prices for their crops. I'll block efforts to send jobs overseas to people in other countries because they make products with cheaper labor which hurts our economy over here in the United States."

"Are you sleeping with colored women? That's the general talk around Washington D.C. They say you spend more time with her than your wife."

"That's my private life and not yours. Polly works with me on important issues affecting colored people in this state. That is all gentlemen and I have to go. Enjoy the meal which my cooks have prepared for you to eat. I need you to write some positive comments in the newspapers for what I want to do for the great state of Mississippi and the citizens living here."

With that all said and done the reporters finished their lavish meal and left.

Reporter Freddy Pots one of the reporters who Senator Wilson felt would write lies about him ordered his assassination the minute he and another reporter left the plantation to write negative things about him.

"Freddy we have to write the truth about Senator Wilson because he lied about everything he told us and has no intentions of doing anything for the people and he wants the lands which has oil on it." Richard Loves said who a reporter was listening to Big Jim.

Before his friend finished his sentence their car went out control going down a hill with trees of all sizes on it and when their car hit a tree it exploded killing both of them instantly. Big Jim said they would not make it back to their newspaper s to print negative things about him. When the authorities checked the brakes of the burning vehicles they were tampered with but no fingerprints were available to find out who made them malfunction. The police were paid to not make a good investigation as to who killed these reporters. One thing Big Jim did was to control the media who might write bad news about him and get rid of the people who would do it.

CHAPTER 27

There was a nearby school in Jackson, Mississippi and as the twins approached the age to attend it, John and Betty took them to Livingston Elementary School and to enroll them into their kinder garden class of students. The school was one of the finest in the state but when Betty and John went to register the kids they met a principal by the name of Mr. Paul Renaldy who met both of them at the administration office. "I see you have two kids and one is white and the other colored and that will be a problem. You have beautiful children"

Dressed in a white dress, Betty and John, who wore a suit, sat in chairs, and Betty said, "I want to enroll the girls in this school and come and pick them up later."

"Who is the gentleman?"

"He is my foreman on my farm and manages the upkeep of it."

Leaning back in his chair the principal said, "We can enroll the white looking child but the colored one it's impossible."

Getting angry." Or these rules?" Betty said.

"No this is the law of the state of Mississippi and I and no one can do anything to change it."

"We cannot separate the twins from each other because they are a close nit group."

"I am sorry," the principal said as he smoked his big cigars. "Take Dora to the school for colored students where she will be accepted and treated much better."

"I hate these types of things because my children will grow up hating each other because of the opportunities that Dianna will have over Dora. Both of them did not enjoy the rejections Dora faced and John said," One day I'll be in a position to stop this discrimination."

"How can you do that when you cannot read or write? You'll be the laugh of the citizens who you want to give you money and support."

Looking at Betty. "I'll do something about my lack of education. Just wait and see."

A knock is heard at the door and Betty went to open it. Outside Jack Benson stood at the door with a humble face that was false.

John was out in the fields working and cultivating the various crops they grew. As they talked John came into the house from the backdoor. "Hi Benson it's been a long time since I've seen you and thanks for giving me some fish to take home to **Betty**. How have you been doing?"

"I want you to go outside and get me some water because I want to spend some time with your woman."

"What in the hell do you think this is the days of slavery. Back then black slave women had no choice in who they could sleep with on the plantation because Massa went to bed with any of the slaves he wanted to. This is not the days of slavery and black men will not take it kindly when you want to molest their women against their will."

"Boy hush your mouth before I tie you to a pole and put a leather wipe to your back. Now get out of here so I can romance your woman."

Grabbing John by his shirt he did not look timid as he told Benson to take his hands off of him. "You will not come into my house and act like you are the overseer. I do not have to answer to you. I thought you were a nice honorable person."

When Jack Benson turned his back to touch Betty, John picked up a stick and hit in his head and the blows knocked him out and he fell to the floor. His body smelled badly and his dress of clothes looked like he wore them for several years.

"Search his clothes John. He might have important papers on him because he is always doing things for my father."

John reached into Benson's pockets and pulled out papers saying there was $25,000 dollars taken from the poor farmers who Big Jim and Benson influenced legislators to go up on the property taxes which the farmers could not pay resulting in their lands being foreclosed on and taken from them.

"Let's get him out of here and call the authorities to come and get Jack."

When Betty called the police they came to where they said they saw a body lying on the road and immediately came and got Benson who could not remember what took place.

The sounds of kids sleeping could be heard as the twins slept in their bump beds and moved from one side of their bed to the other snoring as they breathed deeply and dressed in their pajamas which looked like space outfits. In their rooms were pictures of black and white heroes. As John and Betty slept in their beds, John said, "Betty I'll have to leave you and the twins for a while and came back later. You know Benson will tell your father where we are at and no matter what he would do to me once he finds out."

"I do not want you to go. You have a family here and the girls will want to know who their father was but if you stay your life is in danger."

Grabbing her. "Just take care of my children and I will get back to you once this incident has settled down and people will let us live the life we believe in."

"Here's some money so take it and tell me where you are at and I'll get back in touch with you."

CHAPTER 28

B etty is sitting at her desk and opened a letter from the state of Mississippi's Governor's Office which said: "Your property will be taken from you because there are owed taxes on it and unless you get $200,000 dollars your property will be taken from you."

On the bottom of the document Benson's name was on it. To get revenge Benson managed to persuade the state officials to find any property taxes on Betty's farm. Knowing she could not borrow the money because of her love affair with a colored man the bankers would not lend money to her. The bidding for the default property would take place in three days. Betty went to see several lawyers to show them she owned the property after they placed taxes on it but they feared her because of Jack Benson's connections with Big Jim and refused to take the case.

She had not heard from John in four weeks and did not know where he was at. The only thing left was for her to go to the bidding and try to write an IOU and promise to pay the money back when the crops came in. As once she read the document and smoke could be seen coming from the large corn field several miles away and three or four men were seen running away in a red bus who set the cornfield on fire. Located near the farm was a water hydrant the other farmers used just in case of a fire and when Betty called the fire department and told them about the fire on her property she could not get anyone because someone had cut the telephone wires. A farmer happened to be driving by and saw what was happening and drove home and called the fire department to come and stop the fire from reaching his farm and crops. At first when the firemen came and they knew Betty had a colored lover and refused to do anything about putting out the fire but the other farmers who were white said they would have them fired immediately and they started putting out the fire before it reached their land. Tears flooded Betty's eyes as she saw what damage the fire did to her property and now she knew she had to show up at the bidding for her property to save it from Jack Benson who worked for her father and wanted revenge for what happened to him at the Carol farm.

CHAPTER 29

Betty went to the bidding and took her twins with her and not only did she have to fight the discrimination of having biracial kids, she fought discrimination because she was a woman dealing in a white man's world of bidding for land at the auction when white women had few rights in the state. Women could not hold jobs men traditionally held.

As Betty approached the door with her kids the security officer looked at them. "Are you bidding for land? The colored section is in the back of this crowd. You have to take your house maid's daughter to the back because colored people are not allowed up here with the white people doing the bidding."

Pulling open her blouse and showing her breast the security officer smiled and let her take the twins to their seats much to the dismay of the crowd of white folks who went to other parts of the bidding area and sat by their own race of people to keep from being seen sitting by Dora."

"Yes I am. I lost most of my corn crop in the fire and I plan to get my property back. The corn crop would pay the taxes on my farm. I believe someone did this on purpose to make it impossible to earn money to pay the mortgage on the farm because they wanted it."

"You are up against a stone wall. No women have ever won in the bidding for the defaulted property. I have seen women out bided because they were women."

"She cannot bid for the property, "A mean looking man said.

An officer said," The rules have changed. Now women can bid on defaulted or foreclosed property so long as they have the funds to buy them. For years, women were denied civil rights just as the colored people in this state. They are trying to make more equal rights for white women in this bidding activity."

Betty's kids sat in their seats as cigarette smoke circulated in the air getting on people's clothes and they waited for the auctioneer to bid as he said, "Let's start the bidding and do I hear any bids?"

Betty, "I bid $ 1600!"

"The farmer bided $1700 for that property."

"1800!" another farmer shouted

"I bid $1900 for the property!" Betty shouted but the auctioneer did not even acknowledge her as a bidder and paid her no attention.

"I bid $ 2500 for the property!" shouted Benson who had confidence to know that he would win as usual in these bidding wars with the people trying to get the land.

Getting worried Betty knew she would lose this battle to win her property back.

"Are there any more bids?"

The crowd was silent and many of the bidders watched as the auctioneer began to speak. "Looks like Benson will own the property you folks are bidding on."

Someone in the audience cried $ 4200 dollars which out bided Benson whose face turned to rage but there was nothing he could do about it but he badly wanted to harm the person who won and keep him from getting control of the property.

A stranger dressed in a dark blue suit wearing a white hat with a maturing suit disappeared but had one of his aides do the transaction work to get the property.

Getting disappointed Betty drove to the bank with her children who were hungry and cried. They had no lunch because the bidding on the property took so long. The kids begged other people who ate food near them and Betty tried to stop them from doing this. When Betty got to the bank, she looked at the account and saw there was no money in it. She knew something was wrong and went to see President Runaway Henry.

"Mr. Henry I see all of my savings were withdrawn."

Shoveling some papers Mr. Baker adjusted his glasses as they kept sliding off his narrow noise and he tried to swat at a fly which kept sitting on his forehead as he spread his papers.

"There is no money in the account for you. Your father Senator Big Jim Wilson called and told us to get all of the money out of it and send it to him. It seems you have creditors at home who said you owe them money."

Stomping her feet against the floor. "That's a dam lie. I owe no one anything. I have to get down to the bottom of this matter and it seems like nothing can be done about it."

"Your father has much power at this bank and he always gets what he wants."

Somehow one of Big Jim's friends saw Betty and informed him of her business transactions.

Getting up Betty strolls out the bank disgusted, "My daddy will not run my life and tell me what to do. This is America and we are supposed to be treated equal."

Still having to take care of the girls Betty went into a bar and took a seat. Sam the bartender waited on customers as she came in.

"Those white pants, and white shirt black overcoat looks good on you."

"What are you drinking miss? I do not think the manager is going to like the idea of you bringing your kids in here. It's against the law to have kids in this bar especially a colored girl at that. You would be better off going to the colored section of this town where you can enjoy a drink and meal in peace."

Sitting her twins in a seat at a table, "Sam I want some vodka and I want to get high tonight. That no good father of mine took my property and stole money out of my account. I do not know what to do."

"Now you have to control yourself Betty before you do something you'll regret."

"Sam tonight is my night. I am going to dance with my children so turn on the jukebox. I am lonely and need something to ease my mind. I'll pay you an IOU because I do not have any money."

Going to get some vodka, "Now Betty you have watch these girls and you cannot do it being drunk."

By this time Benson and his friends came in and Betty saw them even though her eyes were glassy. Sam fixed the twins something to eat but Betty hears Benson talking about how Betty lost her property and everything she worked for.

"There's Betty and her half-breed children. I am sorry about what happened to your property," and he and his friends toasted and celebrated with much fun and told Sam to play some blues on the jukebox.

The slow blues comes on and the country singer sings about his woman leaving him for another man who had more money than him.

"Betty let's dance honey. I have always wanted to romance you but you fell in love with that nigger John Carol and that hurt me to my heart."

"You better hold down on that drinking. Its making you smell real bad plus you do not know where you are at so baby come closer and be my honey to night."

"Do not step on my feelings. "Betty said as she tried to avoid stepping on Benson's feet.

Benson at last felt he could take John Carol's place and be Betty's lover but she was filled with revenge and told Benson, "Go speak with your friends while I tidy up and powder my noise. Get my children Sam."

Betty went behind the bar and grabbed a shot gun and pointed it at Benson and his friends and she said, "Now you no good son of a bitch I'll put some buckshot in your ass for taking my property from me. It was probably one of your friends who out bided me."

"Do not shoot me Betty because I and the boys were kidding. Now put the gun up."

Barely standing up, Betty pulls the trigger and people ducked everywhere. Fellows playing cards at a table flipped it over as buckshot hit it leaving marks everywhere. The liquor splattered and you could hear the fellows in the bar saying, "That bitch gone crazy! Why don't someone go and grab her so we can finish our poker game. I had a good hand before that chick went on a wild rampage."

Prostitutes and their clients came out of their rooms from upstairs to see what the commotion was about.

"Nancy I paid my money. Come on back and give me some love and affection."

Sam grabbed the twins and took them in the back of the bar for safety and the look of revenge appeared on Betty's' face as she poured liquor into her mouth. No one dared to bother her as she fired pellets into anything which moved. All types of noises were heard in the bar. The smell of alcohol disappeared into the dress she wore. A big man came into the bar and said, "Betty a night in jail will work wonders for you."

The big man's name was Eddie Franklin who loved being a lawman and his family had a number of famous lawmen in it and he wanted to carry on the tradition of his former relatives who were justices of the peace. His only weakness was women and drinking from sunup to sundown and people wondered how he drink so much and could be sheriff of a town at the same time. People knew Franklin was not always on the good side of the law and often took bribe money to let the dope dealers sell their drugs with a piece of the money coming to him by not trying to enforce the law to stop it.

As Franklin came closer to Betty, she hit him with a whiskey bottle and he blocked her arm and grabbed her as she kicked and screamed when he took her to his police car. At that time Betty was in her jail cell and Jack Benson came to check on her while Sheriff Franklin signed papers.

"Benson what brings you to this jailhouse at such a late hour?" Franklin said as Benson adjusted his eye glasses and chewed on tobacco every fifteen seconds and spitted into a metal can and smiled.

"What are you reading?" Benson said, "It looks like you are looking at sexual magazines. Those women sure look good."

"I know you did not come here to see me. I think you need a favor from me."

"I want to spend some time with Betty so go and open the cell door for me."

"You have not told me what's in it for me. You want sex from Betty but I have to get paid too. I'll charge you two hundred dollars for your humanitarian act for raping Betty."

"Now look you owe me money from our last dice game so deduct two hundred dollars and we are even."

"You know Benson I think we have a deal" and gave him the keys to the cell as Betty slept and snored at the same time. Tiptoeing quickly, Benson unzipped his pants and approached Betty and a fight took place.

"Get your filthy hands off of me you bastard!" Betty screamed which woke up the other prisoners. Benson tried to rape Betty who scratched his face leaving scars on it. The other prisoners shouted for Sheriff Franklin to come and get Benson out of her cell. Slapping Betty in her face she hit him with a punch to his head and did a finger stab to his eyes temporarily stopping him. A finger nail file was in Betty's shoe and she pulled it out of one of them and as Benson gained an awareness of where he was, Betty pretended to want to have him sexually and said, "Come closer, I am sorry,"

Do you really mean it.?"

"Yes I do."

When Benson did this he tried to hug Betty and she stabbed the finger nail file into his chest. Holding his chest Benson fell to the floor and shouted for help as blood came out of it.

"Son of a bitch, if you ever put your hands on me again I'll kill you. You tried to rape me but I got your number this time and you will not be able to rape no one else."

Sheriff Franklin opened the cell door and took Benson to the hospital and the driver who drove the ambulance car made sure he would be half dead by the time they reached their destination but the driver knew he would not survive this trip to the hospital and cheered inside of his heart because Benson once beat his father badly for speaking up against him when Benson insulted his wife and nothing was done about it.

Blood scattered everywhere as the doctors tried to stop the bleeding and ordered more of it because a main artery in his chest was difficult to clamp and he stopped breathing and they shocked his heart so he could show signs of life. One of the main problems was trying to find the right blood type. Needing type o blood was difficult and they went to the section where black people's blood was stored and found the type of blood he needed. In those times white people's blood was separated from colored people's blood.

After getting the right blood type, the doctors found the ruptured blood vessel and stopped the bleeding and for eight hours, Benson's life survival depended on God and he decided to let him live as Sheriff Franklin drink whiskey in the waiting room and got drunk and did not know if Benson would live or die. But for the moment he became happy because Benson owed him money and he could not collect it if Benson would have died from his chest wounds.

When the news hit the papers, Attorney Little Ronnie Hall went to the jail where Betty was put in and spoke with her because in criminal cases lawyers are appointed and he knew he would get paid but his heart was not in it.

As Betty looked at attorney Hall in a frightful way. "That Jack Benson tried to rape me. Is there anything you can do to prosecute him?"

Looking at the evidence before him, Hall tried to explain to Betty. "No one will come forth and fight against Jack Benson for what he did. He has the big time judges in his hand and plus Big Jim will not come out to protect you so you can prosecute Benson who might gain the sympathy of many of Big Jim's friends because they would not think in terms of Benson doing anything to hurt Betty even though he nearly died from the stabbing. Nothing would be said about him trying to rape you."

When word of the raping got out to the public by way of the radio, newspapers, and television news stations, and anti- rape organizations gathered at the police station to protest the attempted rape of Betty.

Groups held signs up protesting and they wanted Betty to be set free. When the higher up people saw this was Big Jim's daughter they wanted to let her go. They did not want bad publicity on Big Jim because he was Benson's friend. When Benson got well, he tried to file a charge of assault with attempt to kill but the charges were dismissed and the judge said Betty's actions were in self-defense.

Betty did not know where Sam took her children and worried about them constantly. As Betty walked towards her use to be plantation she saw some civil rights workers who were in front of a school protesting because colored children could not be admitted and she saw a tall handsome man by the name Fisher Mickles who Betty stops. "Why are you and those people protesting in front of the school?"

Wearing a big straw hat and large white blue jeans, he said, "Why should you ask?"

Instead of speaking to the fellows Betty kept on walking and wondering where her children were located and most of all would she see her beloved John Carol again and it hurt her to think he would abandon her at a time when she needed him most of all in such terrible times.

In regrouping her life the threat of rape could be seen in the faces the men who looked at her dressed in their white and black uniforms with cross like symbols across their chest.

"I want to touch those pretty white legs of yours and spend some quiet time with you also."

The three big men got out of the car and each of them carried guns ready to kill the people protesting to integrate the schools against their beliefs and they felt the white liberals could not come down to their state of Mississippi and tell them to change their segregationist ways. One of the men went to use the restroom in the nearby woods and the other one tried to get closer to Betty to rape her and she has a brick hidden in her purse and hits him with it in the back of his head knocking him out cold and Betty gets his car keys and drives down the road with the other men shooting at her and she drove back to the town she lived in.

Having very little money, Betty realized she needed friends and if she goes to Marry Florence's house maybe she might take her in and hopefully tell her where her daughters are at.

When she drove the stolen car to Mary Florence 's house a note is placed on the door saying," Nigger lover go home."

Betty did not get a chance to even ring the doorbell. Instead of knocking on the door again, Betty got in the car and drove trying to get leads on where her children were located. She knew that Sam got them out of the lounge she shot up but she did not know where Sam lived.

In her attempts to find out where Sam lived Betty looked in the Yellow Pages and saw the telephone number of Fisher Mickles and felt he could help her. With just a dime in her pocket Betty called his number and someone answered it.

"Hello who is this?"

Trying to smile Betty said," You rejected me earlier when I asked to be a worker in your campaign to stop them from keeping black students out of the school. I felt what you did was wrong."

Studying his schedule. "I am sorry but you are the daughter of the biggest segregationist in the state of Mississippi. Now do not call me. How do I know you are not spying for your father?"

At once Betty hung up the telephone and said nothing. This did not stop Betty from driving to his house and this is what she did. As Betty ringed the doorbell Fisher looked out and to his surprise he saw Betty standing on the porch and he opened the door. His eyes showed he was tire and sleepy and his body odor came at you because working on the various field activities made it impossible to take baths and keep a neat professional appearance. The field hands were more comfortable with Fisher's civil rights organization because they wore the clothes of a field hand just like them.

"Now I told you, you should give up working with us because it will damage our cause."

Betty stopped him from closing the door. "Now look I went through changes to get to your headquarters now hear me out. You preach about true equality but discriminate against me based on

166

hearsay and no evidence. I do not share the same prejudice feelings as my father to keep colored and white citizens from living in peace in a non-segregationist world where all of God's children can enjoy the same freedoms regard less of their race, color, or religion. By the way in about three minutes white extremists are supposed to come by here and shoot up the place. You should warn your workers to seek cover."

Still trying to get the sleep out of his head Bill tried to ignore Betty and a loud sound of a bullet hit the house and many people living in the house dived for the floor seeking cover. The people in the car shouted obscenities at the civil rights workers hiding from the possibility of getting killed. Policemen came two hours later asked a few questions and reacted like they did not care because Big Jim would stop giving them raises if they tried to investigate racial incidents taking place. Getting off the floor Betty looked at Fisher and smiled.

"I am sorry for rejecting you the way I did. Is there anything I can do help you help you. You saved many of my people from getting killed."

Taking a look at the pictures on the wall it showed field workers teaching many classes on non- violence and registering them to vote in the rural areas. The right to vote was a very privilege thing because only blacks and Indians could not vote and Fisher's group set their goals very high to get equality for all colored citizens. On the wall another picture showed the lynching of a colored citizen and his group wanted to see that colored people and white folks were treated fairly but in this struggle colored and white civil rights workers were killed to achieve this objective.

"What's in the room causing all of that noise?" Betty said.

"That's the people practicing to be non-violent before we send them out to try to integrate the places of public accommodations such as restaurants."

As the other workers poured food on their heads and called them racial names, some of them tried not to fight back and others took all the abuse and insults to become a member of the organization for civil rights. As Betty watched what the workers went through to see if they could take the abuse from people to use the methods non-violence, she thought about the times John could not go into the different stores and try on clothes or go to a place called Fun Time because of his race. She felt this was something she wanted to be a part of but she had her reservations about it.

Her father Big Jim would have ten heart attacks to see his daughter on television sitting at lunch counters letting white folks pour food on them trying to make them fight back thus destroying the principles of non-violent disobedience.

"I'll have to have time to think about getting into your organization if they have to go through that abuse."

"We could need a good secretary to write letters for us and send them to organizations for money and supplies. Most of these people are college kids from up north and do not know anyone when they come to these rural areas of the South."

"Do their parents like the idea of them getting on the freedom rides to come down here and help integrate public facilities?" Showing her to her cabin behind his house is where the other workers lived.

Fisher said, "We never ask them about that issue but I have heard of much conflict with some of our workers having problems with their fathers, mothers or sisters or brothers who rejected them for standing up against discrimination and coming here to risk their lives for it. It takes courage to do what we do. Maybe one day our efforts will not be taken in vain."

"When do these issues come up?"

"It's usually when we are in our group discussions and something plays on their minds and their inter thoughts are expressed about what they are doing and is it better to live in their rich homes up north or choose to come down here and help the colored farmers and their families enjoy their constitutional rights."

Getting interested in Fishers' background. "What did you do before joining this organization? I've heard you speak some heavy big Standard English words and many legal terms. Are you in the legal profession by any chance?"

"I am a lawyer and my specialty was civil rights but I had to get out of it for a time because I was tire of litigating cases and losing when the facts were pleaded for my clients and the judges and juries kept discriminating against them. I got frustrated and stopped practicing law and it broke up my marriage and I just drifted from one dead end job to another."

"Well this is your cabin. You can stay in here with the other girls. There are other cabins for the men."

"Where did you get the money to build these cabins?"

Kicking some branches up in the air, "They did not want to sell us timber to build these cabins when they found out we were a civil rights group."

Touching the logs connecting each other, "Well how did your group get the logs to build these cabins?"

"I filed a law suit saying they discriminated against my workers and selling wood to others but not my people. I lost in the state court and won in the appellate court and got some enemies who stood in the way to achieve equal protection of the laws. The girls will come into this cabin in a few minutes and introduce themselves. I hope you will like staying with them. I have work to do."

"One more thing before you go. Can you look up a man by the man of Sam? He took my kids when I got drunk and shot up the place."

"I'll try to do that because I know you really need them and they are probably worried to death about you also."

CHAPTER 30

A knock is heard at the Carol house and Peter is busy sleeping and it is quite in the house but Sarah is sewing patches of cloth in his pants which he wears out all the time. As Sarah sews his pants, she yells out loud, "I told him to get some new pants when the crop comes in but he always refuses saying they are too high at the stores so fix the ones I have." and starts laughing.

Outside John tried to get into the house without being seen by anyone. His appearance was bad looking and his body smelled badly because for days he had not had anything to eat or no place to take a bath on the way home to see his folks. As he approached his folk's house, he stopped and looked at the area him, Betty, Sandy, and Kirby played as kids and the markings left in the trees saying" love Kirby and Betty."

John looked at the tree and rubbed his hands against the carving which brought up memories where he remembers saying to himself. "John you are colored and have no right loving a white girl and all of them laughed when she said that but Sandy had her reservations about playing with colored children at that time and tried not to. Kirby and Sandy begged Betty to give John a fair chance to get to know him but that was not the way her father wanted her to think positive about colored people.

Having not seen John in three months, Sarah worried about her son like a mother would about her children. As she sat in her rocking chair a knock on the door made a loud noise.

"Who is it?"

"Momma it's your son John. Let me in."

Going to the steps and yelling, "It's John so get up and come down the stairs."

"Peter, come down the stairs because your son made it back home. I am so glad to see him."

After working in the fields all day, Peter did not like being disturbed and would not get up and he rolled over on his side and kept on snoring making a big noise as he did it.

"I'll fix him and teach him how to get up when I call him. All at once a loud shouting noise was heard as Sarah poured cold water on Peter's face and he jumped out of his bed and yelled, "What in the hell did you do that for! I was going to get up!"

Laughs appeared on Sarah's face as Peter got his shot gun and went to the door knowing he could not hit anything because of his eyesight was failing him as he grew older.

"John is that you? Please let me know you are out there or I'll shoot some buckshot at you.

Do not play any of your tricks on me."

Knowing he had not seen his father in a long time John wanted to play a trick on him and did not answer any questions.

"I'll go around the back and see who is at our door. I am going to put some buckshot in their asses if it's those bill collectors who keep coming around here trying to take our land sent by Big Jim."

Half drunk and cannot see, Peter decided to be the law on his land and get retribution from the agents which were no good trying to steal the land of other people both white and black who they said owed back taxes on their properties with little or no proof..

"Now Peter you have to ask first and shoot later. You can get in trouble for taking the law into your own hands."

With his hard of hearing and seeing, it was difficult for Peter to hear what Sarah said to him. The shadow of John's body showed and Peter not knowing it was him came around the corner shooting and John ran off the porch as he approached the front of the house. Sarah opened the door carrying a shot gun too. The power from Peter's shot knocked him fifty feet backwards and it got his work uniform dirty as he landed near the chicken yard and into the pig trough where one of the meanest hogs were shielding her baby pigs from danger and when Peter crashed into the trough he bit him in the behind and he jumped up and hollowed real loud with a lot of anger in it.

Meanwhile John took off scrambling down the road thinking Big Jim's boys were coming after him. Realizing it was her son, Sarah at the age of fifty-five took off after him hollowing and screaming for him to come back home to the top of her voice.

"John come back. This is your mammy. It's not Big Jim and his boys!"

But John who stride too fast to hear what Sarah said only wanted to make his get away from Big Jim. For one reason or another, John stumbled upon a bear who was going into hibernation with her cubs and they used a cave for this purpose. John felt this would be a great hiding place so he went inside and Sarah who did not know where John was hiding at stopped and rested

As the bear and her cubs slept in came John and a big commotion was heard in the cave. The big bear and John wrestled and John screamed for his life as he tried to get away from the grip of his muscular arms. Grabbing a rock John hit the bear with a stone knocking him out for a short minute and by this time the bear was too mean to give up the fight and Peter recovered and went in pursuit of the bear and tripped firing the shot gun pellets in the air and he landed in a deep gulley and managed to crawled out of it and spotted where Sarah was in front of the cave.

John said," This is your son so do not shoot. I am coming out but kill this bear ok before I attempt to escape."

Sarah took aim and missed the bear and Peter shot at him too but this time the buckshot went right between bear's eyes and he fell dead. Sarah and Peter grabbed their son and embraced him.

Peter said, "Son I did not know it was you on the front porch. I thought it was the tax collectors who keep on coming around here lying to steal our land so I decided to take the law into my own hands but look where it got me a big bear but we can use his furs for a blanket or bear coat for the winter and his meat"

The three of them embraced each other and trekked back to the house to get Peter's mules to carry the bear back to the farm, "But what about the bear clubs which were three of them. Without their mother they would surely die." Sarah said.

Peter replied back," That's none of our business because Mother Nature will take care of them."

"They are so small and need some type of nursing and after all we killed their mother. We should keep the clubs for at least one year and let them go into the wilderness and get on with their lives."

Knowing when Sarah made up her mind Peter knew he would have to support her but he was a stubborn type of person who set in his ways. Sarah read a part of the bible which said the man was the head of the household but she defied it when she felt Peter's decisions were not good and he met resistance from her.

If he did not go along with Sarah on keeping the twin clubs for a year, Sarah might go and stay with her sister BB who he did not like, for a week until he changed his mind, Peter could not cook like his wife, so weighing the possible loss of his wife for a week, Peter finally said as he cut the bear meat, "Ok Sarah keep the clubs but they must go at the end of the year."

Sarah stared at her son. "John it's been a long time since I've seen you. Where is Betty and her twins. That's not like you leaving your spouse and kids by themselves. I've always taught you to stick by your family through thick and thin. Now tell me what took place because your father and me want to know and you did not come back home unless it was a good reason."

Sitting at the kitchen table. "Momma I got into it with Jack Benson and scrambled a way before Big Jim's people would come and lynch me. We lived in a small town outside of Jackson. By the way what are those papers on the kitchen table? You know you and daddy cannot read too well but has anyone tried to read and tell you what's in them?"

Grabbing the papers Peter balled them up and threw them on the floor because he could not read them. "That Big Jim wants to take our land and harass us about it saying we have not paid our taxes and we have three months to do it."

His father told us they would pay our property taxes and now Big Jim is breaking his father Roscoe' s promise to us and now they are trying to take our property for tax evasion. The taxes are too high for me and Sarah to pay them."

Sarah hugged her husband and poured him his favorite moonshine he made every now and then but the bottle was empty and she went out to the meat shed and saw the two clubs high as a kite as they completely drank the alcohol and was sound asleep as though they were in hibernation and Sarah shouted,

"You good for nothing bear clubs. If Peter finds out you ripped him off of his whiskey he would personally come here and shoot both of you. I'll go fetch a bottle from up in the cellar and give him some of it." The clubs were so drunk they just quietly slept with a little heavy snorting.

Peter drink this favorite moonshine to cool his temper. In a few seconds, Peter fell on the couch and went to sleep because this is what Sarah felt Peter needed because he worried himself to death about the threat of Big Jim breaching the promise he made to his father telling the Corals they could stay on the property for life as long as they sold their crops to him and not join labor unions.

Putting a blanket over Peter" That's the problem son. Your father is a member of a labor union because they promised they would stand by us and keep Big Jim from taking our land,"

Trying to eat some food. Did the union make good on those promises."

"You can see plain as day they did not because that is what these papers are saying."

Going into the closet John took some of his father's clean clothes and laid them on his old bed he use to sleep on and it made a loud noise resulting from it.

Weeks of traveling on the road made his body built thin because he could not eat decent meals in the restaurants because they would not serve colored people. His face showed a man who crossed the countryside with the sand and dust shaping the wrinkles in his face and he needed a warm bath and stains covered his dirty shirt and pants and his shoes showed much wear and tire and you could see the soles containing large and small holes in them. His legs hurt badly, swell up as he marched down that lonely road towards home, tractor-trailers traveled at full speed near him, and he grabbed the railing of a bridge to keep from being dragged under the 16-wheeler truck tires.

As he shaved John thought about the possibilities of going to visit Big Jim's hoping he would drop those charges against his father because of morality issues and the fact his father worked with labor unions to stop the state under the control of Big Jim from taking what seemed to be the rich oil lands they wanted and Big Jim would do anything possible to get those properties from the black and white farmers.

For the first time in three or four month, John looked like a human being and after he took a bath felt much better. John took the steps necessary to look presentable to Big Jim and his political thugs he would meet going to the plantation to see if he could settle things with him to not take his parents' farm land.

Putting a small gun in his pocket, "Now son I do not believe in violence but you cannot trust Big Jim because he might try to do anything to kill you. Be careful and I will not tell Peter what you have done because he might come looking for you to keep Big Jim's men from killing you."."

CHAPTER 31

John approaches the mansion and strolls with caution because it was not easy to come into Big Jim's mansion because he made many changes to it. Video cameras surrounded the estate and in one of the rooms, three men worked twenty-four hour a day shifts to make sure anyone on the estate could be apprehended. They liked to drink on the job and could not see people who appeared on the video. In certain parts of the estate, lights came on and gas escaped out the ground choking people who attempted to walk on his lawn. Big Jim 's swimming pool automatically let people trespass into it but if they fell into it when they were not supposed to be on their land, Big Jim sued them for illegally traveling on his property. If a person hiked in certain areas of the estate men monitoring videos surveillance cameras pushed bottoms making the manmade earth fall beneath them causing much injury to the unwanted intruder. Many law suits followed as a result of this but Big Jim's influence on the judges made it impossible to get a fine or conviction on him.

If a person appeared on his property and stepped on a stone laying on the well-cut grass, it gave out an unpleasant scent drifting into the air to the displeasure of the foolish victim who dared to come up on the threshold of Senator Big Jim meant problems for them and he gave his guards rewards and exclusive permission to shoot any anyone on site believing to be trespassers coming uninvited to spy on his plantation's massive crop fields of corn, tobacco, wheat, wild chickens, green beans, peas, and marijuana concealed from federal law enforcement people and when Big Jim wanted to relax he got his possession of highly toxic weed and made some joints and smoked the night away in his favorite penthouse at his plantation.

The leaves crackled beneath the feet of people who made tiny steps and the sight of Big Jim's large plantation with its fine large pillows reminded you of the old south when slaves built those large mansions. With Big Jim Wilson being in dirty politics to preserve his status as a powerful federal politician representing people from the great state of Mississippi, he felt compelled to keep people who desired to pull him down from power would end up dead if he found out about it. With John coming on Big Jim's plantation, he and no one knew anything about it.

When John Coral came up to the gates of the plantation a big bright yellow light showed on his face which blinded him and his feet lost their control on the ground and a rope got caught around his legs and it pulled him high into the air hanging him upside down hollowing,

In addition, John yelled! "Get me off this dam rope!"

The gun in his pocket dropped into the grass hitting the bright lights which made them turn off. By this time Big Jim and his boys were at the gate laughing with him.

As John hanged from the rope attached to his legs, "Cut me down because I need to talk to you about the taking of my father's land."

"I understand your needs about your father's land but I want to know where my daughter is. I miss her so much and I do not get want you and her to get married because it would ruin my political career. I am planning to run for the president of the United States one of these days and the both of you are doing things which can keep me from successfully fulfilling my ambitions."

Still dangling and getting dizzy, "Let me down and I'll tell you anything that you want!"

"Ok boys let's have target practice so when John comes down he is ready to give us the information we are looking for!"

Sweat scrambled down his face, and John's body turned in different directions as Big Jim's men pushed his body back and forth in the air. His men were good shots but one of them had eye problems and came close to hitting John.

"I guess he's had enough so let him down. Now look nigger I do not want any trouble out of you and above all do not get smart with me!"

A control device let John down and Big Jim's assistants came and took him into the compound and to his headquarters.

Sitting in his chair Big Jim smiled at John. "Where is my daughter and are her and the twins doing well?"

"Give me a reason as to why you want to take my father's property and all the other farms lands you have no right to it."

Slapping John, "I do not have to explain anything to an uppity nigger like you. You never did stay in your place when you chased my son and daughter all day and pretended to care about Kirby and Betty. Now I am going to give you one more chance to tell me or I 'll have Get More bang you up a little."

Out comes Get More who weighed about 400 pounds of pure muscles. His body looked like a Mr. America with huge legs, chest, arms, and back muscles and if he hits you once that was the end of a person's life. His body smelled like he had not taken a bath in months and his skin was tougher than a rattlesnake's. His eyes were green and bluish and his front teeth glowed with gold teeth and the pants he wore were made from wolf skins with a matching shirt. On his side he carried a big Bowie knife and a wipe he used to break young colored men with who rebelled against their master and he wore big boots which made a loud noise as he walked and cowboy spurs were attached around the heels of his boots and his hat looked like the ones worn by hunters who wore them doing big game hunting in Africa. Tattoos made him look like the eighth wonder of the world and he chewed on tobacco only to swallow it which made him angry most of the time.

"Your drunk Get More because I smell it. You know my rules are. You cannot drink while on the job. If he kicks your ass, I'll keep you from bringing your women up to the plantation."

Grabbing John and picking him up he threw him into the air and John landed on his back but broke the fall with his hands and as he fell Get More put a scarf lock on his neck keeping him from moving and said, "Where is Betty and the kids. I'll choke your neck off now tell me where they are at!"

Big Jim looked at the situation. "You are going to have to let him up for air. We cannot get information from him if he is too sick or worn out to talk."

Instead of letting John go Get More went into a seizure and choked John until he could not breathe.

At once Big Jim took out his pistol and hit Get More in the head and broke the handle and he stepped into the house and grabbed a shotgun and ran out to where Get More tried to kill John and pulled the trigger and Buck fell down hitting the ground leaving his eyes wide open and all of his facilities shut off and blood flowed down from his head where the buckshot made its last entry to stuff out his African American's life. A picture of a small girl and her mother were on it and Big Jim said, "I did not know Get More had a family. He never talked about it."

One of his workers said, "What are you going to do with the body? He deserves a funeral doesn't he?"

"Just go to the corn field and bury him. I think he would have like that"

Eventually John saw the large pool of blood on the ground as mosquitoes sucked it.

"Now tell me where my daughter is living at!" as he slaps John and orders him tied to a pole to be whipped by him and John said, "If you promise not to take my father's property and their friend's lands hoping to find oil on it. They owned their land for decades and you and your friends will offer them a price they cannot accept and later raise the property taxes where they would not be able to pay them."

Grabbing John's shirt, Big Jim took his whip and struck him in his back with it and smiled at him, John spitted at his face.

"I am not going to hit John again because we have done enough of that. Build a wooden casket and bury him alive."

"You cannot do this to me. It's a dam shame." With that being done, Big Jim's men John placed in a wooden box and buried him in it and he screamed, "Don't do this! ""Don't do this!"

Big Jim's men poured dirt on the wooden box and John laid in darkness as he heard movements of worms coming into it. One worm got into the box and crawled on his face and John's face swelled up because of the bites from bugs crawling on it and he could not do anything to stop them. He saw his life being smothered by dirt and wondered why he suffered for wanting to have the woman of his life regardless of her race. The smell of dirt seemed to be strange to him and he hollowed until his voice became horse where he could not feel anything and his body smelled awful which attracted more blood sucking insects who bit his feet to suck his blood. He hit the tops and sides of the box tied down by rope. There seemed to be hope because the box was buried in two feet of dirt.

A small five-foot girl got through the maze of security on the estate grounds and came to the site of where John was buried. Her hair looked like Scarlet O'Hara in the movie "Gone With The Wind" and her perfumes smelled twenty feet away and she stumbled with a limp due to an accident in a car she drove and crashed into another one. Her body gave out much sex appeal and she wore lipstick with a dark red color and with a skirt and tennis shoes. Sandy wanted to get John out of the ground before he would die from suffocation and immediately she used her hands to get the dirt off the wooden box but she scrambled around the place to find a shovel located in a tool box with an alarm on it. Sandy went into the kitchen and got a glass of water and poured it on the alarm shorting out wires located on the tool box.

The thing which became a problem was she did not have a key to open it. Again Sandy went into the house in a hurry because John gradually lost his sense of where he was at. Meanwhile Sandy sneaked into Big Jim's room to get the keys to the mailbox and this would be no easy task because his dog Rex slept near them and he would attack anything coming into Big Jim's room but Sandy went to the refrigerator and got a steak out of it and went to the bathroom and took a bottle of sleeping pills from the medicine cabinet. Sandy pushed some of the pills into the steak and when she opened the door Big Jim and Polly his colored mistress slept with him but they were drunk from drinking all night. The keys were in between Polly and Big Jim's legs as they slept together in bed with no clothes on.

Giving Rex some meat with the sleeping pills he gradually became sleepy after eating the steak and Sandy tiptoed up to the bed and got the keys to the tool box. Getting back to the spot where John was buried, Sandy stayed and kept digging and her pants got muddy, and dirty but she managed to get to the box where John was buried in and Sandy opened the wooden box giving John some air. The darkness was all around them and Sandy said, "Are you ok John?"

Pulling the top of the wooden box off of him.

"I cannot believe my eyes. It's you. You never spoke to me or the other colored people on the plantation and so why are you helping me?"

Trying to get John out of the hole, "Well I was told not to like your people and I listened to my father but as time went on I resented the way he treated both the colored and white farmers trying to take their properties. I am sorry about everything. By me joining the civil rights group daddy did not pay for my law school tuition."

"I was surprised Sandy. You will find the money to complete law school. We needs more lawyers to help us fight your father's injustice."

They went and hid in a group of trees and John said, "How did you know about Betty and the twins?"

"She wrote me but used a different return address."

"I want to see my nieces. I know they are pretty. My sister and I had our differences about the white and colored folks mixing and I was against it but she still is my sister and I want to help the both of you if I can."

John hugs her and trudged towards where his family is at. He knows it will be difficult trying to hold his family together because he had to endure so much and arrange to get a good education to make a life for himself and the family despite prejudices he would face in the process by those people who opposed it. Staggering his way home to his parent's home, John is stopped by the county police and the arresting officer Mark Housing hollows at him and he hid behind a tree as they approached him and said, "Stop! are you John Carol?"

John did not answer at first. Looking at the fugitive criminal record, he held in his hand he said, "You are who we are looking for. You are under arrest for false imprisonment of Big Jim's daughter. As Mark came to put hand cups on him; John resisted but when he saw Mark's gun pointed in his face, he decided not to resist because if he did; it would mean sudden death for him.

CHAPTER 32

S itting in the jail cell, John knew he would probably be accused charges which were lies. Having the charge of false imprisonment and kidnapping Senator Jim Wilson's daughter, pending against him, he knew were lies. To convict him, Big Jim would do anything to send John to jail because if he married his daughter and produce mixed racial children it would cost him his reelection. He needed a conviction on him if it meant buying the jury to do it and paying off the judges to rule in his favor.

The trial would take place in Jackson, Mississippi. Against the wall hung pictures of confederate generals who served in the army who owned slaves. A big Confederate flag hung on the wall and because of the law it was illegal to have it displayed in the courtroom. It represented a nation who was in rebellion against the United States one hundred years ago and most of the black folks did not stand a chance in the courtroom. Judge Huey Homes presided over the trial. His bottle of wine appeared on the table clearly to be seen and often he took sips of it and made decisions based on if he liked the client or not and not what the law said must be done for charges against accused people. His habit of dipping snuff angered people working in his court. Judge Homes could spit thirty feet in the air and the tobacco contents hit other people sitting in the audience but who possessed the nerve to stand up against Judge Homes who developed a reputation for setting his own precedents instead of following the law made by the state of Mississippi Bar Association.

As John stood in front of the judge he said, "John you are charged with false imprisonment of kidnapping Senator Big Jim's daughter and taking her to another state for unethical deeds like prostitution. Now how do you plead guilty or not guilty? Now plead guilty because you know it's against the law for a black man to mess with white women in the state of Mississippi. You can get lynched for such a horrible crime. Do you know that?"

Looking at Judge Homes John said, "I did no such thing because Betty and I have been friends ever since we were kids growing up on Senator Wilson's plantation. He did not like it but his father Roscoe did not let him stop us from playing with each other and plus Roscoe invited us up to the house on holidays like Christmas and we ate Christmas dinner together and passed out presents."

As John stopped talking, he thought for a second and said, "I do not have a lawyer and it seems like I will not get a fair trial in this court just by looking at the Confederate flags hanging in here. Where's the United States of America flag? You are part of the United States and why do you act like this is a separate nation from our government?"

"Now look here boy. You had better watch your mouth in my court. I'd appoint you a lawyer who 's a public defender of mine's and he's called Goody Good Shoes plus you can always depend on Goody."

A bailiff comes up to speak with Judge Homes and he told him to call the public defender to come and represent John Carol.

In ten minutes the bailiff comes back and said as Judge Homes drink some scotch, "Attorney Goody Good Shoes is at the house of prostitution on an investigation."

Most of the people in the courtroom who heard the comment laughed in a loud humorist manner.

""When I saw him he reminded me this was his day off and he is plenty occupied with sexual opportunities and cannot be disturbed."

"Order in the court!" "Order in the court!"

"Are there some other lawyers who will do prose work for this nigger because he will be lynched if he does not get representation.

Now do I have any volunteers? All the people in this court room who want to see this nigger get a fair trial for stealing Big Jim Senator Wilson's white daughter and taking her across state lines for prostitution stand and hold up their hands or forever hold their peace."

A still quietness went throughout the court and al the white people stood up and the colored clerks in the court stayed sitting down in support of John. John knew he would not get justice in Judge Holmes' court room.

A man walked into the courtroom dressed in a white suit with a red silk shirt, tie, and hat. "I am an attorney and I will represent this man."

"Your honor this man cannot see," John said, "How can he represent anyone. I don't want him because he is blind."

Judge Homes asked him for his law license and the gentlemen said, "I do not have it on me."

One of the judge's assistants came up to him with a magazine on legal court battles and said, "This is one of the best lawyers in the state of Mississippi. He is called Blind Man Andy Nelson and he has years of legal experience and one of the best lawyers in this state. He's a jack of all trades kind of lawyer and he is rich too."

Behind him came ten assistants to help him with his case after he called them on the phone to come to this court where this trial was taking place.

John could not believe all of this was happening to him. Was this a dream come true? The black man never receives this type of treatment so why now?"

"Your honor I want to represent this man because I feel he is a victim of racism and I can help him out. I do not think he will stand a chance in this Jim Crow court anyway. Can I hear what charges are lodged against him who appears to be a victim of racism?"

Judge Homes looked at the charges and said, "He took Big Jim's daughter across state lines and raped her for his own pleasures and prostitution and he's saying he had nothing to do with it. He took Senator Wilson's daughter for his own selfish reasons. We ought to hang him right now without a trial because he is guilty as hell but this is a court of law and I am always fair in civil right cases brought into my court room."

Nothing but boos came from the colored people in the courtroom. This cry of injustice from the colored people section of the courtroom could be heard which was the standard routine for the judge's courtroom showing much discrimination and prejudice in the manner Judge Holmes did things in his courtroom on civil rights cases.

Getting upset Judge Homes said, "Bailiff call the sheriff' and tell them to bring the dogs. I am cleaning out all the colored people who cry out against my court rules which are always fair to them."

In ten minutes, sheriff's deputies waiting in the hallway got ready to bring in their dogs to get order in the courtroom. In his calm way Blind man Nelson stood up and the sunlight coming into the courtroom window shined on the diamond rings he wore and he said, "Never mind your honor. There are many of my clients in here but they do not see any good jurors. John will not stand a chance with this type of jury. But anyway I'll ask the colored section of spectators for peace and order so we can proceed with the court to set my client free because he has not done anything wrong and most of the evidence will be hearsay."

"Ok, Attorney Nelson, do you need time to prepare your case? You have not had time to get all the evidence together to defend your client.

"Well, I'll need a week to collect the evidence to get my client acquitted of any crimes charged against him."

"Attorney Nelson we will have to put him behind bars until the trial."

"Your honor I will post money for his bail. I promise he will not escape and run away."

Looking at some papers the judge said, "There will be no bail set for John Carol because he might escape and I do not want to do that so I will set it high. The bail is set for ten million dollars"

At once the bailiffs took John to jail and he cried out, "They will kill me in here and I will not live long enough to have a fair trial. They will poison my food and do anything possible to see I do not get any justice. Look around in this court. I see nothing but race hatred signs saying something even though I cannot read them and black folks do not get a fair trial in this courtroom."

"Order in the court room. Bailiffs take him to jail and give him only bread and water but make sure he will be able to stand on his feet."

As Attorney Nelson talked to John Carol he asked if he ever intended to kidnap her and take her across state lines for prostitution.

John said, "That's' a lie, Betty's father wants her to be with a white man and not me because I am colored. He's told the voters he is going to be anti-integration and he knows he cannot get support from the segregationists in the state if he allows me to marry his daughter. They would not support him if they found out about me and Betty who is white.'

One of the jailers came and said to both of them, "It is time for John to be locked up."

Attorney Nelson wrote his information down and said, "Don't worry John I'll try to get you out of this jail. You do not belong in here."

As his attorney trudged out the jail and to the outside of the court house Attorney Nelson fell to the floor dodging bullets and narrowly missed getting killed. Attorney Nelson looked to see if he would get some assistance.

One of the guards who knew Big Jim Wilson said', "Let him die. I will not try to save him. He helped send my brother to jail many years ago."

Larry Carson another security officer would not have any of this as he rushed to help the attorney shot at by unknown assailants and the bullets nearly missed his shoulders.

"You ok? Carson said, "They came close to shooting you. You are very lucky."

Carson a man who wore rings on his fingers and sported long hair gave you a great smile Carson wanted to make a deal to get John out of jail with the judge but his efforts were in vain.

Attorney Nelson was not discouraged by the attempted shooting against his life. When trying to get evidence for the case, witnesses would not cooperate with him. If his witnesses knew Big Jim had anything to do with the case, they would back down and not give out useful evidence to clear John.

John's attorney had mounting cases which took up much of his time and decided to make a plea bargaining agreement with the judge in order to get his client out of jail. He grew tire of getting shot at and in one incident his law office was bombed and Attorney Nelson dropped John's case and Sandy took over to represent John in court against her father's wishes and at the time of John's day in court she had passed the bar in the state of Mississippi after struggling to get her law degree.

Sandy appeared in court and said Big Jim forged papers to take over John Carol's father's land with false signatures and deeds. Sandy knew John did not sign those papers and she subpoenaed her father to come on the witness stand to show fraud and opposing counsel was angry about Sandy having her father served to appear in court to testify without his lawyer knowing anything about Big Jim's efforts to take John Carol's father's farm land.

Much drama took place in the court when Sandy kept asking her father about the papers which were fraud but the judge being loyal to Big Jim said the papers did not have real signatures on them indicating Big Jim had anything to do with this scheme. Even though Big Jim stop paying for Sandy's law education she managed to get financial aid to complete it and it was hard for her to get the financial aid because of Big Jim's influence on the people who gave out the funds but Sandy threatened to sue and she was given a loan to complete her law degree and took the bar several times because her father paid the bar examiners to fail her each time she took it. Again the courageous Sandy Wilson filed suit to say her father influenced the bar examiners to fail her and the judge had other bar examiners to look at her examinations and they said she had been graded unfairly.

These events surprised everyone because people thought Sandy would stay on her father's side but this did not take place and her father threatened to get her disbarred but she defied what he stood for to get justice for John Coral her client.

During the court trial Judge Homes did not want to hear anything bad about Big Jim Wilson because he got him appointed to the job as judge when other lawyers did not want him on the bench because of his anti-civil rights beliefs.

"Now counsel proceed to ask your client questions."

Judge Homes said, "Now tell me Sandy do you have any information which could keep John Carol from being placed in jail?"

"My father has deeds written out saying he is the owner of John Carol's father farm but it's all a lie because my dear old father cannot read or write."

That statement brought nothing but humiliation to Senator Big Jim Wilson who shouted out. "That's a lie I can read and write and I can prove it!"

Attorney Ellis Walton who represented Big Jim said, "Your honor this is humiliating to my client because you have to think about the impact this information will have on the people who look up to him as their leader in this state of Mississippi and his colleagues."

Attorney Walton became one of Big Jim's friends when he represented him in a tax case and won it but they did not ever get alone with each other because Big Jim tried to tell him how to run his case.

"I understand your position attorney Walton but we have to let Attorney Sandy Wilson prove her case."

"Thank you Judge Homes."

Senator Wilson conferred with his attorney." I cannot come up here and embarrassed myself. I'll pay you and the judge $100,000 dollars to keep from testifying. The voters who elected me to office trusted me and felt I was honest in handling this elective office and if they find out about my reading problems all hell will break out so go into the courtroom and do whatever is asked of you for the sake of not having a riot in our beloved city between our colored and white citizens. They have already said a colored man cannot get a fair break in this court anyway."

"Now Senator Wilson read this document for me if you can, "Sandy said,

Senator Wilson took the document and read every three words on the page and could not compose the whole sentences. His hands trembled not being able to pronounce the words.

In frustration, Big Jim cried and said, "It's hard to read when my allergies set in. It happens when people smoke. When the pollen from the leaves and plants fall, it poses a horrible time for me."

As Judge Homes saw what took place, he declared a mistrial with no explanation given to the jury and set John free with no explanation for his actions. Some protesters in the court felt Judge Homes did not follow court procedures which he never does and shouted at him.

"This is my court and I do whatever I please!"

Judge Homes dismissed the trial because he knew a riot would result and the governor would have to send federal troops in to stop the rioting which would result in Senator Wilson saying things which would hurt him and implicate other politicians in this plot to steal the land which probably had oil on it. Not liking what took place Sandy said she would file a suit to get John out of the army because he was placed in military service against his will without due process by the judge.

Headlines appeared in the newspapers indicating the North Koreans invaded South Korea and at the same time President Truman issued orders to integrate the armed services and after Judge Homes read those headlines he ordered John Carol be turned over to the military officials to be inducted into the army and be sent over to the South Korean battle lines after he got his training.

His protesters tried to break him away from the guards but it was impossible and the military officials sent him to Fort Oak Tree and John was seen standing with army soldiers in attention and Captain

Jack Benson standing in front of the men who showed a dislike for being in South Korea talking to them.

"Now you niggers are getting a chance to fight in this godam Korean War for the first time with white troops who are much better than you. This is still a Jim Crow army even though your dear old president has allowed black and white troops to live and die together. I do not like the idea of having niggers in this army fighting alone side of me but an order is an order and there is nothing I can do about it."

Because of Senator Wilson's connections, he got Jack Benson promoted to captain without any military experience but Big Jim got what he wanted by saying he would write and support bills funding the troops fighting the North Koreans without delay.

John Carol recognizes Jack Benson but chose to keep quiet, and he did not know where Betty and his kids were located. As Benson read the orders with magnifying glasses a brick came sailing across the sky and hits him in the head which made him curse out loud. As he rubbed his head and took out a cup and poured some water in it which was in his canteen.

At once everyone got quiet to show they did not plot to injure him. On his uniform were many medals and Benson carried pearl handled pistols and sported yellow stripes on his pants and he wore his uniform with his bright yellow colors which made him a shooting duck for the North Koreans. Big Jim made it possible for him to have his way with his commanding officers and he threaten not to vote on legislation approving large amounts of money for their pensions and disability payments for injuries sustained against the enemy if Jack Benson was not allowed to command troops in this conflict and promoted to a high rank.

As Benson looked at John. "I am a west pointer and hold the rank of captain and this is a lot of importance in the army and you will do as I say. Do you hear me because you will pay the price if you do not obey my orders?"

John always spoke his mind about a problem. "This army is integrated and those Jim Crow ways of yours should have left at home or at boot camp."

Some southern drill instructors thought the civil war was still going on and treated colored troops badly."

"That's right boy we did not end the war at Appomattics Court House. It is still going on today."

A war raged between Captain Benson with his Jim Crow ways against the forces of anti-discrimination forces and this bothered John who vowed one day to end the segregation which still existed in the prejudice South he grew up in and forced to die for a county where President Truman's executive order said the armed forces were supposed to be integrated at all costs with deliberate speed.

"I want to transfer to another unit and I do not think I am going to make it in your company. You are going to get all of us killed. You are not an officer and did not attend West Point for officer training." John said to him.

"As a result of your uppity mouth I order you to run up near enemy lines for about an hour so the North Koreans can have target practice and shoot at you. I'll appoint some of our soldiers who come from our national guard from the great state of Mississippi to guard you and plus they were loyal and faithful to the local clan."

Private Bill Clyde and Willie Washington drove up to an area near the border of North and South Korea and they made John walk and he did pushups every ten minutes which made him tire.

"Why don't you give me a break because I cannot hike on this road all day? I might get killed."

Private Clyde asked, "Why is it Benson wants to keep on punishing you like this?"

""Well it's a long story. He got angry because he could not have my white girlfriend and now he wants to take it out on me and hope I get killed over here in this God forsaken place."

Private Washington came from the South and he grew up in Mississippi and did not like colored people.

"To ease your pain, I want you to take your pack off and give it to me."

When John explained things to him, Private Washington put more bricks in it and made him wear the pack and carry them and he said, "Toll the line nigger and march but you cannot stop or we will shoot you."

With each step sweat fell from John's face and his body ached and he looked aged with hair on his body which seemed to be changing colors as the wind blew on it and his tongue struck out due to the heat and they would not give him water.

As John treks in a tire manner he fell down the hill head first with his helmet coming off.

"Get that nigger out of the hole. "Private Washington said.

But the driver of the jeep could not keep it from driving off the road. They were knocked unconscious when the vehicle they drove plunged into a large ten feet hole. By that time John noticed long vines on the side of the hole made by airplanes dropping bombs which left craters in the ground when they exploded on targets.

As John looked at the top of the steep hole made by the American pilots, "If I leave those white crackers down there, Benson would think I did something which caused their injuries. If I save them, maybe I can get a signed agreement which can make life better for me over here."

At once John went about the business of tying tree vines together to lift the two soldiers up from the steep hole. American jets flew by and the pilots thought they saw some North Koreans and attacked without knowing it was an American soldier they fired at. The American pilots saw military vehicles in the area and destroyed them. When they saw John and the soldiers in their situation the North Koreans were hiding on the hill not too far from them thought they were South Korean troops and fired machine gun bullets at them and John ducked for cover and hid behind some large boulders and the other two soldiers did the same thing. After several attacks the American flyers went back to the air base in South Korea. At once John came to the top of the big large hole in the ground.

"Now both of you have two choices and that is to tell Benson to make a better life for me. I do not want to go through too many changes when I get back to camp. You both have to sign confessions stating you will keep Benson from making a slave of me in this man's army. The civil war ended in 1865 but Jack Benson wants to see me in chains again. President Truman said us colored boys are just as equal as the white boys in this army."

Both of the MP's signed a statement saying they would try to bring justice to John if Benson tries to overwork him more than the other soldiers both black and white soldiers. But in the back of his mind John wondered if the MP's would honor what they wrote on paper. Many soldiers because of their race got mistreated and not given leave time to go home or rest away from enemy lines. Military officials always sent colored troops up to the front lines in the integrated army. John placed a rope around the MP 's body which was in the jeep they rode in and pulled him out of the big hole and then he went back and got the other one and both of them suffered much pain from their injuries from the tragic accident.

CHAPTER 33

When Benson greeted them the MP's he said. "Did you search Private Carol and get the message which was sewed in his jacket?"

"We did not know he carried secret information concerning arms deals."

'That's why I asked you two to guard him."

"The secret information on him would inform the North Koreans where and when to pick up the guns we would deliver to them. We stand to make a lot of money but we got to find that jacket because I had someone to steal one of them and that information was secretly sewed into it so when you two came near enemy lines the exact position for the pickup of arms would be sent directly to the North Koreans. They would pay us ten million in gold for the weapons. The two of you are dismissed for now but I want both of you to go into John's unit and find out anything about the missing information sewed into his jacket. Now we do not know where to drop off the guns and the North Koreans will meet us at a certain point between the borders of North and South Korea."

A group of soldiers are at the obstacle course and they are an ugly group of men and many of them saw action fighting at Pork Chop Hill and already battled hardened veterans but needed counseling because of constant fighting behind enemy lines.

"Private John Carol step up and climb the rope on the double!" Captain Benson cried out loud.

Private Carol's body began to tremble as he climbed the rope and his body ached in pain trying to accomplish the impossible feat.

"Sir I cannot because this pack is heavy."

Sweat formed on John's head and his vision was not too good and his hearing seemed bad at the same time and his body odor was not too sweet. He imagined himself fried at the stake with Indians dancing around him with the fire burning his body and his flesh melting as the fire scorched his black skin and at once when Benson shouted at John he came to hold the rope very lightly even though he hung on for dear life hoping Benson would tell the MP's to take the bayonets from under him because with the slightest release of the rope John found himself falling to his death and no longer would he be able to be home with his daughters he had not seen in many years being kidnapped after being placed in the army against his will. Benson wanted the secret papers hidden and sewed into John's jacket and secret orders which told about the place he would ship the guns and get his millions of dollars promised to him and Senator Big Jim Wilson who gained political power in the state of Mississippi. In defiance John refused to cooperate with Captain Benson which made him furious and he wanted to shoot John and punish him.

Benson took out his wallet and showed it to John and it was a picture of his two girls and Betty. John nervously looked at the pictures and he cried with tears of anger because he had not seen his kids in many years and he wondered how Captain Jack Benson get those pictures.

John shouted, "Where did you get those pictures and are my two daughters ok?"

"I will not tell you anything until you tell me about the information which was sewed into your jacket coat."

The rest of the soldiers rested and wished their commanding officer could get the secret information. Benson looked into John's coat and said, "Give me your jacket and I will see what is in it."

"No I will not do it," John said breathing real hard and his grey hair on his face made him look distinguished and his body showed massive muscles on it as a result of all the strenuous exercises Benson took his body through and the smell of soldiers which came from each of them was not difficult to smell as they patiently waited the outcome of John giving up his coat to Benson.

"You have five minutes to hand over your coat for inspection."

Slowly John took off his coat and gave it to Benson who told everyone was dismissed except Private Carol. The two of them went to Benson's headquarters and he watched as he cut into the jacket and said he got the letter which held the secret.

As Benson read the information, he said "This is not what I am looking for. Godamit that Private Carol!

Captain Benson orders the soldiers to take him back out to the rope climbing range that makes him climb it again and he said," I want you to climb each time I shoot off my gun."

As usual Benson orders his men to place a blindfold around John's face so he could not see as he climbs the ropes and John curses all type of obscenities at the troops. While he climbs up to the top of the rope, he takes a brick out of his pack and throws it at Captain Benson which knocks him out and John pulls himself down the rope with great speed. Captain Benson is taken to the base hospital but his men came to John 's room and opened the door. The two men grabbed John but he fights gallantly against the invaders who attacked him.

One soldier grabbed John and said, "Nigger where is the information pertaining to the places we can do some smuggling with the communist agents. If you give us the information, we might let you go home. The thought of going home brought much joy to John and even though he hated being in the army and away from his kids he said, "Fellows if you let me go home I'll obtain the information you want."

John takes off his shoes and pushes a knob on them and a secret compartment opens up and John gives them the messages which show where the pickup of arms will be with the North Koreans.

As Captain Benson looks at the message he decodes the information and said, "You have done an excellent job. You will receive your going home papers tomorrow go to Army Company C and join the troops. I am getting tire of looking at you anyway."

At once John is taken to the barracks where he sees black and white troops arguing with each other about General Douglas Mc Author being relieved of his command.

"I do not understand it. Mack was a great commander in chief, "One of the colored troops said," "You know the general was not fund of colored troops. He did not have confidence in colored troops in the first place especially when President Truman issued orders to integrate the armed forces. The president did not get anti-discrimination legislation through the congress but he fought discrimination in the armed forces by integrating black and white troops into one army."

A white solider who was from the South said, "It was that bastard Thurgood Marshall who came over to this country and made a report saying Mac was not implementing his integration plans and that's why he was fired from his job."

Another black soldier said, "We were not being treated fairly in this man's army. A black soldier was given stricter punishments than the white soldiers and Thurgood reported this injustice to President Truman. I do not believe the commander in chief did not follow the president's orders. I would have dismissed him too for insubordination myself."

Before all the arguments were heard the colored and white troops fought each other and John tried to be a peace maker as the troops hit each other with several of the white troops trying to be peace keepers too. A meeting was held and many of the troops received punishments and sent to the guardhouse because they took part in the fighting. Others who did not want to be involved jumped out the windows and went to other barracks to keep from getting blamed for the fighting and John knowing he wanted to go home strolled out the back door and at that moment the North Koreans attacked the base and the Americans were not prepared for the assault.

Large waves of North Korean troops attacked in full force and the Americans soldiers tried to fight back but the Koreans killed many of their troops as they slept in their beds and no mercy was shown to the American troops they captured in the barracks. John did not know what to do but he grabbed a rifle and shot at the North Koreans troops attacking them. Bullets flew everywhere but the American troops rallied and drove the North Korean troops back at a costly loss of life on their side. Much hand to hand combat took place during the fighting. As John traveled through the destroyed rural townships he saw how the ravages of war hurt many people and the thousands of men, women, and children traveling on the roads to evade being captured by the North Koreans. He saw little kids fight over food left in trashcans just to get a bite to eat. At the base many kids roamed it begging for food. His only wish was to go home and leave this war behind him. Sometimes the North Koreans attacked shielding themselves with local citizens to keep from getting killed when fired at. When he returned back to the base, he was given orders to leave South Korea immediately. When John got on the boat to go home, the clerk at the ship checking passports tried not to let him get on it.

John traveled back to the base to see what took place and it showed where he was given the wrong orders instead of the ones signed by Captain Benson for him to go home. An MP was told to take John back to the ship so he could leave in time for the United States. On the way back the North Koreans soldiers shot up the public streets killing innocent bystanders who ran for cover. One of the bullets hit the wheel of the jeep he rode in as shells exploded around him. Some of the North Koreans saw the military vehicle John rode in and shot at it.

"Get down or you will be killed. I 'll get you back to the ship!"

At once a bullet hit the driver and John moved to the driver's seat and pushed him out it. When the driver got shot the jeep slammed into an abandoned restaurant and destroyed an enormous looking window.

Pushing the driver out the jeep, he put the gear into reverse and drove back into the street, flying glass got into the tire and air seeped out of it but he did not want to be captured by the North Koreans who followed him. Heading towards the ship three miles away, it seemed as if he would not make it in time. The North Koreans' secret agents pursued John because they found out he gave out the information of when they could exchange weapons for secret military information. Overheating of the engine caused the North Koreans to stop their car and meanwhile John made it to the boat and he gave his orders to the clerk and trekked up the gangplank and the boat took off at once with North Korean troops firing at them killing some of the troops on it as they scrambled for cover and many bodies floated in the ocean as a result of being shot.

All of his troubles did not end at once. After an hour out to sea North Koreans pilots flew over the ship and dropped bombs on it as he dashed to get aboard ship with many bullets being shot into it and the sailors manned their guns with bravery and shot down many planes which dropped bombs around them. Seeing one of the gunners injured John who did not know anything about shooting it manned the anti-aircraft guns and shot at the advancing planes as they dropped bombs and attempted to destroy the ship.

One North Korean flying bomber pilot flew closer and shot a torpedo into the ship's side immediately placing a wide hole in it exploding, and knocking John into the water. The alarm sounded and you heard loud speakers saying "abandon ship." Water poured into the ship and men swim out of it which filled quickly with seawater. Screams were heard from sailors and soldiers being trapped by water coming to where they tried to close safety hatches to keep from drowning. Many men jumped into the water with or without life preservers on.

The captain ordered his men to abandon ship but he did not want to leave it and assisted many people to jump over into the water to keep from going down with the ship. Sailors struggled to get life boats into the water but some of them did not know how to handle the equipment letting them cut the boats loose. Fights erupted among the sailors when survivors attempting to get into overcrowded life boats. Men swimming in the water watched as their great battle ship sink deeper into the water. As John and the crew floated in the ocean thoughts of seeing his kids and Betty flooded his mind. The smell of dead bodies floated in the water were burnt badly and no one could identify them and if they had dog tags it was possible to see who they were if they were a member of the crew or not. Gradually the survivors got into groups and tried to hold up the ones who did not have life preservers. The low cries of help drifted from man to man. The water could not be drink. About fifty men formed into a group for safety and hoped a plane would race towards them. Some of the men wondered if the captain sent a message to the nearest ship to come and pick them up. Sharks swim in the distance as crew members prayed help would arrive and take them to safety and many of the men who drink the salt water became sick and as sharks came closer to get a man for their evening meal, they were hit by boots and anything they could use to keep from being eaten up by them. If they jumped into the water with guns; you could hear the cries of men being eaten and the dead bodies of sharps floated adrift from them either dead wounded or dying from the bullets fired from the sailors who managed to armed themselves before jumping in shark infested water and oil from the ship's engine covered many of them and fire covered oil could be seen over the area in the sea water. The fresh smell of blood brought more sharks to the area and open cuts from wounds showed missing body parts on some of the men which resulted as they bit at the arms and legs of sailors fighting to stay alive in the sea water.

The sailors watched as their ship sink and tears fells from many faces of the men who lost friends on it. John experienced cramps and could not stay clear of metal objects falling off the ship trying to swim to a life boat containing a few people in it and John said, "Can I get in it with you all?"

"We do not want niggers in this boat go find another one."

This type of treatment John hated but he knew people do not change their prejudice ways overnight and the dead men and personal effects from them floated in the water such as photographs of family members and their friends. Seeing food in the water sailors and soldiers fought each other to get their portion of it floating in the water. Looking into the sizzling sun blinded many of them as they tried to tell time by looking at the direction it raised in the east and going down in the west.

Sea water tossed some twenty feet up into the air and John tried desperately to stay afloat himself and all at once he saw a white sailor badly burned and struggling to keep from drowning as he swallowed salt water every time he opened his mouth.

Watching the sailor yell for help made John think about if he should help him or not because of the treatment he received over in Korea by the white soldiers he came in contact with who never spoke to him or tried to be his friend.

But the words of his mother always came back to him who said, "John do not treat all white folks wrong who treat you bad. Many of them are good hearted people and will help you in times of need. God wants us to turn the other cheek and love those white folks who hate us. It's better to love your enemy instead of hate him. God will punish those people who treat you cruelly. You have to set a positive example and show white folks love not hate."

Thinking about what his mother said John swam towards the sailor who tried to stay afloat and his name was Paul Smithy and he was white and weighs about three hundred pounds and he could not swim and John wondered how he kept himself from drowning.

"Boy what are you doing? I do not want a nigger trying to save my life. What would my folks back in Mississippi think about a nigger saving my big ass from drowning? Just let me go to the bottom and go save yourself. Now get away from me. Let me die on my own terms."

"Look at this big baby who was afraid to live and wants to take the easy way out"

"Just wave your hands and feet to keep from going under and I'll place my arms around you and try to swim towards parts of the ship floating in the water."

This was a great undertaking on John's part and he fought Smithy as he tried to hold on to him and he pulled John under the water several times nearly drowning the both of them. Knowing he could not keep swallowing water as he struggled on top of the water, John grabbed a piece of wood and hit Smithy in the head knocking him out and he pulled him to some steel parts of the boat and pushed him on it

As the sun rose in the east, Smithy woke up in pain and said, "I just cannot believe this. You could have let me die out there and plus I am a member of the local clan at home. They always taught me you cannot trust people of your kind."

"You know I started to let you drown but what good would it do. Sometimes you have to judge all races of people by the content of their character not their skin color."

"Where do you come from and what is your name? You are the first white man I have spoken to since I was forced into this man's army. This is not the colored man's fight anyway."

"I am from Jackson, Mississippi and my father would turn over in his grave if he knew what took place with you saving my life. He seemed to preach love but it was not for the races mixing together like this."

"I wonder when the search planes will come and pick us up. Man I am hungry and thirsty," John said, "We cannot survive out here any longer without food."

At a great distance they could hear sailors screaming because a shark attacked him and it was a long battle between him and the shark.

One of the Great White Sharks attacked John and Smithy and they struggled with him and used their shoes to keep him from eating his evening meal with their bodies and the both of them pelted the shark with anything they could get their hands on. Eventually the shark bit off one of Smithy's feet and he left with Smithy's foot in his mouth. Two sailors saw what took place and rushed to where they were at and tied his legs with their belts around some pants material taken off a dead sailor to stop the bleeding.

Some American fighter pilots saw sailors in the water and thought they were enemy sailors from North Korea and shot machine gun bullets at them killing and wounding the ones who got hit.

One of the pilots radioed ships in the area where the sailors were located and stopped the firing on their own men. After that a freighter appeared several miles from them and came to pick up the survivors and John was one of them. Unfortunately, Smithy died because he lost so much blood. When this happened, he vowed to go back to the town in Mississippi to speak with his wife and tell her husband he died a brave man and inspired him to keep on trying to survive and get home to his daughters who he had not seen in many years.

But this was an experience John would never forget because it tested his will to survive under conditions which would have made problems for other men. It was time to go home and John could not wait to see Betty and his kids again.

CHAPTER 34

B etty and Fisher are in the living room listening to a television news caster make an announcement saying John Carol had problems with Captain Jack Benson and was placed in jail until he gave information which the newscasters did not reveal anything as to why John was going through so much hell. Betty could not believe her eyes to see John on television and Fisher looked at her and said, "Why are you staring at that man like you are in love with him?"

Sitting in her chair Betty said, "He's going through a lot of pain and needs some support."

"Do you know who he is?"

"No I do not know him personally but I've met him before and he tried to flirt with me and I felt shocked having a colored man rap to me. I could have told the sheriff and they probably would have hanged him but I chose to forget about it."

"If Captain Jack Benson has authority over John he will have a hard time with him because he is a racist and he's a member of the White Citizens League."

As they spoke a headline appeared over the television program and the announcer could barely get the news out because of the commotion from the people who gathered around him as he said, "A US ship was sunk as it carried passengers across the Pacific Ocean from Korea. There were about six men left out of the crew after they battled the sharks and starvation because there was no food."

A picture of John on the evening news showed him as one of the survivors of the destroyed ship.

Betty could not believe her eyes as they looked at John and cried out, "Oh my God that's my old friend John and he's alive!"

A television screen showed the doctor putting large wrappings to cover the infected sores he suffered caused by staying in the sun so much and he lost about thirty pounds. One of the reporters interviewed him said, "How did you and the five other men survive the ordeal in the mighty Pacific ocean?"

"Well sir it was a terrible situation. We did not have nothing to eat and in some cases we drink salt water but it made us sick but God was in our corner and I cannot wait to get back to my family living in Mississippi."

The reporter said," You have a family in Mississippi?"

John replied, "Yes sir and I looking forward to seeing them again."

A doctor came up to the both of them and said, "That's all my patient can answer and they have been through a rough ordeal and need much rest and recuperation. In a few days they will be able to answer your questions much thoroughly but they are not in their best minds at this moment."

Dr. King getting waited on when a women drove
a seven inch letter opener into his chest.
painting by Charles Pointer

Dr. King and Abernathy kneel in prayer on February
1,1965 in Selma for voter registration drive.
Painting by Charles Pointer

Freedom Riders being attacked outside of Anniston, Alabama.
Painting by Charles Pointer

President Johnson signing the 1964 Civil Rights Act
Painting by Charles Pointer

Dr. Martin Luther King giving a speech on civil rights
Painting by Charles Pointer

Dr. King shoots pool with citizens in Chicago to get
support and trust to help in demonstrations.
Painting by Charles Pointer

Dr. King and his wife lead singing on the outskirts of Montgomery

Many of these black people are voting for the
first time in Camben, Alabama, 1966
Painting by Charles Pointer

Dr. King receiving a Nobel Peace Prize at
Oslo University on December 10, 1964
Painting by Charles Pointer

Dr. Martin Luther King with his children, Martin,
Yolanda and Hosea Williams telling people to vote.
Painting by Charles Pointer

Freedom Riders are being protected by National Guard
Painting by Charles Pointer

After April 12 arrest Dr. King wrote his famous letter from
a Birmingham Jail defending the demonstrations
Painting by Charles Pointer

Dr. King fighting for equal treatment when
black people use the bus service
Painting by Charles Pointer

Chicago 1968
King with Elijah Muhamad
Leader of the Nation of Islam
Painting by Charles Pointer

Mississippi 1968
Marching to protest shooting
of James Meredith
Painting by Charles Pointer

Montgomery 1967
Serving short sentence for
Birmingham Protest
Painting by Charles Pointer

Demonstrators get
water shot at them
Painting by Charles Pointer

Demonstrator is
outraged at fireman
Painting by Charles Pointer

Right Bull Connor using dogs
against demonstrators
Painting by Charles Pointer

CHAPTER 35

When Betty got back to Fisher's house, she had a fit discovering the twins were not at home. Getting upset Betty frantically called the police department and gave a report of what took place but the officer knew her father and refused to send anyone following Big Jim's orders not to go after the men who took Betty's children from Fisher's house.

For nights at a time, Betty cried her eyes out and knew she would not see her daughters again. Only the rich people brought their kids to The Good Shepard Boarding School made with red bricks to make this building into an institute of higher learning. This boarding school was under restraints from the state because of rumors of child abuse and the state threaten to take its license for these sexual assaults brought against this state school but when they were investigated for child abuse the school administrators could rely on Senator Jim Wilson to keep the state from closing the center down.

Dianna and Dora both were brought to the school against their will and critics who visited the school said the school did not let the children have enough social life and it was operated as a prison. The kids underwent severe punishment for not making good grades or excelling in sports or anything they wanted to be good in. A tall slim lady came into the school and saw Dianna and Dora getting an examination Dora acted more militant and kicked and screamed as the doctor tried to examine her.

Miss. Pauline Grayson the director and a teacher spoke to Dr. Lilly who taught eleven-year-old Dora in her class. Her sister Dianna who was white could not be with her sister all the time because segregation was practiced at the school. The colored and white students were separated from each other.

In one class, Dora asked her teacher Miss. Grayson "Where is my mother and father. I know I had a mother and father when I was a younger and a sister and now I do not know where they are ?"

"Close your mouth young lady. I think you are talking too much instead of studying your lessons, "Miss. Grayson said, "If you continue to ask about your parents I'll have you punished and put in solitary confinement."

Getting defiant Dora repeated her questioning and asked, "Where is my sister, father, and mother. I deserve to know?"

With that response Miss. Grayson grabbed a rattan and requested Dora come to the front of the classroom and get a beating and when she obeyed her Dora looked at Miss Grayson in a mean sarcastic manner and said," You are not going to beat me again. I only want to know where my sister is. We were kidnapped and brought here by force and separated. I want to see her because it's been five years and I feel like a prisoner in this school."

The other girls looked curious as to what Dora said because they were allowed to go home and be with their parents after the school year was ended but Dora never got this opportunity.

What Dora did not know was that Big Jim paid the school authorities to keep her at the school as a prisoner because he did not want Dora knowing Senator Big Jim was her grandfather because it would hurt his political career even though he had a colored lover living in his estate by the name of Polly who he loved and would defy anyone who wanted him to get rid of her.

Taking a swing at Dora, she reacted and yelled out loud so the security people could come and save her from a beating but Dora and Miss. Grayson fought each other until the girls in the class broke it up. They were both brought to the principal's office and Mr. Guy Rice the person who takes care of bad discipline students said as he rubbed his bad shoulder and took off his wide eyeglasses and said, "You should know better than to fight the students. I might have to suspend you because this girl is 14 years old and too young to be hit by you. She can sue us for you fighting a minor."

Looking at Dora Mr. Rice said, "What do you have to say about this Dora?"

"I am much older now and I have not seen my sister, and mother or father since I was a little girl and no one will tell me anything about their whereabouts and why is this? The other girls get to go home to see their parents after the school year ends but I have to stay here year after year. I want to leave this place to find my mother, father, and little sister."

Before Dora went to see Mr. Rice, Lilly Porter heard what Dora said and kindly knocked on the door and said, "Dora what have you done now?"

"She's in trouble for defying Miss. Grayson's authority. I am thinking about sending her back to another school because she keeps thinking and talking about her parents and a sister. I can only say they brought her and her sister here and left them with us."

"Mr. Rice I would like to know if I can keep Dora at my farm. I get lonely out there and need someone to talk to and help with the house keeping."

Dora looked at Miss. Lilly Porter in a strange way because she never spoke to her while she was at school and talked to her about her health because she was a doctor but other than that Lilly never had anything to do with her.

Every time Lilly saw Dora in the hallway she stared at her all the time. "This young lady reminds me of my daughter Angle and I miss her a lot."

Mr. Rice said, "Dora would you like to stay with Lilly for a while? She might want to adopt you as a kid of her own."

"I have a mother and father and I do not need any replacements."

""If you do not take me up on my offer you might never get a chance to find your parents by staying here at this school but you must live with Lilly while we look for them. You will be in her custody."

Thinking about getting away from the school, Dora said," I guess I can try this out for a while but you must find my parents. You do not let me use the telephone to call anyone and that is wrong."

A quiet silence came over everybody in the office and Dora said, "I guess I can try this out for a while but you must promise me you will find and locate my parents."

With that taken care of Lilly said "Dora I'll take you home so get your clothes and we will leave. I know you will like my place."

As Lilly drives through town Dora gets out of the car and attempts to scramble away from her and Lilly stopped the car and Dora darted into a large grocery store with Lilly in hot pursuit.

"Move out the way!" shouted Lilly as she pushed customers out of her path and Dora ran throughout the store. As she passed by a group of oranges packed up into a pyramid Dora hits the top of them and Lilly stumbled and fell but managed to get up and continued with a limp to chase after Dora who tried her best to get away from her.

Seeing Lilly closed in on her, Dora pulled a shopping cart in front of her but being a track and field champion in the track meets doing the high huddles she jumped over the shopping cart and landed on Dora and put her in a scarf lock judo technique on her neck to stop and refrain her from continuing to escape.

As Lilly chased Dora she remembered what Mr. Rice said about Dora, "Dora does not let no one get to know her and she defies authority."

"Now Dora you're coming home with me. You might find it attractive to you and you can meet the farm animals and my ranch hands who keep things up on the farm while I am away teaching at the medical school and doing medical practice as a doctor in the evening."

"Why did you go out of your way to get me out of this place? There were other girls who needed a home to stay at during the summer months because they had no parents to go home to stay with?"

Still driving," I needed someone to be positive in my life. I get into all types of things which kept me from living a positive life."

"Such as what?"

I took drugs to calm my nerves but it became additive which would help me forget about my problems I dealt with during that time."

"Why is it you wanted to keep me for a while?"

Looking at the traffic as she drove. Lilly said," I looked at you and saw myself as a child who could not adopt to the rules and changes as a younger person, I did not know much about life and no one took the time to help me. It seems like I always got into trouble and I did not feel I was important."

Miss. Lilly why didn't you get married?"

"I had a husband and I thought he was the right one but he wanted me to not finish medical school to become a doctor and I was not going to let him keep me from achieving my goal."

"Dan left me because I told him I was going to become a doctor and he would have to accept my wishes or we could not make it."

"In a way Dan and I were different because he wanted me to be blacker because I spoke Standard English around him and he did not like it and felt I was a sellout to my race."

"Miss. Lilly I do not think you are a sellout. You wanted to be free and did not allow other people define who you should be."

As they approached her farm house, Dora could not believe her eyes as she saw the enormous two story house with so many windows and the huge white columns supporting the front porch roof and the many areas of farm land on her property and several people on the farm helping her.

"Where did a colored doctor like you get the money to have such material wealth as this?"

Dora only thought white people were supposed to live like this and she saw many mansions in the south but they were owned by white folks.

As Lilly got out the car she coughed badly and her servant came and gave her something which could make her breath much better."

"Now rest Lilly you should keep your portable breathing machine with you at all times. Without it you will have a hard time breathing.

The doctor warned you if your asthmas flares up you can die and fall out. You should not be so hardheaded. You got too much at stake to die now and who would inherit all of this property and land of yours. You know Big Jim Wilson is trying to get the property from all you farmers down here if you sell out to him. You have to take your medicine to stay well to be able to make the sound decisions when they come to buy your property,"

Using her breather, Lilly said "I keep forgetting to use it but other times I cannot."

After Lilly said that she and Dora strolled into the kitchen to get something to eat. As they sat down Dora looked at the glass dining table they sat at and saw the beige cabinets containing stylish pots and pans and to the sides of them a refrigerator which made its own ice and there was a dishwashing machine in the kitchen too. The huge oven cooked much food. The marble floors in the enormous kitchen shinned because the house keepers kept them looking nice and good. In the dining area was an enormous table decorated with the latest style silverware and dishes imported from Europe and priceless works of art adorned the walls with elaborate white curtains like they have at the White House in Washington D.C. were in the windows. The white carpets did not have stains in them and the living room contained couch sets. In her bedroom was a restroom and shower and Dora could not believe what she saw because in each of the twelve room were fashioned with all the comforts of a person would want. In the backyard was a pool and tennis court and she owned a gym for the times she wanted to exercise.

When Miss. Lilly got ready to take a rest and go to sleep, she received a telephone call and it was from Mr. Rice and he said Miss. Grayson became gravely ill and almost died and she might need a specialist in her field specialty in cancer and if she could assist her in the medical treatment for Miss. Grayson and Lilly said nothing because she had her own illnesses and would have to take a rest for a while.

"I am glad she is sick because she made life miserable for me while I was a student at the school. She put me on report all the time and kept me in the writing lab just for the fun of it and I later found out she kept my mail sent to me from people I did not know about. I am curious to know who tried to contact me. The other girls always received letters from their friends and relatives but not me. I do not think Mr. Rice is going to locate my real parents for me. He wanted to get me out of the school to keep me from complaining all the time. He is a good friend of Senator Jim Wilson and whatever Big Jim said he did it with no problem,"

"Now Dora I'll try to keep locating your mother and father if I can." Lilly said to her.

CHAPTER 36

As time went by Dora became restless and yearns to see her mother and father but no one seemed to know anything about their whereabouts. One evening Dora strolled down the road without anyone seeing her and hitched hiked to the nearest nearby town by the city of Jackson, Mississippi. As she darted down the street hunger pains hit her stomach and she wanted to eat.

"Oh my God I am hungry and I will need to eat in a hurry."

As she came closer to a food store, Dora looked into the window and decided to steal something to eat because after not eating at the house before she left, Dora could hardly move because she did not have any energy to take many steps. Her flat stomach looked like a board and her underarms smelled for lack of being able to wash up and her eyes showed the anger she felt inside because the hunger pains were unbelievable and looking at the food in the store made her want to eat it because the feel of any type of food would fulfill her healthy appetite to eat anything her body could take in. As she came into the market, it was adorned with good things to eat and she approached a lady who was letting people sample new meat they sold.

"May I have some meat balls? "Dora said," I am hungry?"

"No problem. Take a couple of pieces if you wish because I will make some more of them."

"I have to go back into the freezer and get some food. Pay me when I get back."

Realizing this was her chance to steal food; Dora grabbed the boxes of meatballs cooked chicken and took off scrambling through the store.

"Stop that girl. "One of the security officers shouted at Dora as she strutted through the store trying to evade the officer chasing after her. Two male customers saw what was happening shouted, "He is trying to molest that colored girl!"

As the officer approached the two women customers they took swings at him and he went flying into some boxes of washing powders busting some of them which broke open pouring their contents on his face and they both grabbed him and shouted "How dare you try to molest that little colored girl. You should not do things like that."

The security officer tried to remove the washing powers off of himself and shouted, "Godamit I'll have both of you arrested. That poor innocent colored sister just stole two boxes of some new meat the store was trying to sell."

Helping to pick the security up one of the lady shoppers said, "We thought you were trying to molest this poor innocent girl. The both of us are sorry. We only tried to stop a possible rape of that darling little child. Will you please forgive us?"

The security officer said, "Ok but can you give me a good description of the girl?"

Both of the ladies looked at him and said, "Why should we because she is only a woman who probably wanted something to eat any way."

By this time the clerks in the store called the police and officer Tom Smith asked the two lady customers who the young lady was and immediately bits of information came out of their mouths because the police officer threatened to have them locked up for obstruction of justice and keeping a police officer from doing his job. Mostly what they told him were lies about the identity of Dora who they still felt was telling the truth. Both customers were against harming a woman in any way because they felt women could not do any wrong.

By this time Dora ate the contents of what she stole but people passing by were just as hungry as her and invited themselves over to get in on an uninvited meal. As she ate the meal Dora heard footsteps approaching her and saw the hand of someone grabbed for her prize stolen possession. A man who took pride in wearing a red bandana around his head with three of his front teeth missing growled at Dora and said, "I want your food. I am so angry so give it to me."

"Go to hell, I worked real hard to get this food. You cannot have any of it. His other arm was wrapped with a coat because in his last fight someone broke it and seeing a stick on the ground Dora grabbed it and said, "If you come closer I will use it on you."

With his tongue hanging out his mouth the fellow said," I have not eaten in a week and I will die if I cannot get something in my stomach," as the fellow talked he breathed hard and attempted to look presentable even though his long hair needed cutting and his worn out suit coat appeared to be dirty as if he used it to sleep on the ground for many weeks.

"When was the last time you took a bath? You smell bad and need one"

"Mam I am sorry the way I acted but what I think about the way Senator Jim Wilson pushed me off of my farm for back taxes and came and evicted me from my land I do not know what to do."

The man cried as he spoke to Dora and his hands looked aged with hair dangling on his arms like an ape.

"Why do you keep on scratching your skin? You need to get a good bath. I see lice coming off your body."

Feeling more comforting, she said, "What is your name by the way?" as she gave him some food from one of her boxes of chicken; she managed to provide him and he ate it like a wolf who killed its prey.

"My name is Tim Rays. I own the farm not too far from Miss. Lilly's. One day, this fellow by the name of Jack Benson and his thugs came and evicted me from my property because owed back taxes and I did not have a hearing. Big Jim's signature was on it from the court which evicted me from my land."

"Why did they evict you from your land?"

"I think they wanted the oil on the property. A man from the state's government on conservation said, there was some oil on that huge tract of land and ever since then they have evicted people off their property for any reason they wanted to bring charges to steal a person's farmland."

"Did you try to go to the court to get your property Tim? "Dora said moving the chicken meat from her lips,"

"What good would it do? Senator Big Jim Wilson has the law enforcement officers in the back of his hand and they paid off to do his dirty work."

"Maybe someday I'll be in a position to get my property back, "the gentleman said and slowly went his merry way into a bar.

"Thank you little girl I'll never forget the kindness you showed me. I not was raised by my real mother or father so I drifted from home to home trying to make a living for myself but one day I get my property back but we need someone in office who will make sure the little man gets a break."

CHAPTER 37

"That little girl looks nice," Quick JJ said as he saw Dora strolling down the street eating her chicken and Quick JJ cried out, "Baby where are you going?"

What JJ said scared Dora because every time a stranger approaches her at night they think she is out to have a date with them

"Why don't you come with me pretty little girl, I will not harm you. I'll make sure you're ok. I got much paper and I am a rich photographer."

Still Dora did not say anything and chose not to be bothered with man who seemed to not take the word no for an answer. Parking his pink Cadillac decorated with velvet custom made material complete with a bar, television, and a stereo record player, and eight track player to listen to his favorite music, and he left his car to speak with Dora and said," I don't want to hurt you but I can do something about your future."

Looking curiously at JJ, Dora said. "You mean I can make a lot of money with you?"

Dressed in a flashy pink and green suit Quick JJ said," I have many women who posed for me as models and now stardom is in the air for them. Some of them made the cover of big magazines."

Throwing a chicken bone into the street a stray dog came by picked it up and ate it.

"I am only 15 years old and you will get statutory rape if you harm me."

"Little girl take a look at me. I do not look like the type who would harm you?"

Knowing she needed a place to sleep, Dora asked if he could let her spend the night at his place for a night and then be allowed to home in the morning.

Holding Dora in his arms Quick JJ said, "Its ok you can stay as long as you like. I will not hurt you."

With that being said and done Dora got into Quick JJ's car and he drove them to his studio where he took photographs of people. He owned a big two story apartment with about ten rooms in it.

"Man you have a nice looking place. All of this priceless artwork cost much money."

"You will like this place. It's what a girl dreams of living in one day after I make them rich and famous by putting them on the cover of the most famous magazines in the country and Europe. See all of these girls they are making big money. If you listen to me, I'll give you a life style you will never regret even if you do not finish college."

As Quick JJ talked of giving Dora fortune, fame, and money, she looked at the huge living room complete with pretty couches and love seats sitting on a white and black zebra rug with black and white chandelier lights and silver tainted glass coffee tables and a big wide clock with Roman numerals hands which were gold with a black marble background.

The beds were decorated with black and white silk materials and the bar was about ten feet long and it was glass and if a person wanted a drink he could see the different bottles of wine on the table beneath it for his guest to get their favorite bottle beverage. The rich aroma of meat cooked on a grill Quick and his guest used for special occasions. His walls were decorated with bluish and white designs of squares and circles. If someone came to Quick JJ's, he or she would see different plants in his house and the kitchen contained the latest advances in cooking materials.

They both went into a photography studio and Quick JJ took pictures of Dora in the nude. There were rooms Quick JJ did not show Dora and she asked who was in there because she overheard conversations but could not understand what the people said.

Little did Dora know Quick JJ put drugs into her glass of orange juice which made her sleep and she could not control her actions and did not know where her mind was at when she drink the orange juice he gave her. This made it possible for Quick JJ to take nude pictures of Dora posing in different positions.

Driving into Jackson, Lilly still worried where Dora was and wondered why she would run off because she and Dora seemed to be getting along just fine. Parking in a no parking area, she went into the store to get some medication and a paper man sold papers and magazines in the store.

"May I have a paper young man? "Lilly said," I want to know what is happening in our local news today?'

Inside the newspapers, appearing on the cover was a picture of Dora in a nude pose with another woman and she said, "Who is the person that's taking these pictures. They are awful."

"That's Miss. Dora." the Madame said, "and she is sexy. I'll sell out of newspapers every time they put her pictures on our covers."

"Do you know where JJ's production company is?"

Now as he ate some candy and sucked it to death the sales clerk said, "I have to think about it but with a little money I can remember a whole lot."

Taking fifty dollars out of her purse Lilly said, "Maybe this will help your memory to remember where is my little adopted daughter is."

"His office is located on 25th and Vineyard in a big building which looks like a huge mansion."

Without delay Lilly left her car and strolled down the street to find Dora. Making it to JJ's building, Lilly came up to the large wooden door and knocked on it but before she could a voice said over the intercom, "Hi sexy Quick JJ welcomes you to his paradise of love so just wait for a couple of minutes and he'll be able to come to the door and greet you and make your visit one you will never forget. Man you sure have sexy legs and your dressed to kill," and in ten minutes the door automatically opened and at the door to meet her were three beautiful women dressed in short mini dresses but it appeared they were in a hypnotic spell being programed to do certain functions.

As Lilly waited a portion of the door opened and a tray came out with different drinks and supported by a handle underneath it.

"How do I know this drink does not have drugs in it? "Lilly said," I did not come here to get drunk. I want to see Dora and take her home,"

All at once a tall gentlemen came up to her and said, "Come on in sugar my name is Quick JJ and welcome to my paradise. The ladies love this place once they get in here. Now what brings you to my paradise of love?"

"I see you have a lot of nude pictures hanging showing a good business you are in."

"I want to be a famous model and travel and see the world you talked to many girls about and I see you held the key too many students' dreams to get them on the cover of major magazines in the world."

"Well the first thing you have to do is to get photograph shots for me and I will take a look at them and see who I can send them to."

"That should be no problem Lilly said, "What type of outfit we'll wear to take my first photographs in?"

"Sugar pie you have a sexy voice" as JJ moved closer to kiss Lilly and she pretended to kiss him back but said, "Now JJ you have to wait until we are finished with the photo session and I will treat you with love and affection."

"JJ you smell good and that cologne you have on turns me own. Why don't you dress in some of your sexy silk pajamas and use that good smelling cologne you have on and I'll go into the restroom and change."

Trying to think on what to do, Lilly goes into her purse and writes a note with her eyebrow pencil stating JJ is taking pictures of underage children by making them pose nude and he is trying to make money off of them by selling them to pone magazines. She indicated he is molesting underage girls and attempts to throw the note out a window hoping someone would pick it up. She found a screwdriver lying on the ground floor and used it to pry the window up high enough so the alarm would not go off indicating someone was trying to escape alerting Quick JJ where he could stop Lilly and Dora from leaving his mansion.

"Ok darling is everything ready?" JJ said dressed in silk night room clothes and no women ever came into his building or bedroom without him making love to him and he would not take no for an answer. Softly strolling into Quick JJ's bedroom to another room Lilly locked the door but JJ kept an extra key under the rug in front of the door and he obtained it and opened the door and said, "Now Lilly this is our time to make love so laydown and let me have it."

As Lilly laid down on the bed, JJ did not realize he hid a hammer under the bedspread she would use to hit him with and when JJ tried to take his fill of Lilly's love she wracked him with the hammer and he fell to the floor making him lifeless. Realizing Lilly could not get dressed properly she strolled out of JJ's bedroom quietly and looked for Dora who tried to get out of the arms of Mad Dog King who attempted to molest Dora and Lilly heard Dora screaming and could not open the door but she disguised her voice like she was JJ and Lilly said in a strong JJ like voice "Mad Dog King come out immediately. I am going to give you some extra bread for being a good employee for me. Come and get this five hundred dollar bonus right away."

The only thing which could stop Mad Dog King from raping Dora was money and ever since Quick JJ shot nude pictures of Dora he wanted to have her as a sex partner despite the fact she was underage.

"Godamit just when I was going to make love to this young beautiful girl "Mad Dog King said, "I'll be there as soon as possible," which was the message he said into his hand radio he used when communicating with Quick JJ when he was in another part of the huge building.

By this time Dora tried to put her slip on with Mad Dog King watching and weighing three hundred pounds, she knew he would rape her. A stroke of luck prevailed and as soon as Mad Dog King tried to rape her she hit him with a skillet and he fell to the floor."

"Now Dora let's go. You don't have clothes on but we got to get out of this place before those two men wake up."

Hugging Lilly Dora said," I am so glad to see you. I thought no one would come looking for me. Both of them tiptoed out of the vast studio and before they could get out the place Quick JJ's dog Paluka growled at them and chased them through the house as Paluka came behind Dora and Lilly they slammed the door into Paluka's face and knocked him out. They still needed to get out of Quick JJ' s house before Mad Dog King and Quick JJ woke up.

"That's the way to the front of their apartment so let's go in that direction."

Finally reaching the door they could not turn the knob but a message appeared on a television screen above their heads which said, "Name this song and you will be able to get out of here."

Some music played and Dora picked a selection but it was not the right one. Another song came on and Lilly named the right one and the door did not open.

"Godamit they are going to get us but this is the only way we can escape this dilemma"

Another song came on and Dora tried to name it but the door partially opened but they could not open it all the way. After getting over their headaches Mad Dog King and Quick JJ who were in another room close by tried to name it but the door partially opened but they could not open it at all the way and wanted to stop the women before they could escape and report them to the law but the doors were made of heavy steel and difficult to open all the way without naming the right song when it played over the speaker.

After getting over their headaches Quick JJ, Mad Dog King and his dog Paluka, reached the front door where Dora and Lilly tried escape after JJ named a song which opened the doors all the way.

"Now we got them "Mad Dog King said," I want

Dora and you can keep Lilly."

"No problem," Quick JJ said.

With the door partially opened the police came up to the door and pulled it open to them and they shouted for Mad Dog King and

Quick JJ came out or they would have come in shooting and the police apprehended them.

"We are glad to see you and they wanted to rape both of us. We thought no one would come to the rescue."

"The sergeant said an old drunk came to the police station and thought he found a one hundred bill and wanted us to keep it for him. One of the officers at first wanted to throw it in the waste can until he looked at the writing and read what it said.

We immediately spoke to the man who brought us the note and gave him a good dinner and one hundred dollars for helping us find you."

"I am glad you came and found me. Please forgive me for giving you such a hard time Lilly"

"Well that's ok. I can understand how you felt not knowing where your real mother was at. I'll do my best to help you find her."

Still trying to hold back the tears, Lilly said, "I've been down that same road of loneliness wishing and hoping I would not be lonely all of my life."

"Can I ask you a question?" Dora said," I need an answer but maybe it will take some time for you to answer."

As Lilly gets into her car she said "Well now Dora we cannot keep things from each other so tell me what's on your mind?"

"Will you adopt me? I do not know where my real mother is. It seems as if I 'll ever see her again."

"Well you already have a mother but I can make a good step mother for now."

"I love you Lilly and I think you will make me a great mother and I need you."

All at once Lilly grabs her chest and stops the car.

"What's wrong Lilly?"

"I have been having chest pains and it's because I left my medicine at home before I came to pick you up."

"Lilly do not do that. I'll try to remind you to take your medication when I see you getting sick. You are the only mother in my life regardless to if you are my stepmother. You're all I got."

CHAPTER 38

To award John for his bravery, the Colored and White Farmers Allegiance gave John a reception and thanked him for helping save the lives of both colored and white troops in Korea. It surprised him to see so many colored and white farmers mixed together and not white and black sections of seating.

While he lived as a young man growing up on Big Jim's plantation or when he went to Jackson with the Wilson family he witnessed segregated businesses which he could not go into to try on a suit or a pair of shoes. But this night excitement soared through the air because the Allegiance would give John an award for his bravery under extreme dangerous conditions during the Korean war. The president came up to the podium and spoke to them as they sat at their table eating the best food the great state of Mississippi offered them complemented their wives who did the cooking southern style.

"It is an honor to have Corporal John Carol to come up here tonight to speak to you. He saved many lives when his ship got torpedoed and to survive survivors fought off sharps who killed some of the servicemen after their ship sunk. I know you're getting tire of me speaking and I have a habit of talking forever to discuss the many issues which are affecting your families and your abilities to keep state elected officials from taking your land which they say might have oil on your property. Please welcome Corporal John Carol and another thing I knew his father Peter Carol when he first worked on Big Jim's plantation.

Looking a little tire and worn out John smiled and got closer to the podium and waved his hand and many types of ribbons adorn his uniform and his face is well shaved said," I appreciate you giving me the honor to speak with you tonight. Many years ago who would think colored and white farmers would be sitting down in this beautiful building honoring a colored veteran from the Korean War. Everyone knows race situations in this country has not been good since reconstruction and for the goodwill of God you have come together to discuss bettering the lives of your children and love ones. I've heard stories Senator Big Jim Wilson has not fulfilled your promises and most of them have not been met."

"He is for big business and they are cheating you out of higher prices for your crops and homemade products. I hate to see this happening to you because he tried to take my daddy's land too. The big boys are trying to foreclose on your land and take your farms from you. We cannot let them do this because it's not right and just for a few greedy rich men to live off the hard work your families have put into their farms for over a hundred years or more and it would be a shame to see the hard work go down the drain and have wealthy landowners drive up the interest rates on your loans and pay you low money prices for your crops.

After John said this many people in the crowd stood up and gave him a standing ovation and when the clapping stopped John said, "When I was in the army, I saw a different one. White and colored boys trained, fought, and died together. I hope their dying was not in vain. I hear they are changing our names from colored to black and now I do not know which one to use. As I road home I said to myself I wanted to one day build better schools for all the people of this country and have colored and white children attend quality schools to go to. I plan to get an education and run for political office one day but I need your help to do this. One of the white farmers shouted out. "Why don't you run against Big Jim Wilson? He is the reason many of us are losing our property."

The huge crowd stood up and clapped for him.

"I want to run out the elected politicians who are charging outrageous prices for your crops and leaving you with nothing. I want to help build irrigations systems that can be used to keep crops alive so the dry season will not destroy your crops. I want to keep jobs here in this state of Mississippi and not have companies in this state build manufacturing plants in foreign countries because of cheap labor they charge to make our products. I want to give help to farmers who cannot keep up the mortgage payments on their farms when the weather keeps their crops from growing and provide education technologies to better their crop yields. I want to make sure we get top dollar for our crops when they are shipped overseas where many of our jobs are shipped. I want to knock down the walls of segregation which keeps the races from coming together to create a world all mighty God said all men regardless of their race should love each other and build a better foundation of love for a better tomorrow."

CHAPTER 39

Senator Wilson got word from an informant in the group that John Carol would be speaking to the Farmers Allegiance and Senator Wilson said he would send in men to disrupt the meeting. Senator Wilson said to his buddy Jack Benson who he called the enforcer, I stole one hundred dollars from the Farmer's Allegiance when I sold their properties and got much of the money. By the way I added an extra $1,000 dollars for you. Now do not kill anyone because the federal marshals will be coming down here to investigate for possible charges of discrimination and violation of their civil rights. Let the northerners stay up there and we will handle our affairs in the southern tradition like they did in the old days."

In a waiting car, Polly the mistress of Big Jim who stayed by his side wherever he went acted as an aide to him but only a few people knew she was his lover and everything was kept quiet about their love affair but he managed to pay everybody off who wanted to say anything about it.

Polly a high yellow looking female with long curly hair sat in the car and wondered what was going on and asked Big Jim.

"It's nothing Polly those fellows and John Coral are going to cause trouble in our great state of Mississippi and I mean to stop it. All they are trying to do is have the federal government send unwanted officials to check on if we are letting the colored folks vote and we feel they have no right to come in our towns telling us what to do in our beloved state."

Pouring a glass of wine Polly said, "Baby, my brother is attending this meeting because his farm was taken from him by your rich landowners. Tell them not to kill him because he is my youngest brother who hopes to become a doctor to help the poor white and colored women get decent prenatal care and medical services. It would be a great lost to the people who are counting on him to come back and work in the local clinic for all the people regardless of their race"

Pouring some wine for himself, Big Jim hugged Polly and said, "Now do not worry I know he will be at the meeting and I told my men not to shoot or kill anyone and do enough to disband the meeting."

'Should those people have the right to assemble and voice their opinion about their own survival baby and the right to talk about issues which are important to them?"

"Baby this is their method of them keeping the carpetbaggers in the North from coming down here and taking over. You got to fight fire with fire."

"Even if it means getting my own brother killed in this effort to preserve southern heritages. It does not make sense so why don't you call off this ugly mess you are getting yourself into."

Still drinking Senator Wilson opened the door and stood looking at the big lodge where the farmers both black and white plotted to stop him from taking their land from them.

"Big Jim I do not want my brother killed and I must warn him, "Polly said as she hugged him," I think he must not get injured in this ignorant scheme of yours to keep them from fighting you back and it would be a great lost if he is killed."

"Don't worry Polly I told the men not to hurt your brother."

Big Jim's men wore black clothes to keep from being seen by the farmers inside the forest as his men crawled across the field leading to the building which contained three flights of stairs with rooms for sleeping quarters and to have meetings. For an old building, they filled it with the latest equipment to protect themselves from possible invasions from anyone attempting to destroy the building. Instead of trying to stay awake, Big Jim's men took breaks to smoke some weed and it became difficult to coordinate their plan with each other when they finished smoking which meant secrecy in this operation was important. What Big Jim did not anticipate was frustration developing in the group of men because they found out that one group of Big Jim's boys from another county got more money than them and all hell broke loose among his forces before they were supposed to attack the meeting of the Farmer's Allegiance.

"Big Jim's recruits came from Crawford Country and Taylor County and it was difficult recognizing them because of the darkness and they wore black clothing. By this time the farmers protecting the building saw what underground tunnels which led a way where the farmers could attack the retreating men who wore black and threatened the freedom of the Farmer's Allegiance. Big Jim's policies kept them from growing crop yields and being able to keep their own farms and knew they would take their revenge on them. The farmers came out of the tunnels and began firing at Senator Jim Wilson's men who fought and shot at each other because Big Jim paid one group of men more money than the other group and when Big Jim saw he was on the losing side, he drove off.

"Come on Polly we have to go because I cannot get caught in this. It will ruin me in the upcoming election."

"I cannot leave my brother out there because he might get killed. I've got to warn him."

Grabbing Polly Big Jim said," I cannot let you do that. They will know I had something to do with it."

Stopping the senator, "You do not give a dam about me. I am just another colored woman you are sleeping with. Although evil things they said about me were incorrect I tried to ignore what they said about you and now I see you only care about yourself."

"They are firing at each other Polly and I do think you should not go out there and get killed."

Bullets came flying around Big Jim and Polly and the smell of blood lingered through the air and gun smoke created a big cloud and men fired shots at each other in pitch darkness and no one knew who they were firing at. This noise frightened the herd of cattle down the road and they stampeded towards the area where the gun battle took place. Men caught in the middle of the fighting scrambled for cover and some of the farmers and Big Jim's men were trampled on by the cattle.

Polly scrambled to the site where they were fighting and as the heard came towards her she climbed up a tree but there was nothing could be done to save her as they knocked it down. By this time Big Jim made his way back to his plantation not caring if Polly was dead or alive. He could not be implicated in this incident which took place.

Always thinking about himself Big Jim did not bother to read the newspapers articles on what took place. When the police revisited the site, cars were turned over and dead bodies littered the place and ambulance medical teams tried to get up to wounded people to the hospital.

As Big Jim road back to his plantation, he listened to the reports on his radio and when he found out Polly was dead he almost crashed into another car barely missing it. Instead of going back to his plantation Big Jim rode back to the scene of the crime and searched for Polly 's body but it was nowhere to be found. The love of his life died that night and felt he lost a friend and lover. Big Jim spoke to one of his political friends and he said, "What happened to Polly?"

"She went looking for her brother and probably got injured by the firing from both sides. They took her away to the colored hospital ten miles away. I am not certain if she was killed or not because so many false reports came from the news medias about the number of people killed in the fighting. It's hard to say where they took her because colored folks are not allowed in the hospitals for the rich people."

Big Jim did not like what he heard and said to a worker, "What do I get out of this? My friends will not like the idea I am trying to save the life of a nigger woman."

Criticism from other members of his staff came forth. 'Where is your respect Big Jim. Just think how your opposing party's leaders will treat you."

Pulling out his 45 Big Jim said, "I'll shoot the living daylights out of you if you don't take me to the colored hospital."

Sam said, "Ok but it will cost one hundred dollars to take you."

". Just get in the car and drive to where they took Polly."

At a quick pace, Sam drove fearlessly down the road and headed to Jacksonville, Mississippi where the colored hospital was located. They arrived after having to detour because of heavy flooding and raining. Big Jim wanted to find out if Polly was doing ok but the guards would not let him into the hospital and Lester a black man greeted Big Jim at the door. "May I help you sir. We do not allow white folks in this hospital."

This insulted Big Jim who said, "If you do not get out of my way, I'll kick your colored ass boy. I am senator Big Jim Wilson. I am the only white man who voted money to have this hospital built for your people so let me in to see Polly!"

The fellow by the name of Lester weighed 245 pounds grabbed Big Jim and threw him into the wall with one great throw and Big Jim went crashing into the floor making a loud noise creating much mental anguish in the patients and a very nervous of Big Jim who got back up and did a football tackle against Lester.

"Ok Lester let's see what you got now throw the next punch."

Lester threw the punch and Big Jim who knew martial arts techniques learned from the service executed a back hand strike to Lester's head and his kick broke some ribs as Lester hit the floor. A nurse came and saw Lester lying on the floor with his nose bleeding and his body smelled from under his arms because of the rough fighting and wrestling with Big Jim who felt defeated at the hands of the senator.

"Nurse Jane Patterson said, "You banged this man up badly. You know white folks cannot come in here."

"I helped build this hospital and I am Senator Big Jim and I want to see Polly the women who was hurt in the gun fight when the farmers and my men fought each other."

"Come with me Senator Wilson, "Lester was following my orders. Polly is in this room, sleeping."

Coming into Polly's room Big Jim looked at her and cried to himself and said, "Baby I am sorry this terrible thing happened to you. I told you to stay in the car."

"Nurse will my Polly be ok. I need her in my office working for me. She's my backbone who watches my back. I cannot live without Polly being by my side. She handles all of my administrative duties."

The doctor said she might pull through but she will need plenty of rest. The bullet hit her spinal cord so she might be paralyzed all of her life.

Strolling back and forth in the hospital room Big Jim held Polly's hand but she was unconscious. A news reporter looked and saw this white man holding a black woman's hand and how he loved Polly and Big Jim looked at her as she rose up from the bed and shouted, "You son of a bitch Big Jim you killed my brother!"

Polly sink into her bed and the nurses who played cards ignored her cries and did not care if Polly needed help or not. A reporter by the name of U-tube ran into the room taking pictures of what he saw as Polly rolled back and forth across her bed and screamed out loud about the death of her brother.

"You killed him!"

U-tude's body was short and he weighed one hundred pounds turned on his tape recorder and said, "Mr. I have never seen you in these parts of Mississippi before. Can you tell me your name?"

"Does it matter? I am a big time politician and do not have to tell you who I am."

Looking at a poster of Big Jim showing him running for reelection Lester said, "You are the one on the poster running on a platform of being anti-colored but yet you are in the hospital crying your heart out over a colored woman."

Taking a closer look at the picture Lester said, "You are Senator Big Jim running for reelection in the United States Senate. How dare you not practice what you preach? If the voters felt, you were having an affair with a colored woman it would be the death of your campaign and by the way how much money will you pay me for keeping quiet about this whole matter. I want $40,000 dollars to keep from telling the reading audience of my newspapers you have been lying to them all along about wanting a separate but equal state of affairs between the colored and white citizens of this state."

Lester threats of black mail did not make Big Jim happy and Big Jim grabbed Lester by the throat and he choked him until he fell out.

Big Jim killed Lester and scrambled out of the hospital and got into a car and drove home to his estate. He never got a chance to talk with Polly or knew if she died from her injuries. As Big Jim drove home he could not think about nothing but his Polly who he loved. To lose Polly meant so much to him and they quarreled with each other and he hated to hide Polly from other people and his friends but they knew something strong existed between them. When riding in the limousine, they sat together in the back seat and on lookers were surprised when they saw this and could not believe their eyes because Big Jim gave speeches against race mixing. He would not rest until he saw what happened to the love of his life. With Polly he could be himself and let his hair down and relax. When his enemies wanted to see him, he sent Polly to speak with them to see if she could help settle some of the problems and at first the different white businesses men did not want to be bothered with a black woman or man to translate business deals but to get to Big Jim you had to please Polly first and if you looked suspicious and she felt it would hurt Big Jim you never got to see him and now she laid in her hospital bed in in a state of shock and Big Jim in a rush to leave did not check to see if she survived her gunshot wounds.

CHAPTER 40

O ne evening Betty went to the Starlight club and wanted to ask people if they saw her daughter and showed them a picture of her and all at once several girls came out on the floor and did a sexual dance and one of the dancers was Dianna who performed with them. This outraged Betty and she went up to the stage and pulled her off of it and when Tiger Woodson the owner of the night club tried to stop her from taking Dianna away she threw a bottle of wine at him and the glass landed on the floor and people were injured who scrambled away from it. Taking out her 45 gun she shot bullets into the air and shot out the light located in another room."

"You know I was going to find you because I loved you and your sister very much.

Betty did not have any money in her pocket and she had to do something so she and Dianna could eat. As they glided through the park they saw a man lying on a bench trying to get a nap to finish his list of duties in the bank in which he took the farmer's money and brought land from out of state buyers at lower prices breaking the law.

-"Momma see the watch he is wearing. It is very pretty."

"Yes it is. If I had it, I could take the watch and get some money to buy us something for us to eat little daughter."

Sneaking up to the bench a tall man rested on a bench and he slept because of working half the day and during his lunch break he traveled over to his car parked on a street and took a nap until he went back to work. This is the place where the local prostitutes came and solicited several favors for money. On this day, the local prostitutes saw him and the one thousand dollar watch and attempted to seize it before anyone got near him...

As Sleepy White, attempted to snatch the gold watch Betty grabbed his hand and they fought over it and even though the lady was bigger Betty and Dianna grabbed the woman and hit her with many punches and she got up and rushed down the side walk and went away limping because of the pain inflicted on her by them.

Davey Williams the gentlemen they tried to rob, got up and screamed because he felt he was being attacked and the first thought that came to his mind was to run but he rooted for Betty and Dianna to win the fight. Finally, the prostitutes managed to glide away cursing up a storm. Before grabbing the watch she hit him in his chin, pulled Davey's beard, and rubbed his balled head. As Sleepy did these horrible things, thoughts of being with pretty women danced in circles around his head in a dream with him being kissed by all of them and being assaulted at the same time. This dream put him in a deep trance and as Sleepy pulled his watch from his pocket the alarm went off and he stirred into the prostitute's eyes and screamed and that's when Betty tried to grab her and Dianna helped apprehend Sleepy. The prostitute ran when she saw Betty and Dianna put up a heck of a fight.

Mr. Williams said, "Oh I am glad you two tried to help me. She would have stolen this priceless watch my wife gave me for a Christmas present."

"So you are married I did not see any rings on your fingers,"

"Well I am married but my wife left me."

"Why did she leave you?"

"I did not sell my land to Big Jim because he wanted to dig for oil on it."

"Is there oil on your land?"

"I do not know but he threatened to have my land taken from me if I did not sell it to him or my position as bank president would be taken from me."

"How could Big Jim make it possible for you to lose your land?"

"At first I had rice fields and later grew other cash crops. I was out tending my crops and saw this truck coming and it was about five or ten men in it and I approached them and said, "Why are you coming on my land. You are trespassing anyway. I gave you no permission and he said I owed back taxes on the property and the state was going to take ownership of it."

"Did they show you the legal papers signed by a judge?"

"No they did not."

"Then how were they able to take your land?"

"All it amounted to seeing an eviction notice on it and before I could do anything about it Big Jim's men tore up my property and drained all the water from my rice fields killing my rice crops and they gave me nothing for my loses."

"When I tried to stop them they beat me up."

"That once fertile field has nothing but oil on it and they are destroying the property around here and running off the animals and nothing is being done about it."

"Is there any land around here which is not being developed?"

"Well I know of some land that is rich in lumber that is being foreclosed on and it will be up for sale in a few days but you need five thousand dollars to pay a down payment on it. I want this land because my family can use the money to live off of it. I'll do anything to get that property. Who knows I might marry you. I need a place to stay and if I cannot get a place to live at me and my little girl will wonder all over the county begging for food."

"Well my wife left me and I do not think she is coming back to me. I'll tell you what, I'll get you a job at the bank and you can be my special assistant."

"I do not know sir because I have a little daughter who is mean and uppity at times."

"What about school for your daughter. You know it's against the law to not have kids in school I can arrange for her to get into school."

"I cannot read or write too good but I am willing to learn some fundamentals if need be. I had a difficult time in high school because life was so good that academics did not fit into the program."

"I cannot refuse your offer but I cannot promise you I'll stay here forever."

"It's a deal," Betty said to Mr. Williams

"That's my daughter and she is spoiled rotten. I played a great role in doing that."

"Hi, Dianna how are you doing?"

Dianna did not say anything to him because she longed to see her father John Carol again who she felt deserted the family.

Dianna tried not to say anything but issued a statement to him. "Do not say anything to me. You are all dirty men."

"Now Dianna I will not have you speaking to Mr. Williams like this. He's mother's friend and wants to help us."

"Betty it will take time before your daughter will get use to me. She will enjoy the family and my little daughter Pewee."

Dianna and Betty were driven back to Mr. William's plantation called Cross Oak's Estates. The house like most of the big mansions had marble columns in front of it and much farmland but one patch of land grew nothing on it.

"Why is it nothing growing on the property?"

"I do not know. Every time I tried to grow crops on it nothing would happen."

This puzzled the both of them as they looked at the land.

"Momma how long will we stay here. I want to see. my father, and sister again?"

"I am afraid that will be impossible. I do not know where they are at. Maybe one day that will happen."

All of this conversation made Mr. Williams curious as to what both of them were talking about. Mr. Williams did not want Dianna to see her father and sister but felt he should get their attention.

Mr. Williams did not want Dianna to see her father. All he needed was the love of a woman who would care for him as he grew older. He was twenty years older than Betty but felt she could love him no matter what. Betty saw this was a way to enhance her future by being with a wealthy man. What was love to her? Money was really what mattered and Mr. Williams had plenty of it.

"Where do I sleep Davey? You know I would like to sleep alone for now and besides my daughter would not like it because she is used to seeing me with her father."

His face was round and he wore thin gold eye glasses and Davey strolled casually through his plantation with Betty with him. It became a problem at times because both Dianna and her daughter did not like getting up in the early hours of the morning which did not appeal to them and problems came up as a result because Mr. Williams criticized Dianna for showing no disciplined attitude about living up to the expectations of not being raised like a country bumpkin without social graces when growing up as a young kid.

In his plans for Betty and Dianna, he wanted to groom them to become ladies use to lavish living and he was not taking no for any answers.

"Momma I do not want to be trained to be a rich person. He must have a lot of money, "Dianna said,

"Now Dianna you have to let Mr. Williams take of us. He is rich and I would rather be with a man of good means then a one who is poor and cannot do anything for you and me. There's a chance for you to get a good education and become a lady of good trained manners."

"I have the good manners you taught me."

"It was not enough and besides I have big plans to make. You and I will live off of Mr. Williams 's generosity."

Betty wanted power and Mr. Williams was in a position to get it for her. No more struggling for her and Dianna and she felt getting to know the people in the corporate world could give her what she wanted and at all costs she would get it. Her faults were many and her desires became a necessity. Did she love Mr. Williams? It's hard to say because being poor Betty did not want to identify with and she wanted to live the life style of a millionaire. Would Betty get alone with Pewee and Mr. Williams at all costs?

Betty wanted to keep Mr. William's happy but she was not going to mistreat her own daughter to pacify Pewee who was spoiled rotten. While working at the bank, Daisy May approached Betty and said," I read about you and Mr. Williams 'will in probate court. I think he left you all of his assets. Are you Betty Wilson, daughter of Senator Big Jim Wilson?"

"No I am not. Who told you that? No one knows me at this bank."

"You better keep quiet about this. There are women who work here who have been after him for a long time and his daughter is spoiled and very protective about her father."

Pewee was eight years old and a problem and she did not like the idea of her father bringing another family into the house because of her hold on tight to her father attitude with strangers. A meeting was arranged between Betty, Dianna, Pewee, and Mr. Williams who said, "I've called this meeting because there seems to be a problem between Pewee and Dianna and they cannot seem to get alone with each other. I think the girls should try to show more respect because we are a family now."

Betty, "My daughter can be a bad ass and yours too,"

Pewee said," Dianna thinks she's prettier than me and I do not like it. She said I would never be anything in life."

"Why did you say that Dianna, "Betty said, "You two will have to learn how to love one another? I am getting very fond of your father. He has done a lot for me and you by bringing us into his home when he did not have to and even got me a job at the bank. Pewee I am not your mother but I can help you with many problems you are facing in life."

"Father always did that but now he is too busy at the bank. I do not know when he will come home. I am getting tire of eating by myself with my dog Lacey. I need help with my lessons too. My teacher and I cannot come together so I can move on to the next grade."

"Pewee why didn't you tell me you were having problems with your homework? I will visit your teachers this week but I cannot fit this matter into my schedule. Big Jim Wilson who is the Senator is doing some illegal things with the farmer's homes and he wants to foreclose on them as fast as possible because there is oil on their land. I have to be there to see he foreclosed on their property illegally. If not, I'll lose my job at the bank. I keep the accounting records and make sure Senator Wilson wins on each separate deal. I have to be with him most of the time."

"Now Dianna what do you have to say because this is a family and each of us have a voice in here and besides I love your mother," Mr. Williams said, "I need your input in this matter."

Looking at Mr. Williams with his glasses hanging loose, Dianna said, "This is only a pack of lies. You never invite me and my mother to the big parties your friends throw. You get cleanly dressed and take Pewee with you but never me. Do you call that being a caring father? You do not give a dam about me because we are poor."

With that being said Pewee slapped Dianna and a fight broke out between the two girls.

Dianna. "I am going to kick your ass!" as she threw punches at Pewee who grabbed Dianna and pulled her hair. Both of them rolled over the floor and Mr. Williams tried to grab his daughter Pewee but she was so angry she hit a picture of her mother that was an expensive oil painting and destroyed it with a strong punch which Dianna ducked. The smell of blood filled the air and curse words echoed back and forth from both girls and they hated each other with a great passion and they both wanted to make sure each of them understood what they fought each other for and that was respect and equality. Seeing the girls kept beating each other up badly there was only one thing to do and Betty grabbed a gun from under a couch and fired bullets into the ceiling and knocked down a chandelier which fell to the floor and pieces of glass scattered all over the beautiful wooden table stands costing thousands of dollars'

When the shots ringed out this caused a fire alarm to go off. The local fire department arrived and the farmers did not check to see where the fire was located. They hooked the hose to a fire hydrant that was not working properly and when pressure was applied to the hydrant the water rushed out too quickly and knocked the steel hydrant into the car. A large flow of water shot into the air. The big explosion of water flew into the air and family members and their black maids went where the water came out of the hydrant and they pushed each other for fun causing a big commotion and people helped each other and fights broke out. One of the big problems which took place was most of the people fighting were drunk.

On the way to the plantation, fire fighters went into a liquor store and consumed a lot of fire water called alcohol and it became a free for all with most of the people fighting being drunk and it appeared to be a riot on the plantation. Eventually the alarm was heard by the local police officers who came to the plantation and pulled out their guns because it was a grand alcoholic fight taking place and it took several peace officers to put down the fighting. One of the fighters opened up the door to a coral of pigs who stampeded into the fighting area and dispersed the people who were fighting each other and saying the best curse words they could find to put their point across and even though they were drunk. They felt they fought for a common cause. Most of the people became muddy, dirty, and drunk.

"I'll give everyone five minutes to get back to your homes or places of business. I'll have all of you put in jail for peace disturbance."

Instead of spending the night in jail and court they decided to disperse and go back to their places of business and all over the farm land were dead pigs. Things seemed to settle down and the girls stopped fighting each other and peace at last came to the place. Pewee and Dianna would never stop hating each other. They both were enrolled at the same school but there was a problem because Betty did not have Dianna's birth certificate which state law required it.

"I'll handle it, "Mr. Williams said," I know the superintendent. He owes me some favors."

Mr. Boston the principal lets me have my way on things like that but I always promise him something in return."

"What is it that you want Mr. Boston?"

"I want you and Betty to come to an after hour drank and party at the Swinger Hotel that have 14 flights of stairs and plush hotel rooms and you have to supply the call girls and bring Betty also."

With a frown in his face Mr. Williams said," I do not think so Betty is spoken for. I am in love with her."

"Since when have you ever loved a woman Williams? Everyone in town knows you cheated on all the six wives you've married. Now what makes you a saint and only desire one?"

"Just shut the hell up. Betty is a fascinating girl and I plan to marry her."

"She's twenty years older than you. You are too old for her and plus she only wants you for your money anyway."

"But I will deal with that when we are both lone and that twenty year age difference does not come up. She loves me only because of the way I treat her and her daughter and plus they are in my will if anything happens to me and my wife Happy will not get anything."

"Mississippi is run by the big plantation owners of this great state and they favor the men getting the inheritance when they die and the wealth of the plantation is left to the men and we are talking about two hundred years of the men in Mississippi making the law to serve the interest of men and not women."

"I understand but everything is worked out for Betty to get the estate and not my ex-wife who ran out on me in the early days when I struggled to build up the bank and many other industries. Betty's the perfect person to control things if something happens to me. Here is a copy of this will explaining who shall get what."

"Why are you showing this to me. You know I have a big mouth and love to talk a lot especially when I am drunk?"

"That's ok Boston here's two thousand dollars to keep your mouth shut about this."

Boston took the money and promised not to say anything about it to anyone he knew.

"By the way there is going to be a big party at the King's Delight Hotel are you going?"

"No I have some last minute work I have to complete before going to bed Betty said, "I have to go and represent the bank. I am getting too old for that type of life style."

The King's Delight Hotel was one of the most gorgeous one in the city of Jackson but before the old mayor died he did not like the hotel owners because of the prostitution which took place there. Many of the town's people who knew what was going on in it opposed the heavy drinking and gambling usually had church pacifists picketing outside of the hotel during the week but many protesters in the group did not like to see people getting sloppy drunk but they did not mind the gambling because they sneaked in at three or four in the morning when their Christian friends who they picketed the church would be asleep at that time of the night.

But this time Betty was invited to represent Mr. Williams because their friends wanting to lure more of the rich to set up accounts in their bank. A deal was made with officials from the people at the hotel to have a night when people could come and get free rooms without paying anything especially if customers had charge cards and customers of the bank.

Getting dressed in her best outfit Betty changed her mind and got into a big black limousine driven by Mr. William's chauffer, an Afro American, who wanted something as usual escorted Betty up to the ballroom but did not go into it where the guests are having a good time because of his race but years later all of this changed because of the 1964 Civil Rights bill but now times were ripe for keeping the people separated because of their race.

A person who drink at a table looked familiar to Betty and as she looked at him flashbacks came back to her and the gentleman looked like someone who cheated her out of some money by having her play a lottery which failed to pay if the person came to claim their money but the lottery people would not pay off. Taking a 45 caliber gun out of her purse as she approached the stranger she said, "You no good lousy bastard. You cheated me out of some money in the lottery. I won the money but you know good mother would not pay up."

Being afraid of what was being said to him, the stranger said, "Mam I do not know what you are talking about."

At once the stranger turned around and Betty realized she knew this person but could not recognize him and immediately John looked at her in a curious manner.

At first John was scare and got very shy and had not slept with any women at all. It appeared to be a colorful romance because soft music played in the back and both of them looked at each other with penetrating eyes as if they wanted to make love to each other.

The ballroom looked good and they both sat on a bed when they entered a room.

"I saw a poster and the fellow on it appeared to look like you."

"What did it say?"

"That you were running for United States senator in the state of Mississippi."

"You're, right. I am running against Senator Wilson and he fights dirty. They say I do not have a chance to beat him because he's a powerful man in this state but I will not give up my dream of defeating him."

"It will take a lot of money to beat him. You have to raise funds to beat him to get the word out as to what you are going to do for the people in this great state of Mississippi,"

"I'll do my best".

"You are going down a steep hill because he will use tactics to intimidate you the black voters who want to vote for you. Black people have the right to vote in this state but they are run off by Big Jim and his henchmen and they fear for their lives."

"Do you have a family and a wife to care for you?"

"I have two girls, one who's white and the other one who is black but I have not seen them in ten years. "What happened? I know this can be very emotional."

Getting closer and prancing back and forth across the floor, tears fell from his eyes as he held Betty and said," I left my family because I got into it with a justice of the peace and left instead of staying there to get lynched by the local people. I hope to one day to see them. My lovely Dora and Dianna."

Even though Betty knew she was talking to John; he did not recognize her because it had been so long since they had seen each other. Betty wanted to tell John who she was but it would cause a lot of commotion and if Big Jim found out John was at the hotel he would have him killed. Traveling from town to town in Mississippi, John built a large following of people wanting Big Jim to lose an election and he would do anything to win even if it meant killing the candidate running against him. But this was John's and Betty's night together.

"I've seen you somewhere before", John said as he looked at Betty and tried to remember where he had seen her but due to an injury he got in Korea when he fell and hit his head it was difficult for him to remember who was his woman who looked so beautiful and charming as they looked at each other and Betty said," You're a great dancer. You move good on your feet like it was natural without missing a beat." As the band played soft music in the hotel ballroom.

"It came from me looking at my father Peter and mother Sarah dancing to the old music at home."

The door buzzer ringed and a waiter brought some wine to Betty and John's room and when John opened the door a big bottle of wine sat on the side of the door.

"What's that Betty? It looks like someone has left us a bottle of Champagne and I am thirsty. I'll pour us some."

Each step John took in the hotel suite a soft noise drifted into their room and by this time Betty was in a romantic mood and wanted to tell John he was the father of her two children who he had not seen in ten years.

Pouring the champagne Betty said," I know when there's an airport not too far from here. Let's go and watch the plans take off."

John said," I think we might get in trouble doing something like that. A colored man and a white women riding in a limousine. You must be crazy."

"That would not be a problem. I know all the patrolmen and they will recognize the bank's limousine anyway and I'll be sitting in the back seat anyway."

Looking at the limousine, John said," I would love to drive that limo. Here it is I am running for United States senator and driving an old run down Ford. It's about time for me to be seen driving a car that represent the political office I am running for."

Arriving at the airport, they parked the car and Betty sat into the backseat of the long black limo and John poured her champagne.

"John let's go for an airport ride. I know how to fly."

"Betty you have had too much to drink."

"I haven't and if you do not go with me I'll fly it myself"

Betty who was drunk scrambled towards the airfield where some twin engine planes were located.

"Betty wait a minute. You will get yourself killed so do not do it."

As Betty approached the fence she saw it was too tall and covered with bared wines. Next to the construction site a large pole about twenty feet inches long laid on the ground and she picked it up and ran toward the fence and pole vaulted across it and tore her pretty dress exposing her slip.

Seeing Betty could get killed John grabbed the same pole Betty used and did not want to be outdone by a women and ran thirty feet away from the fence and trek back towards it and pole vaulted across it and the same thing happened to him as the bob wire tore his pant legs off of him.

"Betty stop it!" "Stop it! "Wait for me!"

When their clothes touched the bob wire it sounded off the alarm and opened the doors of the big German Shepard Butch who came striding towards Betty and John.

"Now let me see how am I going to fly this contraction and make it flyable?"

While Betty tried to get the airplane to fly she turned certain buttons on the two seated plane.

By this time the security officers got after him. Known for getting prowlers who dared to come on his airport Butch scared would be burglars from attempting to invade his backyard but it appeared he met his match because chasing John posed a difficult problem as he scrambled towards the airplane and Betty flew it down the runway with John holding on and Butch tried his best to bite off John's leg but by this time Betty pulled the steering wheel up and the airplane lifted into the air with John hanging on and he managed to pull himself into the back of the two seater. Getting into the back he shouted,

"Betty are you hearing me. Let's land this plane so I can get back to campaigning for the senate against Big Jim."

Betty was very high off of cold medicines got dizzy and talking out of her mind without thinking about what she was saying.

"I miss my John I have not seen him in ten years and I will die if I cannot be with him again."

"Betty I do not want to die now. I got big plans with my life. I do not want to die in an airplane crash.

That will not happen if you land the airplane. Just think you will not see Dora if you cash this plane."

"Can you get my daughter Dora back to me and her father John to see me by Christmas?"

Before John could answer Betty she did something with the wheel and the plane went flying toward the ground. By this time John shouted his favorite curse words at Betty and said, "Damit Betty what in the hell are you trying to do. I do not want to die. Land this airplane!"

Betty could not understand what she said and Betty flew the plane up and down and rolled it over. When she straightened it out', she did not see another plane coming toward them and at the last minute dived to avoid hitting it.

"This is fun," Betty shouted at John who by now developed an upset stomach. Flying pass the commanding officer he did not know how to identify friendly planes and called the gun crew to shoot at them and at once shells exploded around the airplane and it frightened the hell out of John but it did not bother Betty because she was high off the wine she consumed at the hotel. Overhead jets appeared over them and they saw the airplane was not military looking but one of the pilots felt it could be a spy plane and wanted to shoot it down. Betty tried to make the plane do different types of turns and the jet pilot's fifty caliber machinegun shells barley missed John and Betty and John kept screaming, "Take the plane down before we crash and get killed. I have an election to win ad I cannot do it getting killed."

The plane descended into a lake and crashed into the water.

"I cannot swim! "John said." I hope some people will come and pick us up."

Betty held him up so he would not drown. A poisonous water moccasin snake swam towards them trying to bite one of them which would cause sudden death if his poison got into their systems. Breaking a branch from a tree John hit the snake and he darted away from them.

"Well you got him John."

"Let's try to get this log to shore so we can get dried off."

The only problem which stood in the way was a big black bear who played in the water with his cubs and stood up and growled at John and Betty. The bear rushed towards them and broke some of the branches with his large paws and picked up John and tried to crush him but Betty grabbed a big floating log and hit the bear in his leg and he immediately got scare and took off swimming to the other side of the lake with her clubs swimming after her. By this time the park ranger came and powered his boat to the area Betty and John battled the big bear.

"You're under arrest fellow because you are out here with a white girl and that is against the law. You kidnapped this white woman and took her across state lines for prostitution."

"Sir you got some papers?"

"Why?"

"Well if I can write out an IOU for five thousand dollars we can forget about this. Mr. Williams is my employer and he always gives funds to the park rangers with my ok and when one of your officers were killed in the line of duty sent a generous donation to the ranger's family.

"I remember, "he said, "I'll let him go but the two of you cannot be seen in this park. A black man and a white woman seen together like this would get him lynched for being with her,"

With grief in her heart, Betty wanted to have her family back together again. Knowing John needed more money she was determined to send it to him. Betty knew John's interest was helping the black and white farmers gain a better life style and finer living conditions and schools all the people of color both white or non-white could attend in the state of Mississippi because the state elected officials spent more money on the white child's educational needs than the black children. Many thoughts came back to Betty as she was taken to Mr. Williams' plantation and because of what happened at the lake her clothes were wet and dirty looking.

"I'll take the girl to where she has to go but soon you have to get to where you come from. Some of the Klan members in this area could get awfully mad if they saw you with this white woman."

Betty stayed quiet as the park ranger drove her home and she thought about the encounter with the father of her two kids Dianna and Dora. The officer's radio kept broadcasting the latest crimes going on and the incident about her predicament came through the radio.

"It seems as if you are very famous Betty flying around up there in the sky with that nigger. What made you do such a silly thing like that? You know this will bring bad publicity on Mr. Williams and the customers who have accounts in the bank. Hope this incident doesn't get to the board of directors. They might get Mr. Williams out of his position."

Betty reflected on the soft music they played and danced to slow music which made her realize she still loved John after years of not being with him. Beating Senator Big Jim would be difficult and she told him if he needed some campaign money she would send it to him because she knew Mr. Williams loved her and would do anything to please her. The board of trustees did not like the idea of Betty getting her position in the bank she was not qualified for. Somehow Betty felt she would one day have her family back together again.

Knowing John needed money she was determined to help send him funds if possible without anyone knowing about it. Betty knew John's best interest concerned assisting the black and white poor farmers to obtain a better life style and living conditions and most of them did not have running water going into their houses and good school systems where all the people both black and white children could attend school together. State legislatures did not spend enough money for the poor income children of its black and white citizens in the state of Mississippi. Corruption took place with the rich business people taking over the small farmer's for closed farms and making them into corporation farming forcing families to leave the South and migrate to northern states to get employment in the manufacturing job in cities like Chicago, New Jersey or Detroit especially during the times of war against other countries.

While John and Betty were at the hotel, she took out a picture of one of the twins and showed them to John who said," Here's a picture of my daughters Dianna and Dora but Dora was taken away from me and I hope to get her back one day."

"They are some pretty girls. If I get elected senator of this great state of Mississippi I will do all I can to help you."

"I had two daughters myself and they were interracial but I left town because they said cruel things to my lady who was white and I stood up for my rights and I escaped from them before they came back to lynch me. I do not know where everyone is and one day I hope to be with my kids again."

"They will not know you because there were little kids when you left,"

Those thoughts came back to Betty as she was taken back to Mr. Williams' plantation to explain to him what happened at the lake and how her clothes got wet.

CHAPTER 41

E very year there is a debate at the Jacksonville College Prep School and parents and friends were invited to see the debate between the last two follow up contestants who happen to be Dianna who is white and Dora an African American.

The education Dora received in the black schools did not have the latest technology like the white ones but through the tutoring of people like Lilly who was a doctor tutored Dora and she became a model student who often felt she was not challenged enough by her teachers and wanted higher math, science, and English classes. Dianna got the best education at the Little Mary academy for girls and she was prepared to debate this black girl who did not have the background Dianna possessed but Dora was determined to prove she could debate on any topic thrown at her to discuss. The audience was separated with one side of the auditorium with white people and black people on the other side. The school located in the white neighborhood in Jackson, Mississippi was equipped with the latest technical equipment to use. It's so modern that contractors built elevators in it which took students to the four floors their classes were located at in the building. In the back of the school, tennis courts, football fields, and soccer fields covered huge tracts of land. The school administration bought the latest up to date books and athletic equipment for their students but the history books excluded black people who made contributions to America and the state of Mississippi. To compete in swimming events with other school districts, a swimming pool was built and school administrators hosted state wide swimming events at their school.

As the two girls strolled towards the podium, Mrs. Gloria Timber waited to introduce the speakers to the audience. Over the ceiling hung fans to keep the audience from getting hot. A panel of five judges sat on the side of them to watch the candidates and award points to the orator who delivered the best answers to the panel who repeatedly ask questions. Many of the visitors were spell bound when they saw one of the colored high schools orators presented in the debate who could speak just as good as the white students in disbelief. The girls looked similar in appearance and people saw some resemblances in both of them especially in the way they fixed their hair and looked at everything in the auditorium as they debated each other. The smell of popcorn drifted into the auditorium which vendor people in the hallway selling it before the debate. Whispers darted across the aisles about this historical moment and each of them studied the debate questions thoroughly and it appeared they did not like each other.

The first one to speak was Dianna and the topic was should there be mandatory bussing of black students to White schools? The debaters could speak their minds and the speaker asked both of them the same questions. Miss. Timber asked Dianna:" Do you think black students should bussed to white schools?"

"I think there should be no bussing of black students to our schools because for years black students have have been educated in their own schools and they can learn without them sitting next to us."

"Dora could you answer the same question. I think the only thing about bussing to another school is we would be learning in an environment that have modern schools built in this decade. Our schools are not built like the white schools are because they are substandard and most of the supplies we used are not new and only hand me downs and they are never replaced."

"The next question is do black students learn in an integrated classroom much?

"I feel we do not want to sit in a lunchroom and have ice cream thrown in our faces and told nigger do not eat in this lunch room and be injured by white students who do not want to overcome and treat us equal."

"Dianna could you respond to the same question?"

"I think that's a lot of bullshit because when the first schools were made black students learned in one room log cabins and were taught and they learned without students sitting next to them. There are many black college students who learn at such institutes as Howard University, Fisk, Southern, and Texas Southern University. Thurgood Marshall who was black could not attend the University Of Maryland Law School because he was black but he later went to Howard Law School and received his law degree. He did not have any white students in any of his classes and did ok."

"Dora could you respond to this questions?"

"What Dianna left out was the fact Justice Marshall became the first African American to serve on the United States Supreme Court and he was able to get a black law school student into the University of Maryland because the school received federal funds and could not deny this black student admission into the law school. I read where a black student could not study in the same classrooms with the white students when she was at their law school. When world war one started they called black troops who died just as the white soldiers and should be treated equal over here as first class citizens. Even in the war between the states called the Civil War black people were put into separate units and fought and died to end the horrible system of slavery. The war would not have been won if President Abraham Lincoln would not have used black troops and later after the north won the battle of Antietam he issued the Emancipation Proclamation."

"Even though black troops were paid eight dollars a month and the white troops $ 10 dollars; they later received 10 dollars after they refused to accept any pay until the Northern congressmen voted and black troops were paid the same income as white soldiers. Dora did not bring out the fact black people fought in the Confederate army as soldiers and were body servants to their masters and helped build bridges and used as laborers and handled supply wagons. A great many of them were loyal to their masters and helped defend the southern towns when the union forces attacked them and received pensions from their states.

"Dora do think it was right for freedom riders of black and white student from northern colleges to come down to our towns and cities to assist to help integrate our schools and public places of accommodations?"

"I am for this because they had the courage to help tire the hated of discrimination in a nonviolent atmosphere and manner. They could not do this staying at home and traveled on busses to get there and help black people get registered to vote and many of them both black and white activist got killed in the process. They sought to integrate the bussing facilities because black people sat in the back of the busses when traveling into other small towns and cities.

The two of them answered their questions to the best of their abilities and when the judges voted in favor of Dianna to win. The judges were anti- civil rights and Dora did not stand a chance of winning. One thing she proved was black high school girls could debate against white students even though they were educated in inferior schools but could hold their own when debating against other students from top high schools in the nation. The audience could not believe those students could speak like college graduates. Dora vowed to come back again and beat Dianna in next year's debates at the same high school.

When the debate was over, Lilly hugged Dora as tears fell from eyes as she said, "I feel I was cheated and they were anti civil rights judges and I would have lost regardless to what I spoke out against. "She is good but I felt I should have won. I will beat her in the next debate because many of the judges will come from northern states."

"You should be proud of yourself because you went up against the Mississippi state champion and nearly beat her. You were black and you beat out the other ten white people who did not come near second place and look this was the first time for black people to prove they can do more than pick cotton like they are slaves with little or no education."

CHAPTER 42

Dora had no other choice but to stay with Lilly because of the strange relationship forged between them. Dora reminded Lilly to take her medication even though she was a doctor. Many arguments took place between both of them but with Lilly, Dora found someone who listened to her opinion even though Lilly won in the long run and told Dora not to take things for granted and she would have to work hard for a living to achieve success. Even though Lilly graduated from medical school it took much work to achieve success.

"What was it like trying to get an education?"

"It was a difficult ordeal. Being black and female made it challenging."

"Why do you say that?"

"I went to a high school which did not want to have girls in it."

"Why did they have rules that were separate but equal?"

"I being female and black; they made it difficult for me to graduate."

"Did you date any white medical doctors while you were there?"

"One of them liked me but when he found out I was black he stopped seeing me. He thought I was white because of my real light skin and I often wondered why he never acted like he did not want to be with me when the white students saw us together."

"Did you tell anyone you were seeing or dating a white male student doctor?"

"No I kept it to myself because most of my black friends would not like it. I think you better get some sleep."

"Morris said he would come and pick me up and take me..."

"No I will not allow it because he is a no good bomb and he is bad for you so get some sleep. He has a bad reputation with girls and he might end up getting you in trouble. I heard he does not know how to treat women like a gentleman should."

"I promise the girls I would be there to practice that new dance with them. Plus I betted them twenty dollars I would win the contest."

"You have to clean up the kitchen and wash my medical clothes so I can meet my patients in clean medical attire."

Lilly went on to bed and Dora called Morris and told him to be watching for her down the street and as she slept you could hear her breathing but she was tire because of her hectic schedule. Dora did not realize Lilly set the alarm so if someone tried to make it out the front door it would go off. The pathway towards the front door was clattered with magazines and medical books left from Lilly's long nights of studying her medical books and as Dora tried to kick them out the way one of the books hit the alarm on the wall situated close to the floor and it went off and Dora darted out the door and as she jumped over the door step Dora tripped and fell but managed to get up and scrambled down the street which frightened one neighbor who happened to be outside and he pulled out his gun and shot at Dora running towards Morris's car. Morris saw Dora running toward his car but thought he was being shot at and turned his car around but waited for Dora to catch up with him.

"I cannot go to the dance with these clothes on. I look a mess and I need some."

Riding down the street, Morris saw some dresses in a window.

"What are you going to do?"

"I see some fine looking dresses behind the store window. How would you like to wear one to the dance?"

"No I do not want to wear stolen dresses because my step mother would be the laughing stock of the town."

A loud alarm sound echoed from the dress shop as Morris broke a large display window and grabbed a pretty red dress and got in his car.

"Here you go wear this."

A patrolman in the area raced towards the dress shop but when they got there they saw Morris drive off quickly down the road and they followed in hot pursuit. Morris pushes on the paddle and managed to avoid hitting other cars on the road. Dianna is hollowing for him to stop the car but Morris had a bad driving record and do not want to be picked up. Instead of constant driving he stopped the car and darted into the forest and hid in some huge bushes. Dianna scrambled with him and they departed ways and they both never made it to the dance.

Strolling into her mother's house "Where have you been"? I've called everyone to see where you were at."

"Momma I just went for a walk because many thought kept occurring to me and I needed time to think about them."

"Well I will not let you play in the game tomorrow. You are going to have to learn good manners.

"Momma I am sorry and it will not happen again. Sometimes a person has to have some fun every now and then."

"Keeping me up all night is not my way of being courteous of my feelings. You are grounded."

A call came from one of her teammates and Dora told her she could not play on the big championship game. They decided to come get Dora when her mother went to treat patients at the prison.

"OK Misty come get me at 11P.M. because my mother will be gone by then,"

"I'll be there as soon as possible. I hear Dianna is bragging they are going to kick us in the ass. We cannot let that happen can we? We have to uphold the honor of the traditional goals of the school."

Speaking to Dora Lilly said, "Dora I have to go do prison ministry so you do all the chores I told you to do. You will have to learn discipline and the rules of my house. I'll keep grounding you if you keep disobeying my rules."

A loud noise is made from a car and inside of it is Misty who is about six foot six said, "Come on girl we have to win this game!"

Strong rivalry took place when Dora and Dianna's teammates played each other.

On the way to the prison ministry, Lilly hears the broad cast of the game and feels awful about grounding her daughter to not let her play but felt she must be taught a lesson. The game starts and the Wild Cats who are under the command of Dianna takes an early lead against the Bandits led by Dora who was team captain.

The game starts out, the Wild Cats who is under the command of Dianna takes an early lead in the game and against the Bandits led by Dora and the game play keeps going back and forth, and Coach Randy Spottsville tells Dianna the following:

"You are going to have to keep Dora from scoring because she is a gifted player."

"I'll do my best to stop her. Dora is out running me most of the time."

As Dianna goes up to take a winning shot, Dora pushes her causing Dianna to slip and fall which causes her to go over to Dora and they exchange words and a fight starts with both teams of their players and hitting each other. Instead of awarding the game to the winner no one is told who won the game. Big Jim paid off the referees to later declare Dianna's team the winner because they made up a list of ineligible plays to say Dora's team cheated the opposing team. This rivalry between Dora and Dianna grew year after year especially after Dora's schoolmates sent decayed turkeys to their school on Thanksgiving Day and some of the students became sick. In another incident at a track meet, Dora won the event when someone came and put glue in Dianna's shoes, someone did the same thing to Dora's shoes, and Dora lost the one hundred yard dash.

CHAPTER 43

The buzzing sounds of insects sounded loud when Betty finally visited her father's plantation and she listened to her father as usual hoping he would not try to kidnap her to keep her from see John after many times of trying to stop her from being with him and she was scare to death to see Big Jim again.

"I want you to marry Jack Benson because he is a rich man and I want you to be with him because I'll be able to get more money to dig for oil on the properties we take from the farmers for failing to pay their land taxes."

"Father I do not love this man. He raped me and I do not want anything to do with him."

"You do not have to love Jack Benson because he's a great catch and he is rich and always loved you for many years."

"Don't you try to rekindle that relationship over again with that nigger John Carol. I cannot have my daughter running around with a troubling stirring nigger."

Looking at his photograph album, Big Jim looked at the pictures of his wins when he ran for public offices and defeated them whether he had them killed before they ran for office or he beat them on Election Day.

"You know you can help me by telling Dianna her father got killed in the Korean War and was a war hero."

Smoking a cigarette, Betty said," I put Dora in an orphanage against her will when she was about two or three. With her being black she would suffer hurt and pain and not be accepted by Dianna's white friends."

"About Jack Benson, I think you should marry him and take out a big insurance policy out on him. I'll have him killed and you will inherit the money he has in this estate. You have to push the idea of getting back with that nigger because it will hurt me politically and keep you from getting money and support for the business you can develop on your own. You'll be come very wealthy by marrying Jack."

"Daddy, Benson has a reputation of not being true to his women and he has thousands of them he sleeps with."

"Do not worry about that I might have him killed anyway so think about treating him nice for right now and act like you love him. You should see his estate. Just imagine yourself in charge of his business interests by marrying him."

A knock is heard at the door and one of Big Jim's house cleaners said Benson is at the door and coming to call.

Betty tries to hold her composure and not make an ugly face at Benson who dresses to please himself and the women he associates himself with and he is always ready to drink with his workers on the plantation.

"Don't you look mighty pretty today Betty. How are you doing? I came over to pay my respects and offer a million dollars to your reelection campaign Big Jim. I hope you can promise me the hand of your daughter to be my wife."

"I do not think so Benson because I heard you have a good reputation for stealing other men's wives."

Smiling at Big Jim and Betty. "A man is going to be a man and get drunk and womanize the young ladies because it's in my blood. I did that in my younger days. I'll do anything to win your lovely heart."

"Do not be so hard on Benson. All that wild life of courting four or five women is over and having poker parties with the fellows and boozing it up stopped years ago. He has not been put in jail in a long time for those types of immature things. It is a matter of fact Benson is a church man and teaches Sunday school lessons to the children."

"All you are doing is covering up for him. The last I heard he was stealing money from the church, courting the minister's wives and trying to baptize sinners to change their ways and your only a hypocrite yourself."

"I'll tell you what. Just give me time to know you and come see me do my first sermon before the whole congregation."

"The answer is no for right now but father said good things about you and I'll come to see you do your sermon at church but I will not tell you when but I do not trust you right now. It will take the time for me to think about it. I am involved with someone else right now and will not tell anyone who he is and besides I might not stay with my father. I only came to visit him and later I will leave in the morning."

"Who is the person you have been staying with? Your father and I would like to know."

"So you and Jack will have him killed. I will not tell anyone about him."

With Betty departing from her father's living to her former bedroom which had been used by Polly she quietly went into the bedroom and went to sleep.

"Benson find out who my daughter has been living with and have him killed if you want my daughter's hand in marriage. We have to stop all the opposition to keep him from marrying your future wife."

After saying that, Betty went up to her room and thought about the challenge and truthfulness to what Benson said. The thoughts of being wealthy by getting Benson's money thrilled her if it meant by any means possible to obtain what she needed to live a rich life style. With that in mine, Betty thought about it but did not fully want to commit herself to the promise but on the other hand if her father would keep his promise to kill him after she marries Benson it might be ok. Betty could inherit his money and his estate after he is killed, buried, and ten feet under the ground and maybe marry Mr. Williams.

As she went into the room anger came in her face as she thought about her father's relationship with Polly and the thought of her sleeping in the bed with Big Jim while Mable her and he were separated.

One Sunday Betty got dressed in her Sunday best to go see Jack Benson preach and just as she thought he was twenty- five minutes late giving his sermon. The people were upset and grew impatient waiting for him so she went back to his guest room to see what was taking him so long. A rage of anger appeared on her face as Betty looked though the key hole and saw Benson on the couch with one of the associate minster's wives having sex and having a good time. They did not think or care people waited for him to give the evening service and Benson and sister Wallace husband Melvin roamed through the church wondering where his wife was at came to the room.

He could not believe his eyes witnessing Pastor Benson in the art of making love to his wife. A rage of anger rushed to his head and his blood pressure went up so high he took his pills but there were not any left as he went to the water fountain trying to get a drink of water.

Other people came to see what was going on and they watched Pastor Benson in the heat of great love making get down with Mrs. Wallace. The smell of drugs lingered out the room and sounds of sweet love making echoed out the door, the crowd grew bigger, and they tried to restraint Billy from breaking the door down to kill Jack and his lover.

Someone shouted, "Call the police because minster Billy is not going to not ask for forgiveness and Benson will be a dead man when he and Sarah Wallace get through making love. He must have had a special key made to keep people from coming into the room because no one could get in it to stop them from making love.

Outside the door church members made bets on if Billy was going to kill Jack or not. When the police arrived, they could not open the door and Sarah and Benson went for a second round of love making and Billy went outside and attempted to find a ladder to climb up to the window which was twenty feet up from the ground to reach Benson to kill him who kept making love to his woman nonstop and Benson heard someone crawling up the ladder and got up and saw it was Billy trying to get to them and he opened up the window and pushed the ladder away from the building and Billy fell unable to get to where Benson made love to his wife.

Someone saw Billy fall and called an ambulance to come take him to the hospital and after all of his effort to kill Pastor Jack Benson it was all in vain. Benson and Sarah saw them take Billy to the hospital as they watched from the window, and finally came out of the room and Pastor Benson gave his sermon on being faithful to your wife. Sarah never came home to her husband and divorced Billy. After seeing that Betty had mixed emotions about marrying Jack Benson and he remained their pastor and the other minsters he trained were out there in the hallway shouting" Benson's getting his."

CHAPTER 44

J ohn is invited to speak at a rally for his election for United States
senator. The summer heat made sweat come from the fore heads
of the thousands of people both black and white Mississippians who
gathered in the three story stadium to hear their man of the hour
give them his message of brotherly love to heal the divisions of issues
which separated them from getting equal treatment before the law and
justice for all of them.

The people were displeased with the politics of Senator Big Jim
Wilson who took care of the wealthy to further his own interest.
Before John gave his speech a letter was sent to the owners of the
building- he could not use it because they have bad unsafe building
codes in it and it was being condemned. Realizing this unlawful
incident took place, John organized a group of citizens and they
picketed city hall and protested the denial of basic freedom of
speech rights imposed by the mayor Henry Richardson who caused
the demonstration. People did not like getting hit with eggs and
insulting curse words directed to their attention. When the mayor
called his firefighters officials and told them to spray water on the
demonstrators they held on to each other to avoid being knocked
to the ground by its great force. Newspapermen, women, and
television news reporters broadcasted the events and photographed
what took place. Women and children were injured taking part in the
demonstration.

To make events appear to be more dramatic, big German Shepard
dogs held by police officers let them loose to attack the demonstrators

and you could hear them scream as the dogs bit at their clothing and they hollowed as the water knocked them down. Sirens sounded loud as patrol cars raced to the scene to put down the unorderly demonstration and reporters operated their cameras. They did not miss taking pictures of the splattering of glass knocked out of car windows and food and packages in some of the cars were scattered on the streets because of the high force of the water hitting them.

Outside the jail demonstrators both black and white folks shouted, "We want John Carol out. Free John Carol," echoed from their voices as the sun gave many of them burns and beads of sweat poured down their heads into their clothes and the smell of perspiration gave out odors.

The men of power in the city of Jackson were in fear of the riot destroying the capital. When the mayor saw what the riot did to his city, he held a press conference and gave into John Carol's demands to give them time to fix up the building to have their rally. Many of the workers lost weight as a result of not eating their food which they felt was awful and then demands to see a doctor but they were ignored.

Clothing shops suffered the same damage because the water flooded their stores getting expensive dresses destroyed. Demonstrators resisted arrest and were carried to the dozens of patty wagons which took them to jail which became overcrowded. To keep united in their efforts, demonstrators kneeled in a non-violent manner and still the police shouted to each other to give no mercy and to keep order and put down civil unrest.

The jails became overcrowded and while they were there. John Carol and his followers signed an agreement to get the city to rehabilitate the building to use it as a community center for civic activities and political rallies. Some of the firefighters refused to continue shooting water at the demonstrators because they acted in a non-violent manner and tears came to their eyes to see they were shooting water at women, men, and children

CHAPTER 45

A date was set for John to speak to the farmers and people of Mississippi. The fellows in John Carol's organization volunteered to help rebuild the three story building. The mayor promised to send three installment payments of $100,000 dollars and many jobs were promised to both white and black people to do the work but as usual fights broke out when the black workers were paid less than the white workers, The black workers who could not read got less wages and also their black women.

Eventually John made it to the building and many people came especially the farmers and he said as he approached the podium,

"I wanted to speak to you about your getting bills passed to make life better for you and your families. Mississippi is a great state but it could be greater if the rich people shared its wealth with the poor black and white farmers."

Some white-collar worker went along with some of the issues John favored but some of those people worked for the big plantation owners who deprived the smaller farmers of getting good prices for their crops.

Trying to get momentum John said," I have to say I am fighting for the white and black farmers too. I want to see equal pay for women both black and white. I want to have the wealthier people pay higher taxes and contribute to programs for the poor."

Cheers of joy came from members of the crowd who wore armbands with picture of John on them.

"Why are you telling these people lies? You know you are interested in gaining money, fame, and good fortune from the people" Larry Nelson said as he strolled to the stage to talk.

"Another thing, this nigger is lying and does not give a dam about nothing but himself and all this talk about colored and white folks getting together is only lies."

At once John's body guards rushed the stage and grabbed him and he fought both them to the cheers of those people in the audience who did not like John.

"Who are you trying to give the impression John does not care about the people he wants to vote for him. He is a better candidate and he did not come from a rich background like Big Jim who only cares for the rich." One of his supports said.

The crowd in support of John Carol shouted praises of joy and approval as they saw their hero came back up to the podium to complete his speech and he said, "Look at what Big Jim has done to you by telling the local boys in power to take your land and cheat you out of your money when you try to get fair prices for your crops. You have taken out much money in loans that you owe Big Jim and his crooks so much money you do not obtain anything back to get you and your families things like clothes and items needed for the house whole. It brings tears to my eyes to see mothers both black and white seeing their kids die at such a young age because they could get no prenatal care. Big Jim sends all the jobs to companies who do not pay much taxes and does it by writing up legislation to support this evil deed and they repay him with big kickbacks of money to furnish his lavish parties he has at his estate in Washington, DC."

Not liking what took place, men sent to the rally rushed the podium and a fight took place. They tried to get John Carol but his bodyguards grabbed would be attackers before they could touch him and escorted him to another way out the building. Big Jim's men fired shots at them and one bullet hit John in his leg. The only thing he could do was hollow as the bullet traveled through it.

Rushing John to the hospital one of his bodyguards fell asleep at the wheel and crashed into an oncoming car and their car was damaged and it could not drive. Getting John out of the car, they flagged down a car and paid the man a hundred dollars to let them borrow his car and when he refused pulled out their guns and took the car by force.

John bled and it was difficult trying to stop it. Driving into a hospital that showed a sign said, "For Whites Only" they had no other choice but to go there.

"They cannot take any colored folks in the hospital," an admission's clerk said.

Taking out his big 45 colt, Jimbo Lightfoot said," I will blow out your heart if you do not take John into the emergency room to get this bullet out of his body!"

"Go to hell!" the clerk said, "Take John in here and lay him on the table!"

A doctor came into the emergency room and looked at John's legs, "It's turned gangrene. We will have to cut it off. He will die before 12.PM this evening."

Lightfoot grabbed him and said, "You did not even look at him so call another doctor."

"Who gave you the authority to be my boss? "The doctor said.

Shooting near his leg which nearly missed it, the doctor called for Dr. Paul Moody who was considered one of the best doctors in the state of Mississippi. Scrambling into the operating room Dr. Moody wore a confederate officer's top coat and he said, "What's the problem in here? You could have done this simple procedure of moving this bullet. His leg is not in gangrene."

Lightfoot pointed his gun at Dr. Moody and said, "This is the next black United States senator of Mississippi and a lot of people in this state are counting on you to save his life. Now take this bullet out of his leg or I'll have to serve life myself for killing you."

The other doctor was ordered out the room and by this time John sink into a deep sleep because he lost so much blood.

"The smell of blood makes me sick, "Lightfoot said, "Doctor can you give him a blood transfusion before he bleeds to death?"

Feeling John's head, Lightfoot cried out, "Can you get some blood from the supply you have?"

As Dr. Moody starts to operate, he said they had no blood for him because no Negro blood is part of their blood bank.

"Have the nurse call a hospital that has a colored blood bank."

"I'll do no such thing, "Lightfoot said, "We will get it from this hospital. Now tell me what type of blood type John has?"

"He has type B blood type," Dr. Moody shouted out loud.

"I'll be back with his type of blood type so prepare to operate on him.

"Which one of you has type B blood?"

"Why do you ask?" one of the people in the hallway said.

"There's a man in that room dying and needs type B blood. Can anyone in the hallway help him out?"

Everyone in the hallway was a white person. You could hear them whispering to each about whether to help John or not. Lightfoot pointed his gun at the person who said he had type B blood and directed him to go into the operation room at gun point.

"I will not give my blood to a nigger. You'll have to kill me first," he said,

As the man strolled away Lightfoot hit him in the head with his gun barrel and he dropped to the floor with Lightfoot catching him and dropping his body on the floor with blood coming down from the gun barrel with type B blood type which he was looking for that could help John survive.

"Take this fellow and get his blood. He is a little knocked out but he'll be ok," Lightfoot said, "Give some of his blood to John."

The procedure was done and they took John to another room. To pay for the medical bill, Lightfoot wrote out a check but it bounced and hospital officials sent the police to John's room because they feared he would leave without paying the bill. A loud noise sounded as footsteps could be heard and a beautiful woman by the name of Lilly showed the policeman John's hospital bill was paid by her and she was a doctor.

"It's hard to believe you are a colored female doctor. They passed you because you were a female and you probably had rich parents which made a big difference."

"You are just jealous. My parents worked hard for a living and my daddy worked as a porter for the railroad and momma cooked for rich white industrialist people who were sympathetic towards me getting a good education."

"I believe they passed you because of your skin color and felt sorry for you, "John laughed out loud.

Sitting on the bed, Dora said," Do not make fun of my mother. She only wants to help you with this election; the problem is that you turn people off when you speak to them"

"I do not think you know what you are talking about. I make a lot of sense when I talk to people."

Throwing a pillow at John Dora said, "You are not professional when you speak to voters. Every group of them are different."

"She is right John. Abraham Lincoln our dear 16th president changed his speech to accommodate the audience. If he knew the people in the audience of voters were proslavery, he tried not to say things which were anti-slavery and reflected on things which they wanted to hear to get their votes. You will have to learn this when speaking to the voters in this state."

John felt both Lilly and Dora gave him a hard time just for the fun of it because he is very ambitious and did not believe both of the ladies tried to help him.

"I know all the time he did not like women telling him what to do," Dora said, "momma we are wasting our time with him. I know he was not serious about correcting his mistakes."

"Dora I think we should go Lilly said, "I have to see some patients and a course you have to get to your lessons."

"Maybe John will realize we are two people who are concerned about Mr. Know it all, "Lilly said in disgust.

CHAPTER 46

As John looked out the window Lilly and Dora left him thinking about what they attempted to tell him. Dora his daughter does not know who he is and Lilly a doctor seemed to care if he became the first African American senator from the state of Mississippi because he played around in his last bid to become senator and did not take the election seriously and let many people down.

At the campaign headquarters on Holly Street in Jackson, Mississippi he spoke to his campaign workers Josh White and Josh said to him.

"Maybe the ladies are correct. I looked at your tapped lectures and you did not look too good when talking to the voters. You sounded too country and you cannot speak to these audiences in the same pitch of voice. There is a certain type of style you develop when talking to the people, "Josh said as he ate his sandwich and looked at the opinion polls which was in the newspapers about the upcoming election.

"See what this columnist is saying about you as he read to John: "He looks like a country boy who does not dress professional and he likes to smack his chewing gum making a loud noise and he cannot provide documentation when he makes statements about the economy or various issues facing our great state of Mississippi."

Grabbing the papers John shouts in a heated rage. "Those people do not know me and they will say bad things about me to make me look bad to the people who will elect me the next US senator from this state."

Josh laughed and said, "I am your friend and I must tell you some of the people in your campaign are saying the same things about you."

Prancing the floor and shaking his head in different directions John said, "Why didn't anyone say something about this to me? I thought we were working for a common cause to help the people."

Josh by now got more serious and poured sugar and milk into his cup of coffee and as he talked he sipped the coffee through his lips.

"John watch yourself and be careful because when you talk about me so much it make me angry and upset."

Strolling on the hardwood floor and trying to eat his lunch Josh said, "I am your friend and a person who loves you and will help you with the rough problems in your life and give you wisdom and good guidance. We cannot force you to get help but if you want our people to elect someone who cares about them this is one of the best reasons to let Lilly to help polish off your social skills and win the admiration of the poor people both black and white people who need better living conditions for them and their families."

Knocking on Lilly's door, John was ready to take lessons reluctantly and speak Standard English.

Opening the door Dora shouted, "What do you want? You're not serious enough so go home!"

Looking at her in disbelief John said, "Now look young lady I did not come all the way up here to go back home so let me speak with Lilly. I want her to help me greet the voters much better than I have been doing."

Dora still slammed the door in John's face and went upstairs and studied her lessons.

"Who was that? "Lilly said.

"That was that fake John Carol. I told him to go home."

"Why did you do that? It seems as if he is very serious and wants to learn some positive things about speaking to the voters."

Running out to the front of her house she did not see John's car and got in her car to follow him and get him to come back to the house before going to her office to greet her patients. Loud music came out of John's car as Lilly spotted him driving towards his campaign headquarters.

"Who in the hell is blowing their horn at me. I hope it's not the police! "John shouted out loud.

Realizing it was not the police, John stopped his car and parked on a side street.

"Well what made you get out of your precious good looking house and came to insult me to like your daughter who despises me? I drove too many miles to your middleclass world to get help after campaign aides said it would be in my best interest to have you teach me things about the voters."

Leaning against the car Lilly said, "You cannot blame Dora for feeling this way about you. She is not convinced you want to win this election. Most black folks Dora comes into contact with do not want to be anything but janitors and waiters working in the restaurants and country clubs owned by white folks."

"I did not realize you were so tall Lilly and you look real cute. When could we begin our lesson?"

Taking out a cigarette, "Come by the house right now and we can start immediately."

'Will the same thing take place when I come to take lessons?"

Shaking his hand.

"I'll make sure my daughter gives you her upmost respect. She might volunteer to be a person in the audience and ask you questions just to keep you sharp."

Now John one of the things you have problems with is keeping eye contact with the people you talk with. This is something you must stop. You cannot rub your head when talking to important people."

"Lilly that's a habit I have had since I was a young boy.'

"Well you'll have to stop it

"You say a lot of uh's when talking. When you talk like that it makes you look bad and you have to research the situation to stay relevant to your audience."

"What can I do to stop it? I did not know I looked like this when speaking to people..."

"When coming to an uh just pause and not use it."

"Start practicing this now as we talk. Just pause when you are about to say uh."

"Sometimes you like to smoke cigarettes when you talk with the important people you meet."

"It might hurt you at times depending if the person who is interviewing you smokes too."

"Lilly I smoke to keep from getting nervous. I cannot kick the habit."

"If you knew that person does not smoke don't smoke in his presence. You don't want to make the interviewer mad to say something negative about you. Many of the people who will vote for you read their columns and articles; you have to make a great impression on the people."

"Where's all that loud music coming from? We can barely hear each other talking."

Going into Dora's room Lilly said, "Why are you trying to keep me from helping John? I will not tolerate that kind of behavior from you."

Throwing her book against the wall. "Why waste your time with him? You are ignoring me to help him and I do not appreciate it."

Trying to settle her down. "You have to give a person a chance. We are not perfect and he has realized his mistakes and want to help the people in this state and he needs our support. You'll only discourage him from wanting to accomplish anything with his life and the people he will represent."

"The conditions of the people in our neighborhood have not changed. Politicians only come around when the want you to vote for them and after that you never see them again."

Sitting next to Lilly Dora said, "I'll be watching him but it's hard to trust politicians. They say what they want you to hear."

Taking a leaflet out of her purse Lilly said, "Look what he wants to do. We need all of these things done in our community and he is the only person who wants to do something positive in our neighbors. How you can sit up here and get mad at someone who wants to help our people live a decent life. Come and help him. He is not such a bad guy"

Reluctantly Dora said," OK I'll help you but the minute I see that he is not for real about winning; I will stop working in his campaign."

CHAPTER 47

This is Election Day and news reporters have come to the city of Jackson, Mississippi to report on which candidate would win the election. His campaign manager Josh White approached him and he said, "Our workers are unhappy and are threatening to not work because they have not been paid. They are all leaving their polling places to speak with you about getting their money."

Strolling towards the window John stood motionless and tried to think of what he would say to the workers who worked so hard to get him in the position to run for United States Senator. His mind drifted to his humble beginnings and the struggles he faced and the adventures of uncertainty kept coming into his life. He dreamed and envisioned a life for both black and white people living in harmony with each other. John thought about his two kids he had not seen in more than twenty years and how dearly he wanted to know where they were at. Maybe someday he'll sit at the dinner table with both of his daughters and they all would rejoice for this wonderful moment in their lives.

"I know you are angry about not getting paid but there was probably a mistake made on the delivery of your worker's checks. They were supposed to be here at this time with your checks,"

Two fellows by the names of Red and Dirty rushed towards John Carol's campaign headquarters with the checks from the people who supported him. They are shooting at the men and shot at his headquarters. The bullets from the men who probably were hired by Big Jim did not care who they hit with their gunshots, it was two cars filled with men, and they shot at the workers with no sympathy not to hurt everyone.

"Come back in here! Said Mquilda whose appearance presented a tall ghostly six-foot image.

"Do not worry, they will not shoot me, God is on my side."

Waving a white towel, she tried to get them to stop but they would not listen to her and suddenly she kneeled on her knees and said a silent prayer.

"Tears are falling from her eyes and a smile is on her face and she knows death is going to take her from here, "John cried out loud.

Before he knew it she fell died from the gun shots.

When the workers saw that they rushed the car and did not care about getting hit by gun fire and dragged the men out of their two vehicles and beat them beyond recognition.

In an hour thirty cars took off down the street and they were late model Cadillac's.

"I hear a lot of noise, "John yelled out loud.

Their cars stopped because someone placed locks in the tires and sugar in the engines.

"Be courageous, "John said, "They want to keep us from getting to the people to explain what our plans are to help them overcome their hurt for being neglected. We will march through town and visit the people to let them know we are on their side and we stand for equality and a thunderous applause came from his supporters both black and with a little discontentment from some of their supporters.

"What if they attack as we march through the streets. You know the police will not do anything to stop this injustice if we are attacked and intimidated by the forces who do not want you to win."

One worker who was white shouted, "You want us to be nonviolent but I do not think they will be nonviolent."

"You cannot act in a violent manner because meeting violence with violence achieves nothing."

"Well I am going to carry my gun with me. I will not let them kill me just for standing up for my rights."

Some of John's workers came later to the meeting and said they will ride in their cars at a slow pace. They did not fare any better because people who were against them threw eggs at them but they continued to march and hold hands and sang "We shall overcome and did not let the threats deter them from their goals. However, regardless of what John and his workers did to campaign to win the election Big Jim's workers passed out anti information on John Carol, which were lies about him stealing money out of the prisoner's funds from the people who supported him.

Lilly I had problems trying to vote, "John said, "I hope the people who oversee black people get the right to vote are on their job in this matter because we need every vote to win this election."

"You and our workers cannot let the threats to keep you from doing God's will because he has brought us too far now, Believe in God and he will help you win this election."

As they marched down the streets a young black girl scrambled up to John and said, "They are making us take literacy test and many of us were turned away from the polls."

Lilly said, "John continue with the election and I'll go and see if we can call the election officials to come and stop this from taking place."

"Ok Lily do what can we do to let the voting officials know about Big Jim's people breaking the federal laws on voting."

Going to the federal building a man who was a security officer stopped her and said, "Black folks have to go through the colored only section. If you do not obey I'll call the police and have you escorted off the premises."

"Man it's noisy in here and I feel very embarrassed going through the colored section of the building and I feel I should go into the building all the people go through

Grabbing her the security officer said, "Ok I'll have to physically throw you out of here. The nerve of you trying to dictate to me what you're going to do in my building."

Lilly manages to get to Judge Fast Roberts a district Judge in the city of Jackson, Mississippi. Lilly stopped him and said, "They are making us take literacy tests to see if we can read or write and that is illegal. Could you do something about it? If you do not, John stands a chance of losing the election?"

"I support Big Jim Wilson and I cannot do it. You have to wait until the election is over and maybe he might win but not against Big Jim and he never loses when running for reelection or a new office."

Out of curiosity, Big Jim visited John Carol's campaign headquarters and as he greets John he said, "You should be out there trying to win this election. You are too over confident."

"You know John you're much younger than me but I bet I can beat you in an Indian wrestling match. All this campaigning is going on and very little fun. To boost morale on both of our workers they need something to take their minds off of campaigning."

"Let's bet $500 dollars I can beat the socks off of you!"

"We can use the money "Lilly said as she smiled at John.

"Now we do not have the time for this horse playing around. We have to win this election."

"You'll just chicken. "I thought you had some backbone in you. Let your people see what you are made of."

Chants from his supporters shouted, "Do it John!" "Kick his ass."

John saw the look in his supporters' faces as he strolled up to in the table to take Big Jim on who never loses at anything he competes in even if it meant losing.

People placed bets in the large room and great intense and excitement could be seen on their faces. John's pride was at stake and Big Jim's reputation was always on the line because the only thing he knew in life was to play for keeps and win at all costs if it meant doing something to make sure he was guaranteed to win.

As John sat down the referee, one of Big Jim's managers said, "Ok gentlemen hold your hands together and when I say go try to be the first one to push the other person's hands down and I will say stop when the winner has the other hand down on the table. The referee said go and the two men tried to put the other's person's hand on the table. Every time Big Jim seemed as if he would win John managed to push his hand off the table. The white teeth of the many people could be seen clearly as they shouted for their leader.

"Come on John! "Lilly shouted," Keep on working even though he outweighs you by ninety pounds but you can beat him!"

Finally John pushes his hands down and he is getting ready to be declared the winner and he spots a white man from Big Jim's camp getting ready push Lilly out the way and John turns around and hits Rugget Larson in his mouth and a big fight starts between Big Jim's men and John's supporters.

Outside a huge burning cross is in the back yard of John's campaign headquarters burning and the flames from it catch on to other buildings and black smoke emerged into the air and people shouted at each other and called one another names and the worst type of Mississippi southern cussing echoed from the mouths of the people fighting each other.

During the fight newspapers lying in cabinets got destroyed by Big Jim's men because some of the editors wrote columns trying to favor the rights of black people to vote and hold public office, go to integrated schools, form their own political parties and encouraged northern people from white ivory league colleges to join black collegians to register black field hands to vote. This would only stir up hatred and cause more problems and the southern way of life would be changed forever in the state of Mississippi and Big Jim's people were committed not to let this take place. Most of the white newspapers supported Big Jim and his people because he influenced advertisers to buy adds in their newspapers and they only printed articles in their newspapers where they saw black people committing a crime and they did not have to live in the state of Mississippi to be written about in a negative manner.

Those people who were too small to fight took chairs and swing them at each other and a lot of the beer bottles were thrown at people causing much injuries. Big Jim grabbed two workers and pushed them through a window. Instead of police officers answering, the call to put out the fire, Mack the firefighters saw all of the fighting going on and said to his commander Steve Davenport, "There is no fire but a lot of people fighting each other. What can I do to stop them?"

"Just shoot the water on everyone that is fighting until they stop hitting each other."

The water knocked down anyone with the force of a fast traveling train until they kept on hollowing to make them stop shooting the huge flow of water at them. Some of them hid behind desks and chairs only to be carried to different directions. When the firemen stopped shooting the water at the demonstrators

Big Jim said, "Well that's enough of all of this playing we have done on Election Day so let's go."

When Big Jim and his men got into their cars to leave the area all of their tires were flat which was done by the black citizens who lived near the area where John's headquarters were located.

"I cannot bring you any tires sir."

"Why can't you. I am running in an election and my people need tires for their cars and trucks."

"Sir I do not know if I have your sizes for all of your cars and trucks. I have a friend who owns a tire shop."

"Call him and have him bring two big trailers of tires of all sizes. There's one thousand dollars in it for you if you handle this for me. Call in the police and have them come and protect us." Big Jim said.

In ten minutes two huge trucks came roaring to the street where Big Jim and his people waited to get a set of tires. His people struggled to put the different tires on their cars and at the same time anti Big Jim people threw eggs and all types of articles at them.

Demonstrators shot a couple of shots into the air and one of the truck drivers shouted at them and many of the rioters scattered scrambling in different directions backing away from the truck drivers try- ing to put the tires on their cars.

"Here come more police so let's get away from here before we are arrested and taken to jail! "John shouted at his workers. We still have an election to win."

While heading to another part of the black community, Big Jim told his workers he wanted to stop and make a speech to try to get more votes from the black wards. As a group of black citizens gathered to hear Big Jim speak he said," I do not have to introduce myself because you already know who I am. I am asking for your support in this election and as you know I am proposing to have new houses built in this neighborhood because I have had my people come back and tell me about terrible conditions you are living under. I cannot make a good living for you if you do not vote for me."

"All you do is come into our community when there's an election but you'll get back into office and forget about us."

Before any trouble started Big Jim and his people left the black areas of Jackson.

"You never did anything for the black famers like seeing to it they get equal opportunity with their white neighbors or colored people could get a chance to attend quality schools with qualified teachers to teach our kids," Lilly shouted out using a bullhorn to get her message across to the people. In addition, you preach anti-segregation when you sleep with black women. As the election results came in Big Jim ordered his people back to his headquarters in the city of Jackson, Mississippi because the polling places were closing.

"There is more campaigning to do John. Take some campaign workers down to the other wards where they do not know you. If you get their votes you might win the election. You have not been down to their ward to seek votes, "Lilly said as she watched the election results on television.

"The electric is off!" Lilly cried out. Now we will not know who is winning or if the race is close! "Lilly shouted at John.

"No my place is with you and the rest of the workers. On the table is a big bottle of wine. Get it out and drink to the winner."

"Don't count your eggs too quickly. Go down the area where you are not known and talk to the people."

By this time John said, "Ok fellows let's call it a day and party"

Turning on their car radio, all of them took out bottles of wine and did not go to the precincts, which could decide the winner of the election but later that morning when they woke up from their drunkenness; John heard the news on the radio that he lost.

"Godamit I took this election for granted in a playful manner. I must make amends with the people."

"I told you to go campaign in the precincts where the voters could either vote for you are Big Jim because he did some positive things for the people by having them get money to fix up their homes. He did it to steal votes from you at the last minute."

It was six twenty three in the morning and John looked at the morning sky showing a bluish light grey color on such a morning of defeat,

"John said, "Look at the trees that appear to be stretching to the sky showing nothing but silhouettes and I can see a pinkish glow coming up in the east," as he faced defeat in agony.

"I cannot face my people and I've disappointed the people to do what was right who depended on me to win this election. I am going away to take a rest. I cannot face anyone at this time. Please forgive me. Strolling out the campaign headquarters he tried to leave without saying anything and Lilly held him by his hand and said. "Come back John and be ready to fight for that senate seat. You have to mature because you were going up against a fierce competitor in this election who does know what it means to lose an election."

CHAPTER 48

Peter Carol laid in bed and the smell of flowers lit up the room. Nurse Lucy Grable is in the room checking Peter's pulse and her eyes appeared to be worried.

"Where's my wife Sarah? She said she would be here. I need her very badly and do not want to die without seeing her."

"Now Peter you are not well and should not be thinking about dying but trying to get well to go home."

"Holding the cross with Christ on it, Peter tries to smile and he said, "I have a weak heart but I have a strong spirit to live and be with my life."

There is much noise in the area of the reception room and Sarah is arguing with an administrative clerk by the name of Mark Bradly who said, "Miss. your husband is going to have to be removed from the room. We only take patients into this hospital who have insurance."

"There must be a problem because Peter has always come here for treatments and his insurance paid for it. See where he made his mark every time he came here for treatments."

"This is a misunderstanding because Big Jim got a bill passed in the senate which said people without insurance cannot be treated here. Without the insurance, he has to be sent home or to a hospital which will treat him."

"That's why my son must run again and this time beat the socks off of Big Jim. He lies to the people all the time and does anything to get the colored man votes and does not intend to keep his promise."

"Another thing, "Bradly said as he held his pants up with suspenders said, "According to Big Jim's new bill affecting this hospital he is in the white section of the patient room. Now poor white folks can come to this hospital but they must be given more priority then you according to the Accommodations Act ordered by Senator Wilson."

"My father is lacking blood and is weak. Will you give him a blood transfusion, "Sarah said, "He will die if you do not give him one."

"This is not a fine time for you to comb your hair and fill your mouth full of food instead of trying to get him some blood because he is he needs more of it."

Putting her arms around Sarah and he said. "I am sorry because we do not have much blood for the colored patients because they separate the white folk's blood from the colored ones."

"Is there something I can do to help Peter," Betty said, "How are you doing Sarah and what seems to be the problem. I hope I can help you with this problem."

"Well here's my old enemy Bradly. Who are you messing with this time. The Carol's and I go back a long way when they share cropped on my Grandfather's land. They have known me since I was a little girl and I do not want nothing wrong to happen to them."

"You know the rules your father laid down on his new policy concerning colored patients and the rules must be followed according to Big Jim's instructions."

Taking the rules and regulations pertaining to the bill to the hospital officials Betty shouted to the top of her voice, "Now look the Carols played a role in raising me as a young girl and Sarah fed me from her breast when I was a little girl and I have the same blood type as John so Peter take the blood from me. It will not kill you. If you think that colored people have contaminated blood!"

The smile disappeared from Bradly's face and he said, "I think we can arrange something like that. I'll get the nurses ready to help with the transfusion."

"Why are you getting the telephone book for?"

"I am going to have the newspapers down here and television news crew to witness the first time a white woman gave the same type of blood to a colored man."

Seeing much publicity would come from the white and black viewing audience Bradly's said, "Ok I do not want folks knowing I gave blood from a white woman to a colored man so I'll have one of my nurses give Peter some blood from our blood bank."

"That's ok I'll go and get some of this type of blood from the white section but promise me you will not tell Big Jim and the head of the hospital Mr. Berry Potts. He'll have me fired if he found out and another thing why is it Peter has not had any medicine ever since he's been in this hospital?"

"We tried to give it to him but Peter is stubborn and does not trust anyone."

Knocking on the door when Betty is talking Dora tiptoes in and watches Betty complain to the hospital officials about the way they are treating the black patients especially Peter who looked as if he could not stay alive for a long time.

"Who are you?" Dora said, "I have never seen you before up close. I remember seeing you at the basketball games with that no good enemy of mine Dianna. I hate her and compete with her in many basketball tournaments. You must be her mother."

As Dora is talking Dianna notices the incision Dr. Jamison made on Dora's neck.

"Wait a minute. That incision looks like the same one which is on my neck too."

Looking strangely at Dora Betty said, "You are my daughter I left at the orphanage."

Pushing Betty away from her, Dora said "You got your nerve trying to say you hated me so you are sorry for deserting me. I needed to know why my mother hated me so badly. I wanted to know what my mother and father looked like."

"Morris said he would come and pick me up and take me back home. I did not expect to see you here telling me you are my mother. Prove it because I always thought Lilly was my real mother. She never said I had a mother who was a part of my life and I do not know who my father is."

"Do not cry Dora, "Betty said," I put you in an orphanage because you were going to experience nothing but hell with you being colored and your sister Dianna would be treated better then you because she was born white."

"I cannot believe you are trying to make up for the hurt you caused me. You knew where I was at but you chose to deny me because I was colored. You must be crazy if I am going to have something to do with you. Get out of my life and don't call me. A mother would never go off and leave their own daughter but you did and I always went to sleep wondering who was my mother," Dora said with tears falling down her face.

Dora quietly strolled out the hospital room in a disgusted mood and pushed people out the way at the same time and those people did not know why she acted this way.

Don't take this too hard," Lilly said, "Betty you are Dora's real mother and as she grew up it shocked her to know you were white and she saw you with her sister and you never tried to identify yourself when you saw the incision on her neck and did not tell Dianna Dora was her sister. For four years you watched your two daughters compete against each other with much envy jealousy, and hate in state basketball games with knowledge Dianna's was Dora's sister. It will take time for the girls to realize they are sisters and need each other."

As Sarah, Lily, and Dora talk with each other Sarah looked at her husband who slowly breathed but managed to open his eyes and he spoke barely being able to breathe.

"Peter please try not to talk. You are too weak. The doctor wants you to rest and not say anything. "His wife said to him as she held his hand.

"It does not seem I am going to make it. I am getting tire and my heart is failing me. I want you, Betty, Dianna, Dora, and my son John Carol Junior to come together. You need each other."

As Peter speaks, Dianna comes into the room to see a grandfather she has never met before or her father John Carol Junior but only as a baby at the age of one years old. Some of her basketball teammates told Dianna she needed to go to the hospital to see a relative who was gravely ill.

"Can all of you come together and hold hands and pray?"

Sarah held Dora's hand and Betty held Lilly's hand and Dora feeling much resentment chose not to hold anyone's hand at all especially Betty's or Dianna as Peter her grandfather said, "I see you all are still harboring resentment towards your mother Dora. This is a time for healing the hatred you have for your mother. You cannot bring back the times when you could not see her or wish for the times when you wanted her back when you achieved success in school or when the holidays were here and you wanted to celebrate it with her or but you both have each other now and can look towards a future with her now. Life is full of ups and downs but we have to forgive each other and overcome the pain which caused that hurt and move towards better life styles. God wants us to love one another and to let by gones be by gones."

"Peter you have talked too much so get some rest."

"He is not breathing "Sarah said, "I think he is dead."

A doctor came into the room and took his stethoscope and listened to his heart and said, "Misses Carol your husband is dead and now he is free to go home to his father who created him from a child to adulthood."

A tall looking man came into the room with smelly clothes on and it was John Carol Junior.

"Daddy do not die, you'll be alright. This is your son John so do not die on me."

Sarah said, "John he's gone and you should have been here for your father. He constantly asked for you but you never came back home to see your family. You just disappeared into nowhere."

"But momma I was fighting myself. I gave up and felt I let many people down including everyone in this room."

"Well I got to tell you something. John this girl you have been arguing with is your daughter Dora and this is your little childhood playmate Betty and you were with her at the hotel but you were too drunk that night you did not recognize her. Of course you know Lilly and she is the one who adopted Dora when Betty placed her in the orphan home."

John said, "Why does it take the death of my father to bring us all together to see the reality of how we are all related to each other."

At this moment Sarah became the spokeswoman for talking about family matters and said, "You have another daughter that you do not know but I will tell you about her. Another thing she is white."

"How in the hell did I become the father of a white and black daughter?" John said as he took the covers and pulled them over Peter's head and closed his eye lids.

After the trauma of Peter's death and relatives seeing each other and sharing the death of a love one, Lilly said, "Let's have a family union and us as a family can get to know one another."

The family members strolled out the door with nothing to be enthusiastic about but Betty said, "Let's drop that sort of thing. I'll try to get in touch with you in couple of weeks from now. It will take time to overcome what has been taken place here today. I'll never get to know my daughter because she hates me."

"Lilly I know the people around here do not like race mixing of any type but it will take time to accept each other but we are relatives and we will one day live as kin folks." Betty said.

"I do not think so!" Dora cried out, "My real mother is Lilly because she raised me from a small child and did not abandoned me to another family or orphanage because of my race or being with her would bring shame to her. I do not want to be with my real mother. She does not have anything coming from me."

Betty tried to hold Dora and said, "I was not there for you when you were a small child but you were in my heart. I kept clips of when you became a star baseball athlete and attended the baseball games and cheered silently when you tried hard to rally your teammate to win against impossible odds."

"I do not need you to tell me this now and it's too late to make up for the times you should have been there for me."

"The money you received mysteriously came from me, "Betty said to John, "I wanted to help your father because I am a wealthy person. I wanted your father to win this election and I did what I needed to do so you could pay your workers and they could help you get a great amount of votes."

"One of the things you never realized is my father gave out thousands of perks to people in your ward so they would vote for him. Big Jim threatened to cut off aid to their area such as money to repair homes, and scholarships for our seniors going to a black college, and promised they would get increases in their welfare checks if he did get more votes than you. He beat you with the power to give promises to people who said they would support him in this election. You did not stand a chance. If you would have set up organizations in their wards, they could not easily be bought by my father but you chose to do it your way and ignored people who told you to set up organization in that area."

CHAPTER 49

"Your father wanted to see you before closing his eyes," Sarah said to him as they made their way to John's car.

"I could not tell Peter you lost the election because he would give up his desire to live. Your father always dreamed of you becoming a lawyer a doctor, senator, or a schoolteacher. He wanted you to become something greater them himself. He did not want you hurt by getting close to Betty when you were kids because when the white kids get older they have to follow in the ways of a southern prejudice culture which is staying with their own white people and the friendships you had with each other is over."

"But momma we always enjoyed dinner at the Wilson's Christmas parties when Roscoe, Big Jim's father allowed us to come and share Christmas with them and white folks came too."

"Son you must understand those people owed Big Jim's father money and they would not dare offend him and avoid coming to his Christmas parties every Christmas and plus they owed Big Jim money too. That's why he knew they would come because he gave them a long time to pay him back."

"Did Big Jim like his father by telling us to come to the Christmas party?"

"He did not like it but Roscoe Wilson was master of the plantation and Big Jim did not defy his father's rules."

"Why did all of this change when Christmas time came when Roscoe died?"

"Well Big Jim changed all of that when his father died and as you see we have not been invited up to the big house ever since."

Big Jim resented his father giving Kirby gifts without him working for it and he felt this would make his son lazy if things were given to him. When Roscoe died, Kirby could not enjoy the lavish life style of not working on the plantation like the black kids he played with. Big Jim did not care if Kirby got sun tanned and made him work in the cotton field from sunup to sundown. That's one of the reasons he resented Big Jim and he let Betty and Sandy have their own way and groomed them to become what southern ladies with a higher class background showed having the last name of Wilson.

"Now father did not like for you to go to town with Roscoe when he took the kids and John to town because you came back crying when you could not go into the stores and restaurants and had to get your food and eat it in the back of the place." Betty said.

"Before you arrived Peter said slowly, "Make sure my son graduate from college and make something of himself."

"With you having him work in the fields he did not get a good education, "Sarah said, "At least the hospital officials will not have to move his body to the black section of the hospital. This man fought for his country in World War 1 and he cannot be treated in the same manner as the white folks in this hospital."

John Carol did not do any work or thought about what he wanted to do at Peter's funeral and some white folks knew and loved him might come to his funeral.

"He looks as if he's not dead," Lilly said, "Now he is resting in peace."

To everyone's surprise, Betty came to the funeral with Dianna and Dora attended also. As usual no one knew where John was at but the funeral went on as planned.

"There's your sister Dianna "Betty said, "I would like to introduce you to her."

"I do not need no introduction because I met her when I competed against her when our basketball teams went to state. I do not want to meet her. She thinks she can beat me in basketball. I want to go home," Dianna said.

Lilly tried to get Dora's attention and said to her, "There is your sister Dianna. You have played against her basketball team many times but you did not know you two were related at that time."

"I do not like her because she and I competed against each other and I grew to dislike her and plus she is a white girl. I will not have anything to do with her."

Dressed in a black morning dress for a funeral Sarah said to Dora as the choir sang a religious song which was Peter's favorite said, "Now Dora Peter would not like the thought of his two granddaughters hating each other at his funeral. This is a time to cherish his memory among our family members."

When both of the sisters were told about their relationship as sisters they just stirred at each other and tried not to say anything. A white fellow came down the aisle and went directly to Sarah with a bouquet of flowers in it and left the funeral as it was beginning to start.

"Sarah who sent those flowers to you?" Lilly said, "I bet it was from your son John."

Holding up the card tied around the flowers Sarah said, "I cannot read it. You may have to."

Being very curious to read the card, "Lilly said, "This is from Big Jim and the card said, "I am sorry I could not make the funeral. I flew back to Washington to be sworn in. Your husband and I go back to the days of when I was a kid. I never got alone with him because of my ant-integration attitudes but I am very sorry about Peter. If you want to sell your property, please let me know we are going to get it anyway."

"That no good bastard, "Lilly said, "He does not know when to do something unless he stands to make money from it."

"Look at the beautiful flowers they have placed on the casket Dianna said, "I never got to know my Grandfather. What type of man was he?"

John said," Your grandfather did not approve of me getting to know your mother. Southern society said it was not right for black and white folks to fall in love with each other."

Dianna wanted to know more about her father and said, "Why not. I just don't understand so please tell me more. I only heard about this history of southern life styles from my grandfather Big Jim."

Holding Dianna John said, "Because your mother and I were different races and your grandfather Big Jim would not have his daughter being courted by a colored boy who shared cropped on his land."

"Stop filling that girl's head with a lot of lies." We are supposed to be mourning the death of your grandfather, "One of the people in the row of visitors coming to the funeral said, "Have respect for something than your own needs." Someone shouted at them who knew Peter and love him very dearly.

Instead of getting into the funeral car, John strolled away from them saying he would visit his mother in the future. They could see the tears in his eyes as they brought his father's casket out to the team of mules pulled a wagon by which Peter requested in his will.

"This was in his will to be carried to his maker being placed in a wagon pulled by mules. He was a simple humble person who lived a decent life and he felt all people should treat each other like brothers instead of this racial hatred he saw and experienced growing up in the state of Mississippi. He saw how the schools for black children were in bad shape and the teachers did not have good teaching credentials like the white ones. That's why he wanted our son to be someone he could be proud of," Sarah said.

When they got to the cemetery angry white citizens picketed the cemetery because they did not want Peter buried in the white section where their relatives were buried. Before you knew it, John and Peter Carol's relatives were fighting white folks who did not want colored folks to be buried with the white people on the same plot of land.

Approaching the police officers Lilly said, "Officer Louis Miles we cannot bury Peter in that colored section because they do not keep the area clean and it's located near a river and it floods into the cemetery. The caskets are lifted to the top of the ground because of the flooding and many bodies of the relatives have been lost because the river washed them away. We do not want this to happen to Peter."

"We will stay until my husband is buried in a part of the cemetery where his casket will not be washed away."

A news reporter came to the scene and asked questions and reported what was going on and their stories appeared in the evening news. With that taking place, waves of people came to the cemetery and supported Sarah to have her husband buried where the river would not carry his casket away. The group of people came together and sympathetic white people prayed together and sing and different churches provided food and blankets for the people who wanted to see justice come to the Carol family to have Sarah's husband buried in a better part of the cemetery.

John scrambled down the road and he flagged down a driver after being refused by many drivers traveling in the direction the cemetery was located with food for the demonstrators.

"That's my father they are talking about and I would like to know if I can go with you?" John said.

"That will not be a problem sir because this is a black and white issue because both races must fight together to end the evils of racism and bigotry in Mississippi, 'Maggie Watson said, "I am gay and experienced the same problems of prejudice because I want to be with a woman who is the same sex as I. We have to keep everything quiet about our relationship. We want to marry each other but no states will grant us a license."

Shaking her hand, John said," Thanks a lot we will somehow overcome the perils of discrimination and bigotry in this matter."

Approaching the site where people are demonstrating and singing civil rights songs, John saw a big crew of people praying and eating and trying to keep encouraging each other but arguments broke out among them too as to what strategy would be used to get Peter buried.

The heat became overbearing and the conversations of many people responded to each other as the police formed a barricade around the entrance to the cemetery and sent messages to the protesters they had to come out of it and bury Peter in the black section of the cemetery.

More state troopers converged on the cemetery dressed in full anti- demonstration attire complete with helmets and hard plastic shields, billy clubs, and carrying canisters containing gas used to disperse the protesters.

A message was sent to them with a message from Governor Bill Morrison who said they could not bury Peter in the white section of the cemetery because he did not want to have a blood baths to take place with the opposing groups shooting at each other. Already several people had been injured and Dora was not hurt at first but when one of the police hit Dora for getting smart with him, Dianna hollowed at him, "Do not hit my sister!" and took a brick and hit him in the face and he let Dora go and he and the other protestors grabbed the both of them and took them to safety.

"Why did you do that Dianna I thought you hated me."

"You are my sister even if you are colored. I realized we are family and must stick together"

When Sarah announced the good news they could bury Peter in the white part of the cemetery there was nothing but clapping and praying. Peter was buried after hours of people fighting each other over this precious right to be buried in a part of the cemetery where the river water would not overflow into it which might raise up his casket.

While John was there Betty and Lilly tried to speak with each other but it was difficult because of the conflicts which came into their lives. As usual John said he was going away and strolled taking slow steps from the group saying he had to take care of some business and he would keep in touch with them.

Tears fell from both sisters when John scrambled down the road.

Both sisters gave him their addresses and told him to write them. They felt too many years passed and all the hating might one day stop. Both of them resented him but they saw he was their father and had full of love for the both of them.

CHAPTER 50

As John strolls down the road he passes a group of state officials who escorted men to a state facility if they could not show identification papers showing they worked.

"May I see your identification papers? "One of the officials said, "You cannot walk the roads of the estate of Mississippi without showing proof you have identification papers and a job."

"Sir, show me a law saying you have the right to do this."

"I guess we have to take you to the facility to work off your fine."

"I was not aware of my fine,' John said as the police officer approached him he hits one of them in the mouth and scrambled down a hill into a bunch of trees. They fired gunshots at him but the thought of dying kept John trying to escape them.

His heart pumped and he breathed large breaths of air. The tree limbs hit him in his face as the state men fired at him. John managed to climb up a hill covered with rocks and as the two men climbed it they fired their guns at him but John threw rocks at them causing them to get behind trees located on the hill. Behind him John spotted a beehive and he took it and threw it at them and they turned around and darted back down the hill at rapid speeds and hollowing as the bees took deadly aim at their skin and stung them. Looking at the men stride down the hill made John talk to himself...

"The thought of them thinking they could catch me and make a slave of me. They got their nerve!"

This did not stop the state men from starting all over again trying to catch John. They needed men to work on state projects and got paid two hundred dollars a person if they brought men to a facility where they could work for several months at a time until they satisfied their debts owed to creditors.

Trying to get some sleep in a cave, John looked at a big shadow standing over him and it was a huge grizzly bear getting ready to attack him. The bear grabbed John and he stood up six feet tall and squeezed him and John yelled out loud, "Godamit put me down. I do not want your babies. Bear you must be crazy!"

With a lot effort John was thrown out of the cave and he made a loud growl at him and pounded his chest with his big paws. By this time John crawled under some weeds and trees to hide from the bear. When the state men came near the cave, they both did not know the big grizzly nursed his cubs and when they came into the den the bear grabbed both of them and crushed them to death. Their mangled bodies were thrown out the den and the smell of blood drifted into the area where John hid from the bear. He could hear the hideous sounds of the men as the bear kept throwing them against the walls and biting them at the same time.

Still sore from his ordeal with the bear, John strolled towards a building that was made for the homeless. Still very tire. John is taken into the facility called Our Blessed Home

"This place looks like a medieval castle. Where am I at John said, "You are at a heaven for the homeless and we help many people who come to us."

This fellow sported big earrings on his ears and wore big red suspenders with matching pants and his face was covered with scars from many fights with the patients and he walked with a limp and his two front teeth were knocked out.

Break It said, "You will like it here and maybe you might want to join our cult. I am the high priest and will need men like you who come to our facility looking for hope to achieve some thing with their lives."

"How long can I stay here?"

"You are here for life. You have certain obligations to fulfill and you might become a permanent loyal priest at this temple."

"I don't think I want to stay here sir. I have other plans to do with my life."

The high priest held John.

"All of a sudden I have to leave this place, "John said," I have business to do. I am a politician."

The other disciples hid in another room listening and four of them armed with guns came and escorted John to a cell. "I cannot stay in that place. Let me go."

"You have to stay here and help us destroy the city of Jackson."

"Man you're dressed to kill with that uniform on. Where I come from the preacher dressed in different suits all the time especially the ones who have a lot of money."

"You cannot leave this facility. You know too much now. You must give me your word you will not say anything about our facility and what we do here. Big Jim wants those properties owned by you and the farmers both black and white who live there."

"There is a bridge we will build to bring dynamite over to the dam to destroy it and the water will flood the fertile farm lands owned by your family and other farmers living in the area near and around Jackson, Mississippi."

However, I will have you confined to a dark cell where you will have crackers and water for two weeks until you give your loyalty to me and the brotherhood."

The guards took John to a section of the facility that is dark and he cannot breath too good.

John did not like the ordeal he was in but what could he do but take part in a dirty cult which wanted him to do criminal things to hurt other people and go along with the program to help build a bridge to carry explosives to a dam to blow it up so his friends and neighbors living there would lose their properties and Big Jim and his henchmen would for close on the properties and take their lands by declaring it a disaster area and get their properties and drill for oil on it.

If the farmland is flooded, this means disasters like yellow fever would fall on the area and death would occur leaving many people homeless and destitute without a way to make a living and all they worked for was tied up in their farms and flood water would ruin their crops."

"So you will not eat the food, "the guard said," You will die from starvation."

The guard stood about six feet and felt he was a nice looking man who wore nothing but black colored clothes with big white spots on his uniform and high heel boots colored black. A grayish looking beard grew around his big cheeks.

"They call me the Beautiful One. I am kind to the new disciples and they like me because I sleep with them. John you be good to me and I will get you out of here. You will get better food too."

The beautiful one opened the door and made an advance and attempted to molest him.

"Do not touch me! "John cried out," I will kill you if you attempt to have me. I am no homosexual!"

The Beautiful One grabbed John and started taking off his clothes and held a big bowie knife in the other hand.

"You stink so take your hands off of me or I'll be forced to kill you. You look so weak with those ugly tattoos on your face and earrings hanging on your ears."

"You will be mine."

The beautiful one shouted at John and attempted to kiss him and John hit him in the mouth with his fists but it did not bother him that much.

"Stop licking me. I am no girl!" John slapped his ears with both of his hands, and he threw a ridge hand strike, right cross and a jab to John's body and he blocked the blows with his leg and threw the Beautiful One with a hip throw and a thunderous sound hit the concrete floor.

"You sonofabitch I'll take care of you." and the Beautiful One put John in a headlock but with the combat training he learned in the army John hit him in the stomach and stomped on his foot and as he bended over he let John go and John hit him in the head with a steel chair.

The Beautiful One dropped to the floor and died instantly. With all that noise the guards came scrambling to see what happened. They were stunned when they saw the 250 pound, The Beautiful One dead and the 140 pound John Carol standing over him in victory.

Velvet said, "Where did you learn to fight like that? The Beautiful One was unstoppable and no one could beat him and a little runt as if you did what none of us could do. We will take you to our master and see if you can teach the guards hand to hand combat. Our honorable priest. Break It Jackson would be glad if you could teach his men martial arts and maybe join our organization. John you will be in some heavy activities such as over throwing the United States government."

Taking John to the courtroom, he saw a beautiful courtroom where he received his guest and Brake It said, "My guards told me you are good with martial arts and my men will need a teacher. The Beautiful one trained my guards but now I see you killed him and this is something no one has done before. You are very suitable to teach our priest the martial arts." Velvet said," You defeated the Beautiful One with his large size with no problems and the Beautiful One was our best martial arts teachers. You killed The Beautiful One as small as you are."

"Sir he kept beating me and I had to do something."

"You have to join our temple if you want to stay alive," Velvet said, as he tried to save John's life because if he refused it would mean getting killed and the thought of seeing his kids again would be impossible.

"Ok I'll take over teaching your priest in martial arts but you must let me be free to move in the temple at well."

Leaning back in his comfortable chair, "Break It said, "Get this disciple dressed up so he can worship me as a God and give him a plush room with all the trimmings. Tomorrow we will show him the plans to flood these lands for Senator Big Jim Wilson who was voted back into office."

A messenger came delivered a message.

"My friend Big Jim Wilson has come to pay his respects. He did not tell me he was coming to see me."

Break It wore silk made colorful robes and a mask to cover his face as senator Big Jim Wilson walks in to speak with the high priest dressed in a black yellow robe with gold zig zag lines on the front of it and his feet rested on a soft stool which sat in front of him.

"The fragrance of the perfume smells very good Brake It."

All at once four men came and sat some expensive gifts in front of him.

"My, my, my what beautiful gifts sir," Big Jim said, "I am honored for such hospitality"

"I have been receiving the money from the sales of license plates your prisoners are making. I will use the money to finance my reelection for the senate seat and give you everything you want like money, and girls, and men slaves to help with the growing of pot and more equipment to work with. I see you and your engineers are building a tunnel to take supplies over to the big dam to blow it up to flood the farm lands then the governor can declare it disaster area and my friends who have given money for this project can benefit from it."

Being part of the celebration, Brake It clapped his hands as Arabian music sounded coming out of speakers.

"Yes we are making tremendous strides to build the tunnel and sometimes we work at night putting parts of the hard plastic tunnel in place under the lake surrounding the dam and solder the parts done by my divers and they have connected a sucking hose to pump water out of it so more space can be used to plant the dynamite near the dam. We have place bricks to help hold the tunnel on the floor of the lake so the current will not make it drift away. The tunnel was four feet wide. Which is big enough for my men to crawl through to plant the dynamite on the dam? When the dynamite explodes they will not know what hit them."

"When will you blow up the dam?"

"In about two months we should have everything in place."

"You are going to have to tighten security because some of the prisoners have managed to get the word out on what's been happening at the facility. Have some of your people on the news stations to give a different picture of what is going on up here. Don't be surprised if some reporters will be coming up here to see what the prisoners are talking about."

"We call them disciples not prisoners. Even they are here against their will. I have proclaimed myself God and they must do as I say."

"Let me show you what I mean."

"What do those bottles contain in front of him? "Big Jim said.

As the disciples came in front of both of them, Break It said:

"Do you honor and love me and if you do drink the liquid portion of this drink in remembrance of me."

The priest immediately did what was asked of them and within minutes they all dropped and their bodies were taken and put in a big fire and their ashes were thrown into a nearby lake.

"Magnificent they do exactly as you tell them. They think you are a god and do not hesitate to please you."

Giving Senator Wilson some marijuana Break said, "We will send up some weed and drugs to you and your friends so they can be distributed to anyone who will buy it. You 'll need the money to hire and pay workers to drill the wells once we flood the valley with water and most of land will be evil to your people so it could be refined and sold to the rich people in your state and across the United States and all over the world."

"Another thing Break It, I will be sending you more people to help you build your temple since you are God of the universe. There's rumors my wife Mable might be a member of your temple. She always read your literature at the house. It's hard for us to stay together because I have to have more than one woman. I get tire of making love to the same woman. If she is in the group, please notify me. I cannot have her around me saying I am a womanizer so if she turns up in here please notify me or you can kill her."

"Ok Big Jim we have had a productive conference and I wish you a safe plane flight to Jackson."

Hugging Break It. Velvet visited John's room and warn him to escape because he overheard the disciples saying he would be put to death by poisoning and he should make plans to escape.

"Why are you telling me all of this? What will you gain from telling this me dangerous information? I do not know you. Can you give me an explanation why you want to help me?" John said.

Velvet's eyes sparkled as he talked and he spoke many languages and his skin changed from white to velvet and his clothing consisted of white silk beautiful material and he adorned himself with great smelling perfume and he said, "My brother was once a disciple but was killed because he saw much wrong doing by Beak. My brother spoke out against the enslavement of innocent people and the raping of kids who were 13 or older and made the people worship him as if he was a God and killed many of the people who refused to believe he was a God. My brother was murdered because he spoke out against what the cult stood for and that was corruption and wasting the citizen's money to have a temple built for him was ridiculous."

"Now I see what you are saying. Big Jim and his cult must be stopped or it means problems for the citizens of Mississippi."

"He's making drug deals involving little children who are three or four years old up to adulthood and using them as slaves and just think about the fact the parents have not seen their kids since their childhood after they were kidnapped."

"Thanks for telling me this Velvet I'll try to get away from this place and tell the world what is happening up here. I see they are putting all types of people in this place."

"They are cremating the bodies and picking the gold out of their mouths and peeling the skin off of their bodies and making colored wigs out of it and in some cases feeding their hogs the body parts and they do not get a decent burial whatsoever. Somehow something must be done to tell the world these people are being treated like the Jews who died in the concentration camps."

CHAPTER 51

A white girl came to the facility which kept John as a prisoner and presented a document releasing him to do some work at another facility with Senator Big Jim Wilson's signature on it.

A smiling John Carol came strolling towards the gate and the person who managed the walls pulled a switch and let the both of them out.

"I am surprised to see you. How did you get me out of here?"

Trying to hurry up to get into her car, Sandy said, "It's a long story but I looked at some of those news broad castings of what was happening at this center and one of the members of the cult mentioned your name and said you were a model disciple and helping to bring more people to their temple."

The guards called out on the loud speakers for the both of them to not go anywhere because they wanted to speak with them immediately.

"They caught on to what I did and realized those signatures were forged by me to get you out. A letter came to me from a man named Velvet, he said you were going to be poisoned today at 8 p.m. in the morning, and I did not want that to happen."

"How did he know how to get in touch with you?"

"Pow Pow" came the bullets as they hit the car and Sandy pushed on the gas making the car go much faster but the gas pump did not work properly and they stopped and it slowed down.

"I got to see what the problem is or they are going to catch us."

The disciples closed in on them and John looked under the hood and he saw a spark plug was not in its socket and when he put the spark plug in and yelled," Sandy step on the gas pedal and get the hell out of here."

Pushing on the gas, "I will leave you if I did that!"

"Just do what I am asking you to do."

Reluctantly Sandy did what John told her to do and the car took off and John placed his arms around the area where the windows let down and held on with his the leather on his boot heels dragging on the road.

"They are firing at us. I have to slow down and stop the car so you can get in are you might get killed."

Holding on the car windows. "Go down that hill. They will be afraid to do that. I think we can do it so just control the brakes. I'll try to get into the car at the same time."

As he crawled through the window, Sandy made a sharp turn to avoid hitting a tree and John was lifted back to the side of the car in the same predicament holding on to the frame of the car window and his legs were tire and sore and his fingers attempted to hold on and his head pounded against the car window frame with his heart beating hard and fast.

By this time the disciples tried to hit the car and Sandy dodged trees and weeds trying to get to the road which could lead them into another county. What John could not believe was Sandy had negative feelings about equality of the races sharing the same public facilities. As she grew older Sandy saw the poverty the share croppers experienced at the hands' of her father's henchmen as they cheated people both blacks and whites and how her law professors notified her father when she attended African American city affairs in Jackson and criticized Big Jim and his racist policies and he threatened to cut off his financing of her tuition. Big Jim and Sandy clashed about the integration of black and white people and she quickly rebelled when her father tried to tell her what she could and could not do when it came to associating with black people. One evening she witnessed the lynching of two black service men who were not given a trial and it was mob justice and nothing could be done about it.

Many evenings she heard her father in his parlor talking what they would do when the freedom riders came to their places of accommodations to integrate the lunch counters and bus terminals and she debated him so much and for weeks they would not speak to each other and he got angry at her because he and Polly who was black had an intimate relationship which drove his wife Mable away from him. In their heated debates, Big Jim said what he did with his private life was his own business.

In her professional lawyering world, Big Jim told Sandy if she took on civil rights cases in favor of black folks he would find ways to keep the law firm she worked for from getting business and Sandy left the firm because her law partners would not take civil rights cases and she formed her own firm which was fired bombed many times.

"I'll drive you to your mother's house so you can spend some time with her. By the way, Betty told me you were at the facility and I wanted to help you so here I am to do whatever I could," John said to her.

"Dad put me out of the house because of my opposition to his racist policies and his influencing the newspapers to print articles which are anti-civil rights and because I would not file law suits against the farmers to take their land because they could not pay their monthly farm bills. And another thing daddy wants those properties because they are rich in oil and other natural valuable resources."

CHAPTER 52

"**M**omma how's Betty doing. It's been a long time since I've seen her. I still have feelings for her."

"Son you have many goals to achieve and getting to know Betty will not help you. It will only turn away people who will be able to assist you win the congressional senate seat for the state of Mississippi and help our people You will be able to influence many white folks to write legislation that can help give our people a better way of living. Many of our black women who have kids are dying for lack of prenatal care and this is a big problem. You cannot let the people down again by getting caught up in trying to court white women."

"But momma I understand but times are changing and people cannot tell you who you can marry or not marry in this country. The days of telling colored people what they can or cannot do are over. I got to see my two daughters and the last time I spoke to them; I had obligations to take care of and I would get back in touch with them."

"Now John I promised your father I would speak with you about getting your GED and hope you'll go on to college."

"I want to see Betty Momma. I think I might still be in love with her..."

"Son, Betty is in another world which is a rich life style. The times you shared with each other are over. Try to move on with your life without Betty. You said you were going to get your degree and finish college."

For a moment John thought about what Sarah spoke to him about getting an education to better his skills in writing and reading. So many times he went to the store with his father and saw how he was being cheated because he could not read or write or understand numbers or words.

"John you have to get an education so you can understand the language in the different papers you will read pertaining to the bills submitted that affects your district. Do not forget you will be representing colored and white people. You must get their trust."

"Momma I have a lot to be thankful for. I'll do the things which will make you and the citizens I will represent in this state proud of me."

Looking out for the best interest of her son, Sarah wanted him to achieve success but not waste everything he worked for to get involved with Betty because those relations would hurt him in the long run because many white and black supporters would resent it.

CHAPTER 53

"John you have a great challenge in front of you trying to get to know your real daughters who are mixed races and their mother may not want to renew relations with you even though you are the father of Dora and Dianna." Lilly said.

Lilly goes on to say how she got Dora from an orphanages and raised her from childhood because she had difficulty living in a white environment and how she adjusted to not being raised by her real mother and the pain she felt when she saw Betty was on the sidelines rooting for Dianna's basketball team to defeat Dora's team which developed into a bitter hate between both of the girls. Before coming to Lilly's house, John wanted to make amends with Dora because he was not in her life when she needed someone to be a father to her. Believing he could get to know Dora and be there for her he got a chance to meet Dora after years of not knowing her.

Lilly said, "It will be difficult to know both of your daughters because each of them saw two worlds. Dora faced discrimination being black and Dianna did not know how she could be born white and have no trace of blackness in her.

"I know it can be hard on both of them but they have to work out this problem somehow."

As mentioned earlier John stopped at a drug store to buy a gift for Dora to show her he was serious about being the father he knew he could be. He went in into the store and saw some perfume lying on the counter.

"This perfume is what I want and it could be a perfect gift for my daughter."

"It's one of our best perfumes said White Pearl and it smells good."

"Sir you will have to go to the back and I will sell it to you. Colored folks are not allowed in the front to purchase goods in this store. Go to the back and I will serve you."

"Why is it I have to go to the back of the store to buy this perfume? My money is just as good as the money being spent by people who are white and Chinese who come into the store. If I cannot be served in the front of the store, I will go somewhere else and buy this perfume!" and John walked out the store in an angry mood without buying the perfume.

Immediately John left and anger filled his face. The thought of being made to be look like a second class citizen did not make him feel good and he wanted to stage a non-violent demonstration in front of the restaurant and perfume store to make them serve them just like they did white citizens. Making it back to Lilly's house, John was hot and angry and wanted revenge against the people who kept him from being served like the other customers who were white.

"Now there you go again trying to wage a war against people without support. The people who you are going up against are powerful with a lot of big named supporters, who do not want to give up power."

"I know Lilly but something must be done to stop this injustice they are subjugating my people to."

Handing John a cup of coffee Lilly said, "The only thing that will happen is they will put you in jail for non-violent demonstrations but sometimes they turn out to be violent and you must unite with black and white civil rights groups who have clout with the office of the president of the United States who can send in federal troops to protect your workers from the anti-integration forces trying to stop things from happening so the people in this state can enjoy all the civil rights guaranteed by the Constitution of the United States.

Constantly looking at his watch John said, "Lilly you have a great idea which might work because we need an organization of grassroots people who will go into the farms and assist the farmers and organize an organization which will get equal voting rights for all the people in this state."

Lilly smiled and said, "The civil rights people who come down here do not stay with the farm hands and see what problems they are facing. They come and pass out literature and then leave them to struggle with the problems all by themselves."

Stilled filled with curiosity, the coffee pot steamed and made loud noises from the oven and produced a rich aroma and John felt comfortable having a lady cook him breakfast because he never had those types of services did for him. As Lilly and John talked, Dora walked into the kitchen and it surprised her to see her father. Instead of speaking to John, she went into her bedroom without saying anything to him.

"Well what did I do? She is not too happy to see me. I should not have never come here. Dora harbors a lot of anger against me. I cannot make up for lost time but I'll try to get a better relationship with my daughter because she is uptight about what I did in the last election but I have to break the ice between us and be her father and it will not be an easy task."

"John those types of things take time. It will not happen overnight."

Before going to Lilly's house, after leaving the first store he tried to buy her a present at another store for being a good athlete and one white fellow came into the store and grabbed John and took him to jail stating they would speak with him about the stolen perfume.

"John thanks for leading us where the jewels were at," they said, "Come on and go with us."

"I do not know who you are." John said.

With that the fellows scrambled out of the store to an awaiting car and they stumbled on some bubble gum struck on the floor. Their driver did not wait for them to get into the car and drove off and left them. The police arrived and they searched for the men who robbed the store.

"He was with them!" One of the customers shouted at the policeman who responded to the call for help.

Immediately they grabbed John and escorted him to the police station and placed him in a cell stating they will speak with him about the stolen perfume.

"May I see the charges of what I am being placed in this cell for. It seems as if police wanted to put me in jail without any proof I was involved in the crime and I was not given a lawyer to speak to."

The sheriff said, "We will take care of this matter in about a week."

John felt this was wrong and at least he could be given the privileges of eating in a restaurant of his choice or vote on the people they wanted to represent their thoughts and needs guaranteed by the Constitution of the United States. As John sat in his cell the sounds of men both black and white citizens vented their negative feelings about the state police authorities and the manner in which they treated wealthy prisoners better than poor ones. The emotions in their faces showed a disappointment in the judicial system operated by Big Jim and his favorite people he put in office to keep control and stop those people pushing for equality for the masses of people.

His thoughts reflected on his father who fought for this country in the great World War 1 and how he said to get involved with a white woman would cause him problems in the future. He thought about getting a good education and what it would mean to him to do this and learn the necessary tools to be able to write bills that could be used to ask congress for help for the people who elected him into office and he wanted desperately to accomplish his almost impossible goal. Sitting on an uncomfortable steel chair made him uncomfortable and his back ached and he knew he might get out of jail.

CHAPTER 54

The police officers took John outside and said, "We'll let you go if you can give us fifty dollars apiece for me and my friends or off you go to jail."

"There is no proof I knew the men who robbed the store and they acted like they knew me and the clerk thought I was in on the robbery. A big fellow who was with Officer Ray Robinson said," We'll let him go this time but we want one thousand dollars at the end of the month."

"This is extortion. You are police officers of the law but you are no different from the so called law enforcement officers of the law."

With that being the case, they let John go with the understanding he would have to raise one thousand dollars by the end of the month or be arrested and placed in jail again. This is an ongoing crime Big Jim used to raise money for his elections and spend the taxpayer's money without them knowing about it. With his lavish life style, Big Jim had money coming to him from many sources but he was never charged with any crimes because local officials who ran the wards covered for him. The ward leaders endorsed Big Jim and encouraged their people to vote and reelected him to any state office he wanted or federal civil service office.

Knowing how stubborn John was, he wanted to beat Big Jim at the voting polls but for thirty years Big Jim ruled his office with a strong hand against the will of the people who were too afraid to stand up against the injustice and racketeering he was involved in. His family was torn apart by the competition people linked them to because of their ruthless father. Big Jim's horses won at the race tracks because he paid off the other jockeys to not attempt to win the race and he supported a bill which could lower taxes for the wealthy. But his eyes were on the oil rich lands his neighbors and friends owned but would not help him obtain passed down to them from many generations of families in the state of Mississippi since the formation of this state. While John was in jail, Big Jim visited him and he suspected him of setting him up to be placed in jail for the robbery at the jewelry shop.

"Why are you coming to see me Big Jim? You never took the time to know me when I played with your kids why now."

"Stop taking those pictures of me and John talking, "Big Jim shouted at the reporters trying to cover the story!"

"You mean to tell me you are refusing to get free publicity and why are you trying to act like you are a humble person."

"They tried to finger print me and reporters took pictures for their newspapers to embarrass me. I will make a charge of defamation of character filed against them for that."

Sitting in a chair Big Jim lit a cigar and asked John if he wanted one.

"You must be crazy. You know we cannot smoke in this place."

"Never mind I tell the people what to do in this town."

Big Jim said, "Why won't you get out of this election. Big Jim never loses elections. I guess you know by now, plus, I want those oil rich lands your people are living on. I have great plans for that area once we take it from your black and white farmers."

Smiling, John showed much confidence when he said, "You think you can wave a magic wand and people will do what you want them to do. Those days are over with. The poor farmers will rise up and organize themselves into unions and decide their own destinies for their families."

"That's a lot of bull shit. They owe me a lot and I lent many of them money to start their farms and now they are forgetting the person who helped them get to the mountain top."

"All of this means nothing to the families you are talking about because all you are is lie to them."

The ugliness came out of Big Jim when he ordered the guards to come in and make John drink some water which made him choke. One of the cooks who worked in the jail called John's mother and told her to come see her son, who waited patiently for this to take place. No one showed up. While he was in jail Big Jim's men came into his cell and showed him pictures of made up photos of him kissing homosexuals and laying nude in the park and they circulated them throughout the community and newspapers friendly towards Big Jim ran topics on John to slander his name to keep him from getting votes needed to stop his opponent.

"This place stinks, "John said as he tried to use the toilet and it needs painting.'

There's no good living conditions in this cell he told his faithful mother Sarah who came to visit and it took two weeks for the officials to let her see John beaten by the local police who hated him.

"They are only trying to discourage you and keep you from serving the people who want you to beat Big Jim so hang in there and do it. If God is for you, they cannot stop you."

"Another thing John when was the last time you took a bath? Do they let you wash up? It is unsanitary and something should be done about this."

"Don't worry Momma God is not going to let us suffer for a long time. We'll overcome. Injustice will not be allowed to destroy our rights to keep our property and send our kids to decent schools which are modern and have them not study from outdated books which did not show their own people doing positive things with their lives such as them being owners of businesses or being lawyers or doctors teachers or scientists in which they can achieve great success in those types of endeavors."

While John and his mother are talking a loud noise is heard outside the jail house and he sees many students outside holding up picket signs saying let John out of this jail and we want freedom, justice, and better schools in our neighborhoods. Other signs said we wanted more African American placed in the textbooks. Other signs said we wanted John Carol to be the next United States senator from the state of Mississippi.

Joining them were teachers who wanted better conditions for their students to get relief from the overcrowded classrooms lacking air conditioning in the summer and bad heating during the winter and increases in their salaries because the teachers have not had a raise in ten years. They wanted the separate but equal policy to end where black and white students could learn together because the problem was they both had prejudice feelings against each other because they never had a chance to engage each other in positive dialogue.

"You see John it is your destiny to run for the United States Senate because the people both black and white people are showing you must get into the senate and write bills that can help them out. Don't get discouraged because most of the senators are millionaires. If the people are for you, who can be against you but it will be no easy job to accomplish. The teachers and students have gone on strike for this cause to end injustice."

"I heard your daughter is taking part in this strike and I am proud of her for taking a stand on this issue. They are trying to be nonviolent in this effort to get better conditions so their kids will be able to study in comfort and many of them come to school and are hungry when they get there. How can a student learn and be hungry at the same time and many of them have to stop school to work in the fields before walking many miles to attend schools far from their neighborhoods."

Looking at her in amusement, John said, "Mother Peter would be very proud of you standing up against racism and encouraging me to run for public office which will enable me to do something for the people of this state who need it especially the poor black and white farmers and city people. Your very right mother our kids use too much slang in their everyday talking and it's difficult for the kids to speak Standard English because it is not used in their house wholes. When they come to school, it becomes another world to them when speaking Standard English. That's why many of our kids drop out of school."

Taking part in this strike by Dora was not liked by Lilly because of her conservative viewpoints and John said, "Lilly is sensitive about those types of things even though she faced discrimination as a doctor and African American. At first when she opened up her office for business, the white people would not visit her to be treated. But when she saved the life of a person who owned a bank he encouraged citizens to go to her for their medical needs who at first stood outside her office protesting and wanted her to leave and go practice in another town in Mississippi where there were more black people. There will be a major clash between Dora and Lilly when she finds out Dora became one of the protesters. She does not want to lose white patients who are rich and keep her in business all year long."

The Mississippi State Board of education called out the state national guard to put down the demonstrations by the students and warned not to use real bullets but only blanks.

Dora and the students organized and marched for many hours without food and water and held meetings outside the school. A letter was sent to the governor of Mississippi Joseph Lonely indicating they wanted better conditions for their school such as clean restrooms toilets that worked, gym equipment, better curriculums, better landscapes on the school grounds that provided trees and flowers, nine month school years, and students being allowed to finish out the school year instead of being made to stop school and work in the fields. They wanted better organizations for sports activities, buildings for recreation, and college preprograms, and lunch programs. They requested classes for special needs students, better science equipment so the students could perform experiments when they studied about the earth. They requested electrical equipment for studying electricity, and inspection of their schools for lead paint that the state ignored for years and many of the kids in the preschool contracted it and became ill but nothing was done about it. They protested the fact no trash truck drivers came to pick up the trash every day and by the end of the week plies of trashcans needed to be taken to the landfill but much of it laid on the ground with rats spending much time eating food from it that led to the spread of disease.

After reading those demands, Big Jim said, "Those kids are trying to run this state and I will tell the governor to call out to National Guard to stop the students from winning in this latest outbreak of civil unrest."

"You know that principal will defy your authority Big Jim because he is a pro integrationist and will support the teachers, "One of his workers said.

I will have Governor Lonely fire the teachers supporting the students. He will help me because he owes me favors and I'll have the local politicians throughout the state to support him when he runs for reelection. Tomorrow I'll have Governor Lonely send letters telling the striking teachers to come back to work or they will lose their jobs and we will replace them with teachers who we do not have to pay much money like substitute teachers."

In the gym, Baker called a meeting with the striking teachers and said, "A letter has come from Governor Lonely which said all of us will lose our jobs but we must stand tall and support our students for better working conditions. All of you teachers who are for supporting the students in their fight for justice please raise their hands. I hope the demonstration is something that will make the state government listen to us. I am tire of seeing my students studying in cold rooms in the winter and hot ones during the summer months without air conditioning."

"But Big Jim never supported legislation for our students to get the best teaching materials money can buy. I recommend we support the students who are getting the feeling of full equality to be educated in a modern day teaching school."

Some fights broke out between the teachers who wanted to join the striking students who were determined to stand up against injustice at all cost those who did not want to strike. In some cases, they would not speak to each other.

CHAPTER 55

B ig Jim holds a press conference sitting in his soft leather seat and smoked long Cuban cigar and said,

"It takes time for change to take place. For years the southern politicians have been against integration and helping those colored school districts to provide quality education like the white school districts received. They did not appreciate it when Lincoln abolished slavery in the state of Mississippi. They lost their main source of income when this was done and during reconstruction the carpet baggers came and bought up all the land from them they could get. Under federal control, colored men ran for elective office. .This type of behavior got the northern white soldiers out of the South when a deal was made at the Warmly Hotel and ever since black codes have governed the control of colored folks in the South. Southern life style gained back its dignity and controlled the upward mobility of the colored race. That's why black people were treated like this."

"But why is it you are against the black and white liberals coming into Mississippi getting black folks organized?"

At his office on Capitol Hill the reporters asked him several questions

"Is it true the teachers and students want better working conditions and school equipment to give quality education to the students?" One reporter said.

"That's only people who are my enemies who are staring up more racial strife. I have not ignored their demands and this time I 'll have my workers drafting up papers which can eliminate the complaints they are raising and writing up the bill giving funds to all the school districts."

Paul Snowball said, "I've looked up the history of the state and I have not seen any funds appropriated to the black school districts but are you doing this now?"

One of the reporters in the crowd said, "Big Jim one of your daughters is out there trying to get upfront and speak her mind. It seems as if the reporters will not let her in and your aides know her but seem to not want to be bothered."

Smoking on his cigar Big Jim said, "I do not want my daughter up here talking while you reporters are losing the big picture of what I am going to do for the farmers."

"Why don't you want her to speak at this conference? Maybe she can tell us something we do not know about."

"That's nonsense," I always want to hear the opinions of my kids but now is not the time for opposition gossip."

"Let me through here. You have no right to do this. I want to address the reporters and give my opinions about the conditions the people are living under."

Leaning back in his chair trying to present a pleasant smile, Big Jim said, "Well here's my lovely daughter. What brings you to my headquarters up here in Washington D.C. That is a pretty dress you are wearing. Fellows this is my daughter Betty and isn't she attractive. She looks like a rainbow shinning after a rain shower has fallen."

"Aren't you going be a gentleman and let your daughter sit down and talk with the reporters? I am sure they want to hear what I got to say."

A reporter had his tape recorder with him and he unbuttoned his collar and made his tie loose.

"What can you tell us Big Jim is not explaining to us about? Make sure it is important and news worthy. I have to sell magazines with this information."

"Now gentlemen my daughter is just showing off to make herself look good. Just ignore her."

"My father is swindling the those farmers and wants to use them so he can get cheaper prices for their products and he is pretending to give aid to those teachers and students who are protesting for more school supplies and warm buildings during the winter months. He wants to see the land go into waste and have the farmers grow weed on it to sell and make money by digging for oil."

Throwing his cigar at Betty Big Jim said, "That is a lie. How in the hell do I know about oil being in this state anyway? I am a politician not an oil man."

Noises filled the air because the reporters wanted to print this in their newspapers to bring attention to the people and Big Jim's rivals would probably make an investigation into every piece of legislation he has produced and passed promises of giving the people much needed improvements in health care for their families and better prices for their crops. This information Betty provided to the reporters would make the federal government step in and see if the civil rights of the individuals were violated.

This outburst by his daughter would not let Big Jim stand and listen to her slander him in the eyes of his friends and political enemies and he said, "Now you cannot believe my daughter because she is in love with a black sonofabitch I hate. Betty was raised to not associate with colored people. When she came to me saying she wanted to marry a colored man, I raised so much hell about it and told her I would dismember her from my will."

"Why are you standing up daddy? I see the look in your eyes when your mad and you are about to explode."

Pushing her to the side, the reporters came and kept them apart and Big Jim said, "She's doing nothing but lying on me. I am the best person those people voted into office. See all of those pictures of me being accepted with the white and colored people. This shows they like me."

"You lie to the people to get what you want from them. I got a copy of your voting records and it indicates you have not voted any funds for the colored school districts and it shows you are supporting an effort to push the people off the land because oil is probably on it."

"Directing his aides to come and get her, they escorted her out of his office with her shouting and swearing many curse words at him and she pulled off one of her shoes and threw it at him because she knew as usual he lied to the news reporters and they believed him.

As the students picketed the school for their rights noise could be heard coming up the road. It was the sound of armored personnel carriers with troops to disperse the crowd with canisters of gas being shot at the group and they were ordered to go home until something could be done about the bad conditions their students studied under. Dora got overcome with gas but kept a determined spirit to keep on protesting for their rights. Fireman arrive at the school and sprayed water at the students and the national guard was supposed to have blanks in their rifles but one soldier did not check to see if live rounds were in his and fired at some students and injured them.

John got the news from his mother when she visited him while he was in jail and vowed to get bills passed by the federal and state governments to get better working and training internships for the students in various trades. Dora's side of her body ached in pain and it took four hours to remove the bullets from her arms and legs and one of the bullets near her heart was life threatening and doctors had to leave the bullet near it for the time being because removing it would probably kill her and a decision was made to remove it when she was stronger. Dora would have died because Big Jim ordered the president of the hospital not to admit students hit by bullets. Ambulance drivers took them to clinics not designed handle operations but once they got to the clinics the hospital technicians would hit and abuse them and federal marshals ordered staff members to stop this insane behavior.

Some of the students were taken to other out of state facilities to have their wounds treated and lost a lot of blood in the process. At one hospital they would not treat them because of their race and the other students following them in their cars took over the hospital administration and held their workers as hostages until their friends and comrades were treated.

Later police arrived and broke into the area where the students held the hostages and shot gas canisters into the room and stormed the building and took them to jail but the students got treated which resulted in high medical bills charged to the ones who did not have insurance. The students lost the fight and were told to go home. Only promises were made to the school officials but were never kept after the demonstrating stopped and only a few conditions changed in the education of the students and state officials said something would be done to better the learning environment of the black and white poor students. John felt he had more to gain fighting discrimination against white and black people, gay, and same gender people.

Something would have to be done to make improvements in the education system because the demonstrations caused much destruction to the property and loss of life and tourism would stop because when people heard about the way black folks were treated in Mississippi, they would not come to the state for vacations and hold conventions in the state leaving vendors unable to provide the things they needed like food, transportation, hotel accommodations, and entertainment services.

This is why John Carol wanted to be the next United States senator from the state of Mississippi because he felt he could make a difference by writing legislation to improve the living conditions of the people and he promised himself he would do this. Dora recuperated from her injury and the bullet removed from her body but vowed to take part in future demonstrations for equality for her herself and her friends. As part of the agreement John was let out of jail with him saying he would not take part in any civil rights demonstrations in the state but the minute he said it he knew he was lying and would join future protests to fight for equality in the state of Mississippi.

CHAPTER 56

The college stood on a big hill by the name of Greenville and had an assortment of buildings and huge lengths of concrete marble stairs started from the entrance of the school. Before the long roll of steps was a narrow roadway lined by trees and cars parked on each of the narrow driveway and big buildings located to the north and south of it with trees in both directions of the narrow lane. To the south was the architecture building and the arts academy and to the north housed the science academy where some of the best scientist taught courses in the sciences which resulted in many students failing their classes but John was determined to get his degree and make something of himself.

When he was getting his GED, he mailed off letters for scholarships to various colleges but none of them came through and each morning he waited for the mail carrier to show up and put something in the mailbox it saying he won one. When rejections piled up to get his scholarship Lilly said, "You will not solve the problem talking about it. Why don't you take a ride up to Greenvill College and see. You might have a scholarship."

A tall man with a height of about 6'7" could hardly see. He loved playing Black Jack but he could not make out anything when he read papers and said, "I know why you came." as he rubbed his cat that was prohibited on campus but other professors had birds in their offices that he always argued about but was bent on breaking the rules. Every year students come to my office to get their scholarships and never say thank you."

"Sir I drove up to this campus with little or no money and I would like to know if I got a scholarship card to continue my education and not have to pay anything."

"Thousands of records sat in front of him and he said," I have work to do. We do not give scholarships to niggers so boy get out of here!" As he got a cup of coffee but instead of coffee he placed some noodles in it and got uptight when he saw bugs running around it and shouted, "Those dam college officials know we have a bug problems but never do they call out a professional exterminator to kill them,"

In his office bugs crawled on the floor looking for food and the trash piled up for weeks before it was collected because the trustees of the college spent money intended for the maintenance of the college spent the funds given to them from the state legislature on lavish trips to the islands and called it business education meetings. Much corruption took place because money given to the college ended up being spent unwisely but nothing was done about it because the students feared they would not get financial aid if they told about the miss use of funds by the college. It was wasted for purposes not intended to make a good learning environment for the students.

"We do not give scholarships to nigger so boy get out of here !" he said as he went to get a cup of coffee and placed noodles in it and bugs crawled out of the cup which as usual made him angry..

"They are not going to give you a scholarship to let you into this college boy so go away from here and you did not get a scholarship anyway. There are too many of our white students who need the scholarships so what makes you so special?"

Looking at the scholarships applications John spotted the word John on one of them. The last name showing Carol was covered by some other papers. He wondered if that was his application but an administrator came in and said he had to leave because they were closing the office that resulted in an argument.

"Young man you must go before I call the campus police to escort you out of here."

Knowing he wanted to get the much needed information to see if he received a scholarship; John decided to break into the scholarship office to see if he received one because he did not have the money to pay his tuition and he knew they would make it hard for him to get into the college. They security officers placed alarms on the office door when the employees left their place of work and would go off if they attempted to go back to get something they left in their office.

Digger Jones usually patrolled near the scholarship office and wanted to sneak into it and get some rest even though he was supposed to be on guard duty. Precious one of the campus prostitutes wanted to get her money from him because he promised to give her 50 dollars the last time they went to the hotel. He did not have the money to pay her. She followed him to the scholarship office and he smiled and said, "Pretty Precious I have been looking for you. I owe you from the last time. Let's go into the scholarship office and get down and I will give you your money."

"You look dressed to kill Pretty Precious and you are wearing just the right romantic clothes. I like smelling that perfume you wear which always drives me wild and that sexy body makes an older man like me wish for younger days."

"Digger you say that to all the girls you want to screw but this time you have to pay up or I'll go to your commanding officer and report what we have been doing on campus and you will be fired if they find out so are you going to pay me this time."

"Baby it a piece of cake. Just follow me into this office and lay on the couch."

"Why don't you go into the office and get undressed and leave your pants with me."

Getting very excited Digger rushed into the bathroom leaving his pants for Pretty Precious and why did he leave them with her for because she got money from his pockets and cut her hands because he had needles in his pockets to shoot heroin into his arms and fear gripped Precious as she shouted to the top of her lungs and scrambled out into the campus trying to get away and when Digger came out of the men's room his smile changed into one of ugliness as he realized he had been ripped off by Pretty Precious and as Digger ran after her he left the door open and John went into the office to get his scholarship card. He did not have much time to find it. The wind blew wild as John searched for the right drawer to look in. Seeing problems came his way when he saw a lock on it and could not figure out a way he could open it but on a a table he saw a paper with a list of combinations on it but by accident someone placed heavy office furniture on it.

Time was running out and John pushed the furniture out the way and back pain in his muscles ached with every effort made to retrieve the lost folder containing his scholarship information and when he pushed off the furniture sitting on the folder the alarm went off and John rushed out of the room and made it back home the best way he could and police officers fired at him as he scrambled across the big large field of grass trying desperately to get away. It made John very mad to think someone would not tell him he received a scholarship.

The next day John enrolled into school and started his classes. Being black created a problem because all of the students were white and did not speak to him and he managed to get to his English, history, and mathematics classes. The one class he wanted to take was public speaking. Knowing his financial problems would take place he needed a job and went to see about working in the lunch room but he was rejected because the supervisor did not like the idea of him being at the school anyway and he said to John "We do not have any openings at this time so come back in a month."

Seeing what took place John said, "The sign said you needed people to work right now and I see you just hired those two students ten minutes ago. Either you hire me or I'll go to the head of the college to get them to give me a job."

"Get the hell out of here nigger and go back home. You are not wanted in this school!"

The next day John is seen carrying a picket sign saying the kitchen supervisor is discriminating against him because of his color and he feels he is entitled to a job just like anyone else. As John picketed outside the cafeteria students threw rocks, eggs, and anything they could get their hands on at him but this did not stop him from fighting to get a job at the cafeteria. When he went to his locker, the students tore it open and threw manure over his books making John turned into a rage but he felt to lash out violently would cause them to dismiss him from the college and he did not want this to occur and John called his trusted friend Sandy who came and spoke to the college president and threaten to sue them if John was not given better treatment and a job working in the cafeteria. Seeing Sandy was not playing orders were given to give John a job in the cafeteria.

The students called John "Short Dog' and 'Nigger Boy" and John gets into many fights as a result but finally he overcame the problems. When he ate in the cafeteria, the students put milk on the floor making him slip and fall when he left to get something to eat but he was determined to graduate and take all of the punishment they dished out every evening. Lilly and Dora came to pick him up and John complained because he received grades which he felt were not fair. Going to his locker, he sees different signs with ugly racist markings written on them but he tires them and off and makes it back to his class.

Because many of his books were destroyed, John went to the library to get books talking about the same subject matter to keep up with the class to not fall behind. After John went to the restroom he saw signs saying colored folks had to go to the gym three miles away and he called Sandy again and said they were putting signs up saying colored folks had to use separate restroom facilities than white folks and she came again to see the college president Mr. Harold Collins and asked him why the signs were being placed showing prejudice against John because he was black.

"You know it is not fair for you to have these signs on the walls and John's locker and for white only signs on the facilities he must use on campus."

College officials said, "Everything will be all right. It's hard for people to change their ways about integrating black and white folks together."

"This sort of disparate treatment is not good for John who is under much pressure to graduate and he must be treated equally. If this mistreatment continues, I will call the local NAACP and have an investigation of what is going on with the mistreatment of John. It is not good for him to study under these conditions. This is the last time I will have to come up here to see John gets treated equally."

"Sandy you're a life saver. You always come up here to bail me out. You know your old man will not like this so be careful."

"John I 'll always fight for the civil rights of colored people because I have seen how they have been treated and denied equal rights the United States Constitution say they should be enjoying. Just hang on in there and get your degree. There are too many people hoping you graduate and do something positive in this state."

CHAPTER 57

A strange looking woman came into the office while Sandy and John and President Collins spoke with each other and it was Betty and tells her sister to calm down and she will help John get his books back.

"What are you doing working here? I thought you were keeping your business going?"

"I am but I have business with the university. I supply them with books to use in their classes.

"I moved away from father and had my own home built located in Grenada County. You and John ought to visit me sometimes."

"I do not want John lynched going to Tara County. I read in the newspapers where they have hanged a colored boy who had come home from the war with his uniform on. I do not want this to happen to John," Sandy said.

"It seems like you still love John Betty."

"That was a long time ago and I have moved on. I have other lovers."

"You have John's daughter and her father longs to have a relationship with Dianna."

Later Sandy took John to Lilly's house and traveled to Betty's office.

Going to her book closet Betty said, "What books do John need?"

"He needs his math, science, and history books. I'll make sure he gets them Sandy."

To get more information from John on what books or other materials he could use Betty traveled to Lilly's house after Sandy gave her the address she rang the doorbell while John is sleeping but did not get a good reception from Lilly who by now had fallen in love with John.

"Why are you leaving. I was taking a nap and heard your voice." John said as Betty strolls towards the front door, "It's been a long time since I've seen you."

"Betty has to go. Now you have to get back to studying to get out of that college." Lilly said in a quiet voice," I'll make sure you get all the books you need."

Leaning back in his chair a loud noise was heard as Dora hit John in the head with a plastic bottle and ran upstairs.

"I'll kill you! You ways want to play games when I am studying!"

Lilly laughed because Dora wanted to get his attention and Dora never knew what it was like to have a father and she sure wanted to find out. Just to have fun Dora hid his books from him and would later bring them back and place them in his room while he slept in bed.

CHAPTER 58

John went out for the football team and got banged up by his own teammates and this is the first time he got into the game but he could not hang on to the football when going out for a pass and he never had a chance to play in a game because the coach felt he was not good enough so he was dropped from the team. In most of the plays none of his teammates blocked for him and he walked around hurt all the time.

Other concerns came up when Big Jim paid John's instructors to give him low grades because a well-educated black man would appeal to some of the liberal white educated white folks in the state of Mississippi during election time."

"They are putting me in the writing lab. Mr. Paul Collins, an English professor, loves to poke fun of my writing Lilly but I have to do it against my will. I'll do anything to graduate." John said to Lilly.

"John," he said, "You are a colored boy and is the first one of your people to come to this university and there are people who are hope you give up and throw in the towel."

"They already kicked me off the football team but I will make my mark at this school. I am colored and proud of it."

In this room were tables and books on writing and Mr. Paul Collins said, "John you are going to have write much better than this if you want to beat Big Jim for the senate seat. He is afraid of you because he does not know how to read or write himself. He hires other people to write his bill for him"

"White folks are always telling us we cannot write. Damit I get tire of hearing that shit. White folks write just as bad as us."

"But you got to be better than the average white boy to make any success in this white man's world. You wanted to study public speaking but they burned up that building when they heard you were going to major in that field.

Asking for a cigarette John said, "That will not deter me. I will take other classes for public speaking. You see those white folks on this picture of the college graduated from this college. I will be one of them. I am not going to lay down and give up."

"You know you are up against a stone wall trying to be the first colored boy to graduate from this college. I do not think you have it in you to graduate from our campus and get a degree but if you want my help I'll tutor you in your public speaking before class starts."

The sound of jazz music is heard coming from his radio and the announcer said, "Big Jim is running for a third term and it looks like no one is going to beat him. His staying power is enormous and supported by most of the rich people in the state of Mississippi. The opposing candidate should give up because Big Jim is calling all the shots and every candidate who runs against him should increase their life insurance policies. People who run against him end up dead if it appears he is going to lose the race, before the election is over. Pouring a glass of wine Berkington took a smell of it and said, "See what you are up against because Big Jim is no one to run against and if he pays off the election officials he is assured a win because they can throw out your ballots."

CHAPTER 59

Trying to learn math, English, and history and other courses were not easy and when John tried to get on a social club it became difficult because he was told they had enough people.

Reading an article in the college newspaper, John saw that their debate team lost all of the competitions and needed people to try out for the debate team and decided to go and ask Mr. Donald Case could he try out.

"Come in. What can I do for you? It's a great surprise lately and all I have been getting is loses from the competition and if I do not win more debates they will get rid of me."

Dressed in a white a white robe which said, "Keep trying Mr. Larry Case,"

"What can you do for my debate team? We have not won a championship yet and I do not want to hear no sad stories today."

"You have many trophies your club has won. That's a great achievement."

Showing John a letter from the administration it said: "This communications is from the faculty. "If you do not win your next debates you will be fire."

"I see you are about to lose your job if you do not win any debates."

Sitting in a chair John said, "I know the first debate hall was blown up when the students saw I wanted to major in communications and debate."

"Come to my house located in Bering Heights and I will spend time helping you with your speech. Now my wife Maggie may not like it but if I lose the debate I will not be employed and its hard trying to get a job teaching at the college and plus I am Jewish. I need to win all three debates to keep my job."

Buttoning his shirt and making himself look much neater.

When John arrives at Mr. Cases house, Butch a big black Dobermans comes after him and tries to tire his leg off. Instead of staying to find out if the dog would bite, John climbed up the tree with Butches' teeth on his pant legs trying take to take a plug out of it. A white woman came from around the back of the house with a black patch covering her eye and a big shot gun and while her dog pulled at his legs his woman shot into the tree and the buck shot sprayed through the tree branches which fell like little rain drops and the smell of metal pellets made John cough and the smoke turned his eyes red looking and holding on to the tree with his frail hands, they kept slipping as the old bark fell off as his hands desperately tried to keep him pent to the tree. The growl of Butches mouth grew stronger and John listened to Butch who seemed to have a vengeance to eat him alive.

Pushing toward John and Butch, Mr. Case stood there and laughed at the whole incident. Fear filled John's face and the thought of being eaten a live did not feel too good with him but Mr. Case called off Butch and made him become non-violent with the snap of his fingers.

Coming into Mr. Cases's house, it looked a mess with holes in the walls and roaches running into little cracks in the ceiling trying to keep from being exposed to the light. To make things worse, his grass on the lawn needed cutting and when going up the stairs they rocked back and forth making it difficult to scramble on it. Faded bright red and white paints peeled off the house and in the attic broken windows allowed the bats, owls, and birds to come in and made it their living quarters and a strong smell came off the rug and it was impossible to breath and cats and dogs littered the place and every now and then Mr. Case broke up fights between the different pets he kept.

"We can go into the basement and you can start reading the subject matter to this first topic of the debate which is white and black folks going to school with each other.

"Now remember John you have to be opposed to black and white people going to school with each other. I'll go upstairs and fix us something to eat. I'll make sure you'll like it. In another room the sounds appeared to be that of someone sawing off body parts and blood scattered from under the door and the smell made it impossible to study methods of doing speeches.

Coming into the basement Mr. Case had a big bowl in his hands which trembled and shaked as he handed John a paper on how to speak.

"This soup tastes good. Just keep on reading the instructions on being a good speaker and use your hands as you speak on the different topics."

As he watched Mr. Case eating he could not believe his eyes seeing a college professor with a bowl of human eyes and body parts and eating them which made John throw up because he never knew a professional college professor who taught speech and practiced cannibalism at the same time and he hoped he was not going to be the next meal for Mr. Case.

Maggie, Mr. Case's wife, opened the door and said, "Why is he here? I do not like colored folks coming to my house. My great grandmother told me the carpet baggers came to our great state with freed black folks and took land from us white people and I hate black people for this."

Looking at Maggie John said," You look like a witch ready to eat someone up. Why don't you be easy on me?"

"Maggie go into the house. I have to tudor John on giving a speech."

Dressed in a black dress and black blouse Maggie said, "Darling I will bring your supper out in a minute."

Sitting at a table getting ready to eat, Mr. Case said, "Now you have to have your facts straight about what you are going to talk about You have to say your words with clarity and like you know what you are talking about."

Minutes later Maggie came strolling into the room and she carried two bowls covered by a soupy red color and which smelled bad and to touch it with your lips made you want to spit it out and you could hear the funny noises as Mr. Case sipped the solution into his mouth and the bones shaked inside his bowl as he consumed it with pleasure.

"Take some of this soup. It will make your ribs quiver and your tongue stick out of your mouth."

Knowing he leaned better manners to not taste food made by strangers and John kept saying no when Mr. Case wanted him to drink it. The hunger pains immediately bounced back and forth in his stomach and John said, "Well I guess I'll try this stew because I am hungry."

As John put the bowl up to his mouth he spotted a round looking object which looked like a human eye and he threw the bowl in the air.

"What in the hell! Is this a human eye?!"

"Yes and we want to eat you too!" Mr. Case cried out. We were paid by Big Jim to kill you."

At that instance Mr. Case grabbed a big sword and tried to cut John's head off and nearly did it. Throwing the bowl at Mr. Case John said, "You only brought me here to do Big Jim's dirty work and I'll go to the cops about this."

His wife Maggie came into the room with Butch her big dog and said, "Get the colored boy Butch!" and as Butch jumped into the air to bite John he grabbed one of Mr. Cases long rifles and fired it and Butch fell to the floor.

"You killed Butch. I'll kill you!" and Mr. Case pushed the dinner table into John who jumped on it and Maggie kept throwing anything she could at him and when Mr. Case pulled out his derringer to kill John and said, "Big Jim is giving us $10,000 thousand dollars apiece to kill you. We can use that kind of money. Now you have to die!"

As Mr. Moody pulled the trigger on his gun it exploded killing him and injuring his wife and John jumped out of the room into a large 10 feet pool to escape to safety but he hurt his leg and it was difficult for him to get out of it because his ankle hit a portion of the concrete side of the pool wall. Moving his legs in a slow motion Mr. Cases's crocodile woke up for his evening meal and saw John getting out of the pool but Maggie arrived and tossed hand grenades at John who dove deeper into the 12 feet swimming pool which speeded up his efforts to get away from Maggie who wanted to collect the $10,000 dollars for her reward and to please Big Jim.

If John could escape and tell the police, she and her husband would be put in jail for cannibalism and murder because they had a number of dead bodies in their house which they preserved and no one knew anything about it. The pet crocodile saw Maggie was not paying attention to what she attempted to do to kill John to collect her bounty money from Big Jim. The hungry alligator normally got fed human leftovers Maggie and Mr. Case did not eat but he was hungry and did not care who would be his next meal. Getting her last grenade out, Maggie started to hit John with it hoping she would kill him but Crock the name they called him sneaked quietly up behind Maggie and grabbed her by her legs and pulled her into the water trying to eat her but as John swimmed away very quickly the grenade went off and killed Crock and Maggie instantly and the bluish water turned red with blood. This event saved John, he made it out of the yard and back to Lilly's house who sat in the living room with Dora, and they talked about the events, which took place at Mr. Case's. House. Searching the place, the police could not find out why did this incident took place because no one was there to tell them and the motive behind both of the murders. Going into Mr. Case's study, they found him in an in sane mood talking to himself.

"Have a seat John. You are going to have to make it home or call and tell me if you are going to be late."

"He will not graduate anyway. He does not study when he is at home anyway and by the way when will he help pay for his food he eats here?"

While staying at Lilly's conflict always developed between Lilly and Dora because she was always said things to put John down because she felt he was lazy and no good but she did not realize Lilly was growing fund of John because she saw another side of him and always tried to encourage and inspire him but John stayed in his room studying and did not give Lilly love and affection because he did not want to be hurt by any woman and he still had deep feelings for Betty so he shielded his heart from the affections of women who took an interest in him. Constant conflict erupted when Dora played her music real loud which irritated John and sometimes he and Dora got into bitter arguments about why he was not there for her as she grew up.

"Now listen young lady I am your father and I feel you must respect me and call me father instead of John and other names except John. You must show me more respect and stop playing loud music up so loud."

Trying to mediate between John and Dora became a problem and Dora would say to him. "I have not seen you in twenty because you deserted me and my sister Dianna and now you want to come into my life as if you were there all the time. You got to be crazy!"

"Well I am here now for you regardless of if I was in your life as you grew up. I have home chores for you to do like take out the trash and clean up your room if you expect to eat at this house.!"

Throwing a pillows at John Dora shouted," Go to hell! I'll do whatever I want and you cannot do anything about it!"

In the scuffles at Mr. Case's house, his wallet contained a credit card, it was found at another crime scene, and the police knocked on Lilly's door and asked about John's whereabouts.

Each time detective Willie Davis called to speak with John, Dora said he was dead and do not call back to their house again.

Going to Lilly's house Detective Davis knocked on the door and asked if he could speak to John who studied in his room getting ready for his exams. Pushing open the door Lilly said, "Why are you coming into my house. You do not have a search warrant."

Pushing her out the way, Detective Davis strolled into the house and at that moment Dora attacked detective Davis with a bat swinging it at his legs for assaulting her mother as she shouted, "You have no right to come in here without a search warrant now leave this house immediately!"

Seeing what took place, John came down the stairs with a shot gun in his hands and said, "You came into Lilly's house without a search warrant which is illegal. Now what is it that you want.?"

Taking a seat Detective Davis said, "Now there is no need for you to keep pointing that rifle at me. I came to talk with you about Mr. Case and his wife's death.

Going to the top of the stairs John said, "I went there to take some speech lessons and they tried to kill me but I escaped without a scratch. If you check their house, you'll find the body parts of several people and they lured people to their homes and drugged them. I managed to escape by fighting my way out of it because it was a matter of self -defense."

Writing all of this information down he said, "I guess you are telling the truth because my men did find those dead people's bodies because one of those victims was my daughter whom I had not seen in ten weeks and all of a sudden she just disappeared.

Big Jim immediately sent his PR people to see what happened because he paid Mr. Case good money to kill John but a miracle of fate took place and John escaped death again from Big Jim who wanted him to be killed before he took his senate seat.

CHAPTER 60

One of the students saw John walking on campus and asked his some questions and John said, "Why are you asking me if I want to join your debate team? It seems as if colored folks cannot do anything worthwhile around here but be cooks and janitors."

His name was Teddy Washington, he had a heavy voice, and in his hands, he always carried chewing tobacco because it made him feel good and calmed his nerves when he chewed it... His long hair came down his back like a hippie with colorful bright colored symbols on them which he caught hell for because his family and friends wanted him to be different and dress in suits but Teddy rebelled at everything his parents wanted him to do. Rich life gave him no opportunities to be himself but he searched for an answer to what was his goal in life but he wanted to reach out to John for some reason and the conversation went into high gear.

"Aren't you the one I saw out there holding a sign saying "Nigger go home when me and my attorney came to enroll in this college?"

Pulling out a bottle of wine Teddy said, "Yes I guess you are right. I sided with the people who protested your arrival because my people told me colored people are the dumbest people on the planet and they are lazy and shiftless and I grew up believing it all the time until one of those colored fellows stopped in front of a bullet and died when it could have been me."

"Big deal. A black man has to die for white people to be accepted and I bet you still hate colored people."

It impressed Teddy to hear John speak and Teddy said, "Continue to speak because I and my friends never get a chance to talk with colored students and you are the first one to be enrolled in this college."

Throwing his books on the floor John said," Regardless of this education I am getting very discouraged because I might not graduate from this college. They are giving me all low grades and I cannot do anything about it."

"I thought you were getting a fair break around here."

Still disgusted John threw his books against the wall and said, "I am barely making it through this college. Every time I sign up for a speech class it is always full and I need them very badly. I plan on debating Big Jim in the coming election."

"Ok you're having problems with your books and up until now you cannot get the courses to graduate."

"Well I am ready to throw in the towel and go to another college which will treat colored folks much better and maybe I'll be able to debate Big Jim because he is not representing the poor white and colored families in this state. On July 5th go and enroll in Dr. Brewster's class because he has formed a public speaking class for people like you."

"Thanks a lot. I'll be there in two days."

Approaching Dr. Herbert Brewster class for public speaking John went to him with an enrollment form to take his class while there were only white students in the class.

Standing at five feet tall professor Brewster wore sandals which made a loud noise and he smoked cigarettes when he lectured to his students sitting on a desk with folding legs pointing in the direction of his students showing holes in his shoes and in a few weeks if he kept on wearing them and they would hurt his foot and this made his students laugh at him when they witnessed this taking place and the smell from his feet made some of the students sit away from his desk.

"I did not know a colored boy would be in my class. You cannot come into this class without taking public speaking one."

Holding his head up John's heart beaded fast with sweat and his nerves kicked in and he could barely speak. One of the white students yelled and said, "Tell the nigger to go back to Africa where he belongs." and all the students laughed at what he said.

"You see they do not want you in this class or on the debate team. You know how it is. They will not allow you to debate the white students."

Nellie Bacon stood up and said," Why can't you give him a chance to be in this class and make a positive contribution to what we are trying to learn and also to our school as a whole. You always say the colored students are dumb and cannot represent our school but if you do not give them a chance we will never know."

Another student said, "Why don't you sit down and mind your own business. You are trying to speak up for the niggers. Let's decide if we want the nigger in this class. They are always coming down here to our state of Mississippi trying to tell us how to run our schools and places of accommodations. We should be able to let who ever we want to sit at our lunch counters."

Looking at the excitement the students caused Mr. Brewster said, "Let's take a show of hands and see if we want this colored student in this debate class with the possibilities of him representing us in the national school debate. The room thirty students grew quiet as one after one raised their hand to deny John the opportunity to join the class and debate team except Nellie Bacon who kept to her conscious of free equality for colored folks and John Carol especially. Standing up and walking to the front of the class Dr. Brewster said, "There's nothing we can do to put this student out of this class even though I disagree with Miss. Bacon. This student will stay in this class but representing us at a debate program is out of the question. He will not be able to represent the viewpoints of this college fairly because he will be against the segregationist policies our college stand for."

Not being outdone, Nellie wearing a dark blue cotton dress with a white stylish white collar said, "This college was built by colored workers but you look down on and many of your parents and great grandparents were breast fed from the colored slaves they kept in bondage and worked in the hot sun picking cotton and getting nothing in return but a life time of slavery only to see their own daughters and sons sold into slavery never to be seen again. We owe them to enjoy the same rights as white people."

Boos lit up the room and the students who smoked kept blowing it out of their mouths and many of the white girls kept folding their legs to let John see them but John dared not to look in their direction. Many of them never dated colored boys and were willing to find out by flirting with John but he was reluctant to do this because he did not have an interest in social integration with white women. He mostly studied by himself and lone.

John hated Earth Science because he did not feel no interest in this because the professors never answered his questions when he asked for help. None of the students spoke to him in the classes he took. The only student who spoke to John was Mary bacon who came from a wealthy family and plantation owner and she always spoke about the human plight of the people on the different plantations who suffered from not getting much needed food and healthcare for their families. Sometimes John and Mary Bacon studied with each other getting ready for the debate which would be in a few weeks from now.

For rehearsals Miss Bacon came over to Lilly's house where John stayed and Lilly did not except this at first and Lilly told Miss. Bacon John was her man and not for sale and sometimes Lilly showed hostility towards Miss. Bacon who started liking John as they studied together.

To add to this dilemma Dora always played her record player up loud to keep him from studying properly and John came upstairs and took the record player and threw it out the window and broke it.

"Why did you throw her record player out of the window? That's not the proper way to get respect from your daughter. Now say I am sorry and you will not do that again and furthermore your tutoring lessons over here are over. I thought me and your daughter were going to help you with your lessons anyway."

"You could at least told us about your plans to hire that bitch to tutor you for your speech classes."

Seeing the atmosphere was bad he did not waste no time getting out of Lilly's house never to come back after she came home and caught John and Miss. Bacon kissing each other in her bedroom while she and Dora shopped for groceries.

Lilly pushed John out of the front door of her house in anger and John said, "Thanks for the help. I deeply appreciate it." And Dora threw some of John's notebooks at Miss. Bacon as she left the front door and Lilly said, "I should have told you to go to the back door like they tell us to come in from the back door of grocery stores instead of the front entrance of the store."

Realizing Lilly wanted to bang him up John he went out to the quest house and could not get in.

Coming towards John Lilly grabbed anything she could get hands on and threw various items at him and John ducked his head to keep from getting hit by the objects and Lilly pranced back and forth in her living room and complained he was such a dog and womanizer.

"How could you do such a thing while I and Dora shopped at the store for your birthday present? You are no good and do not deserve to be helped and you are taking me for granted and I love you. I hope you do not graduate and stay a nigger field hand. You should leave my house and do not come back until you say you are sorry."

Ignoring Lilly John took off down the street making light footsteps vowing never to come back to Lilly's house again.

Knowing he owed Lilly much appreciation for letting him stay at her house rent free and eating her food made him think about what she wanted him to accomplish in life. Looking into the mailbox Lilly saw a letter from John's debate professor asking him to stop by his office to get information on the debate which was going to take place at the huge auditorium in Jackson. After seeing the application to join the debate team and John saw this as an opportunity to show his ability to gain some experience as a debator. Going up to the white people's section of the library John wanted to look at some books on public speaking to gain valuable in information on that subject.

Strolling into the library someone said, "We do not allow colored folks in this library now get out of here!"

Trying not to get angry John left the library without saying anything because he saw the sign on the wall which said no colored folks allowed in this library and he sat on the steps of the library with tears falling from his eyes because he needed more material on public speaking. Not to be outdone John went back to the library two blocks away and he saw the same sign saying the same thing.

"I'll never be able to get the books I want because they will not let colored folks use those the library," John said to himself.

As John gazed down the steps of the Dolson W. State Citizen's Bank he saw a man trying to make his way up the white marble stairs holding a cane and he struggled to make it up the stairs. Seeing the fellow having trouble getting up the steps John rushed to the rescue to help him. The elderly gentleman wore a black suit with a white color which indicated his profession which said he was a member of the clergy. His body frame made him look like he played sports and lifted weights and he made a limp as he barely touched the steps and each time his foot touched the steps he made a noise and tried to refrain himself from looking helpless and in need a shiny cross hung from his neck and in the other hand a bible. No one would think this man which took John's interest wore gun holsters around his waist. The mustache he wore made him look like a sheriff and his black boots shined brightly and his pressed suit made him look like a dignitary and a bright white handkership neatly folded over the suit pocket on the right side of his shirt. The puzzled John went to the blind man and said, "May I help you I see you are blind and need some help."

"I guess you have noticed this so why don't you go away and mine your own business."

Feeling rejected John made his way down the long flight of stairs and he slipped on a banna peal bringing his body to the ground below him.

While the fellow opened the maple-wooded doors, a big man looking like a wrestler with tattoos on his face and all of his body grabbed the gentleman and tried to take his money. The commotion made John hurriedly get up and came to the rescue but as he started up the stairs it became impossible because of earlier injuries he suffered in an accident trying to help the pastor.

Calls for help echoed from the gentleman's voice and the man wearing a dark suit hit him in head and witnessing this ordeal John managed to lift himself up and made it to the blind man who by now was holding on the robber and hitting him.

"You should be worshiping no person by the name of Jesus Christ. I'll make you pay for this. Pulling out a metal idol that contained diamonds in it he said, "You should be worshiping our God Jesus."

Making it to the Top of the stairs, John tried to stop this big man from robbing the gentleman but it became impossible and he hit John knocking him down. The police came and rushed up the stairs and were getting ready to arrest John but the gentleman said, "Do not arrest this young man who came to my rescue.

"Take the crazy man who do not like gay people like me. The colored person came to help me when no other person would."

Seeing that was the case, they took the wild ugly looking man to jail and he kicked and screamed and the police officers hit him upside of his head with Billy clubs repeatedly until he could not standup as he cried. "Please do not hit me no more. I'll obey you."

"By the way what is your name and I am pleased you came to my rescue at the cost of you getting hurt. I am looking for a book on my gay rights but I'll have a hard time finding it. It seems many gay people write books but this library never seems to have them and my friends say this is the building which appears to have books on gay rights."

Dusting the dust off of the gentleman's suit and giving him his walking stick John said, "They will not let me in the library either because I am colored."

Listening to what John said the elderly gentleman said, "Lead me to the library and I'll pretend you are my servant and you can get my books on gay rights and look for something on debating."

The library looked like former President Thomas Jefferson's house at Monticello with a big white pinball on the roof of it and going through the large maple doors made you feel like you opened a medieval castle door that ringed a bell letting people know you entered the library adorned in red carpet going through out the library floor. As usual you saw the white and colored sections which angered John but he felt this was not the time to get involved in racial conflicts if he could help it. The various volumes of the book consisted of many different topics and clerks assisted people to get books but every time John tried to get a clerk to help him they just ignored him and helped other white customers.

The gentleman said, "Act as if you are pulling the books off the shelf and tell me if the little one is talking about gay rights."

Wondering what the gentleman attempted to do, John asked him why did he want books on gay rights and he said, "John this is difficult for gay people to get jobs, or openly admit they are gay and it appears we are persecuted just like colored people and I want to be able to sue people when they mistreat us and form an organization which fights for gay rights."

Still looking into the section John spotted a book that listed some rights gays have and do not have in Mississippi. A tall looking person came rushing them saying," You are in the white section of this library. Now go back to the colored section where your kind is located."

Getting angry the gentleman said, "Now mister I have to use this fellow as my personal aide so let him help me get what I want about gay people."

Taking out a notebook. Easy Jenkins ran the security of the library and he dressed in black pants and a blue shirt like law enforcement officers wore and shiny black shoes adorned with two picture Ids, a five year pin of service, a black tie and name tag but his name fitted his personality because he gave John and the elderly gentleman much difficulty just to get their books and posed a problem and Easy wanted money before they could take the books out of the library.

Easy put on a big smile with his 250 pound frame and long white blond hair and he said, "I know both of you. The nigger has raised so much hell trying to integrate into our white schools and colleges and you are gay."

Setting in his seat John said, "What does our backgrounds have to do with us using the library?"

Putting out a cigarette which he was smoking Easy said, "These are difficult economic months in this state and if I let you use the library with the nigger helping you, I could lose my job and plus you haven't said anything about compensation for letting you get books out of here."

Regardless of the rules Easy lit up another cigarette. And did not care about the rules which said there would be no smoking in the library and after he finished the cigarette he threw it on the pretty carpet. Immediately the other gentleman told John to write out a check he took out of his bankbook and gave it to Easy and a big smile appeared on his face as he said, "The going rate is $4000, for the both of you to use the library."

Taking a big look at Easy John said, "This should be enough money. All we want to do is check out two books."

Chattering among several people kept looking at what took place and smoke journeyed through the air and sailed into the nostrils of patrons using the library and they read all types of books. You could see the smoke from the rug quietly started to make a small flame but someone accidently kicked a bucket against it keeping the ever growing flame out of sight from the patrons going through the dozens of books they examined out of curiosity with their fingers flipping pages back and forth examining each one of them for knowledge, which either aroused their sense of awareness or increased their enthusiasm to plow through the volumes of information exposed to them by the authors of these precious books.

But somehow the smell of smoke reached the fire alarms and instantly they went off after getting the books they wanted and Easy shouted for the patrons to run out the door before the library went up in flames. An anti-gay person saw the gay's rights book in John's hands and took it out of his possession and scrambled away from him. With all of the trouble it took to get those books John ran after him to retrieve them leaving the old gentleman in the room wondering in bewilderment what took place. Seeing the young man kept going faster than him John grabbed a book from one of the shelves and threw it at his feet and he tripped and fell but when he grabbed for the book the stranger who weigh about 300 pounds and full of muscles pulled down a shelf of books and they fell on John and the stranger left in a hurry leaving the books he stole from them on the ground and John got the books they both wanted and went to get the old gentleman out of the library.

"Where's are the books? Easy said." Your friend the old blind gentleman wrote a bad check because I called the bank and they said he do not have an account with them and you he are a fraud and fake."

The flames got thicker and attempts made to put out the fire failed because the fire extinguisher would not work and everyone had to get out of the library and Easy got impatient and wanted his money for letting John and his friend get their books and he wanted to get paid. The supervisor came to Easy and said, "You have to help get these people out of here in a hurry and that's an order." And he left helping the other people escape death from the fire which spread through the library.

"I have to have my money now what are you two going to do? You two are not going nowhere. The smoke is getting very thick in here."

"We do not have it and another check will have to be made out to you. Just look at this place you should be trying to help people get out of the library instead of making a profit and I will report you for keeping us in here against our will."

As they held the books they became very hot and the old gentleman said "Here's a 100 year old watch my grandfather gave me. You can have it and let us go I cannot take another breath of this smoke."

"Well guess this will work. It's a deal. You are getting what you want and I and am satisfied. It was nice doing business with the both of you."

"That dam Big Jim said he would help improve the safety conditions in this library but as usual he lied to get the support of the library commission when he ran for reelection but he did not take care of their concerns after he won reelection."

"John said and all three of them left the library and battled to get out of it.

CHAPTER 61

A big crowd is gathering in Jackson Mississippi and the debate teams arrived at the great capital building and in front of the big two story building dignitaries came to witness the great debate John was going up against the University of Arkansas debate team and he was a member of the GreenVill Debate team. People from all across the country came to see the great debate teams of Arkansas State and Greenvill who defeated all the candidates who debated against them and now it was time to decide who would prevail and win the Gold Cup Debating Award and the topic of debate was: Is it justified to give civil rights to gays and colored people. In the auditorium a large table had a number of judges setting at it and two podiums for each team member from Greenvill and Arkansas State would speak on the given topic with a pitcher of water on each side of their podiums.

In the colored section of the auditorium sat Negro visitors who wanted to see who would win especially because of John Carol the only black person would speak and this generated much interest because of the prejudice shown by Arkansas State to integrate their college to black students. The news media made a spectacle of it and predicted Greenvill College would lose.

The announcer requested for the first speaker from Arkansas State to come up to the podium and speak on the topics and his name was Billy Satson and he weigh about 150 pounds and he dressed in a brown suit and white shirt and black shoes and when he spoke he kept blanking his eyes and smiled as he spoke. His proud parents watched from a distance but the only problem dealt with was he identified with gay people's rights, but was against integration of the races in any form and he was against women's rights and had many issues against speaking up for topics which he was against even though the objective of their debate team was stand united as one on the issues.

A nervous John Carol came to speak and all the hard work he put in to debate would mean a lot to him and the other colored people who wanted to into Greenvill College. The look in his face became a mass of nervousness because he wore stolen clothes from a clothing store because he lacked the money to buy them and the clothing managers put out rewards to have him arrested. Trying to drink some water, he spit it back out because of the length of time it sat on the podium table. Shouts of boos came from many of the people in the audience.

One of the clothing managers spotted John on television wearing the only suit that no other sellers of suits in Jackson, Mississippi had in their inventory and wanted to attend and see the debate and have John arrested but the owner Thomas Big Hog Williams said, "Do not have him arrested because he might win wearing our famous suit and we can have him say he wore our famous brown more hair suit and get a lot of people to buy and wear it. They say millions of people around the world would be viewing this debate and we would be getting free advertising for our suits. I'll get to that debate to see to it that John wins this debate."

As usual the colored folks sat in their segregated places in the balcony and white folks sat across from them. Betty came to hear John's speech about civil rights and gays and he wiped his forehead of sweat which came down and hit his hands carrying the topics on the papers he wanted to speak to the audience about who gathered to hear his viewpoints on the civil rights of black people and the rights of gay people being able to live in our productive society in the state of Mississippi. His big round ears heard whispering to the left and right of him as the crowd drank and the smell of cigarette smoke danced in the air hitting everyone in its path and who tasted the rich nicotine aroma on their lips which spoke of who would win this debate and what it would be like if he lost to a colored boy but would John Carol be wasting his time because the forces that be said the colored boy could not beat a white boy and get away with it. The colored race was seen by the white Mississippians who did not believe in the creative mind of the colored people who were looked up on as people who could only till the ground for their white masters who for almost two hundred years grew rich off the long hours colored slaves worked from sundown to sunset. The audience consisted of white people who did not believe in segregation of the races and many of them felt true equality should be given to the non -white population of the state and some of them were in the audience to support the speaker who championed the rights of true equality of civil rights for all people not just for colored citizens in the state because many white folks went to jail urging black folks to register and vote and suffered the humiliation of having soda and ice cream poured on them trying to integrate the lunch counters and got beat up participating in the freedom rides on busses taking them to the deep south to assist poor colored farmers to organize themselves into constructive non-violent groups to form unions for better working conditions and higher wages and wanted these issues addressed to inspire the people who were risking their lives to achieve the civil rights given by the United States Constitution.

Looking at the audience Billy said, "I think you for coming out here this evening to hear a debate between John Carol and myself on the issue of if gays and black people should have equal rights with white people. I must personally say I am gay myself and no one knew I developed an open relationship with a male gay friend of mine I did not tell anyone about it until right now. I grew tire of keeping everything a secret which I felt very much in love with my gay companion. I feel that people should be able to be with whomever they want to be with. Many years from now laws will be passed when gay people will be able to adopt children and get the same benefits for health care and social security and not feel uncomfortable when strolling down the street holding hands. Gay people have been killed just because they were gay and teased by their relatives when it was known they were gay. We have a right to love who we want to regardless to if our mate is of the same sex. In his speech Billy had much to say and was not finished with his speech and what he said did not go too good with the audience who did not agree with what he said. And he sat down without saying anything about other problems concerning women's rights and black civil rights.

"We want to know how you feel about women and black people's civil rights and that is what we came to hear what your viewpoints were about these unpopular topics which is part of the debate so tell us. "One person in the audience shouted.

Still not out done Billy felt it was his duty to tell the people what they wanted to hear and said, "Well it hard to say if I want to speak in favor for black and white people. Civil rights. I came from a family tradition where my relatives owned many black people and my momma did not breast feed me. A black person did it because momma had other things to do instead of breast feed me so she hired a black women to do it so you can say that I grew up around black people. I was raised to think white folks were superior to colored people because that was the way it was. I was told I could play with the colored boys as kids but when we got older I could only play with white boys. How could I have a twenty year relationship with Jason who was black and toss him to the side when we got much older and he became my lover and we are like that now. I had to get into the college and have anti-gay and anti- black civil rights to get on the debate team so I let my true feeling to not be known because I championed the rights of gay and black people but I was afraid of losing my scholarship so I went along with their anti-black and anti-gay rights so I could pay my tuition and graduate. As for as the right for woman equality I think they should not be in charge of important positions of power because they are women but times are changing because I was at home and called a policeman to come and take me and my child to the hospital because she choked on a chicken bone and a women policeman came and put the hemlock maneuver on her and saved her life. Many of my friends are women but I think men should run things and we all know the bible say man is the head of the house whole and the woman is his help mate and that is all I have to say about these issues and hope the best speaker wins. I know I'll lose my scholarship but I have to speak my peace and say what I feel. I'll be proud of myself many years from now because I said what I believed in and would pay a price for it."

As he sat down with a smile on his face, Billy felt good to be able to speak the truth about an issue which is something most people in Jackson, Mississippi did not agree with and the judges he felt should be open minded about his beliefs instead of being bias about them...

News casters asked the audience who would probably win the debate about gay rights and a soda bottle came sailing at Billy but this situation did not deter him from coming back to debate John Carol from wanting to win this debate. As Billy spoke people had to be carried out because people who did not like what he said and someone tampered with his speakers making it hard for him to speak but in one case a young lady in the audience became overcome with what he said and fainted but with him being gay Billy did not feel compelled to comfort her.

The Master of Ceremonies strolled up to the podium and addressed the crowd and said "That boy sure has courage to speak on those topics against what the school he represented stood for and against in the areas of civil rights that I do not agree with but in some cases gays should have rights just like the colored citizens and it took courage for him to speak his constitutional beliefs. What Billy said went on back in the days of Jesus Christ and I feel that God made us to be with the opposite mate but we cannot condemn people because they want to be with each other. I am against two people of the same sex to be mating with each other because the God I worship is against this."

In the crowd Dianna shouts at Billy and said "You are misleading these people because you have both male and female lovers. "Look at these pictures showing Billy hugging male and females."

The officers in charge of the debate team came and grabbed Dianna and she does not leave easily and hits one of them in the mouth and they haul her off which did not set too good with Betty'.

Looking at Dianna did not make John look too good but he absorbed the boos from the crowd and the announcer asked John to come up to the podium to address the need for equality for black and gay people and he said, "I do not see that colored and gay folks should be judged on the same level. Both white and black folks have built the great state of Mississippi also."

Getting angry about what Dianna, said Dora passed by her and said, "How dare you say things like that about my friend Billy because he is only speaking his mind?"

"What your problem. You have always been uppity and thought you were too good to be around your own black sister which is me but you still hate it that that you have a black daddy," Dora shouted.

"That's something you'll have to deal with on your own account" Dianna shouted back. For years you knew I was related to you but could not stand the fact I was white and could mix with white folks and you could not stand it."

"I was raised as a little girl with you and you act like it never took place and tried to hide it when you went to a white school."

Seeing what was about to take place in the sister's confrontation with each other, Betty knew Dianna temper and lily knew Dora's temper Betty got in between them requesting that they stop this fighting of each other so the debate could go on and with the reporters in the crowd they would be printing stories in the newspapers about the incident of what was taking place.

"You cannot solve your problems like this. Everyone is entitled to their own opinion and no matter how you two sisters do not like it that's the way of the world. You are going to realize that one day you will need each other as time goes on. You two must stop the hating of each other. This type of behavior will have to stop" Betty said.

Lily came over to the area where Betty, Dora, and Dianna confronted each other about their disagreements and said, "Guess who's coming to dinner. It seems like there is difference of agreement and no one is winning. It would be nice to have some type of unity with each other. Remember the old saying "Together we stand.

Divided we fall. By this time security came and requested that they take their seats are all of them would be thrown out of the building.

"Big Jim sent us over here to stop all of this. I do not think he is going to enjoy that. He cannot hear the debate especially since he put $10,000 on the white boy to win so let's settle down and all of you get to your seats. Plus he has two women with him instead of his wife Mable."

In a rush to get to see the debate Senator Wilson paid our guards $1,000 dollars apiece to keep her from coming in this area where the debate was going on. Curiosity appeared on their faces when they saw Senator Big Jim Wilson sitting at a table with Polly who was a constant companion to him for many years posing as a public relations person for him against the wishes of her family because they felt they were using her.

Looking at Big Jim and Polly his black mistress sitting at the most important guest seat angered Betty and Dandy but sandy said, "This is nothing and now our crafty no good daddy of ours have always pretended to just be a married man and have an employer type of relationship with Polly. Daddy has to leave his colored women alone and its rumored he has several colored children by them and we do not know anything about this but eventually it will come out in the open so let him do his thing. You know daddy has to have a new woman in his life since momma left him."

"She left for good reasons because daddy never took the time to be a good husband and wanted more women to sleep with. I guess it's in his blood to be a womanizer."

The announcer spoke to the audience and said, Now John Coral come and speak on civil rights for the colored man and the lands that the state is trying to get from them and the rights that gay people should have in this state of Mississippi."

"Ladies and gentlemen I want to speak about segregation and civil rights in general."

A frightened look appeared on Big Jim's face as this was said and he did not like it because him and his political buddies planned to take those lands by saying it is has atomic wastes and declare it a hazard for people to live on and seize it and promise to give the people living on it a place to live in financed by the state government of Mississippi. This would be the greatest lie ever told."

People served drinks of all kinds as the two speakers tried to win the debate.

John said, "This is not a problem of only black people getting their civil rights in the state of Mississippi. Civil rights to me means keeping your lands and stopping men of greed from taking them and using them for their own needs which means much more money for themselves. I feel colored and white folks should live in peace with each other and judge each other by the content of their character and not the color of their skin. This is a country of haves and have nots but we the people in this great state of Mississippi must share in the wealth of this state both colored and white and unite and rid ourselves of the political forces which are trying to take oil from lands in this great state of Mississippi.

As Big Jim listened to John speak about his hidden plans to take the oil rich lands and he witnessed something he did not expect and his wife Mable stood before both of them with a gun in his hand and said, "I knew all alone you and that colored woman slept with each other and I'll shoot both of you."

"Now Mable you do not want to do something you will regret."

People saw the commotion and moved out of the direction a bullet would fly to kill Big Jim and Polly who sat quiet and said nothing to keep Mable from pulling the trigger. As Mable pulled the trigger Big Jim took a plate and held it as the bullets broke it and Polly dived for cover trying to not get hit and people scrambled out of the way. Another bullet hit the cocktail glasses and Big Jim pushed the table over and bullets made their path into it. While Mable kept firing a police officer came from behind her and grabbed the gun hand and took it from her.

Even with the events surrounding what took place the announcer shouted over the loud speaker everything would be ok to finish the debate.

John tried to adjust to what happened and said, "You see I hope the forces of justice will give Mable her rights of duprocess but I know Big Jim. He will make things work for his wife to not be put in jail. That's what my speeches are about full equality for all the people colored and white people both straight and gay should be able to work in harmony and build this great state together. Black folks tilled the ground and picked the cotton and the plantation owners became rich off of their hard labor. Now there is trouble brewing because integration of the school is needed but there are people who do not want equality to work. They want to see the races fighting each other instead of trying to build a greater Mississippi. The rich people in this state want to control and charge our poor black and white farmer low prices for their crops but will make sure their high profile friends in the state of Mississippi and federal government profit from the higher prices when their crops are sold around the world. The establishment is not working for the poor farmers.'

All of a sudden the sound system stopped and there was no sound coming out of the speakers and John and his supporters are getting upset about what took place, The announcer said, "The winner will be announced in about ten minutes."

When the announcer came up to the podium, he declared the other candidate the winner and John and his supporters were surprised and they felt he the officials cheated John and felt he should have won because of the manner he presented the different issues and arguments to the listening audience. The chants of unhappy people were heard from the supporters wanting John to win. .You could see the disgust in their faces and the anger they showed as they tore up the brochures about the debate. The taste of victory could not be celebrated because of the unfairness of the referees who followed Big Jim's directives to score him so low he would end up losing regardless of how professional he looked giving his speech. The noon sun scorched many of them as they listened to the two people giving their speeches.

On this day John made his hard earned right to graduate from college. As John sat on the stage to graduate with those students his mind raced back to the times he tried out for the football team to play the quarterback position and the football players and his teammate on the offensive line would not block for him and he got hit many times. He never gave up, and nn all of this drama John felt he could make a contribution to the team.

Constantly thinking about his earlier ordeals at the college, he saw in his day dreaming the time when the coach made him do more wind sprints and other exercises than the other football players but he never gave his teammates the joy of making him quit. As time went on his teammates gradually helped him because they saw John had the heart to keep on getting knocked down but he never complained and his coach still had no inclinations to let John make the team but when his teammates heard about it they protested against this prejudice because they felt John possessed the skills necessary to be a great football player especially when he was given a chance to show his skills and talents to help his school win their division and they staged sit ins when other college football teams would not compete with them because they had a colored quarterback and Big Jim paid the officials to cheat against those team who played against John Coral but despite the prejudice his team won a national championship with John quarterback when he threw a winning pass touchdown pass with three seconds to go in the game and the fans went wild when John did this.

At the prom a sign hung on the wall saying niggers go home that insulted John and he and his date turned around and walked out of the prom room in tears but his fateful seniors friends who played football with John stopped them and said." If you and your date cannot go to the prom, we will do something about this."

All the football players came and tore down the poster and dared anyone to put John and his date out of the prom and this made John and Lilly proud to see his teammates stood up for him that night.

As he sat on the graduation stage memories of him, debating white students did not get the approval of all the student body. Many of the white students expressed angry remarks when John said the student body should be integrated more then what it was because too many of his classmates hated colored students they knew little about.

The criticism John faced as a student came his way and his English teachers made him do compositions in the writing lab because his instructors did not like the way he expressed himself in words. In the long run, John appreciated this ordeal when he campaigned for Big Jim's office because after long hours of practice he improved in being able to write any forms of written communication.

To John's surprise, Big Jim attended the graduation and hugged John saying he was glad for him but John was very suspicious of him because he tried hard to influence his professors to give him low grades to keep him from graduating. Liking to be in the company of pretty women Big Jim as usual escorted Polly to the graduation who was disliked by Mable and Betty her daughter and Sandy did not like it either because she felt Mable gave him the best years of her life and never cheated on him. Knowing Big Jim knew many judges, he influenced them to place Mable in a mental health institution for life. Big Jim felt Mable needed help. The only problem that developed was Mable got into fights with Big Jim's staff.

This day would never be forgotten because Sarah cried when she saw John walk up to the podium to get his Bachelor of Science degree and she thought about the many times her husband Peter was cheated out of his money. Peter lacked the education basics to add and subtract numbers and he wanted his son to get a good education and represent the people in a professional manner and speak with dignity.

John took classes in speech because proper English was needed when addressing the senate and at the same time speak to poor people on their level and not use big words which would confuse them. Sarah saw in John a positive role model for the children both black and white who lived on the farmlands in the delta of Mississippi because the only black men they saw were waiters or workers who were in the fields harvesting crops.

But now John's friends and himself felt he could run for Big Jim's senate seat and beat the opposition pitted against him and his mother felt proud of what her son did to get a good college education despite the discrimination he faced obtaining it, Even though Peter did not live long enough to see him graduate from college, John made a pledge to his father he would graduate and become the first United States senator who would be an African American from the state of Mississippi.

In his mind, John wanted to help organize the farmers into an organization to control what took place because the farm crops provided money to buy house whole goods, take care of their families, and keep food on their tables and the necessities to live a comfortable life, despite the desired forces who wanted to take their lands from them. Their desires were to form an organization which could uplift the spirits and especially the poor farmers who were constantly being cheated by Big Jim and his political allies. John vowed to not let that happen if it meant risking his life to stop it. He was up against a powerful man who would do anything to stay in power and no one had ever defeated him in anything he did and Big Jim never lost an election.

To get more money, Big Jim wanted to build private prisons in parts of those lands and write laws to have the prisoners learn different trades to build and make things like clothes, boats, grow crops, learn to take care of fish and market it to various stores in the state of Mississippi but this angered John and the farmers because they could lose money because of the cheap labor costs Big Jim would use to prepare their crops for market lowering the prices of the farmer's goods and get paid some of the profits made off the farmer's crops. It took hard labor to produce them. Money was needed and the farmers wanted someone who would work for them and not let the corporations take over their lands in search of oil.

But John began to organize his organization and continued to communicate and argue with Lilly and Dora and as time went by Lilly and John began to get closer and she wanted to know if John would marry her He still lived in a world where marriage did not play an important role in his life and they argued a lot about it because Lilly fell in love with him but John still loved Betty and could not explain the reason why. His friends told him to go on with his life and forget about her because of the many years they stayed apart from each other. Betty was on the side of big business and broke all of the labor laws and the farms she owned did not pay good wages and as usual Betty did what her father Big Jim said to stay in power and keep on making big money.

As Big Jim and Benson strolled on his plantation, a conversation started between them and they smoked their favorite cigars and Big Jim was eager to talk with Benson for his further ambitions to get farmlands which he thought contained oil.

"Benson I want those oil lands the farmers have but if you run for governor you will have the power to persuade the state legislators to vote and declare those lands a hazard and force the people to sell their properties."

"What do you propose Big Jim? You know that uppity college graduate John Carol is running on your coat tails and wants to get your senate seat."

"Over my dead body. He will not beat me regardless of what education he has. If he gets elected, John will have those black and white freedom riders coming down here stirring up trouble trying to help the colored folks organize to vote and send their own representatives to congress."

"I want you to run for governor and get the votes necessary to get those properties that are rich with oil. While John is busy going after my office, you will raise hell on the farmers who have the oil on their lands. I worked like hell to pay off his instructors not to give him failing grades but my daughter Sandy came to the rescue and bailed him out."

"That sounds like a winner Benson we have to keep him from organizing the farmers because we will have to pay higher prices for their crops to take to market."

"We can bring some insects over and drop them in their crops which will eat them up and to speed things up for us to take their farm lands."

"Now you got the right idea. Take the land at all cost."

"But Big Jim I want your daughter Betty as part of the deal so talk to her for me and convince her I have changed and want her in my life."

To get his plans taken care of, Big Jim knew Benson could do many things as governor to help him out and he wanted to persuade Betty to marry Benson so he could use him to get the farmer's oil rich lands and he was sure oil was on the lands himself.

CHAPTER 62

B etty went to the horse races and one of her horses she normally bets on was going to win the race and she betted $1,000 dollars on him and lost her money. She could not realize why her horse Wild Furry did not win. Wild Fury was considered the frontrunner to win. One other person had his horses in the race and that was her father Big Jim who betted $5,000 on Lighting to win. He knew Betty's horse was in the race.

Instead of wondering what took place, Betty went to the stall and saw fellows putting drugs in the horses' water buckets before beginning to race and when their handlers were not watching their horses or going out to lunch. The drugs would slow them down as they raced around the track.

Betty noticed Big Jim's handler guarded his horses 24 hours at a time and never left them alone for fear someone might poison them. When she saw what was happening, Betty wondered what she could do about the situation. At this particular time, Big Jim and Polly came and sat by Betty who did not like seeing Polly with her father and gave her an ugly look and decided to get up and leave.

Big Jim said to her, "Do not leave I saw you sitting there and I wanted to talk with you. You know Polly because she helps me in my office and she is a life saver. I almost lost her in a firefight."

People who knew Big Jim came up to him during the races to get his opinion on who to bet on and asked who was the colored woman with him but Big Jim ignored them and said she was a part of his staff and they should not worry about his private life. In some cases he said,

"My wife Mable is sick and recuperating from a bout with alcoholism and hopefully she will recover from it."

"Betty you know who this person is?

Dressed in a pretty red dress with flowers on them and a white straw hat and white slippers Betty said,

"I know this is the black woman who takes up most of your time while your white faithful wife of 30 years needs your help. How could you leave mother for this no good black bitch. Mother stayed by your side when all your other girlfriends wanted you for your money. When you went out and stayed with the other no good women, mother took you back."

'That's not true Betty I loved your mother but she did a lot of drinking in public and this did not look too good for me. Rumors kept circulating Mable went into public places shouting out loud the misery she a went through because of my many women who I worked with in the public service business."

"That's a lot of bullshit and now you are disgracing our family name running around with this no good black woman. How dare you!"

A crowd gathered as Betty criticized her father for his intentions on keeping Polly by his side as Betty tried to get Polly's attention. Dressed in a white dress Polly tried not to say anything but this time she could not take no more of Big Jim's family saying things which humiliated her and pushed Betty with Big Jim getting in between them.

Polly said," Let's get something straight. Your father came to me and he was lonely for love and affection. You feel you are losing a father but I love him and he loves me."

"That's a lie "Betty said, "He's always had affairs with any woman which took his eyes and he does not know what it means to be faithful to his wife and now she is in a nursing home and she is insane because of father's many years of having affairs with other women."

Trying to keep the two women from fighting each other Big Jim smileed and ordered one of his body guards to take Betty away.

"Another thing Big Jim you should give these people their money back because you have been paying people to inject chemicals into their horses to slow them down so your horses can win their races."

Slapping Betty Big Jim said, "That's a lie. Big Jim never cheats the people. I will not stand for that type of talk now get the hell out of my face!"

A reporter who worked for a newspaper happen to hear the commotion walked behind Big Jim's guards and made sure Betty could not interfere Polly and his horse betting and as usual Big Jim's wrong doing helped him much money. Going to pick up his money his guards took Betty away from him and Polly. One of Polly's brothers by the name of Randolph approached Big Jim and said,

"Why are you messing with my sister and using her for your selfish needs and when you finish with her you are going to find another colored woman to sleep with and you are not going to leave your white wife for a colored woman anyway. As of today you will leave my baby sister alone."

Counting his $10,000 dollars Big Jim said, "Now boy go to the colored section of this race track before you say something that's going to get you in trouble. Just mind your own business boy. I and Polly have things to do and a lot of money to count."

"That's a lie. Will my sister be able to sit at the table with your white friends or will you send her to the colored section of the country club you never eat at?"

Putting his money in his pocket Big Jim said, "Boy take this five dollars and put it on my horse, the colored horse and win a bunch of money now get."

Before Big Jim could turn to leave, Randolph pulled out a gun and to shoot Big Jim and he grabbed Polly and used her body as a shield and the bullets holes went into her chest and body. The commotion brought Big Jim's guards to the scene and tackled Randolph and took him to jail for trying to kill Big Jim but the bullets fatally shot killed Polly who was pronounced dead on arrival and probably would have lived but she could not be taken to the white hospital because of the segregation laws not allowing black patients into their hospitals.

CHAPTER 63

Big Jim visited Betty at her farm she purchased by foreclosure to speak with her about marrying Benson because he decided to run for governor and he would convince the legislators pass bills to declare the oil rich lands a hazard and the farmers would be evicted off of it. The estate Betty lived in came as a result of taking it from an owner who foreclosed on the property and Betty's bribed the owner and bought it for $100,000 dollars instead of the asking price of $300,000 dollars. Using blackmail Betty's lawyers threaten to expose him to the public for selling poorly fed beef cows who were diseased.

"I will not marry that no good bastard who raped me many years ago when I was drugged,"

"That man can do a lot for us if you marry him especially when I back him to be governor."

His face looked angry as Betty told her father she would not obey him and Big Jim hated to be injured by Betty not to follow his plans and Big Jim said, "If you do not do what I say I will have you taken out of my will which is about 200 million dollars at this time."

Throwing a newspaper at him Betty said, "You cannot run my life and control everything I do. This is America and I have freedom of choice and I prefer not to marry that no good son of a bitch."

"If the citizens of this state find out you have been helping yourself to their pension funds, I think those no good evil friends in the justice department will press charges against you and have you arrested so in a few days let me know what your decision is. I've spend too much time trying to get those oil rich lands and you will pay a price if you do not help me secure them."

Pouring her some wine in a cup Big Jim smiled and said, "Please think out about the circumstances of what you are doing before you refuse."

"Damit why is it you have to have your way all the time. It's your way or no way at all. One day someone is going to break your belief no one could ever beat you in an election. Your Waterloo is coming and you will go down in defeat because you do not represent the needs of the people who voted for you and they are the rich people who benefit from your unfair decisions against the poor people."

As Big Jim strolled out the door he waved at Betty and she tried not to wave back because her father asked her to do something that would be difficult to perform because she did not want to marry a man she did not love.

Chapter 64

To get the word about his daughter Betty marrying Benson, he travel to the local radio station KBBM to announce the marriage of his daughter to Benson the next candidate for governor and Benson sat next to Big Jim smiling and thought Betty gave her permission to marry him. Over the radio Big Jim assured Benson he would support him when he runs for governor of Mississippi. Knowing it would help him to get Benson elected he said he would form a coalition to bring his enemies back to work together because Big Jim knew it took more togetherness to get Benson elected because his viewpoints were similar to his but more radical. To stop the controversy Benson said, "I know I have radical ways about race mixing but I am willing to compromise on some things and start to work out some problems our farmers are having trying to keep their lands and send money to them by writing funding bills to take care of their needs."

Calls kept coming in and most of them were the critics and enemies of Benson and Big Jim. Picking up the telephone one caller said," Benson how can you change all of a sudden when you always demonstrated against black folks wanting to vote and eat in the places of accommodation?"

"Well I grew up in the state of Mississippi and I did not know many colored folks and as a boy I was taught colored people were to only live in their own separate world and associate with each other. I have a lot to learn about race mixing and will be fair to represent all the people of this state."

"Are you still running around with your colored woman and going out partying with her?"

"I do not know what you are talking about. You know everyone is trying to frame me all the time and most of this is hearsay information."

Another caller said, Big Jim I hear you are trying to get legislation to get the lands of where some oil might be located. How can we trust you are trying to mislead the people into believing you are not interested in grabbing their lands?"

"Well there is no proof of this and mostly lies and I will support groups who uphold civil rights for all the people in this state."

One caller said, "Benson you are deceiving the people because you never hired black people in any of your businesses and were opposed to groups who demonstrated against bussing black students to white schools which were better. Now explain that situation to us."

"I feel students should go to neighborhood schools where they live at and not be bussed to schools so many miles away from where they live."

"I think you should judge Jack Benson by his current viewpoints not when he was a young person at the age of 19 or 20 because he changed for the better to represent the people rather they are black or white."

An event would take place that would be hard to accept where Benson's son Mark Benson saw an African American traveling through a white neighborhood and he followed him home. The young man was 17 and a junior in high school. The boy's name was Chamberlin Grays who traveled back to his home after playing a game of basketball at the high school. He normally went home with the boys but had to go back to the school to get his wallet containing his ID and other papers and went through a white neighborhood to get back to his house much quicker.

While going through the new unfamiliar neighborhood, Mark followed him and reported that a black fellow was walking through their neighborhood and that he looked suspicious. The officers told him not to bother the young man who only was trying to get home.

Instead of doing what the police told them to do by staying in his car and letting them take care of it. Mark got out of his car and engaged in a dialogue with Chamberlin and said to him "Why are you walking through our neighborhood? Do you live here?"

"Why do you ask? I am trying to go home so mind your own business."

"I am part of the neighborhood patrol and you have to show me your ID boy."

"Go to hell! "And Chamberlin strolled away with the police coming to the area where the both of them were located and saw them wrestling on the grass and shots came from the gun Michael held in his hands. Bullets from the gun hit other cars nearby and broke windows at the same time making the inhabitants drop to the floor to keep from getting hit with the bullets.

"Put the gun down and stop wrestling with each other or one of you might get killed!" yelled the policeman who held his gun on both of them.

If the police would not have tried to stop the shooting innocent people would have been killed and they took both of the people to jail. The reason Chamberlin got a lot of attention was because he wore campaign shirts saying he wanted to have John Carol elected to the United States senate and this angered Benson's son who retaliated against him. This action by Mark outraged John Carol to go out much harder to win the United States senate seat. Hearing about what took place, John sent lawyers to defend Chamberlin who was placed on probation and made to do community work and since the judges owed Big Jim some favors ruled against Chamberlin and as usual Big Jim won in this case because he managed to get Chamberlin a suspended sentence to get the black citizens to vote for Benson and donated $10,000 dollars to black church leaders to repair their churches where needed. This did not sit too well with some of the black and white people in favor of civil rights for all the people and racial demonstration took place in front of Big Jim's senate building to his dislike and Big Jim called the firemen to shoot water on them to break up the crowd.

CHAPTER 65

A big rally took place at the Jackson State Commission and Sandy organized a group of black workers to attend. She was prepared to show a film on the bad living conditions the farmers both the black and white farmers lived under.

Before she presents the film Sandy said, "I am showing a film about the poor standard of living the black and white farmers are living under. Civil; rights workers are coming down here and trying to get better living conditions for the poor white and black farmers and those people living in the cities too. Poverty is in the cities in Mississippi and on the farms. You notice I used the word black. The freedom riders used the term because it identifies them as people who are proud of the color of their skin. Our candidate is running against Big Jim Wilson to take his seat because he only represents the rich when it comes to getting their interests taken care of."

As Betty her sister walks into the audience, the crowd begins to boo her because she has cheated many of by charging high prices to take their crops to venders but buys them at lower prices from them. To get over Betty bought their farms from them at lower prices and sold them triple their cost to gain a profit. John's supporters at first told Betty she could not attend but John who knew her said, "Let this lady in!" This angered Lilly who did not like Betty she said, "Why let this segregationist lady in this meeting because she does not belone in here."

This became a family affair because Dianna backed her mother one hundred percent and said, "My mother has a right to come in here and should not be denied because of her bad business dealings with the people in this gathering. If she has done wrong dealings with the people, why is she willing to come in here and another thing why isn't she locked up in jail because of it."

Knowing Dora could not control her thoughts she said, "Even though you are my sister I feel you are taking up for your mother because you hold the same prejudice ways she has and her father is always ripping off the farmers and writing bills not to cover their pensions if their employers will not to do it."

"Sandy you cannot show this film Betty said, "It will ruin our father's reputation as a United States senator. What right do you have to come in here telling me not to show this film? We need change in this state and the First Amendment protects this precious right."

After Sandy said that Betty's supporters were part of the audience too and a fight erupted with pro-Big Jim supporters fighting John Carol's supporters. Anything they could get their hands on the supporters of Big Jim fought John Carol's supporters who were the majority and threw Big Jim's people out of the auditorium telling them never to come back and disturb their rally again.

Betty became outrageous when Sandy said her speech that her father broadcasted she and Jack Benson would be married in a few weeks after Benson wins the governor's seat. To make matters worse, Sandy showed pictures of Big Jim sleeping with a lot of women while he still was a United States senator indicating he cheated on his wife Mable for a long time including the times he slept Polly his black mistress.

The backers of John managed to get Dora, Lilly and Sarah out of the area where the fight took place. Food was destroyed by the fighting and in a few days many of the people felt the food was contaminated with diseased meat and John became sick and he found himself in a colored hospital and doctors told him he would have to watch the food he ate at the functions he went to because some of his own people wanted him killed too. Sarah, Lilly, and Dora visited John while he laid in bed trying to get over the food poisoning he experienced. While John rested in the hospital, he took a look at their problems and wondered what steps he could take when Big Jim Interrupted his political campaign.

The supporters of John Carol sent him letters and petitions requesting Sandy be appointed his legal counsel for the group that supported John Carol. Seeing Sandy representing John Carol regardless of her father Big Jim being against it she would protect their civil rights taken from them. The coalition of both black and white citizens tried to get more black citizens registered to vote. Many of them experienced the pain of getting black people registered to vote and the freedom riders both black and white people left the peace and comfort of their homes to speak in the deep South at places in Mississippi where people were killed for doing activities designed to make poor black and white people build better schools, be able to stay in hotels or attend movie theaters or concerts in towns and cities in Mississippi and not be put in separate facilities for black people only. The group John Coral represented were prepared to get killed to stand up for civil rights. His group wanted to unite all the people to fight for civil rights in the state.

The period of the sixties made Sandy take on the role of being the first white women to attempt to elected into public office in the state of Mississippi as attorney general and bring about reform in its politics. The election comes up between Ronald Patterson who thought like Big Jim as an anti- civil rights person. Sandy felt with Big Jim would be up to his old tricks and within days Sandy's headquarters were bombed several times and her workers still tried to get the vote out for her were attacked but John kept up the pace to get Sandy elected attorney general. One of the main problems Sandy faced was trying to convince many black folks to vote for her. People wearing "Vote to Get Sandy Wilson" elected went into a bank with guns and robbed a bank but when they were apprehended her people were not the ones doing the robberies. In a tour to one of the school districts, Sandy made videos of the poor facilities the black students used to get an inferior education and in school districts where white students attended and how run down the buildings were which had no indoor plumbing and many of the schools used odd houses.

According to the documentary many of the students did not have certified state teachers and the school districts were not accredited making it difficult for many of the high school graduates not qualified to attend college. In her speeches, Sandy wanted to unite all the black and white people in the state for a common cause for equality to use the ballot to pick the candidates who wanted to represent their interests. When Sandy gave her speeches, she felt the pressure of her sister Betty and her father to change her views but it became too impossible because her supporters would be disappointed throughout the state. Over looked and over shadowed by her sister Betty throughout their years of growing up together, Sandy held center stage to become the first white female to become the attorney general of Mississippi. Not only did Sandy talk about the school system going bad ;she attacked the gambling establishment who cheated their customers at each of the casinos operated by the owners who gave money to Benson's race for governor because things would stay the same and more of the money they paid in taxes who be used to build huge condos instead improving the highways and roads people traveled on because many accidents occurred on them and the state failed in their efforts to repair the roads or place adequate lighting on the highways.

The polls showed Sandy a little behind Patterson because of Big Jim's connections with the people in public offices within the state and Patterson tried to tell the people he would look out for their interests better than a woman and he said Sandy was too liberal and wanted to turn the state into a communist state and make the farmers form collective farms and would be given very little for their crops and goods they made in the state.

Pictures of the women were shown in a negative manner because Patterson placed the term "Petty Coat Law" on most of the pictures trying to run things in the city and county. When Sandy's backers saw those ugly pictures of Sandy they tore them down.

In some cases one of the workers from Patterson's camp sent some bad sandwiches wrapped in fancy paper as it said on a card From an unknown supporter as a gift to your workers. The workers who were hungry ate them and threw up and taken to the hospital but when they saw they came from Patterson';s support group they threw them away and some of the workers were taken to black medical facilities not capable of treating so many people on a large scale. Trying to vote became difficult because Big Jim influenced the state legislatures to pass laws saying voters must have photo ids in order to vote and most of Sandy's supporters did not have picture ids when coming to the poles to vote. To further confuse the voters, Paterson put Sandy's name in foreign letters to confuse the people and said she was on the ballot in another state because most of the voting machines were broken down in the state of Mississippi. Scare tactics were used by Patterson's people to keep them from coming to the polls to vote. At the end of the day it showed that Patterson won the election to the dismay of Sandy's supporters and rumors circulated some of the places where Sandy got her greatest support the polling places close at 5 p.m. instead of 8 p.m.

Witnesses said they could not vote because the voting polls closed too early and this is where Sandy could have wrestled the election away from Ronald Patterson who did anything he could do to win the election. Sitting at her campaign headquarters with her supporters and workers Sandy said, "Thanks for giving it all you had and we put up a good fight."

Hugging Sandy John said, "We have to have a recount of the votes because Sandy should have done better in those wards where she had the most support. We'll have an investigation made."

The box of fireworks stayed closed because everyone wanted to see them burst into the air to celebrate the victory. Tears came to Dora's and Lilly's faces because of the lost to Ronald Patterson even though Sandy and them did not agree on many issues about race relations but they felt she would serve the needs of the people both black and white because her sister Betty campaigned for Ronald Patterson against Sandy and pressure was placed on her by her father Big Jim because this would show a unified front on the Patterson team. Tears fell from Betty's eyes to see her little sister lose this election because she knew Big Jim and Patterson cheated Sandy out of it and knew the greed of her father Big Jim who always got what he wanted. Thinking about his wrong doing Betty called Sandy and told her about the wrong doing and how she got cheated out of the election. To get the evidence Sandy and John Coral attempted to break into Patterson's headquarters. Taking a crow bar John opened up the door to Patterson's headquarters and they both searched for the information on if they did illegal things to win the election. Seeing a big white wooden box John shined his flashlights and this box contained a combination and all at once the alarm went off and Sandy and he panic and scrambled out of the door but it closed shut and the thought of being caught in the headquarters of Ronald Patterson would prove to be embarrassing. Seeing a nearby window, John moved the table near it and he kicked the window out as they scrambled out of it Patterson and his people came into the building as Sandy and John rushed to her car which failed to start. All at once a young girl came riding on a horse and John asked if they could borrow his horse to get away. The gentlemen said give me one hundred dollars and I will let you ride him just tell me where I can reach you."

"I do not have a pen to write the number down the gentlemen said, "Tell me your name. I'll remember it."

John and Sandy mounted the house who kept on bucking and jumping on his heels but they hung on and John hollowed for the horse to go and he took off with Patterson and his men running after them but John who carried a gun shot out the tires of the fellows as the horse kicked and got angry as he took off on his long run. Sandy lost some of the information when the box came open showing evidence Patterson did unlawful things to win the election.

Taking the evidence to court proved to be fatal because the court judges said Sandy could not prove Ronald and his people stole the ballot boxes showing most of the votes going to Sandy. This became an outrage to Sandy and the voters who cast their vote for her at the polls to only see that their votes did not count and were stolen and hidden in the back of Patterson's headquarters. To get the word out to the public, Sandy held a press conference but very few reporters turned up because they were loyal to Ronald Patterson and Senator Big Jim..

CHAPTER 66

Dora is nearing her new senior year and she wondered about a scholarship she applied for at a college and got worried because no colleges officials contacted her. Every evening Dora came from school looking in the mail but nothing was in it and the ordeal drove her into a state of shock because she bragged she would get a scholarship to a big name university whether it is populated by white or black students. Her mother told her it would take time for things of this nature to occur. A teenager is not free of bad habits which get them into trouble. Dora had her bouts with drug addiction when she went to a party and people put drugs into her drink when she was not looking. The boys saw it. and got her high and they gang raped her and took pictures showing her nude body. At the party were kids who supported Jack Benson and Big Jim and they held a news conference and showed those pictures to the medias which embarrassed Lilly who got angry about it. Confronting Dora Lilly said, "Why did you do such a silly thing. That type behavior will hurt your chances of getting a scholarship and you might be pregnant as a result of the rape."

At night Dora experienced nightmares of what took place at the neighborhood dance and wished she never would have gone to it. With so many supporters of Big Jim, they would do anything to ruin John Carol's reputation by saying his daughter is on drugs and she should be serving as a good role model for the kids who looked up to politician's kids to create hope to achieve their career objectives and stay out of groups of people who mean them no good because if her friends do drugs; this will influence them to do the same negative things. Because of her hideous behavior one of the college recruiters hesitated to invite her to the college to interview for a full scholarship.

When the college officials saw she was black, they did not give her the scholarship. Dora never did put identify her race on the application she filled out. No reason was given as to why she could not get the scholarship. Dianna saw Dora at the same interview and they did not say anything to each other and did not tell anyone they were sisters. The interview process was about to give Dianna the scholarship until he saw she was not completely white but Dianna called Betty and she called Big Jim and he called the officials at the college and they apologized and Dianna got the full scholarship because of Big Jim's powerful influence in the state of Mississippi. Rejection is something Dora did not to accept and felt because of her skin color she did not get the scholarship but there was nothing Lilly or John could do to have the college administrators change their minds at that college. As for Dora she did not receive a scholarship offer and her hopes drifted endlessly into despair and wondered would college officials give her a scholarship. Dora's sense of hurt touched her ability to keep on fighting to achieve success in the world she lived in. Would Dora achieve success in the world she live in and be able to face the fact she was black and a female and could she live with the truth her sister and mother were white? Would she one day sit across from Dianna at a dinner table and say?"I love my sister and mother who are white who abandoned me because of my skin color and would I wonder why she never got to know her father but spent many years dealing with the topic?

Vowing to achieve success, Dora felt it would be hard to achieve it. Her world knew about the prejudice environment she lived in trying to stand tall which became a challenge. She tried to not hate the white folks who were not willing to accept her right to be free and go anywhere she wanted without being told to go to the back of bus. Dora could not escape the stigma of going to the colored section of every public facility in Jackson, Mississippi because sometimes she looked in the mirror and said "I am someone even though I am persecuted because my I am African American".

Even though the discrimination came her way, Dora developed that keen sense of I am black and proud to be whom I am and would not feel inferior to any race of people.

CHAPTER 67

In the high school auditorium Dora was at the podium speaking about the bad manner Big Jim served the interests of the people and Dianna sat in the audience making loud noises as Dora spoke against his policies which affected the people living in Mississippi. By voting on Big Jim, she said race relations between the colored and white students and citizens of Jackson, Mississippi would not improve but get worse.

A loud sound was heard from a group of 25 motorist came roaring into the auditorium after tying ropes on their bikes. They attached the ropes to a door and pulled it down. They carried cakes and pies in one arm and as they circled the auditorium their leader drove up to the table with white and black delegates sitting at it and threw custard pies at them.

Seeing people riding on motorcycles racing at 90 miles an hour doing trick riding, the crowd went wild and threw money on the dirty floor meant for people performing the stunts. One of them got off his motorcycle and collected the money. Some of the spectators witnessed money being tossed at the bikers and got into the action to pick it up too which resulted in a fight between the bikers and spectators who outnumbered them. Venders sold popcorn and got into the action trying to get their share of the money and popcorn got scattered everywhere. Technicians operating spot lights shinned them on the people participating in the fight because it was dark in there and someone cut the wires controlling the lighting.

CHAPTER 68

While driving through Calhoun County to see a client, Sandy saw farmers pulling up plants which looked like marijuana but was unsure of what it could identified as. Three of the farmers smoked weed and the smell lingered into the air and strangled Sandy's sense of where she was. To her surprise, she saw Betty directing men to hurry up and get in the trucks to take the marijuana to one of her factories. Sandy knew this was against state law and Betty used the land to grow marijuana instead of crops like beans, cabbage, corn, and cotton which could stabilize their incomes to support their facilities. Dressed in shorts and matching top Betty said to Sandy," Are you here spying on us? You should be working to help those poor farmers who shout they are not getting treated fairly and crying inequality like it's going out of style."

Taking her glasses off and pointing to the marijuana fields Sandy said, "I will report all of you for unlawful use of these lands which is illegal. You should be growing something which can help the people make a decent living. You are breaking the law and I'll tell the state officials about it."

"I'll say you took part in it too so you better watch who you are reporting on."

"Go to hell!" Sandy said, "The people need crops to sell to make a good living from it. You are taking part in what our no good daddy is guilty of and you know he wins as usual. One day he will pay for his crimes he committed in this state against the farmers."

While they talked disputes erupted because some of the workers felt they did not get paid enough money and fought each other.

Dirty Red said, "Betty I was promised $ 500 dollars but I never got paid. Call your boys off of me because I need my money."

"I'll see about it later. Big Jim must approve giving you more money than you are supposed to get."

"I'll go to the authorities if you do not give it to me. That no good father of yours promises raises for his workers and never pays us and I've had enough of this nonsense."

Going to Betty's church Dirty Red spots Big Jim's papers laying on a table with some money and grabbed it and said, "I'll take his. It will cover the debt and more. I'll see you later."

"Get him Randy and Frank!" Betty shouted.

"Let him go before someone gets killed!" Sandy shouted.

The two men grabbed sticks and attacked Dirty Red resulting in a fight and he shot Randy in the chest killing him instantly and Frank put Dirty Red in a bear hug and squeezed the air out of this small body. Realizing he was about to be killed Frank spit some snuff into Dirty Red's eyes and Dirty Red dropped Frank and a shot ringed out and the bullet hit Dirty Red in his leg but he managed to get to the truck because Frank could not be revived because air in his lungs kept him in a unconscious situation.

Seeing that Dirty Red said he would go to the police, Betty called Jack Benson who she hated and told him to gun down Dirty Red because he said he would tell on her father and his operations of wrong doing and smuggling drugs.. Running after Dirty Red, Betty jumped on the side of the truck as it slowly drove off and held on trying to steer it off the road but Dirty Red socked her in her face and Betty fell and rolled down a hill into a beehive and they chased her all through the woods until she ran into a cave and dropped ten feet into a hole without being able to get out.

Jack Benson spotted Dirty Red racing toward Jackson, Mississippi in a helicopter with a co-pilot and took out his Thompson Machine gun and fired at him but the road curved at every angle. Seeing Benson might get accurate in his shooting to hit the truck he said, "I'll shoot one of our missiles at him and I am sure his truck cannot escape these heat seeking weapons".

"Fire one!" The copilot shouted at Jack Benson who pulled the lever and the rocket raced toward the truck Dirty Red used to escape in. The missile hit the side of a mountain located near a bridge and big rocks fell into a river and several cars and people landed in deep water drowning many people attempting to use the road located on the side of the mountain.

"Fire two!" The second missile hit a passing truck carrying explosives which went out of control causing many explosions and started a forest fire and it spread over three miles of land owned by farmers who called the fire department but they could not be contacted because the burning trees spread to the telephone wires and burned them up.

Seeing what happened, the smoke from the fire made it difficult for Benson to hit Dirty Red with his last missile. As he pursued Dirty Red he spotted a dam ahead of him as he drove in that direction and fired a missile at it to release water which would stop him from getting to Jackson, Mississippi and testify against Big Jim and Betty.

Off went the missiles hitting the dam that destroyed various sections of it and water shot out of it like a cannon shooting an explosive shell at rapid speeds which hit Dirty Red's truck and he could not swim. No one knew if he drown when the large amount of water covered his truck and scattered marijuana into the dam and polluted the water and killed many farm animals and destroyed homes, crops, buildings, and damaged smaller towns. Looking for Dirty Red was difficult in the darkness and no one knew if he drowned in the flooding. No trace of Betty could be found and Jack Benson radioed the local authorities she was missing and maybe dead and he would attempt to find her.

CHAPTER 69

At KTKMOZ television two news casters and a hooded man set at the table and the topic consisted of Sandy and the hooded man explaining Senator Big Jim Wilson was involved in growing marijuana and influencing them to grow that instead of regular cash crops which were illegal. Spotlights flashed around them and Sandy said, "I have to go powder my noise and as she put her make up on a loud explosion made the employees scream. Sandy hid in a bathroom stall and prayed for her life because she felt Big Jim plotted to kill her to keep her from explaining his role in forcing the farmers to grow weed and poppy plants.

Sometimes Big Jim went to schools to tell kids not to do weed and drugs but managed to take a hit on drugged cigarettes after he left the school. Doing this civic service Big Jim felt would give him a positive image on the people who voted for him but one day a school member spotted him and said he would tell the news media about it. The explosion killed Dirty red and one of the news casters. The blast killed many people who worked for the tv station and it was difficult for them to get the teletype wires working because of the flooding and sandbags got stacked all around the city.

The capital was in a state of emergency and prisoners were transferred to other locations in the state. Leaving the restroom Sandy got out of the t v station to find many homeless people roaming the streets braking into places of business and looting the stores and big dry good companies. Mosquitoes bit them all the time. Big Jim who stayed in Washington with another black woman who was Polly's sister Molly called Jack Benson to put out a hit on Sandy who he felt was a threat on his ability to stay in office without being impeached.

Parts of the city of Jackson suffered from the flooding. The newly elected mayor Ringo Nivens of Jackson, Mississippi asked Attorney General Ronald Patterson for aid to these people who lost their homes in the flood. Patterson did not send help in the form of food and medical supplies to the people in the areas that supported Sandy in the election. Those people waited for hours before state national guards came and rescued them to take them to other areas not affected by the flooding as people swam towards the boats Patterson's men let the people on the boats who supported him in the election in which he won. People in Sandy's voting districts rested on their roofs and many died because no water or food was given to them. In all of this confusion, catfish floated in the water and died. The bodies of dead people were seen floating in the floodwaters and were eaten by animals who survived the flood.

Trying to get from one destination to another people hijacked and stole their boats from them and threw the occupants out into the flooded water and did not care if they could swim or not. Now Sandy got to dry land and wanted to go to John Carol and tell him what her father was planning to do to make himself rich.

To get to Lilly's house, Sandy went to a place which sold boats where there was dry land. When she reached her destination all the boats were gone except one and old man Servanson a former navy man would not let anyone use them.

"I cannot let you use my boat because you will not bring it back. Plus they are out there hijacking people who have boats like yours. You will have to give me $100 dollars to use this boat."

"What if I write an IOU and I promise my father Big Jim Wilson will pay for it."

Taking his fingers and pulling out several IOUs from his folder he said, "That no good father of yours is not going to do nothing but lie and not deliver anything and he's always trying to brainwash the people into believing he is looking out for their best interests."

"Well I oppose his racist policies and that's why I need to use your motorboat."

Looking at her Servanson said, "You are his daughter and fighting against the most powerful man in the state of Mississippi and that takes much courage. You know Big Jim is known for killing anybody who stands in his way."

"I remember he allowed people to come on my land with an illegal permit to look and drill for oil and I could not do anything to stop him."

"Why didn't you go to the law enforcement officers to have them stopped.."

"After your father paid them off, they said he was in his legal rights to let them trespass on my land." "Well I am fighting for the farmer's rights."

Taking out a picture of his wife he said,"My wife died standing up against the injustice your father's henchmen did to them by trying to go steal their lands unlawfully and as he drove back and forth to the protest area delivering food and medical supplies to civil rights workers gunmen pulled up beside her and shot through her window."

"Did the law enforcement officials do anything about it?"

"They claimed it was too dark and no one saw a thing. There was much bitterness against my wife and the civil rights workers and she did not care what skin color they were. Sometimes she fixed dinner at our house against the wishes of our friends and neighbors who were opposed to equality for the races of people living in this state.

"I loved my wife because she changed my feelings about the races because I did not like colored folks but my wife encouraged me to give my life to God and seek his ever forgiving grace and the will for me to realize I was wrong. Some of the colored folks helped me harvest my crops when it looked like the added rain we received would damage them when my white friends would not help me. I'll tell you what I'll let you use my boat."

"I'll let you use my boat with the motor that's riding good so just promise to bring it back to me."

"It's a deal."

CHAPTER 70

B y this time the flood waters destroyed many buildings and people traveled by boat to where they tried to get to Lilly's house but she did not know if her house was destroyed but Sandy wanted to touch base with him to explain her father intended to do evil things to acquire the farmer's lands and he hired henchmen to blow up the new conference tables at the television station.

As she guided the small motor boat through the city; Sandy saw the destruction done by the flood waters as people tried to beg to get in her boat and Sandy fought them off with paddles which laid in her boat and people who tried to stop the motor had their fingers and their hands cut off attempting to hold on to the blades of the propellers.

The mosquitoes bite her and she felt an uneasy feeling navigating the boat and loud noises were heard in the woods and the dark water made it impossible for people to know what creatures' lived in it. Green plants and house whole goods flooded in the water and Sandy heard the sound of people shooting alligators attempting to injure other people as Sandy guided her boat through the city and a building came tumbling down near her making the boat bounce in the water. Sandy's boat filled up with water and their situation frightened her and her body shook and her small fingers griped the paddles as she hit the alligators who tried to tip her boat over and they chopped off sides of the boat with their large jaws.

As one alligators came down with his mighty jaws, Sandy jumped on a tree branch to keep from getting ate up by him who promptly crashed the boat into with his jaws.

Meanwhile Betty struggled to escape out the large hole she fell in. Her stomach ached and her face showed fear and the moisture on the mud kept her from crawling out of it. The coldness of the weather made tears appear in her eyes. The thought of being buried in this deep six feet hole made her upset and her clothes smelled badly.

Earlier in her life, Betty turned away from God and he could not worship a being she could not see. Taking her fingers and a stick, she attempted to dig small pockets in the sides of the hole so she could use them to step into to get out but each time she put her foot in the pockets to elevate herself up she slid back down with water raising above her head. She managed to grab some weeds hanging above her head and pulled herself up.

Again more mud slid down the hole and a water moccasin fell into it and seeing the poisonous snake, Betty grabbed it and screamed and attempted to tire off his head but before this took place it bite her arm. The poison made Betty weak and she could barely keep afloat with flood water filling up the hole.

Warnings to not fly over the flooded area came over the radio in the helicopter and Benson ignored them because he had to find Betty. The helicopter got hit by hard rain and wind making it difficult to fly it. A big gust of wind knocked the propeller blade off the helicopter and it glided down into the area where Betty was buried in the hole and landed against some trees injuring Benson making it hard for him to walk. Benson could only crawl when lighting hit the tops of trees and the limbs and branches fell over on him and he laid underneath branches covering the helicopter.

Not too far from the helicopter Benson heard a voice crying out from nowhere saying, "Please help me O God. I have to get out of the predicament I am in!"

Knowing she did not believe in God, Betty thought about the times when her mother taught her to have faith in God and put him first in her life but she never believed in what Mable told her. Betty felt she made it to the top of the corporate world without God helping her but now she realized there were other things her money could not buy. It would take a miracle of God to get her out of this tragedy she dealt with and the muddy water kept getting into her eyes and the smell made a person vomit with the ugly taste which touched her tongue making her want to not believe God could help her out of this dilemma and she was confronted with fear and mixed emotions.

Would this be a test in her belief in God or would she be going through the motions to believe she could worship the one living God who she felt had to make a physical presence for her to believe he could work wonders to get her out of the jaws of death trying to take her last breath of life from her. Could she handle this challenge confronting her? Would she be able to see her daughter and friends again? Would her bite from the snake keep her from believing she would walk out of this situation without fearing death knowing the poison from the snake bite would kill her or all the wrong things she did in life against people would be forgiven?

The echoes of Betty's voice came to the spot where the helicopter crashed and immediately Benson yelled back to her. Even though his legs were broken he managed to crawl away from the damaged helicopter to the hole where Betty tried to get out but could not climb to the surface to level land.

"You ok Betty. I heard your voice. I'll try to get you out of this hole."

Grabbing a long tree branch, Benson passed it down to Betty who grabbed it and Benson pulled her out of it but she fainted once she got on the surface from tiredness and the snake bite.

"A snake bit me. I need to go to the hospital immediately."

"Go to the helicopter and speak into the radio and see if you can call for help."

Benson said," My leg is busted and broken too."

"I should leave you here. You are a no good bastard because you raped me many years ago."

"Now Betty that was years ago but now I am governor of Mississippi and I plan to do good positive things for all the people both black and white folks who voted for me. I'll see if we can get help plus you got bit by a poisonous snake so let me suck the poison from your leg."

Looking at her wound Benson sucked some of the poison out of it and grabbed her and attempted to rape her but Betty fought off his attempts by grabbing a branch which fell on the ground during the storm and hit him in his head knocking him out. Helicopter crews came from the state to pick Benson and Betty up and both of them were flown to a hospital for treatment.

CHAPTER 71

Meanwhile Sandy stayed by the tree until some local politicians traveled in their boats to rescue victims and take them to dry land and to Lilly's house which was flooded and she needed food to eat. They were glad to see Sandy who fought against her father's attempts to commit larceny and take the lands of the farmers land rich in oil. In visiting Lilly's house Sandy said, "I know this flood is going to hurt many people but I wanted to help them."

Sandy told John, Lilly, and Dora she insisted on having a press conference to inform the farmers of what lies her father told the farmers and citizens living in the state of Mississippi so they would react with a positive attitude about the whole situation. Lilly and John clashed on women's rights issues and John felt women should be a helpmate to her man but not assume a leadership role in the relationship and he knew Sandy was a true friend who could be counted on and defied her father's policies on civil rights issues. An official from the state government of Mississippi came and left a note with Lilly saying her house and property would be seized if she did not fix it up in two weeks from Governor Benson even though her house could not stand up any longer because the flood waters damaged it. People affected by the flood sat up tents in the area on high ground.

Lilly said, "Big Jim is not going to allow you to have a press conference to tell the people about his bad deeds to take rich oil lands from the farmers and deceived them like he does when he campaigns for their votes."

Trying to find the right words to say, Dora said, to Sandy, "You have to do more persuading because you are trying to find the right words to say. You must convince the voters very strongly because your father and Benson cheated the people out of their lands and property who did business with them. How can we trust you because you want to hold a press conference to tell the truth and you are his daughter?"

"We have a fool to deal with this time and your father is drafting flood relief funds legislation for the counties whose citizens voted to put him back into office," Dora said.

"Let's get down to business," John said, "Something must be done to stop this greed from men like Governor Benson who is sending out letters to people to give up their houses and property to the state and mostly the farmers who supported Sandy when she ran for attorney general. The time to act is now because Benson is not going to help the farmers who did not vote for him. Since we cannot have the meeting on dry land a group of us will have it on our boats and invite the news people down here to see we are not affiliated with Governor Benson and that he will not help us and he sends money to people who supports him for his reelections which he always wins and do illegal voting practices and lies to the voters to get their support."

Word circulated throughout the state a protest would take place anywhere the people could meet regardless to where it would be held and John Carol and his supporters would take boat rides to different parts of the state affected by the flooding for two days and a press conference would take place on a boat with Sandy showing stolen documents of what her father and Benson planned to do. The people got word of this and responded to it.

Some of John's friends and allies were fired upon as they carried flyers to other people who came by boat and many of the boats sink when bullets holes opened up their sides and overflowed with water where alligators ate them up and poisonous snakes bit them.

Regardless of the setbacks some of the areas not flooded received news of a meeting at Dixie Lakefront.

Workers flew supplies to flood victims and one of the planes crashed into the river killing all aboard because Benson's men put bombs on it. They tried to help those farmers who protested against his stand as an anti- integrationist. On a sunny day people from the state of Mississippi heard Sandy talked against everything her father stood for and held that press conference despite threats from Benson's supporters to disrupt the meeting. People who lost their love ones still continued to get to the hearing after their dead relatives' bodies were recovered from the river. When John heard about the deaths of his supporters, he held a memorial prayer for them and postponed the meeting for a day to wait for the surviving member of those who lost love ones when alligators found a way to get into the flooding waters and capsized their boats. Nothing was done by the state to help get those victims to a hospital because Governor Benson knew they were protesting about his unfair policies which favored the rich and not the poor farmers.

On the main boat, Sandy, Sarah, Dora, and John sat on the deck of a big motor boat. The people came from all around the state to hear what Sandy had to say about her father's dirty politics on how they urged state officials to take land and get rich at the expense of the poor people who had three or four people in the boat with them. Someone in the boat had riffles and guns to shoot alligators and people who wanted to infiltrate the group and cause problems and despite the problems facing them bright lights were placed in trees above the water which shinned brightly and the wind blew quietly and people prepared to eat their sandwiches. Looking at the many people despite the problems they faced did not prevent them from having this non-violent gathering.

Sandy came up to the microphone and said as she turned the pages of her book of notes:

"Thanks for coming to this meeting even though we are having it on this flooded area. We cannot give up because we need someone in office who will serve the needs of all the people both white and black citizens. This is not a black problem and it is about true equality for all of our people. As I look at a lot of you sitting on your boats, you have not received any equal rights and decent prices for your crops when Governor Benson gave higher prices to the farmers and citizens who supported him in his bid for governor. I have documents in my book showing where my father and Benson stole your hardearned farm lands from you to dig for oil. They promised you would get relief from this flood but as we can see at this moment no aid has come to this area to help feed our people and move them to dryer ground.

Reading the information about what the rich politicians did to get money many of them angry but they wanted to have good guidance and advice to keep their lands from someone they could trust who would represent their interests. Sandy showed them records where the people paid property taxes and when they came to discuss the matter with state officials but no record of this could be found and Govenor Benson issued orders to confiscate their lands.

Television crews recorded what took place and many of them slapped at the bugs flying in the air and people listened to Sandy and John make their speeches. Sandy urged the people to cast their votes for John Carol because he would represent their needs and interests when they needed help and try to get bills passed to help them obtain better farming machinery and prices for their crops and relief from the flood and she said," Now I want you to welcome John Carol up here who will be our next United States senator from the state of Mississippi."

John's speech:

"Man that was a great speech from Sandy and I declare she did not lie about her efforts to provide needed social services to our people such as prenatal care, legal aid, and higher prices for our crops. Now I am asking for your help to spread the word throughout the state of Mississippi. I am asking you to please tell the voters John Carol graduated from college and studied many issues they faced and he understood their plight and that better conditions for the people of Mississippi must be improved and they needed someone who cared about them and wanted to help you keep your lands and property from being seized by Benson. Many of your friends and love ones lost their land and their due-process rights were ignored. Someone in the crowd asked will he stop Big Jim from stealing their properties and John replied, "I will do anything in my power to stop this unlawful practice done by him."

CHAPTER 72

Sitting in his office in Washington D. C. Big Jim watched television and did not like what he saw when his daughter got in the newsroom and spoke out against his policies in regards to the oil rich lands he wanted so badly. He wanted her to be silenced and killed because his followers would question his initiatives in that state on his plans to take over the land filled with oil.

Governor Benson was summoned to come to Washington and he wanted to have Sandy silenced and kept from practicing law in the state of Mississippi. While this conversation continued between Big Jim and Benson, Betty hung on for life and seemed to be trying to talk with her mind going in difference directions and her saying she could not recall what was said the next day. Nurses and attendants buckled her down as Betty kicked and screamed the night away. Trying to feed her was difficult and before being buckled down to her bed, Betty swung her hand against the IV bottles and knocked them to the floor and plasma and medication spilled over it. Betty's hollowing and screaming woke up the people in her ward and the snake poison made her shout to the top of her lungs. The lady patient in her room could not stay and take her crazy behavior Betty produced.

They pushed the patient out the room to discover Betty who was full of drugs and poison, broke the belts and got out of bed and medical staff tried to stop her because they were on the 10th floor and they were higher in the sky which looked dark bluish and you witnessed thousands of lights shinning in the darkness and the smell of carbon dioxide circulated through the air making Betty sick and the sound of voices as she ran into the kitchen and saw the dish washing machine taking dishes and pulling them through a rack and decided to throw them at the orderlies who ducked and dodged every plate thrown at them. As she saw a window opening, Betty opened a window and the orderly rushed her and kept her from diving out of it and gave her a shot so she could go to sleep.

CHAPTER 73

News arrived at Big Jim's office saying Betty tried to jump off the tenth floor of the hospital due to the effects of the snake's poisoning in her wound. In their meeting, Benson was told to arrange to have Big Jim's daughter killed and he wanted Benson and his men to kidnap her and if this did not succeed he was to have her shot and killed to keep her from exposing his plans. As Sandy drove to John Carol's house after trying to contact some of her clients a helicopter flew above her and Sandy wondered what was taking place.

Men from Benson's staff shot at her tires and they exploded making her car glide into a lake and it sink into deeper water. A group of fishermen tried to catch fish in the lake saw what took place and paddled to the spot where Sandy's car went into it. In desperation, Sandy let her windows down to get out of the car but it became a difficult problem because they would not function properly and she frantically kicked and punched the windows. A tall big African American by the name of Randy Champion dived into the water to rescue her from drowning and he saw Sandy trying to hold her breath but she could not do it much longer. Her eyes opened up when she saw Randy trying to open the window. Thinking it seemed hopeless, Randy swam to the surface and yelled to his friend to give him a flashlight. Grabbing the flashlight, Randy swam back to deep water to get Sandy out of the car. Before he could break out the window, he encountered a poisonous snake and he tried to bite him. By a miracle of God, Randy hit the snake with the flashlight and it dived to the bottom of the lake, as a result of Randy's defensive action and died. Swimming towards the car, Randy broke the window with the flashlight and kicked it in and dragged Sandy out of the car and placed her in his canoe. His wet hair made him look like an African chief and his body contained colors as he tried to pull her to the surface of the lake. Sandy screamed and shouted and attacked him because of fear and the tragic experience of drowning and having a lot of water going into her lungs. Randy and his friend Hank paddled to shore and helped revived Sandy who struggled to get the water out of her lungs and finally she came to.

"You could have been killed and I see bullet holes in the car. Whoever did this meant to kill you."

"It's probably my father's goons who attempted to do this. He does not want me to speak out against his racist policies. I am supporting John Carol to be the next senator from the state of Mississippi against my father and he is the type who will kill you if you get in his way."

"Thanks for helping me and I will never forget it. After that Sandy was taken to Lilly's house which was damaged but still livable and Sandy told John about her ordeal and he praised her for her courage and dignity to go against her father 's pro-segregationist ways.

CHAPTER 74

R eading the newspapers, Betty sees in the bylines how momentum is spreading for John Carol to win the election for her father's senate seat from her hospital bed after getting over her near death from the snake bite. She developed problems with the staff because they wanted to ask her questions about her father and his ambitions to help with the state that attempted to recover damages from a vast flood which brought about death and destruction and what would it take to fix the dam so the farmer's crops would be restored and business as usual. Betty saw how John Carol's forces were directing all the black and white people in their state to get rid of the old segregationist ways and try to unite the people to form unions and elect people to office who would represent their interests to bring industry and federal aid for their people who could not afford to take care of their problems which constantly keep dividing themselves on the issues at stake.

None of the family members came to see Betty while she stayed at the hospital for fear her enemies would kill her. One of the nurses recognized her last name and asked her was she some kin to Mable Wilson and she said yes.

Laura Bell Whiterspoon said, "I go to the mental ward all the time and this lady cries out a name and it's similar to yours."

The hospital room looked old and the beds made loud noises when Betty moved from side to side and her back ached from reacting to hard surfaces that hit it resulting in many bruises. When Mable disappeared mysteriously, Betty knew nothing about it and felt the police should have been notified. When speaking to Big Jim about the matter, he said he did not know where she went to because they always fought each other about his woman chasing and heavy drinking and never taking her to social gatherings with him.

When visiting Big Jim in Washington, he stayed out most of the time and came back drunk with other women who were secretaries asking for a job from him which caused a confrontation with Mable who fought his girlfriends and ended up going to jail. This ugly behavior by Big Jim made his wife mentally ill and an alcoholic that made it impossible to deal with without her threating his many girlfriends' lives.

"Why are you coming into this mental health ward? It is forbidden for you to visit this mental health ward. One of the patients might attack you with a club or bat, "Smithy said to Betty as her face grew angry. I cannot let you in here unless you have permission from a fellow by the name of Senator Big Jim Wilson."

"Why is it you have to get his permission? Some of these women Big Jim courted during the years but he did not love them. This love affair with these women meant nothing to him but now her mother Mable is insane because of her father's misdeeds of his bigger than life image.

"You are going to let me in to see if my mother is in where. I have not seen her in two years!"

"Your father will fire me if I let you in here!"

Broadway Hudson a hospital security officer came strolling into the hall way making his rounds and said, "Miss. Can I help you because you look too pretty to disappoint."

Pulling her dress up Betty caught the eye of Broadway because he loved women and that became his weakness as he grew into manhood but he wanted to help this innocent good looking woman. Weighing about 300 pounds of muscle Broadway said, "Come with me and I will take you to see who you want to visit."

Looking at Betty, Broadway saw how beautiful she looked to him and grabbed her and pushed her into a room and said, "Lady you have to reward me for taking you to see your mother."

This behavior angered Betty and she said, "Don't come near me or I'll kill you."

"I just want to hold you in my arms baby. Broadway always gets what he wants."

Broadway starts to take off Betty's clothes and he pushed her towards the bed and he locked the door to keep anyone from coming into the room.

"It was lousy for him to rape my sister. I watched as this took place as my sister's scream and my father molested her. I have to do you the same way."

"Now Broadway come to your senses. If you touch me, there will be no trial for you plus I am not your little sister who was raped. A black person would get lynched on the spot if they find out about it. You will never make it to the jail. You are mentally ill."

"I will revenge the rape of my sister by taking it out on you at this moment."

Betty screamed "He is trying rape me, help!"

At that moment people heard her scream and hospital staff and other patients come to the door and took crow bars and opened the door to find Broadway in bed with Betty trying to have sex with her. Three of the hospital staff attacked Broadway and he fought them off but more people came and someone hit him in the head with a kitchen pot.

"Let's lynch him! "One of the hospital staff members said. They placed his body in the trunk of a car and drove off to the nearest forest and hung him and did not attempt to take him to the police. Later they burned his body and placed branches over it to conceal any trace of it. Even though Betty went through her ordeal she still wanted to know where they kept her mother. While searching for her mother, Betty heard many people trying to talk.

Hearing all the noise coming from that area, Betty rushed there to catch an elevator to see what all the commotion was about and it seemed many people came up to that 11th floor to stop someone from killing herself. When Betty attempted to go to the 11th floor, the elevator kept going up and down and she experienced a difficult time stopping it.

Getting off on the first floor, Betty strolled up the stairs to the fourth floor gashing for air and could barely get up there and as she opened the door, it made a weird sound and Betty softly slid her hands on the door to open it but the lock was struck. Beating frantically on the door the people would not open it.

Realizing who the person was they tried to keep her from seeing Mable. Betty pulled a fire alarm switch and people ran out the building. Standing on the balcony, Mable spoke to herself real loud and she did not know what she said but her insanity reached the point of no return and she jumped eleven floors to her death. Tears of emotion came to Betty's eyes to see her mother drop to her death and because of her father's behavior of womanizing Mable could not take it any longer.

To get rid of this demon lurking inside of her, Betty chose death by suicide to relieve her of the thought of her husband sleeping with other women. A funeral took place at the local church and to everyone's surprise, Big Jim showed up with Polly's sister. The alcohol on Big Jim smelled all over the church. People stood up and said nice things about Mable who looked decent in a white grown and her hair and smile glowed as the preacher said wonderful things about her as she laid motionless in her casket..

Big Jim approached the casket with his black woman. Betty raced up to the casket and slapped Big Jim in his mouth and said, "Why did you bring that nigger to my mother's funeral and disgrace our family like this. It was ok when it was done behind our backs but you bring this woman to my mother's funeral. Now get the hell out of here with your black bitch and you got the nerve to be hugging and kissing her at my mother's funeral. Now get out!"

Not one to take this sitting down Big Jim said, "This is not the time or place to be carrying on this way. Your mother ran off and I never saw her again. I did not know she was in a mental institution."

"That's lie. I checked with the hospital!"

At the institute Mable suffered from mental anguish and she rebelled most of the time and some of the black people like Annie Table Brook who remembered Mable got up and said positive things about her. "Mable and I go back many years. When I came to the plantation looking for a job, I remember what she said to me." We do not need any help at this time. I'll call you if we have to hire other workers."

Mable said, "Where's my appointments!?"

"Miss. Mable I can do that for you."

"You know how to read and write?"

"Show me you can take dictation."

Annie read out loud some writing and was hired immediately.

"I remember the nurses fussing with Mable and said her white relatives ran away black and white kids who brought her Christmas gifts because they kept up so much noise and she read us fairytales and made us feel important. The nursing personnel did not like the idea of black and white people sitting together but she ignored their prejudice rules on race mixing. Everywhere she went Mable fought bigotry and discrimination and that's one reason Big Jim and Mable broke up their marriage."

As he pranced up to the microphone Big Jim grabbed a microphone and shouted," Thanks for coming to my wife's funeral and I want to say I deeply appreciate the kindness you have displayed by showing much respect. I want all of you to remember and vote for my reelection to the federal United States senate. They think John Carol who went and got a good education will beat me this year but I do not think so and after that Big Jim took out a bottle of vodka %100 proof and drink it down.

This action did not take too well with John who came out of the black section of the church and said,

"Wait a minute this is not the time for a political rally at Mable's funeral. Don't you have any respect for her? Your wife's attitude about the races were just like yours but some colored folks who I know became her friend and she saw the color of a person' skin should not decide if they are good or bad but by the content of their character is what decides the manner in which they should be treated." Cheers from the crowd erupted because some of them felt it was time for a change.

The election caused much commotion with the people gearing up to vote for their candidate who could help restore the confidence people would benefit from the candidates who tries to deliver on promises but the person with the most popularity and money usually wins the will of the people of Mississippi and they will vote for the person who will write legislation which brings about improvements in the lives of the people.

There was so much division in the Coral family on who supported Big Jim. Diana knew her father in this period of John Carol running for the United States senate seat and Dianna clashed with Betty on deciding to work for John's election to the United States Senate and she decided to leave and find her way to his headquarters. Betty attempted to stop her and a fight started and Dianna as strong as she was assaulted her and Betty fell and hit her head on the floor. Dianna locked all the doors and escaped to help John win his election. Coming back to her senses Betty woke up and went to the windows and attempted to open them but Dianna placed locks on them to keep burglars out and she changed the locks on the doors keeping Betty in the house. The only thing she wanted was to help her father John Carol despite his race even though it conflicted with Betty's wishes because Betty felt the family must stick together in times of turmoil and suffering. The bad press Big Jim got could mean his first defeat in his political career.

Calling the fire departments Dianna said, "A fire is starting at my house and spreading to other houses."

When they arrived, the firemen took their axes and broke down the doors to see Dianna rushing out and scrambling down the street. At first the firemen attempted speak with her but their attempts failed and Betty woke up and told the arriving police to stop her but Dianna quickly ran and jumped over a fence with dogs chasing after her and she broke it and injured a bone in her hand but the police chasing her turned back when four German Shepherds broke loose who were chained up and chased after them.

Big Jim's men chased her and shot out her tires and took Dianna to Big Jim's headquarters and raped her and put her in the alley where some mixed groups of colored and white kids helped her. Colored people drove down the alley doing some junking and took her to the hospital where doctors tried to dress her wounds but she refused to tell them where she lived at because being in her teens she could be brought home by her mother who decided she would not take part in John Carol's election to the United States senate seat. This would be an unpopular move on her part because while in high school she joined racist groups who were anti- integration of the races getting civil rights but she witnessed a colored student being shouted at by crowds of white students telling her to go home instead of trying to integrate the high school and felt because of her black skin color she should not be subjugated to this type of treatment. They started not to treat her because they knew Aunt Sandy was always in the news taking civil rights cases to court and losing them being subjugated to improper illegal procedure from the southern judges who were prejudice against the lawyers who brought discrimination cases to their courts and experienced the 1960's type of law before the civil rights bills were passed and not quick to change their anti- civil rights attitudes.

CHAPTER 75

When Dianna scrambled into his head headquarters, John could not believe his eyes when he saw Dianna and did not know what words to say to her because he knew Dianna loved her mother and worshiped the ground she walked on but clashed with him on the civil rights issues he stood for.

When she saw him on television protesting and the civil rights workers holding sit ins and protesting the unequal accommodations for black people, Betty, and Dianna cursed up a storm about the protests but now John questioned why she wanted to help him knowing Dora, Lily, Sandy, and Sarah would be opposed to her helping him in this next election thinking she only came to spy on them and give feedback to Big Jim.

"What brought you back to this place?" Dora said, "Go back to the white folks who are trying to make us stay in our place and keep us from going into their places of business and movie houses or hotels."

"Take it easy Dora this is your sister and you have to treat her with more respect than this. Hating her for her racist attitudes will not solve our problems." Said Sarah.

"We how are you doing Dianna. The last time I saw you was at Mable's funeral and she really surprised me when she changed her attitudes about integration and I am glad she wanted to change on that issue. What brings you to your father's headquarters in this moment of history when we'll make headlines in the newspapers all over the world?" Sarah replied.

Sitting in a chair Dianna looked puzzled as she attempted to answer this question.

"Well it's not hard to explain because I really did not like colored people and I joined clubs at school which were against integration but all I heard was colored people were bad so it became a way of life to hate them. I saw on television how colored people could not eat at lunch counters or visit parks and the zoo and felt it was wrong and they could not vote made me look deep inside of myself and wanted to work for true equality for all the people. I am willing to change to see all of our people both colored and white enjoy the institutions in our great state of Mississippi."

"I still do not believe her Sandy said," As she came from another room in John's headquarters." I say send her back to her prejudice uncle. We cannot treat her like an aunt because she has not changed a bit. The first time she gets information she will go back and tell my father about what we are doing."

"You are being prejudice towards her before you see if she will betray us or not." John said, "Judge her by the deeds Dianna but hating her will not be the answer."

Reading some newspapers on the upcoming elections John said, "Look at what the papers are saying. I do not stand a chance of winning this election and Big Jim is the favorite son to get elected but it's not over yet. Leave Dianna alone and let her help out where she can."

"What's that in the mailbox?" Lilly said as she pulled it out and read it." You and your campaign workers have to clear out of this place because a contractor declared eminent domain and you have to move out in two days."

Dianna said, "These are people who support Big Jim and they want to have you disorganized so you will not have a campaign place to run your election."

"I'll go and get an injunction to stop them from evicting you because you were not given notice of this eminent domain and that is illegal. You cannot run an election on a street corner with rain falling on you."

A knock is heard on the door two days later and people from the IRS came and tore the place apart and grabbed important election strategy papers and John Coral and his workers fought the IRS agents and they were taken to a nearby jail and demonstrators picketed the police station asking to get their friends out. Policemen shot canisters of gas at them and in many cases the crowd ran in different directions because of the smoke and effects of the gas. Sandy went to court to get John Coral out of jail and the court officials said he did not pay any taxes on campaign funds and used them for his own personal reasons. To get these questions answered, the people took telephone books and placed them over John's head and slammed them into his hands as he held them and several of his fingers were broken. The sight of his hands appeared to be red and blue from the slamming of books into them and, the smell of blood and sweat circulated in the room as John thought about his ordeal and wanted it to end. This situation of keeping John in jail kept him from running for the United States senate seat. Sitting in the chair tied up humiliated him and her and the people who beat him laughed about beating John Carol up. The perspiration on John smelled and his breath out of his mouth at a quick pace and his legs and arms ached but his incident developed into a never give up attitude.

The judge did not want to grant John and his follower's permission to get out of jail but Sandy showed papers with John's group representing a non -profit organization and did not have to pay taxes on funds which came to them and there was no proof John's organization members used funds for their own personal use. The group held out in jail and immediately got released from it and paid their fines which broke the group and kept them from buying posters to advertise his goals to become elected United States senator from the state of Mississippi.

CHAPTER 76

A meeting is held between Big Jim and Jack Benson to set up a plot to kill John Carol when he comes to a political rally the day before the election.

"We should kill Betty to keep her from getting the lands when the farmer's properties are foreclosed on for their failure to pay property taxes.

"I love Betty and you cannot kill her Big Jim. I've been after her for a long time and I feel I have a chance to get her in my corner."

"Let me show you something," Big Jim said, "Look at this letter and it is addressed to John Carol saying how much she loved him and wanted him to come to her after the election."

"If you do not believe me look at the hand writing which is Betty's. You're in love with the wrong woman. It's not too good being in love with yourself is it?"

When big Jim said that tears fell from Jack Benson's eyes and he wanted revenge to kill John when he thought of John and Betty being lovers which he hated to think of losing her to John but the thought of killing Betty he could not stand for regardless of what Big Jim wanted.

"I'll pay you a million dollars to kill her because she knows too much and is going to tell the authorities because I will not give her fifty percent of the oil which is being taken from those lands."

"Just think Jack we will be millionaires. The feds would come down on us and put us behind bars so when John Carol and his people get out of the car I'll have someone deliver him a campaign present cake with a small bomb planted beneath it and it would blow up in about twenty minutes hitting Betty and John Carol. I have never lost an election yet and I be dam if I'll lose this one to that uppity nigger."

"Is there a debate being held between you and John Carol before the election?"

"Sure there will be a debate but he might not make it because of a pending accident he may get."

"You are a governor of this state and you can do a lot for us by saying those lands are unsafe."

As they spoke a news announcement came over the television screen which said, "Thirty long 18 feet kites were seen in the air many miles away dropping chemicals on the farm lands contaminating everything in sight but no one knows who was responsible for it."

Later reports said a group of cult people controlled the kites as they dropped chemicals on the houses and setting a big fire celebrating as if they worshipped a pagan god and they made loud noises with their voices.

Fixing bottles of wine Big Jim and Jack Benson toasted each other because Jack would declare those properties as disaster areas. While they spoke, Big Jim did not know his daughter was outside the door listening to their conversation with a secret listening device attached to it looking very cool and collected. She pretended to visit her father to get her cut of the oil which would be taken after the land was considered a hazard and Jack Benson being the governor would prohibit people from coming on it. Instead of clearing up the contamination, Benson hired drilling companies to drill for oil on the property. The Enlighten One and his followers did what Big Jim asked of them and he promised to give the one million dollars to his followers for this.

One of Big Jim's men came scrambling up the stairs and witnessed Betty listening to the conversations with her device and grabbed her and she kicked and hit him in the mouth. Using a judo throw called a hip throw, Betty threw the man and hit him in his neck with a karate chop but by then other people who worked for Big Jim arrived and grabbed her and brought her into his office.

"Boss one of the men said she was outdoors spying on you with this listening device."

"That woman put a hell of a fight but I put a hold on her and you and Jack Benson came out as I got her under control."

As Benson looked at Betty his heart pumped heavily and that love for her was there for Betty. To punish Betty, Big Jim told his men to take her out to the country and give her a beating to teach her a lesson and kill her. They grabbed her and before she goes Betty said, "You killed my mother and brother and now you are going to take my life."

Slapping her Big Jim said, "You know I cannot have you doing what you want to take more than half of the oil revenue for your own purpose."

Spitting in her father's face Betty said," You will not get away with this because I will tell all the big important people and your enemies about your wrong doing ways.'

Slapping Betty Big Jim said, "Take this bitch out and kill her."

When Big Jim said this, Benson got angry and pleaded with him not to kill Betty because this was his daughter. The two big men took Betty by her arms and as usual she resisted all the way out of the office and to avoid the crowd in the building; they took her out the back way to Big Jim's farm not far from his office, which was bought from campaign funds in earlier reelections, he took care of election expenses without telling government officials about it.

In the car being driven by one of Big Jim's men called Lonely Ed, he tried his best to hold Betty who was determined to get away from him but hand cups made it difficult for her to escape as rain poured on the car making it hard to drive for the other driver, by the name of Max, who looked like a hippie with long black air hanging down his back, and his body odor made everyone sick who dared to come near him.

He smoked weed as he drove the car and nearly ran into another car as the distance to Big Jim's farm came closer. With a white cloth tied around her mouth, it was too impossible for her to talk. The farm contained a big house in the style of a southern plantation with a second floor and eight pillars in front and an assortment of plants in the front of it like the White House in Washington DC. It looked beautiful on the inside with antique furniture in it and elevators took people to the second floors and when they strolled in the place it was impossible to hear the person's footsteps because with the touch of their shoes against the rugs laying on the floor ..Orders had to be carried out to kill Betty from her father Big Jim. When they got to the farm, Sam the butler answered the door and at first refused to let them in when he saw Betty struggling with the two men.

Holding a shot gun at them he said, "Let this girl go. I do not know you and Big Jim did not tell me you were bringing a girl here so you are going to have to shoot both of us."

All of a sudden the telephone ringed and Sam picked it up and Big Jim said, "Are the two of my men and my daughter at the house?"

"Yes they are here. I was going to shoot your friends for disrespecting me because one of them called me a nigger."

Smoking on his big cigar, Big Jim said, "Let them do their job and kill Betty. She's going to rat on me. It's a raise for you if you make sure no one bother's them in what they are doing."

The only problem with obeying Big Jim was he failed to give Sam his raises when they were due and this made Sam ungrateful to him. The men tied Betty to a tree and took a rope as instructed by Big Jim and one of them chewed and spitted out tobacco juice from his mouth as he hit Betty in the back with the wipe carving cuts into her back until Sam came out with his shot gun and fired into the air shouting for them to stop. "Let her go before I shoot both of you."

"Shut up old man and go back into the house." Lonely Ed raised his hand and hit Betty again who yelled each time the wipe hit her back and Sam shot at Lonely Ed hitting him in the legs and he limped off towards the house to get his injured legs patched up. Trying to get away from Max, who raised so much hell by dodging shotgun blasts fired by Sam, had a score to settle with Big Jim because he blackmailed him in order to make him work at the farm against his will.

Sam was a felon from justice because he failed to pay child support and did not want to be locked up because of warrants when he failed to appear in court. Max took out his gun and it was an automatic against Sam's shot gun and Betty still tied up feared for her life because Max 's automatic fired more shots than Sam's shotgun. Trying to get an advantage over Max, Sam dived into an area containing a lot of wild horses in it.

Seeing that Big Jim invested much money into his horses; he did not dare shoot at Big Jim's prize horses but Max was hidden behind some trees and bushes that easily concealed him from danger. The thick rose plants had thrones with sharp needle like branches which hurt Max as he struggled to keep from getting hit by the shotgun buck shots but on the other hand, Sam ducked and dodged the heels of the wild horses trying to defend themselves from Sam's intrusion into their place where they mated and ate their oats and did not like the idea of a human being in their grazing area.

But never the less both men fired at each other hoping to get a fatal shot in to kill each other. Dust from the horses covered Sam as he crawled near the fence to keep from getting hit by many bullets being fired at him. The only time Max could shoot was when the horses went in different directions leaving an open target to shoot at hitting the horses which meant strict punishment to Max if he killed one of Big Jim's top mares who might win the Kentucky Derby. Seeing Sam tried to keep from being trampled by Big Jim's horses, Max reloaded his gun and shot at Sam and did not care about hitting any one of them but Sam opened the gate letting the wild horses out racing toward Max who could not get out the way and he paid for it with his life as they kicked him with the heels to death. After that Sam untied Betty from the tree and treated her back and tried to make her stay until she healed but Betty insisted on getting back to Jackson. Intensified pain gripped Betty's back and Sam nursed her the best way he could by keeping her wound from getting infected.

Big Jim kept calling to see if Betty was dead but could get any answer. Lonely Ed kept bleeding from the shot gun pellets in his leg and when Sam finally found him Lonely Ed said," I am going to die so please kill me I do not have anything to live for."

Sam pulled out his shot gun and wondered should he take Ed out of his misery because he always disrespected Sam when he came out to the farm with Big Jim and called him coon or boy when he needed something. These thoughts came to Sam's mind as he decided whether to kill Lonely Ed or not. Could he find it in himself to inflict punishment or revenge on him or not. As he talked to Lonely Ed, Sam watched Ed slowly closed his eyes and died in peace and before his death he asked Sam for forgiveness. To get rid of the dead bodies Sam dug two graves and placed the two men in them and covered the bodies with dirt and trees to leave no trace of them but to burn the bodies first. The phone ringed and Big Jim said he would come home and see Ed and Max because he had not heard anything from them.

"Betty you will have to leave because your father is coming to see what has happened to Max and Ed. I'll think of a good lie to tell him."

As she ate her bacon and eggs, Betty said, "Sam you cannot stay here. My father will have you killed because Ed and Max were his top men and did everything they could to help him plus he paid them good."

"Betty I cannot leave because he will notify the authorities and have the law enforcement authorities raid my wife's home and probably put them in jail for withholding evidence from them about me. I am wanted for so many crimes against society and I have been on the run ever since."

"Sam come with me. They will kill you when he gets her and finds the graves of his two men. Trying desperately to persuade Sam's was next to impossible so Betty got into one of Big Jim's cars and rode off towards Mississippi with no money in her pocket. As she drove towards her home state a broadcast came over the radio saying that an Afro- American by the name of Sam was found dead and buried in a shadow gave on the surface where forest animals ate his body and left only bones.

Immediately Betty knew it was Sam they talked about. Wanting to find a way to get home, Betty stopped at a filling station to inquire as to where the nearest airport was and the clerk told her which road she could use to find it. Knowing she did not have any money, Betty gave the clerk a fake credit card and charged thirty dollars to it to have enough gas to make it to the airport.

Getting into her car, Betty drove down the road at a fast speed towards the airport. When the clerk saw he sold Betty gas on a fake card, he called the authorities and they chased after her when a car came by them matching the description the clerk gave them.

As Betty drove down the road she saw police officers driving after her and knew the clerk alerted them. Pushing on the gas paddle Betty did not want the police to catch her because she would have to testify to the killings of Ed and Max which she felt she did not cause. As she came racing down the road a big tractor trailer blocked the road. Betty stopped her car and got out and scrambled down it and spotted a man sleeping under a tree with his motorcycle not far from him. The policemen got out of their cars and glided around the tractor trailer too and went after Betty. Seeing the motorcycle parked, Betty got on it and escaped.

Seeing the owner lying on the grass, Betty went over to him and grabbed a tree branch and hit him in the head which knocked him out and took the keys out of his pocket and started up the motorcycle and the only problem was he had so many other keys on the key ring she kept trying to fit the right one in the ignition to turn on the engine. Soon as the officers got ready to grab her Betty placed the right key in the ignition and drove down the road on the motorcycle and made her way to the airport. The police officers made their pursuit after Betty got on a plane that would take her back to her beloved Jackson, Mississippi. As usual Betty went into the area where the stewards dressed and put on one of their uniforms and walked towards the airplane going to Jackson, Mississippi and went to a part of the plane which served lunches and dinners to the passengers. One of the stewards asked was Betty a new flight attendant and Betty said yes and she was hired and sent to their plane, after she signed the papers in the personnel office.

"I already knew what to do Betty said, "I do not need any training."

Orders came in for the flight attendants to bring food to the people and Betty acting like she knew what she was doing brought the dinners to the wrong people and they complained because food was brought to them they did not order and medicine was given to people who used the wrong ones causing much pain to them.

Seeing spoiled greens in the freezer Betty gave them to passengers who kept rushing to the restrooms. To really make the passengers more comfortable Betty brought some sleeping pills to the pilots on the plane thinking they were pain relievers for painful joints. As they flew the plane towards Jackson, Mississippi the pilots could not fly it because the sleeping pills made it hard to maneuver the plane and passengers screamed and shouted, "See the airplane going up and down in altitude."

Other technicians rushed to the cockpit and pulled the pilots from their seats and put the plane on automatic pilot and called the tower which guided the plane into the airport and at the same time another jet headed straight towards them and they radioed them they had to use the controls to lift the airplane above it towards a collision.

They had 15 minutes to get their plane out of the other plane's path flying towards them way. The traffic control people frantically notified the other airplane they were about to run into another airliner Betty rode in because their radio had blacked out and was damaged. The flight attendants struggled to follow the directions from the traffic control towers at the airport who were all in a nervous panic to see that four hundred people with two hundred people on each plane were about to perish in this tragic situation to avoid running into each other. Coming close to each other the technicians on Betty's airplane pulled the right controls lifting it above the airplane heading towards it. The pilots on the other plane did not know what was coming towards them because they placed the plane on automatic pilot and got high and were eventually suspended as airplane pilots.

When the plane landed, Betty scrambled off the plane and after calling Sandy who arrived in her car and greeted her and took her home which was being repaired for flood damage.

"That was a scare Betty; I thought you were going to be killed. John is holding a meeting at his headquarters tomorrow and will you attend it?"

"Sandy father is a dirty man and I still have to respect him for that even though he tried to kill both of us to keep from telling about his corrupt attempts to steal valuable farm lands from the farmers for what might be some oil on it. Let me put my thoughts together."

"Sister dear look at your place. Benson will not give you no aid to fix up your farm because you will not marry him and he sat back and watched father's attempt to kill us and did nothing about it. Plus, he ordered Benson to increas your property taxes. John is on the side of the people and they are tire of the corruption and want a change. Lets support John because he can be trusted and he is what the people need and they do not care about the color of his skin."

Other people who Big Jim paid to spy on Betty called Big Jim and told him Betty was active in John's campaign and she was going to see John at his headquarters that was moved because of the great flood that destroyed many buildings.

Sitting down thinking about her ordeal she just experienced Betty decided to attend the meeting because she and no other choices because her father was determined to have his way and he must be stopped from hurting innocent people and taking their rights away from them.

As she gets out of a car an assassin waited in the trees surrounded by bushes and shoots at Betty and she drops in John's arms and Sandy, Lilly, Dora, and Dianna gather around her as she speaks to them.

"Call an ambulance!" someone yelled but it was impossible because Jack Benson's men cut the telephone lines to keep them from calling an ambulance to get her to the hospital.

All the familiar faces of her family gathered around her as John held Betty in his arms and she said," I do not know how long I am going to live but I have to confess many things to my family. Dora I am sorry for abandoning you like I did. I did not want you to grow up in a world where people would not like you because you had a white mother. You would not be accepted in the white world I lived in. I did come to some of your baseball games to see you play against Dianna who you do not know was your sister. I kept thinking about what my friends would say if I brought you out in public with me. I thought about myself instead of keeping my family together. I could not be married to John and raised you and Dianna in this town and see all of you mistreated because of it and I am asking for your forgiveness."

While Betty was at Big Jim's farm in Washington D.C she remembered she looked into Big Jim's drawers and found a note in it saying a bomb would go off at about 10 p.m. at night and kill a lot of people in the building. Immediately John read the note and attempted to tell everyone to get out of the building before it blew up and warned other people but Benson's men under the orders of Big Jim locked the doors and they could not get in to tell the other workers to get out of the building.

Dianna managed to get into the building to call the ambulance drivers and could not get out of the building at the indicated time it would blow up in twenty minutes. John tried to give out a possible combination number just by guessing and Dianna tried to use it but the door stayed jammed and would not open. Lily, Sandy and Dora kept on coming up with numbers for her to open the combination lock until they were dead tire.

Getting angry, Dora grabbed a heavy object and slammed it into a big glass windowpane near the combination locked doors. The glass broke into small pieces and Dianna runs through the big opening when there was one a big glass paneled window but going through this opening enabled Dianna to get out the building and many other trapped people. As they attempted to scramble out of the building, you could hear screams of people running as fast as they could to keep from getting killed. They took deep breaths and it took a lot of energy out of their bodies and the sweat came from their under arms leaving a smell that made them feel bad. People both young and old helped each other to avoid sudden death and as John was the last to leave the building dived out head first as the explosion sent parts of the building in different directions. Big Jim and his men hid behind their cars shooting at the people who did not have guns on them and they threw explosives at the campaign workers running to get away from the parts of the building falling on everything beneath it from parts of the concrete walls.

The local police and state police would not come and rescue John and his workers because Big Jim controlled what they did and Governor Benson would not send state police officers to stop the shooting or the Mississippi National Guard. Many of them were shot down as they left their cars.

Big Jim managed to get away before federal army troops arrived and stopped the shooting and captured the men responsible for killing innocent women and children. Many people were arrested but they would not tell on Big Jim who got on a plane and few back to Washington D.C. and made up alibies saying he was at his estate outside of Washington entertaining some friends and trying hard to get campaign funds to defeat John Carol to keep him from winning the election.

CHAPTER 77

There was much intimidation going on before the election took place because many of the black people would lose their jobs if they tried to vote against Big Jim and if they had literature found on them supporting John Carol it meant they could lose their jobs and be placed in jail. In one town 200 black people came to vote but only five got a chance to vote because they could not pass the literacy tests and on the voting machines it had a message written on them saying support your White Citizen's Council. When the people came to take the test even, PHD's failed to pass it and white folks with less education passed it with no problems. In many cases, one of the instructions said, read or interpret the states constitution later was changed to read and interpret that document.

When Sandy found out about this she filed injunctions to stop the use of those tests and the people were allowed to vote without being tested.

In George County, one white applicant's interpretation of the section. There shall be no imprisonment duit was "I think that a neorger shourd have 2 year in college before voting because he don't understand. He passed the test.

John's people worked in Mc, Comb voter registration drives and lawyers from the north came to Mississippi to help black folks to register to vote and taught non-violent methods in protesting and their headquarters were often bombed by Big Jim's forces. This was an election fought by the young and old and many grade school students were jailed for protesting against efforts to keep black folks from voting. The people who held meeting for such activities got incarcerated for contributing to the delinquency of minors. When the civil rights workers attempted to eat at restaurants while on the campaign trail, angry white folks sprayed them with paint and paper was thrown in their faces. While this went on, they sing freedom songs. At Decatur, Mississippi John's workers were met by gun welding whites when they attempted to register black folks to vote.

Some of the things John's organization showed was black people wanted to vote. Many black people in the state of Mississippi never had a chance to participate in voting for the person they wanted to represent their interests when running for public office. His organization wanted to expand voter registration and constitute a legally constituted Freedom Democratic Party that would challenge the whites –only Mississippi Democratic Party and establish freedom schools to teach reading, and math to black children. They wanted to open community centers where indignant blacks could obtain legal and medical assistance.

The lawyers taught black history to kids and secured their constitutional rights. John's workers faced the police brutality when campaigning in the many towns in Mississippi when traveling to Lorman and Tugaloo. In Jackson, Lorman, and Tugaloo youth chapters were formed and provided workers to help in voter registration drives. Most of the youth arrested came from Lanier, Brinkley and Jim Hill grade schools.

Students from Campbell staged many protests having an Easter boycott of white business owners because they would not hire black workers. Whites from Millsap's, College supported John's organization to fight for full equality for whites and black deprived of their constitutional rights and John's organization recruited workers who came from southwest Mississippi in Pike's County. Organizing efforts were evident throughout the state from Holly Springs and Marshall County in north Mississippi to Hattiesburg in Forest County in the southern tier of the state. When John's organizers marched they had followers coming from all parts of Mississippi such as Grenada, Greenwood, Philadelphia, and Canton, Mississippi.

One of the rules John's organization stressed was for them to bring about 500 dollars for bail money, living expenses, medical bills, and transportation home.

CHAPTER 78

On the day of the election the people came out heavily to the polls to cast their votes and John made his workers see no fraud took place but Big Jim paid people throughout the state to vote for him but it did not do any good and the vast majority of the citizens ignored his people who tried to give them money to vote for Big Jim but in the end John won the election after a hard bitter campaign to become the first black person to be the United States senator from the state of Mississippi.

Later a group of John Carol's supporters filed charges against Big Jim for violating the civil rights of black and white citizens of Mississippi and using fraud to take their farms to use the land for their own purposes and Jack Benson was indicted for conspiring with Big Jim and both of them received 25 years in prison. Betty received five years' probation and five years in prison for conspiring with her father but because she only did unlawful crimes because of the fear of getting killed by her father she received a lighter sentence. After all of his procrastination about marrying Lilly, John married her because she tried her best to help him when no one else would and Dora and Dianna said they would try to get to know each other and both of them pledged to love each other no matter what. Signing on as John's legal counsel Sandy changed her opinion about integration of black and white folks living together and worked with John to help write bills that would help the people of Mississippi get decent prices for their crops, integration of the schools with black and white students attending high quality schools together, and all the people getting good health care benefits, better voting rights, and no picture ID be required to vote or show proof their relative voted in elections two hundred years ago. John wanted to write bills that would give black folks the right to serve on juries to help with the judicial process. Senator John Carol now had a lot of work to do to bring about equality to the citizens of Mississippi.

Printed in the United States
By Bookmasters

Printed in the United States
By Bookmasters